Garry Disher grew up in rural South Australia, where he was born in 1949, and now lives in Melbourne where he is a full-time writer. His publications include novels, short story collections, anthologies, children's books, crime fiction and writers' handbooks. His award-winning short fiction has been published overseas and widely in Australia. Forthcoming Collins/Angus & Robertson titles by Garry Disher include *Flamingo Gate*, a novella and stories collection, and *The Bamboo Flute*, a novel for children.

D1826300

Also by Garry Disher
and available in Imprint

The Stencil Man
The Difference to Me
Steal Away
Personal Best 2

IMPRINT

PERSONAL BEST

Thirty Australian authors
choose their best short stories

edited by
GARRY DISHER

An imprint of HarperCollins*Publishers*

AN ANGUS & ROBERTSON BOOK

An imprint of HarperCollinsPublishers

First published in Imprint in Australia in 1989 by
William Collins Pty Ltd
This edition published in 1990 by
CollinsAngus&Robertson Publishers Australia
Reprinted in 1991
CollinsAngus&Robertson Publishers Pty Limited (ACN 009 913 517)
A division of HarperCollinsPublishers (Australia) Pty Limited
4 Eden Park, 31 Waterloo Road, North Ryde, NSW 2113, Australia

William Collins Publishers Ltd
31 View Road, Glenfield, Auckland 10, New Zealand

HarperCollinsPublishers Limited
77-85 Fulham Palace Road, London W6 8JB, United Kingdom

National Library of Australia
Cataloguing-in-Publication data:

Personal best: thirty Australian authors choose their
best short stories.

ISBN 0 207 16908 X

1. Short stories, Australian, I. Disher,
Garry, 1949-

A823'.018

Cover illustration by Michael Fitzjames
Typeset in 11 pt Times Roman by Midland Typesetters, Victoria
Printed by Globe Press, Victoria

5   4   3
95 94 93 92 91

ACKNOWLEDGEMENTS

The following stories have been published previously in the sources mentioned: 'Reading the Signs', *New Yorker*; 'American Dreams', *Nation Review*; 'The Brush Bronzewing', *Overland*, No 83, 1981; 'Amateur Hour', *The Canberra Times*, 20 September 1986 and *Fiction Magazine*, Vol. 5, No 7, 1986; 'A,B,C,D . . .', *Transatlantic Review*; 'Precious Bane', *Strange Attractors*, Hale and Iremonger, 1985; 'The Archbishop or the Lady', *Meanjin*, Vol. 43, No 2, 1984; 'Junction', *Paris-Metro*; 'Wednesdays and Fridays', *Quadrant*, 1981; 'The List of All Possible Answers', *Age Monthly Review*; 'The Hair and the Teeth', *Woodpecker Point and other stories*, New Directions, New York, and *Australian Short Stories*, No 24; 'My Father's Axe', *Australian Playboy*, 1983; 'Sandcastles', *The Dwarf*, Darling Downs Institute Press, Toowoomba 4350; 'Inside the Oyster', *King* magazine, 1966; 'Black Genoa', *Mattoid 31*, 1988; 'To be Congruous with the Sea', *Meanjin Quarterly*, Autumn, 1974; 'A World this Size', *The Bulletin*, December 1982; 'Only a Little of So Much', *The Canberra Times*, 15 December 1984.

The editor and publishers would like to thank the authors and publishers of the following stories for permission to include them in this collection: 'The Appearance of Things' by Jessica Anderson, from *Stories From the Warm Zone and Sydney Stories*, Penguin Books, Ringwood, 1987; 'Dream People' by Barbara Hanrahan, from *Dream People*, Grafton Books, London, 1987; 'Reading the Signs' by Michael Wilding, from *Reading the Signs*, Hale and Iremonger, 1984; 'A Snake Down Under' by Glenda Adams, from *The Hottest Night of the Century*, Angus & Robertson, Sydney, 1979; 'American Dreams' by Peter Carey, from *The Fat Man in History*, University of Queensland Press, 1974; 'The Brush Bronzewing' by James McQueen, © Panama Productions; 'Little Helen's Sunday Afternoon' by Helen Garner, from *Postcards from Surfers*, McPhee Gribble Publishers, 1985; 'Sister Ships' by Joan London, from *Sister Ships*, Fremantle Arts Centre Press, 1986; 'Amateur Hour' by Garry Disher, from *The Difference to Me*, Angus & Robertson, Sydney, 1988; 'A,B,C,D . . .' by Murray Bail, from *Contemporary Portraits*, University of Queensland Press, 1975; 'Precious Bane' by Gerald Murnane, © Gerald Murnane 1985; 'Through Road' by Jean Bedford, from *Country Girl Again and other stories*, McPhee Gribble Publishers, 1985; 'Gates' by Barry Hill, from *Headlocks and other stories*, McPhee Gribble Publishers, 1983; 'Ladies Need Only Apply' by Thea Astley, from *Hunting the Wild Pineapple*, Penguin Books, Ringwood, 1981; 'The Archbishop or the Lady' by Gerard Windsor, from *Memoirs of the Assassination Attempt*, Penguin Books, Ringwood, 1985; 'The Commune Does Not Want You' by Frank Moorhouse, from *Tales of Mystery and*

CONTENTS

INTRODUCTION

In this book, stories are returned to their authors. The authors choose, and they have their say.

In most short story anthologies the stories are chosen by an editor, who usually is not a fiction writer but a critic, academic or teacher with tendentious aims or particular standards, themes or criteria in mind. Often the stories are justified, assessed or dissected in the editor's introduction or in accompanying notes. A story selected and explained in this way tends to pass into public knowledge as being its author's best or most representative story, even the one he or she might choose.

Writers are troubled by this. I have often heard them (and, indeed, readers on their behalf) complain: 'Why did they choose "Y"? "X" is a better story. It takes risks and achieves more. "X" is more truly representative.'

Personal Best helps to restore the balance. I invited thirty writers to nominate the published story they consider the best they have written—or the one for which they have most affection—and write a brief introduction to it. Significantly, few writers chose a standard anthology piece.

But all anthologies, by their nature, raise the issues of exclusion and quality. Why has the editor chosen these writers or works, we want to know, and not others? Are they, or are they said to be, the best? If a canon of best writers or of best works exists, who chooses it, and can it ever be fixed, given the constant changes in writing, reading and critical tastes? How might another editor—with different tastes, or of a different class, race, gender, age group or historical period—have chosen?

No critical inference should be drawn from my omissions. I decided simply to choose writers I admire (reserving editor's privilege for myself). That said, I believe that I might have compiled several *Personal Best* collections, or one large one, if problems of cost, space and market saturation did not exist. I also believe that there is room for specialist collections: for example, of experimental writers.

In making the final selection of thirty writers I was guided by these factors: first, I was keen to hear more from writers who I knew had made astute observations about writing and their own work in public or in published interviews; second, I wanted to hear writers speak about stories other than their standard anthology pieces or the stories with which we are familiar; third, I aimed to give readers a reasonable idea of the variety of Australian writers who have worked with the short story form since the 1970s. Here are established writers (for example, Beverley Farmer and Michael Wilding), emerging writers (for example, Carmel Bird and George Papaellinas), and accomplished but under-represented writers (for example, Fay Zwicky and Barry Hill). All have had books of fiction, poetry or non-fiction published. Some are better known as novelists, poets or non-fiction writers, and others may not have published short stories in recent years, but all have contributed to the diversity of styles and concerns in contemporary Australian short fiction.

This collection of stories comes at a time of great interest in the writing, publishing and marketing of short fiction in Australia. Authors' reputations, and forms and themes in fiction writing, are the subjects of articles and conversations; the publication of short story collections is not the commercial risk it once was; many successful anthologies have been published in recent years; more and more poets are writing short fiction now; and one of Australia's newest and richest literary prizes is the $10 000 Steele Rudd award for a short story collection.

At the same time, there is a growing interest in public readings, writers' festivals, workshops and writing courses. Curiosity about the relationship between writers' experiences and their writing is reflected in the popularity of collections of interviews with authors, such as *Rooms of their Own*, *Sideways from the Page*, and the *Yacker* collections. It seems that writers and readers alike take an interest in the origins of written pieces, how they are 'made', working habits, and writers' views about creativity.

Short story writing in Australia is also surrounded by debate. Authors have been criticized for not taking as their subjects government, business, the workplace, or the problems and public issues of the age. Some critics are hostile about what they term 'the women's story' and issues in 'women's fiction'. Australian short stories are said to be too concerned with domestic life, relationships, personal matters, the self. On the other hand, it is argued that the local and the personal are suitable subjects for art, that they impinge on so-called wider or more significant concerns, and they are very much the important issues of the day. Finally, writers who work with traditional forms and subjects have been labelled as out-of-date, drab stylists, or ideologically unsound, while experimental writers have encountered variously dismissals, bafflement and fulsome praise.

In *Personal Best* the stories are the writers' own, free of prevailing notions about quality and representativeness. A detailed examination of them would be inappropriate here. One notices, however, the concentration and precision of style and language typical of short fiction, and the persistence of certain themes despite the range of settings, characters, situations and voices. I am pleased by the number of long stories: little magazines, competitions and anthologies tend to give the false impression that stories are or should be about 3000 words long. *Personal Best* includes several stories shorter than 1500 words and several longer than 7000. The arrangement of the stories is not by category, and nor is it entirely arbitrary. I have grouped or paired stories that inform one another or offer varying approaches to a theme or subject.

Each story is accompanied by an author's 'introduction'. I suggested, but did not stipulate, approaches to these (for example, Why this story? How or why did it come to be written? What problems or pleasures did you face in writing it?), and I'm as pleased with the withholding, flippant or elliptical introductions as I am with the straightforward.

What are we to make of the authors' introductions?

Most contributors were reluctant to nominate a *best* story. They would echo Elizabeth Jolley's sentiment that a best implies a worst. Helen Garner states that she hasn't got a best story because her opinions about her stories 'change constantly, according to who else I've been reading and what progress I'm making on my current work'. The *Personal Best* stories, then, tend to be *favourites*: favourites because they are recent, early, an innovation for the author, or a stage in a career. Several writers also mention professional ramifications: the fame, recognition or opportunities their stories earned them.

I think, too, that we should heed Helen Garner's remark: on the day she submitted her story it meant something to her; she found it 'less awkward to contemplate' then than on another day. We should read this book in the knowledge that the contributors' choices and attitudes may not be fixed or final.

Some of the writers are reluctant to reflect on their stories or writing methods, and a few prefer instead to discuss how their stories might be read. David Malouf believes that his story 'now has its own life to lead, among readers', and any comment he could make would be superfluous. John Bryson has addressed the readers' attention by way of another story. Thea Astley has chosen simply to say where the idea for her story came from. Carmel Bird finds it difficult to comment on her story because 'the story is its own comment'.

In spite of all these cautions, *Personal Best* is instructive about writing, reading, and the hopes, fears and concerns of authors. If we ask: 'Where do writers get their ideas?' we learn that Thea Astley read an advertisement and asked, 'What if . . .?'; Gerald Murnane followed unknown signs, exploring the images unfolding in his mind; for Jessica Anderson and Glenda Adams, writing was a stimulus to memory; and a number of stories were prompted by personal experiences—though we don't read them as auto-biographical pieces, attesting to the writers' skills at transforming reality.

If we ask: 'What issues, problems and pleasures of technique do writers face?' we learn that Barbara Hanrahan worked to achieve a style that would mirror the freshness and poetry of her mother's conversation; Jessica Anderson feels that the short story form does not suit her; Archie Weller aims at a natural storytelling voice; Joan London was unable to start writing her story until she had found a form and a voice that worked; Jean Bedford deliberately tried the present tense; George Papaellinas would like to move away from using the self as subject; Barry Hill found it liberating to cast off the impersonal, reticent model of short story writing; Fay Zwicky was conscious of dismantling a restrained, correct voice; Finola Moorhead wrote a great many drafts of her story; Peter Carey likes to meddle with his after they have been published.

To express the meaning held in the imagination entails a struggle, in which intention can mean different things at different stages of the composition, and aim is not always achievement. Perhaps we should be mindful of D. H. Lawrence's injunction, 'Trust the tale, not the teller'. The authors' introductions might themselves be fictional. No matter: I believe that readers will enjoy the stories in *Personal Best* while learning much about the way writers work, and if the writing process has also been demystified a little, then so much the better.

THE APPEARANCE OF THINGS

Jessica Anderson

AUTHOR'S NOTE

I used to have a friend who hated autobiographical stories of childhood. He used to say that, ideally, writers ought not to have childhoods at all, but since they are a biological necessity, some treatment should be devised that would erase that period from memory, thus saving the reading public from the autobiographical childhood story.

That was in the thirties. I was a young adult then, and I liked to agree with him, but in the fervently exaggerated case, half comedy, we made against the childhood story, we did not take into account the obliterating treatment taking place in ourselves, even then, simply by the passage of time.

Four decades later, I thought about our conversations when I surprised myself by wanting to write a story about an incident that had taken place in my fifth year, and which had apparently escaped the treatment. My only clear reason for wanting to write that story was to pay tribute to the warmth and invention and wit of my elder sister. She was dead, and there was a sense of pain in beginning it. I put it off, but began it at last, and discovered that I was not, after all, a suitable case for treatment. Too many deposits had remained, and were substances like rust or coral, capable of expansion.

The act of writing is itself known to be a stimulus to memory. By the time I had finished that first story, 'Under the House', I knew I had more to write. But I was engrossed in a novel, and again, I put it off (the editor of this collection will attest to my habit of putting things off) until a space occurred; then I started on the second story of the series, 'The Appearance of Things', which is the one presented here.

I chose it as my favourite because it is the one in the series that best stands alone, and because its theme allowed me to gather together all six members of my family. The incident described is one in which we all had an opinion, or took a stance, and expressed ourselves on it in our different ways. It could have easily been called 'At the Table', but I chose its present title because it extended the theme.

The wish to extend a theme will mark me as primarily a novelist. I have always admired, but have never succeeded in, the wonderful art of the short story as a highly suggestive fragment. My short stories, including this one, are obviously the work of a writer accustomed to keeping all her clubs in the air at once. I would gladly throw all my clubs away but, so far, they have kept flying back into my hands.

Readers may want to know something about the truthfulness or otherwise of this story. The narrative base is certainly true. Those events took place, and I tried to recall them faithfully, but sometimes failed. The 'truth' is in the deposits I mentioned earlier (my sister's remark at the table, 'Much is metaphor', is one such deposit); but the expansion required coaxing and invention; and the inverted commas enclosing 'truth' signal my inability to describe a process which, if it could be described, would make the writing of stories, autobiographical or otherwise, irrelevant.

Jessica Anderson

THE APPEARANCE OF THINGS

'Rhoda wants to go to church,' said my mother.

'Now why?' said my father. 'Why should Rhoda want to do that?'

'She has become friendly with Helen Scott.'

My father postponed his reply by picking up his newspaper or magazine and starting the browsing that accompanied his evening talks with my mother. When he came home from work, my mother, hearing him mount the side steps and cross the verandah, would go to the door of the dining room. They would kiss and murmur each other's names—'Charlie', 'Iris'—then he would hang his hat on the rack just inside the door and take his seat at the big table. While he sat in silence, getting his breath, my mother quickly made him tea, or, if he were very pallid and exhausted, would first bring him a tablespoon of brandy mixed with water.

If he failed to recover his breath, he would get up and go at his swinging, stiff, defeated gait to lie propped on pillows, coughing dreadfully, in their bedroom; but usually, at that stage of our lives, he would recover, and drink his tea, and then pick up the *Courier* or the *Bulletin* or one of his foreign magazines, and talk to my mother as she came and went from the kitchen. He sat sideways at the table so that he would face the kitchen door.

At these times I liked to come and loll behind or beside his chair. If I was, say, eight, he was fifty-eight. I read over his shoulder and asked the meaning of words. I would take his free hand and pinch the skin along the knuckles into a ridge that remained until I wiped it away. If he had loosened his collar and tie I might ask him to shrug so that I could examine the huge hollows behind his collar bone. I also liked to turn inside-out the upper folds of his ears and smooth his back hair, which was not grey, but that dun colour left by the retreat of a blond brightness.

He was a man of unreliable temper, but under these inspections he was always patient and humorous. I don't recall my sisters Rhoda and Sybil often being present, and my brother Neal had started work in Brisbane, and, as Neal loved to yarn, and was easily waylaid, he was likely to reach home long after my father.

By these inspections I hurried to the dining room to make, I vented an anxiety about my father I was not allowed to express, but there was also an attraction in my parents' conversation, which often had the tantalizing significance of something I felt I was on the very verge of understanding.

I knew that Rhoda wanted to go to church, because she had told me, but when my father said, 'So she wants to follow the sheep', I was attentive to the sharpness of his tone, church not having been presented to me before as one of the banned or scorned places, like the creek or the picture show.

'I don't suppose church would hurt her,' said my mother.

'Isn't it enough, by Jove, that they have compulsory religious instruction in their schools?'

'Not for Rhoda, apparently.'

My father lowered his newspaper and looked directly at my mother. 'Which church does she want to go to?'

'Well, Charlie, if it's to be any church—'

'Of course! She wants to hear the Anglican bleat. Well, next week it will be something else. Next week she will want to play the banjo.'

My mother laughed. I sprang to the rung of his chair and cried, 'What is a banjo?' and my father raised his paper with a satisfied crack and said, 'Give her a week. See if she doesn't get over it.'

My interrogation of Rhoda ended by her taking me to see the church. Sybil came too. Sybil and I, close in age, were still dressed in identical gingham or Fuji silk dresses made by our mother, but Rhoda, fourteen, had started high school, and by helping to make her clothes, had achieved a wobbling approximation of the modern styles she demanded. In this and in other ways she and I had moved apart since we had come into the suburbs of

Brisbane. When we had lived on the outskirts, on Old Mooloolabin, the land once farmed by our paternal grandfather, that rural monotony had found out our natural affinity and had closely bonded us; and even now, when we lived among houses and shops and tramcars, and had each made other alliances, an invisible ligament remained, and it was always to Rhoda I went for information withheld from me.

The three of us walked across the park. 'I've seen the church before, you know,' I said.

'Not the inside,' said Rhoda.

'Everyone else goes to church,' said Sybil. 'And it's not far to walk. Only over the park and down Murdoch Street.'

Pictures from books were amassing in my mind. 'What does Notre Dame mean in English?' I asked Rhoda.

'We're not up to that yet.'

On the rough beige expanse of the park, both earth and grass being that colour, rectangles had been made smooth here and there, and on these, brilliant green or clayey pink, tennis and bowls and croquet were played, in all the subtropical seasons except the stormy end of summer, by adults dressed in cream or white. We walked down Honour Avenue, between the two rows of trees running from the little concrete cenotaph, which was behind us, to the big gates of the park. At the foot of each tree was a white-painted post, to which a plate of some alloy was nailed, and on each plate was engraved LEST WE FORGET, and beneath it, a man's name.

'Imagine thinking those trees would do well there,' my mother would say. 'Imagine the ignorance.' Many of the trees were stunted, and some were dead, and in the rows of posts there were also spaces, where the white ants had been busy. 'I see McCulloch is down,' said Rhoda blithely as we passed.

'Ooooo,' said Sybil and I, shocked. On Anzac Day she and I were among the hundreds who marched from the school down Honour Avenue to the stained concrete cenotaph, each carrying a wreath. Our wreaths, assembled with impatient help from our pacifist mother, were among the worst, but all the same, the ceremony, or the bloody legend of the war itself, did touch some awe in us.

It was a Saturday afternoon, and not hot. To reach the park gates we had to pass the school. When I hung my head and pulled paspalum grass, and diverged to kick the little russet stones of anthills, Rhoda dropped a hand to the nape of my neck, holding me lovingly, keeping me walking. The school stood (I am still convinced) raised above its surroundings on a wide low mound. Although the buildings were on stilts, and had verandahs, they were not pleasantly domestic, nor shaded by trees. There were no jacarandas, figs or eucalypts, not even a military palm. Moreover, the buildings were painted khaki, with brown railings, while the posts on which they stood were grey, as was the concrete area beneath, where we played on rainy days. I was at present assigned to the newest of these buildings, around which hung a smell of damp concrete.

I hated this school quite as much as it deserved. When told to answer a question in class, I stammered. But when I leapt away from it on Friday afternoons, I could forget it completely until the very hour of my return on Monday, a respite which relied, however, on my keeping the school itself out of sight. As we walked alongside its fence, Rhoda tightened her grip on my neck, and shook me slightly.

'If we go to church,' she said, 'we won't walk. Helen Scott's father will pick us up in his car and take us round by the road.'

This was too facile; I did not believe it. She was more successful in diverting me when, without releasing me, she cried, 'Why do I have to fight for every single thing I want? Look at the way I had to fight to get my hair cut!' For I also felt our parents' edicts as too final, their explanations not enough. At the park gates, Rhoda released me and tossed her head very fast from side to side, so that the cut ends of hair flicked in triumph on her cheeks.

The church was built only a few feet above the ground, which was not trodden and dusty like the school ground, but simply weedy and unkempt. It was built of brick, with a stucco exterior painted cream. Wishing to be impressed, I looked up at the small tower.

'The inside is best,' said Rhoda. 'Come on.'

'Don't we have to ask?' I said.

'Churches are always open,' said Sybil with sudden authority.

'Yes,' said Rhoda. 'Criminals can seek sanctuary in churches. Even if you murder someone, you can go and lie at the altar, and no one can touch you, not even the police.'

'That was only in the olden days,' I said.

'And only in Catholic churches,' said Sybil.

Rhoda took my hand. 'You go home, Syb, if you like.'

'No, I'll come,' said Sybil.

I shrank back, rolling my eyes. 'What if there's a murderer in there?'

'You're not supposed to make jokes on holy ground,' said Sybil.

'That's right,' said Rhoda.

The concrete floor of the porch was stained like the steps of the cenotaph. Inside, in her hailstone muslin, Rhoda decorously spread her arms. 'See?'

I saw that the two rows of seats were more interesting than those at the school, being deeper, darker, shinier, and having carved uprights at each end. On the carpeted aisle between I could not imagine Miss Rickard's dogmatic sauntering, nor Mr Alpin's strolling pace as he kept his cane in practice on the palm of his own hand. I rather liked the look of polished brass and flowers at the other end, too, and the stained glass reminded me of our front door.

'They've made a man in the stained glass,' I said to Rhoda. 'Jesus Christ.'

'He looks different from his pictures.'

'It's the black lines.'

'There are no statues,' said Sybil.

'I should hope not,' said Rhoda, in our mother's tone.

'Josie Carr let me look in the door of her church. They have statues.'

'They worship idols,' said Rhoda.

'And graven images,' I intoned, from some deep place in my mind.

'*You* like it, anyway,' said Rhoda to me.

'Yes,' I said kindly.

'Why don't you?' accused Rhoda.

I looked at the altar, where I could not imagine a murderer lying, then up at the ceiling. 'It's not spooky enough.'

'What's this thing?' said Sybil, at a slight distance.

'Don't touch that,' said Rhoda, running to her on tiptoe.

Sybil gasped, and pulled her hand away. 'That's the *font*,' said Rhoda sternly.

'Where babies get baptized?' panted Sybil.

'Of course.'

'Is that all? Josie Carr's is big and black, with gold on it, and steps all round it.'

I joined them. 'It looks like a bird bath,' I said.

We all suddenly giggled, then Rhoda said, 'Shh,' and pushed us both on the shoulder.

'Where were we baptized?' asked Sybil.

'In the different towns we were born in,' said Rhoda, 'when dad was a stock inspector. Which means I was baptized in mum's old church, up in Toowoomba.'

'Let's go and do something else,' I said; but Rhoda said, 'Shh, here's Mr Gilliard.'

I recognized the man who had opened the vestry door. I had seen him at a distance, at the school. But as he came down the aisle towards us, I saw that although his church was disappointing, he himself was a genuine storybook clergyman: tall, thin, light-boned, with a narrow head, shining silver hair, unused hands, and the smile appropriate to that sort of collar. He inclined his head to all of us before speaking to Rhoda.

'I thought it might be you, Rhoda.'

'Yes,' said Rhoda breathlessly. 'This is Sybil, and this is Beatie.'

Sybil, to the amazement, I am sure, of all of us, suddenly slipped into a pew, dropped to her knees, shut her eyes, and raised her hands in prayer. Mr Gilliard looked at her with an unexpected expression, curious and rather hard, before turning on me his benign smile.

'What do you think of our church, Beatie?'

I stepped behind Rhoda and hid my face in her folds of muslin. Rhoda said, 'She thinks it's not spooky enough.'

Mr Gilliard's laugh sounded very bold in the silent church. Rhoda was also laughing: I felt it with my forehead. Looking sideways at Sybil, I saw that she had bowed her head lower and was moving her lips.

'I understand very well what Beatie means,' said Mr Gilliard.

I came out from behind Rhoda and instead leaned against her. 'Only,' said Mr Gilliard, 'we must remember that God is everywhere.'

Rhoda absent-mindedly put an arm round my shoulders. 'But that's what dad says.'

'Oh?' said Mr Gilliard. 'Then you are mistaken about your father, Rhoda. He isn't an atheist, nor even an agnostic.'

'No, wait,' said Rhoda, with amazing familiarity, 'what he says is that if God exists—you see, he always says *if*—*if* he exists, he exists everywhere, and not only in churches.'

'Except that there is no *if* about it,' said Mr Gilliard with his peaceful amusement, 'he is quite right. But some of us like to build a meeting place, where we can gather together and raise our voices to the Lord.'

'Oh *yes*, Mr Gilliard.'

It was so unlike Rhoda's usual voice that I twisted my head to look up at her. I had never seen her long greenish eyes so rapturously fixed. Mr Gilliard was smiling down at her.

'I hope you and Helen will come and have tea again soon, Rhoda, with Mrs Gilliard and me.'

Sybil slipped out of the pew and joined us, with her hands folded in front, looking modest.

'Oh yes, please, Mr Gilliard,' said Rhoda, 'we will.'

Rhoda did not speak to either of us until we were out of Murdoch

Street and through the park gates. Then she turned on Sybil and pushed her shoulder. 'You were showing off.'

'I was praying,' said Sybil.

'Praying!'

'I was. When he laughed, I prayed for him.'

'*You*,' said Rhoda, laughing angrily, 'you prayed for *him*?'

'Yes, because it's a sin to laugh in church. And I'll tell mum you've been having tea with the Gilliards.'

'Ha. Mum knows. I told her.'

Foreseeing that we would dawdle past the school, cavilling, I shouted that I hated the church, and ran away. I didn't stop when Rhoda called me, but ran as fast as I could, cutting out of Honour Avenue, passing the tennis courts, crossing the bleached grass, and slowing down only when I came to the row of houses, among them ours, which abutted on the park. I did not go home, but went through the back gate of my friend Clare's house. On their lawn, which was fresh and dewy, Clare and I raised our arms and twirled. We twirled until our heads were emptied, then were filled with such bliss that we fell on our backs, panting like dogs, on the freshly watered grass.

My father's opposition to church-going must have lasted some months, because on the day of the trumpery rubbish, the mild spring or winter weather had passed, and it was hot enough for me to be sitting, as I often did in summer, on the cool linoleum under the dining room table. I had some nonsensical homework with me. It is possible that I was learning by heart the imports and exports of Chile. My father sat with crossed legs so that one boot was suspended beside the table, and as I read I regularly tapped the toe and kept his foot at a gentle jog.

My mother's footsteps passed to and fro from the kitchen, my father's newspaper rustled, and they spoke of politics. They did not speak of the old days, or of their former hopes, or of imperialist wars, or of the yellow men who would take the white men's jobs. They spoke of Theodore and Gillies, which I had only recently understood was not the name of a shop. Without heat, my father called Theodore a blackguard, and my mother mechanically asked what else he had ever been. But when my father went on to call Gillies a turncoat, and my mother said, 'So much for his early ideals,' my father's tone changed.

'And how much for ours, sweetheart? Bit by bit, we fall back. Do we want the whole shebang to fall down?'

My mother advanced from the kitchen. 'It wouldn't take much, when it's been so undermined.'

I saw her feet halt at the table, her narrow laced-up shoes set together. And now her tone also changed. 'Look, Charlie. Just look at this trumpery rubbish.'

That tone, so intense with disgust, disturbed me as little else could do. I knew that her mouth was turned down as if she were truly tasting some disgusting substance, and that her eyes would be accusing. I heard my father say, in soft astonishment, 'Where the blazes did they come from?'

'Sybil's bag. Sybil has been going with Josephine Carr to their instruction, after school. That's how they induct them. Oh, it is! And you know yourself how they got control of the party. Just look at this. Saints, if you please. And these. And there's something else.'

But now the sudden silence told me my father had remembered my presence. He was pointing, I guessed, at the table top. I bent assiduously to the imports and exports of Chile. The tablecloth was lifted, and my mother appeared in a curtsy, raising with both hands the white starched cloth that yet passed straight across her forehead.

She smiled. 'What a little possum you are. The places you get to.'

My mother was twelve years younger than my father. Her brown skin, dark brows, and broad high cheekbones were cited by my brother Neal as evidence of Spanish blood, one of Neal's current enthusiasms being the story of the castaways from the Spanish Armada. He said some of my father's family looked Spanish, too, in a quick nimble way, but my father was one of the tall fair sort.

17

My mother looked at my book. 'Good girl. But go and do that somewhere else.'

'It's cool here.'

'It's cool in the room under the house.'

'Neal says we can't use his desk any more.'

'I will speak to Neal. Run along, dear.'

In Neal's room under the house, Sybil was doing a heading in Old English lettering in one of her exercise books.

'Mum's got your holy medals,' I said.

'I know,' said Sybil. 'They fell out of my school bag. But she wasn't a bit angry. She asked to borrow them. So I took off my rosary and gave her that too.'

The next day, Rhoda came dancing down the verandah, singing, 'We're allowed to go, we're allowed to go.' And I, thinking for one ecstatic moment that at last we were allowed to go to the pictures, jumped up asking, 'When?'

'This Sunday. To morning service.'

Her hug lifted me from my feet. I did not want to spoil her joy, yet had to express my own unwillingness. 'But,' I wailed, 'what will I wear?'

'Your Fuji, I suppose. I'm going to run down and tell Mr Gilliard.'

And now Rhoda hugged herself instead of me, and her eyes took on that rapturous look I had observed in the church. 'Mum says she will buy you and Syb gloves,' she murmured.

'Does this mean I'll have to do all the weeding?' Neal asked our father.

Moths and big beetles hurled themselves at the white table-cloth, the suspended light. When they came in numbers, we were squeamish, and put saucers over our cups and glasses, and waxed paper over the sliced pawpaw.

'As well as cut the grass and do the hedges?' asked Neal.

'I would help you if I could, son,' said my father. Though

he still did much gardening, his spine was fixed, and he could not bend.

'You girls can do your weeding,' said my mother, 'before you go to church.'

'All right,' said Rhoda and Sybil.

Their assent was taken to include mine. 'Three reformed characters already,' remarked my father.

Neal, his father's acolyte, flung back his head and gave one of his long rolling laughs. Rhoda said with disdain that she could see the food in his mouth. Between her and Neal was strung the same kind of discord as between Sybil and me.

I said that I wouldn't mind staying home from church to do the weeding, but my mother, with the haphazard propriety she could make sound so logical, said that if two went to church, three must go.

Helen Scott's father did drive us to and from the church. My father, who conceded that Scott was a decent enough little fellow, gave him a curt nod as the car drew up, but Neal, working beside my father in the garden, and in equally disgraceful clothes, did not repress his derisive grin.

In church I was hit by a desire to sleep. I was quite alert as the congregation was settling down. I was interested in their clothes, and in their prayer books, some of which had white celluloid covers decorated with gold crosses; but the ceremony had hardly started when I began to glide in and out of those dozes I found so delicious at home, when curled into a chair or under the table while the voices of my parents' group purled and washed and receded around me. These tides advanced on me also at the school, where they were not delicious, but there I had my enemies to keep me awake. I looked at Rhoda, and at Sybil beyond her, but both were as engrossed as at a play. I picked at a hailstone on Rhoda's muslin dress, but she did not notice. In desperation I told myself that if I went to sleep, a tiger would jump on my head and start eating me. His glaring yellow eyes, his bared teeth, his twitching whiskers, kept me awake during the sermon. Perhaps there was some other event before we were told to rise. I lumbered to my feet. Rhoda pointed in my utility hymn book to the words we were to sing. Miss Thurlow took her place at the organ.

I had never heard an organ before, and thought it would sound something like a piano. As the echo resounded from its first fulsome notes, the tiger jumped, his body huge, and soft as ashes. I was thought to have fainted, and was carried out. 'The little one,' said Mr Gilliard later, in the porch, 'may be too young for church.' He put a hand beneath my chin and raised my face to his benevolent curiosity, which, as our eyes met, was touched by that slight hardness I had noticed when he had glanced at Sybil praying alone in the church.

'Perhaps,' he said, 'for this one, Sunday school would be better.'

Mr Scott was displeased with me. I was the last one to get out of his car, but was not slow. 'Go on,' he said. 'Out you get.'

On Sundays we had a hot midday dinner. White curtains with faded blue borders moved at the open windows. My mother looked puzzled. 'Too young? But Sybil is only nineteen months older. Did you like it, Sybil?'

'Oh, *yes*,' said Sybil. She looked round the table. 'There is no hellfire,' she announced.

'What idiot told you there was?' demanded my father.

Owing to his inflexible spine, he could direct a question sideways only by turning his head and torso as one, and this, when combined with the angry blue blaze of his eyes, had a very intimidating effect. Sybil sank low in her chair and mumbled that she had forgotten.

'Charlie,' said my mother. It was some kind of warning, or reminder.

'There is no hell,' proclaimed Neal, 'and no heaven either.'

'Heaven exists for true seekers,' said Rhoda serenely. 'Mr Gilliard explained it.'

Neal gave his laugh. 'Did he tell you how to walk on water?'

'Much is metaphor,' said Rhoda.

I did not know what metaphor was, but could see that Rhoda

was having one of her successes, and did not want to spoil it by asking. But Neal first flushed red and then broke the respectful silence by saying that metaphor was what people used when they wanted to get out of speaking the truth.

'Tell old Gilliard to read Shaw,' he shouted.

'That's enough, son,' said our mother.

'Mr Gilliard may even be a saint.'

'That's enough, Rhoda.'

'Quite enough.' My father pushed away his plate and leaned back in his chair. 'Let them sink into superstition,' he said in a faint tired voice, 'if that's what they want.'

Neal reached across and patted my head. 'The only one with a bit of commonsense.'

'I'm not going to Sunday school,' I took this chance to say.

'If one goes to Sunday school,' said my mother, 'three go to Sunday school.'

'No, no,' cried Rhoda and Sybil. 'Church! Church!' they begged.

'This beats Bannaher,' said my father, in weary affront.

'But I don't have to do their weeding, do I?' I asked, 'as well as my own?'

At first, when I saw Rhoda and Sybil climb importantly into the Scotts' car, I did not feel much excluded. After my weeding I could take a book and lie on top of the bags of feed in Pickwick's stable, while the ageing horse snuffled and tramped in his yard below. Or I could go to see Clare, free after early Mass, or Betty, who went only at Christmas and Easter. Or I could wander down to the creek where the poor kids hung out. These children of vagrants, boys and girls, who lived in tin shacks and humpies or any old bit of bush, beat the school system by the sheer admirable persistence of their truancy. They were forbidden company, yet were to be pitied, both for reasons unexplained, except by their classification as Undesirables.

I did not like all of them, but attached myself to a few. A display of the genitals, by both boys and girls, was one of the rites of admission to this society. It was called a 'showing', and was referred for 'passing' to a boy named Les. I have wondered since from what official Les derived his glance of inspection and peremptory nod of approval. 'Pass.' As he was Scottish, he may have remembered passing through Customs. These boys and girls taught me how to catch yabbies, and to roll cigarettes of tobacco mixed with grass. I brought them matches and tinned peaches I stole from our pantry. As I approached down the slope, through the scrub and thin saplings, they would call out, 'What you got?'

I did not mention them to Rhoda, as I would once have done. She had retreated into her own age group, which at that time consisted of three other girls equally devoted to Mr Gilliard. They quietly talked about him as they sat on our verandah or in our living room, each embroidering a small square with some heathenish design, such as a fairy or an elf on a toadstool, which were then to be made into a quilt for the Children's Hospital. Towards the end of these sessions, they brought Neal's portable gramophone upstairs and sang along with Richard Crooks, or they talked about John Gilbert. Secured by this company, Rhoda was now allowed to go to the pictures once a month.

I don't remember Sybil working on these squares, but she knelt each night by her bed to pray, which Rhoda did not. Sybil and I shared a room, or, on hot nights, slept side by side on the verandah, and, as I watched her rise from prayer, briskly dust down the knees of her pyjamas, and get into bed, her look of adult satisfaction, of repletion, made me shy before her. Nor did she talk any longer about demons and bats and pitchforks (which, instead, found a repository in my dreams) but went straight to sleep.

One night I was wakened by my father's cough, and heard my mother moving about, and I jumped out of bed and turned on the light in a panic, sure that the dreaded moment had come, and that this time his frame must be broken by those terrible convulsions. Sybil was kneeling by her bed, praying with closed eyes. I ran weeping into the kitchen, where my mother was preparing an inhalation. 'Stop that crying *at once*,' she said, 'and go back to bed.' To Neal, who came upstairs as I ran out, I heard her say, 'It's no use, son. He won't allow it.' I ran to Rhoda's room, and though the dreadful cough was much less audible from here, found her sitting up banging the bed with both fists. 'Oh, why won't he get a doctor, like everyone else?'

'Because they're all blackguards,' I sobbed.

'Of course they're not. That's just silly. Oh, all right, you can get in with me.'

My father reduced his smoking to one pipe a day. At his chair in the evenings, he taught me how to roll tobacco in the hollow of my left hand with the heel of my right, how to fill and tamp his pipe, then solemnly to light it. By both of us, the solemnity was maintained because it gave the right emphasis to the next moment, in which, after a few puffs, he would turn his eyes to my expectant face and say, 'Best pipe I ever smoked.'

Passing Rhoda's room one day, I heard her weeping. I went in and put my face against the mosquito net under which she was lying, like a runner in profile, blinding her eyes with her hands. I said her name, and asked what was wrong. She turned on her back, still crying, and began to pull up the net. I helped her, begging her to say what was wrong, and by the time she was clear of its folds, and sat upright on the edge of the bed, and had prepared the drama of her reply, she had stopped crying.

'We have never been baptized.'

'But you said we had.'

'That's what I *thought*,' she said bitterly. 'That's what *any*one would think. And now, because I haven't been baptized, I can't be confirmed.'

'Can't you still be baptized?'

'It would look stupid. I'm too big.'

'I'll go and ask mum.'

She gripped my arms. 'Don't you tell a *soul* we haven't been baptized.'

I was confused. 'But mum must know.'

'Oh, of course. I don't mean her. But don't you tell a *soul* outside this house.'

* * *

My mother did not, as might have been expected, proclaim that if two were baptized, three must be baptized. This supports my belief that she never did manage to coax or argue my father into agreement, but that to avoid presenting a disunited front, they came to a compromise, which demanded of her that I was not to be included unless I asked to be, and of him, that he would remain silent. Neal may have been commanded to the same silence, but, if so, it was asking too much.

Neal would tickle Rhoda and Sybil on the shoulder blades. 'No wings yet?' And Rhoda would not hit him, nor Sybil run to tell, but both would merely collect themselves, draw themselves inward with a determination just too dignified to be called prim.

My mother, too, in those weeks before the baptism, bore herself in rather the same way, though to her demeanour was added a touch of uneasy defiance, which made her march rather than walk. One day I saw her put on her hat, pick up her handbag, and leave the house. I assumed she was going to the shops, and, when looking out of the kitchen window a little later, did not immediately, because of that assumption, recognize the small sturdy dark figure walking down Honour Avenue as my mother. There had been rain; the park was green, the playing fields almost indistinguishable, and only the rutted track of the avenue beige. When I saw the figure twitch the right arm in a gesture unmistakably my mother's, I was filled with alarm. If she was crossing the park, it could only be to the school, to receive some complaint about me. But it was a Saturday. I ran to ask Rhoda, and learned that she was going to see Mr Gilliard, to ask his advice, and to explain why Rhoda and Sybil could not be baptized in his church.

'Because if we were, everyone would know we hadn't been baptized before. Mum says it would not look well, so the ceremony will be at one of the big churches, somewhere else.'

I began to be jealous of Sybil and Rhoda. I would not let Neal teach me greetings in Esperanto, nor laugh when he sprinkled me with water from the kitchen tap and told me I had just been baptized by Saint Neal. Rhoda was always sitting now with her head bent, spreading her hair on her fingers and muttering words from a small dark blue book. When I went to read beside her, she put an arm round me, but did not stop muttering. One night, when Sybil and I were in bed, I heard Sybil say slowly, in the dark, with intense satisfaction, 'We are going to be baptized in a big—stone—church.'

I felt lonely, but did not want to lose the approval of my father. Thoughtfully I wiped away the ridge I had made across his knuckles; regretfully I stroked the back of his head. In the words he spoke after those first few puffs of his pipe, I heard a new confidentiality, a comradely intonation.

I may have continued to resist had it not been for the naming. We had all been given only one name, but now Rhoda and Sybil were each allowed to choose a second name. The *Women's Mirror*, novels, volumes of poetry, the *Girl's Own Annual*, and Shakespeare's plays, lay open on Rhoda's bed, where the sight of them would not irk my father. Rhoda and Sybil asked each other, What about Georgia? Isobel? Katherine? I hung round the doorway, pretending to be interested only in practising the dance steps Clare had taught me. Film actresses were evoked. Bonita? Greta? Marion? I sidled in at last, and looked over their shoulders.

'As long as it isn't just one of your fads,' said my mother.

'It isn't, is it?' said Rhoda, my sponsor on this occasion. 'You'll make a new start at church, won't you?'

'Oh yes,' I said.

I knew my father had learned of my defection when, instead of saying this was the best pipe he had ever smoked, he patted my shoulder, sympathetic, yet, to my guilty mind, dismissive too. I left him quickly, skipping through the house and along the verandah to Rhoda's room, where the books now lay open on the floor. I flopped to my knees, and with tearful resolution, considered Marguerite. And though on many evenings afterwards I read over my father's shoulder, and filled and lit his pipe, I never resumed my inspection of his person, nor sat beneath the table while keeping his foot at a gentle jog.

When I was older and crueller, I used to copy that curious twitch of my mother's upper right arm, but now that I am far older still, I wonder if by that quick indignant pumping movement she was obeying an instinct to send energy into some reluctant part of her, to shake some laggard nerve or gland. Nowadays I find it easy to imagine her, with just that movement of the wing, marching out of her mother's house to marry my father; but then, as she supervised our dressing for the baptism, and ushered us down the side steps towards the gate, I had no idea that anyone had ever dared to disapprove of my father, nor that she had ever been imperfect enough boldly to defy her mother. I trusted the example they showed me, though doubted if I could attain it.

My father and Neal stood at some distance to the side gate, converting a vegetable bed into grass. I expected Neal to laugh at our cavalcade, and my father to give a humorously exaggerated wave. I did not expect that they would simply stand and exchange what looked like amused adult remarks, and then wave quite casually, and that, even as we waved back, they should resume their work.

The church was big, and built of very pale stone, and was so new that blocks of used or spoilt stone were still heaped nearby, and the earth was still turned and trampled by the builders. Inside, I saw that it was lofty and had many complicated arches, with sharp new edges, and much strong light from the windows. From somewhere near the font I could faintly smell damp concrete.

I scarcely remember the ceremony, except that it was a calm mumbling affair. I was not much disappointed. As we left I saw that my mother and Sybil looked satisfied, and that Rhoda had that exalted expression with which I had become familiar. My mother had been given our certificates of baptism, and at the tram stop we made her unroll them. I gaped at my name written there. It suggested a thrilling and inescapable fate. On the way home, dangling my legs from the tram seat and rolling my ticket into a cylinder, I looked out of the window and saw it again, written in well-formed, slightly shaky copperplate, among scrolls and flourishes of the palest sepia.

But the name was all. Church was no less anaesthetizing. The hats during the brief winter period were brown or black or dun felt, and for the rest of the year brown or black or natural straw; the hair of the boys and men was greased. The smells of sweat and scented grease, the rustlings, the responses, the weighted singing, the pleading organ, the wandering echoes—all were soporific. Mr Gilliard moved along the altar rail, his head bent to the communicants, his hair like a medallion of polished silver, while I called up my new assailants, creatures from my dreams, with bat wings and black talons. At the creek the light foliage of the trees would be stirring, the kids would be watching intently as the yabby rose to the bait, or would be rolling on the ground in fights or curled like cats asleep in the stippled shade.

It seemed useless to try to get out of going to church. Both our parents, and our mother especially, greatly valued what she called stickatability, a virtue we could only attain by absolutely persisting in any practice we had begun. Misery, however, made me try.

'What? When only two months ago you were begging to be baptized?'

It was what I had expected. But then she said reflectively, 'It would not look well to stop so soon. Do keep on for a little longer, dear.'

This was as good as a promise to let me off. I was mystified. What would become of my stickatability? But as the weeks passed, it became apparent that my mother had cooled towards the church. My father maintained his silence, but when Neal's teasing became more frequent, she hardly rebuked him. Soon, even I understood that she was worried by Rhoda's excessive devotion to Mr Gilliard. No extremes were acceptable to her; Rhoda's present stickatability was exempt from her admiration.

'The Rushton girls are joining the tennis club in the park,

27

Rhoda. Why don't you join?'

'There is the dress,' said Rhoda vaguely. 'Fees ... the racquet ...'

'We would manage those.'

'And they can only get the court on Sunday mornings.'

'You could go to evening service.'

Tears sprang to Rhoda's eyes. 'You know perfectly well we all go together, all the ones who are to be confirmed.'

My mother found no reply, but in her evening conversations with my father, I heard her energetic praise of tennis.

'It is a good, wholesome game. And splendid exercise.'

'Some of those dresses are darned indecent.'

'Rhoda's need not be so short.'

Sybil did not share Rhoda's devotion to Mr Gilliard, though she said he was very nice, or lovely. From the start, she attended church in the same settled spirit with which I had seen her dust down her knees after praying. It was much more puzzling to me than Rhoda's ardour.

My father was seized by his sickness, and for a week had to stay in bed, coughing and raging. When this happened, my mother was always tired and dispirited, and licence was possible. On Sunday morning I said at breakfast. 'I'll sweep both verandahs if I don't have to go to church.'

Rhoda gripped the edge of the table. 'No, *come*. Come to church.'

My mother looked at neither of us. 'Nobody need go to church unless they want to.'

Neal (who was to become a Roman Catholic in his thirties) gave his laugh. 'Wild horses wouldn't keep Ro from Saint Silly Gilliard.'

Rhoda jumped up and ran from the room. 'I wish you wouldn't, son,' said our weary mother. I said, 'I'll do the verandahs,' and Sybil said that Rhoda and she would have to walk to church today, because Mr Scott's car was being mended again.

Soon after Rhoda was confirmed the news was given out that

Mr Gilliard was to be moved to a parish in northern Queensland. He asked Rhoda and her three friends—those Neal called the Gilliard Gang—to the rectory one afternoon and talked to them with a seriousness that was reflected on Rhoda's face when she came home. I think he was trying to ensure their loyalty to the new man, Mr Alyard. In the few weeks before Mr Gilliard's departure, Rhoda was sweet, composed and distant.

We all allowed her her distance, Sybil cheerfully, my mother and father gently, and myself with timidity. Neal stopped teasing her and addressed her in such a low voice that with a flash of her former spirit she turned on him and cried that he needn't treat her as if she were just about to be burned at the stake. Neal abbreviated his laugh.

Sybil said to me, 'Mr Scott says Mr Alyard's name is Martin.'

I went eagerly to Rhoda. 'Martin Alyard is like a name from a book.'

'Yes it is. And Mr Scott says he is young and dark. But what really matters,' she added, 'is that he is ordained.'

On the day of Mr Alyard's first service, Mr Scott's car was in trouble again. I was lying with a book on the stacks of feed in the stable, and through a crack in the wall I saw Rhoda and Sybil walking home with the Scotts along the beige track.

By the time they got home I was hanging about in the dining room. My mother came from the kitchen when she heard them cross the side verandah.

'Well,' she said, vivacious and perhaps rather nervous, 'how was it?'

'I would rather have Mr Gilliard,' said Sybil, 'but he is very nice.'

'I'm going to put my hat away,' said Rhoda.

'You put yours away, too, Sybil,' said my mother resignedly. 'Then both of you come out and give me a hand with the dinner. And you,' she said to me, 'I've been looking for you. You may set the table.'

In the distance, at the school, I saw Mr Alyard as a tall young burly man who crossed the ground with boisterous and uncoordinated strides. I did not see him lunge, as demonstrated by Rhoda for my benefit.

'When he wants to emphasize a point, he bowls a sort of underarm. Look.'

She stamped a foot forward, drew her right arm back, and bowled an imaginary ball.

'And he spits. Come here and I'll show you.'

'No thanks,' I would say, running away. If she caught me, I would cover my head with my hands, giggling, while she showered me with spittle.

Sybil came across us one day. 'Ro, you're not fair,' she said. 'Mr Alyard is really sincere.'

'Oh yes,' said Rhoda, 'he is sincere.'

She continued to go to church until the day when Mr Scott's car broke down on the road through the gully. She told the others she felt sick, and walked back home. 'It was too late to go anyway,' she said to me. In a hurry to finish my weeding, I merely nodded at her shining shoes on the grass beside my working hands, and wondered why she lingered.

All of us, with a diplomacy that often went awry, would make a bid for what we wanted at the table, where one parent might catch a mood of approval from the other. Here, that Sunday night, Rhoda announced that she would join the tennis club.

Stung by her daughter's presumption, my mother said, 'Will you indeed?' before catching, from the other end of the table, the required mood. 'Well, I know it was my suggestion.'

'Yes,' said Rhoda.

'You won't wear a downright indecent dress,' said my father.

'Dad,' said Neal, 'they can't wear them down to the ankles.'

'Trust *you!*' said Rhoda with fury. 'As if there's nothing in between.'

'She doesn't like Alyard, that's it,' said Neal.

'What's he like, this fellow Alyard?' asked my father.

'A bit like Neal, in fact,' said Rhoda coolly.

'You will make your own tennis dress, Rhoda,' said my mother.

'Make it out of your confirmation outfit,' said Neal.

Neal so seldom got my father's stiff-backed blue glare that he withered beneath it. My mother spoke calmly to Rhoda. 'You could ask Gwen or Helen to lend you a pattern, dear. And you can go to evening service.'

'You said no one need go to church unless they want to.'

'Fair enough, mum,' said Neal.

I sat next to my father at the table, and perhaps it was only I who caught (such a fine shade it was) his mood of assent.

Next Sunday, dressed for tennis, Rhoda said to me, 'Come out to the front. I want to see Mr Scott looking more hurt than angry.'

When Mr Scott fulfilled this prediction, Rhoda brazenly waved to him with her racquet. '*Oh, Ro!*' said Helen Scott, standing by the open door of the car protectively to usher Sybil in. When Rhoda and I were adults we were still mournfully breathing it out. '*Oh, Ro!*'

Rhoda told me that if I could contrive a good alibi, she would take me to the pictures. As our local picture theatre was fobbed off with films the more powerful operators would not accept, the first film I saw was a German *Faust*. We sat in canvas seats, our upturned eyes reflecting the light as it pounced and retreated. I was fascinated as by my parents' evening conversations, in which plain patches were interspersed with enigmas I felt I was soon to understand. This Faust, about to be claimed by Mephistopheles, was saved, or so it seemed to me, by a vision of Gretchen— a vision which incorporated, anyway, a feminine face, and which came in a burst of silver to the screen, flowering fast, then lingering, then nailed by the subtitle, LOVE.

We had to let everyone go out first at interval, because Rhoda was crying. She sidled with her head down past the ice-cream and lolly stall, letting me scuttle behind her. When we reached the street and she turned for home, I realized she had really meant it when she had said we wouldn't stay for the second half, because she had seen it in the city.

'But *I* haven't,' I said.

31

'It was what we agreed. You have to keep promises. Oh, it was a sad ending.'

She was walking fast; I skipped indignantly beside her. 'I was never really religious at all,' she said in a burst. 'I feel ashamed, as if it was all a pose. But *honestly*, it felt so real.' She began to cry again. 'Oh, it was sad.'

Mr Scott's car broke down completely, and, as he could not afford a new one, Sybil walked with the Scott family down Honour Avenue to church. I saw them come and go from the kitchen window, from the stacked bags of feed in the stable, from the boughs of Clare's mango tree. When they passed the tennis courts Rhoda would give them an exuberant wave, and later would show me how neatly they waved back.

'Still,' she would say, 'you can't deny that Syb really means it. I don't know why, and neither does she.'

At high school Rhoda played on the tennis team, joined the choir, and was sometimes home as late as my father, or even Neal. More and more, now, she belonged with those who dressed every weekday with dutiful care, who wore serge or worsted even in heat of a hundred degrees or more, and whose footsteps could be heard morning and evening as they walked between the two rows of timber houses to the tram stop at the top of the street. From the broad road set with shining tramlines the street dropped sharply down, then flattened out. If my father and Rhoda came home on the same tram, they would walk down the street together, Rhoda smilingly responding to neighbours' greetings, my father giving his stiff halfturn and lifting his hat. If Neal and Rhoda came home on the same tram, they might start down the street together, but when Neal stopped to yarn about this or that, Esperanto, the plaiting of stockwhips, or the League of Nations, Rhoda would impatiently cross to the other side of the street, our side, behind which lay the park. Going across the park to school, Sybil and I would start off together, but would drift apart as if by instinct, to walk each alone or in separate groups. On the trodden dusty ground, in front of the ugly school, beneath the Union Jack and the Southern Cross, we hundreds fell in at first bell into soldierly lines, were commanded to stand straight, to stand still, were inspected, and at second bell were marched in to shouts of *Lep*-ri! *Lep*-ri! From these ranks occasionally broke one of the poor kids, always a boy, pounding away, showing his hardened heels, his spirit crying *Enough*! resounding in my heart, while from the ranks of the good kids rose that soft shocked feminine sycophantic Oooooooo! On the verandah, Mr Alpin, with his flexible cane, very lightly, and all in good sport, hit the calves of the girls' legs as they passed. It was said to be one of the best state schools in Queensland, and so it may have been, in that society where brutality and gentleness rested so easily side by side.

I wept long and hard when Rhoda died. I was in my thirties, she in her early forties. Later, speaking to her widower, I mentioned the religious feelings of her girlhood.

'I thought perhaps when she knew she was to die,' I said, 'she may have asked for a clergyman to visit her.'

'We talked about that,' he said. 'She said only if it could be Mr Gilliard. You know how I feel about these things, but I rang and enquired, and it turns out he's dead. They told me he became a bishop.'

'He would become a bishop.'

'That's what she said. She had hardly even mentioned his name before. What was he like? Do you remember?'

'Oh yes,' I said. And I went on to describe him—his manner of bending, his fine light bones, his narrow head, his unused hands, his silver hair, never once pausing to reflect that that was not what Rhoda's widower had asked me. He had not asked me what Mr Gilliard looked like.

DREAM PEOPLE

Barbara Hanrahan

AUTHOR'S NOTE

'Dream People' is my mother's story—it is also my own, because I'm the baby who looked like a little Chinese doll on a stick. It is set in an enclosed world where the big things are the small things. Somewhere there's a war, but it all seems so far away. The war is only real because three days after it began the baby was born.

The story is made up of many of the different stories my mother has told me over the years. It is the sort of story you could keep adding to. My autobiographical novels, *The Scent of Eucalyptus* and *Kewpie Doll* deal with some of this material. The past that is always present in life fascinates me.

My mother's past seems like a dream; its stories are so familiar they seem like legends. She's talked her past out so often she tells of it dispassionately—with time, even my father's death is just something that happened to a young man who might be a stranger, who said he was too young to die: but he died. So the dreaming is weighed down by the hard facts of reality, and I wanted the writing to reflect this contrast. I was continually paring away as I tried to fashion a language that would mirror the freshness and poetry of my mother's remembering.

Barbara Hanrahan

DREAM PEOPLE

She was always dreaming when it was a lesson she didn't like at school. She hated sport and when it was basketball practice she'd hide with the girls who smoked behind the shed, but she got caught and they made her the scorer—she was sitting there, supposed to be scoring, but she went into a dream and didn't put anything down. She'd rock herself backwards and forwards and dream about being beautiful, like Constance Bennett in her first talkie film, *Rich People*, and Miss White would creep up behind her and give her a whack over the head and make her stand in the corner. Once she went into her dream when it was geography—she was rocking and dreaming and when Miss White said to point to the place on the map, she just pointed anywhere and it was the exact right place, some place in Africa.

The Black Nun was a dreadful book about the wicked things Catholics did, but it was popular among the Protestants. She read it inside the cover of another book when they thought she was doing her homework, and she read her mother's Marie Stopes book that way, too. Her mother must have done it with her father and it had taken two days for her mother to have her and now her father was dead.

Two nurses up the street did abortions; one had cross-eyes and big thick lips and a daughter who went to the Methodist Ladies' College, and they had girls going in and out the gate all day; Granma said they put some soapy stuff in a syringe and syringed it up. Old Hoppity-go-kick lived one side next door; he was lame and an old devil, and Granma said he'd grab his wife by the hair and drag her inside to do it with her in the daytime. Sucklings' girl lived on the other side; she had all the blokes coming at night, but she said when she got enough money to buy her new false teeth she wouldn't have them come any more.

Sometimes at the tram stop she worried she'd be late for school, so she'd count up to fifty with her eyes shut and hope that when she opened them the tram would have come. Her girlfriends were silly as wheels and once on the tram they kept saying, 'French letter' and giggling; the conductor was the young one who flirted and when he asked what they were laughing at they giggled worse. The boys at school were in different classes to the girls, but one room was divided into two by a curtain and the boys kept nudging the girls through it all the time. Some girls went behind the bushes with boys.

Once in drawing lesson she drew a pansy and Miss White said it was the worst pansy that was ever drawn and made her hold it up and everyone laughed. When she left school, she got a job as a commercial artist at a big shop in Rundle Street. She drew cups and saucers, bedroom suites and kitchen suites, but she always wanted to draw fashions. One of the other artists got a lump on his head that grew bigger, and then he had funny turns where he fell down unconscious, and he wore a bracelet to say who he was; he went into hospital to have an operation, and then he had a white bandage round his head that he'd undo to show you what was underneath; then he left work and died. She saw an ad in the paper for someone to demonstrate hosiery but Granma said she had lolly legs so she didn't apply.

The brother of the girl round the corner took her to the pictures, and people complained when he kept his sombrero hat on through the film—he was a boundary rider from the country and was dressed like a cowboy. At the interval he didn't stop talking about how he'd driven a team of nineteen donkeys and eaten snakes and sleepy lizards cooked in ashes, and how goanna meat tasted something like butterfish, only sweeter. Then her shoes started to smell, because they were white satin court shoes she'd bought cheap and dyed black with Raven oil. But the oil wasn't dry and the smell got stronger and stronger and she felt like going home barefoot.

Ray Shegog took her to a dance at the King's Ballroom. One of his friends looked like Tyrone Power and he just sat there reading the racing pages of the *News*; he didn't seem to take any notice of anyone. But after a while he asked her to dance and they both lived at Thebarton, so they went home together on the tram. She started going out with him to the pictures and for walks down the Beach Road where they'd have a lemon squash spider in the shop opposite the billiard hall for a treat. Her favourite tune was 'The Last Waltz' and they danced it on Saturday nights when they went to the King's with Ray Shegog and the Ryan girls and a girl who married one of the Junckens. When she won the Belle of the Ball she got a box of chocolates, and she wore a blue crêpe dress her mother made that had blue crêpe flowers round the neck and a fishtail at the back. But when he took her home he wanted to do it round the side of the house—he said it was a proposition, not a proposal.

She didn't meet his father for ages and then one day he stopped in a taxi, and they got in, and she thought what a big fat man he was. His mother lived with his Aunty Agnes and the night he took her out to meet them they weren't home, but his sister was in the sleepout having a passion scene with her boyfriend. His grandfather said her forehead was the only decent thing she had.

Her mother went with her to buy the woollen crêpe material for her wedding ensemble. You couldn't buy the blue she had in mind, so they bought as near as they could at Miller Anderson's and had it dyed the colour she wanted—a soft darkish greyish blue. She made the dress with a flared skirt and sewed silver bugle beads in a leaf pattern on its waistband; the coat had a grey rabbit collar made to look like squirrel. She sewed lace flowers on to her scanties and Granma threw off and said, 'The best thing you can do is to elope, and go off without all this stupid fuss.'

On her wedding day she sat down the yard and painted her nails with pale pink polish and Granma said, 'You won't be doing that long—that'll all be washed away doing the washing.' They were married in the Registry Office, and she thought it was terrible when he went and played football in the parklands afterwards. He wouldn't have his photo taken, and he didn't tell his mother or his Aunty Agnes or his sister because they were Catholics.

They bought a bedroom suite and a kitchen dresser on hire-purchase and lived with his father, who shut his door on a piece of paper so he'd know if they went into his room. If a letter came for her she couldn't get it, because his father locked the letterbox. And his father cooked a stew, left it in a saucepan on top of the stove, and kept adding to it all week; and she'd never seen anybody eat a whole leg of lamb for lunch before.

But he ate his father's stew and he liked curry and gambling on horses—he'd gamble on whether a fly was going to crawl up a wall. He went out with the boys, he was a terrible torment, he'd sulk if he didn't get his own way. He'd won a scholarship to the Christian Brothers' College in Wakefield Street, and when he'd left school he'd gone for a white-collar job in the railways, because it was a big deal to get into the government in the Depression. He had the qualifications, but they reckoned his eyesight was bad and wouldn't let him in, though he didn't even need glasses to read. He was so disappointed he took a job at Holden's in the machine shop and wouldn't look for a better one.

There were ads in the *Truth* for women's complaints that everyone knew were ads for abortions, and she was scared stiff every month because she didn't want to be pregnant. But then she was, and told her mother, and felt cheeky as she sat on the kitchen table, swinging her legs. When her mother said she didn't have to have it if she didn't want it, she said she was going to—for the first time in her life she'd do what she wanted, she was sick and tired of being told what to do.

She sat out under the fig tree day after day and knitted a shawl—she had to sit on her own, she couldn't let anyone near her when she was knitting, because it had fifty-eight rows to the pattern and she'd make a mistake if they talked. She sewed dresses with pintucks and lace, and wound pink thread round a needle, then pulled it through to make snail rosebuds. She knitted dresses and bootees and decorated a cot up with spot muslin. Her mother knitted a pink cot cover in moss-stitch and plain-stitch squares; and she made bonnets, all very flash, with lace on them and ruching.

He used to drive her nearly insane with his tormenting. One day he chased her with a dead mouse, and she was terrified of mice. He only stopped when his father said it'd do some damage to her, in her condition.

When she took drawings into the Co-op, she wore a navy-blue suit with the coat left undone and a fox fur round her neck, hanging down over her bulge. Though she wore her wedding ring, the advertising manager always patted her hand and seemed to think she was an unmarried mother. She didn't tell him she wasn't, because she thought he might stop giving her the work.

One day she was cooking a roast dinner but when she took it out of the oven to turn the potatoes, the pan tipped up and fat went all over her feet. It hurt so much that at first she couldn't feel it; she was alone in the house and just stood there and started crying. Then she remembered reading that you put flour on burns, so when he came home from work she was sitting with her feet in the flour tin. The whole of her feet were great big blisters and the doctor had to bandage them up. She had to cut the tops off the blisters with scissors, and put disinfectant on them, and she was worried the baby would have something wrong with its feet. She met someone she knew when she was wobbling across Victoria Square on her bandaged feet to pick up some artwork from Moore's, and she thought, I bet they think I've gone off.

Someone hung a wedding ring on a string over her and it swung this way, not that way, and predicted a girl. She kept eating oranges—once she ate eight straight off. Towards the end, she felt dreadfully uncomfortable and could only lie on her back to sleep; she didn't like lying on her side, and if she lay on her stomach it was like being up in the air.

Chamberlain had gone off with his umbrella to see Hitler, and people in Adelaide didn't think the War would happen, it all seemed so far away. But it started, and three days later the baby was born.

It was a Wednesday—a hot, awful, windy morning in

September—when her pains started, so he took her in a taxi to the small hospital called St Ives on the Beach Road. When they examined her the pains had stopped and they said she'd be about a week or so yet, she shouldn't have come. She said she couldn't go home, there was no one there, and they said she could sit outside on the verandah till he came home from work. But it got so hot she couldn't stand it and felt sick, so they said she could go into one of the delivery rooms—there was nowhere else for her to go. They took her into a room with great big lights and put her on a skinny little table; they weren't very sympathetic, and said she was a naughty girl, and went away to look after a lady who was having a baby. She was lying there all on her own when the pains started again and then she felt something go queer—it was the waters breaking, she could feel water all round her; she'd read books about it and knew what was going to happen, but she was still dressed ready to go home. She sang out, 'Oh, for goodness sake, something's happened, the baby's coming, I know it's happening.' But no one came, till one of them popped in to get something and then the doctor was there and said, 'Good God, the head's out.' And it was the worst pain in the world, it felt like her whole body was being split open, she thought she was going to die; it didn't seem worth it, nobody could be worth such pain, and she'd just about had it on her own. They said, 'Why don't you scream, make a noise?' and she said, 'What's the good of doing that?' and they put a pad over her nose. Then the doctor held the baby up and said it was a girl and she saw them smacking it to make it cry. They were pushing on her stomach to get the afterbirth out, and she was half daft, and threw the pillow at the doctor and said, 'It's not a girl, it's a boy, and they're going to send it to the War.'

The first thing she looked at was the baby's feet and it had eyes that were sort of shut, not properly opened, and black hair all over its head in curls and two bright pink cheeks, and it looked like a little Chinese doll on a stick. The nurses carried it round the hospital to show it off.

But when she was on the pot, a horrible thing came out—

41

a thick snaky thing—and the nurse wouldn't tell her what it was. She had dreadful ideas of cancers and all sorts of things; she found out later it was part of the cord that should have come away before, but didn't.

The baby's gums were like razors, they used to hang on, and she thought her nipples would be bitten off. It really hurt, it felt funny. She worried her breasts were too small—some people had big brown nipples, but hers were only very small and a pinky colour. But the doctor said size wasn't important.

She stayed in hospital ten days and then they went to live in a hotel in Light Square in the city, where one of his boyfriends worked in the bar. She hated it there, it was awful. The cook was a huge woman, as fat as she was tall; one day she said she didn't feel well and went to hospital and had a black baby. There were boxers and wrestlers and prostitutes and bad language and an old lady wandering round, drunk, with a candle in her hand, and she thought she'd burn the place down. Nearly every day she walked home to her mother in Rose Street, with the baby in its white wicker pusher lined with pink leatherette. If it was windy the baby loved it; its feet were kicking and it was screaming.

The first time she bathed the baby, she felt almost too frightened to do it—it felt just like a little rabbit; it was so small she thought it was going to slip out of her hands under the water. She washed the nappies with Velvet soap to keep them soft so they wouldn't scratch its bottom. The first thing it ever picked up was a piece of bright red chocolate paper.

She drew farm machinery from photos and when she took the artwork in, she'd put the baby in its cot in front of a mirror so it could look at itself, and give it a whole lot of toys to play with. The girl who did the rooms was supposed to be looking after it, but she worried all the time she was away as it was always crying when she came back. One day he had the baby in the bar with her best handbag round his neck, making out he was a bookmaker, and all the prostitutes were there. She said she wouldn't stay at the hotel any longer, so they went to live with his father in Dew Street again.

She drew gasmasks and people doing first-aid to one another for a book of hints on what to do if the War came to Australia, but she never thought he'd have to join up—a lot of the men who worked at Holden's didn't, because they were making things for the War.

Then he got wet riding his bike to work for the night-shift. He had an annoying little cough, but wouldn't do anything about it; his cheeks were flushed and, though he still ate curries and stews, he kept getting thinner. At last he went to the doctor on the Beach Road, who sent him to be X-rayed, and when he went for the results it was galloping consumption; both his lungs were affected and there wasn't much that could be done. He didn't want to go to hospital, so she looked after him at home, and had to disinfect everything and wash his dishes separately. Sometimes he spat up blood, and when his ankles swelled the doctor said it was a bad sign, and he had to go into the Adelaide Hospital where they gave him oxygen.

One night when she was there, he told her to take the tubes out of his nose and shift the cylinder—he kept at her till she did it, and then water shot everywhere and the nurses came running. One day they called her in because he wasn't expected to live, but when she got there he was sitting up reading the racing page. He was very thin, his nose and eyes stuck out, he looked like a parrot. He said he was too young to die, but he died the day after the baby's first birthday. For ages after she couldn't bear to look at a parrot and she couldn't be in a room with anyone coughing; it made her feel like screaming.

The night before the funeral, there was a wake at his father's house. His mother and father's Catholic friends sang songs and talked nearly all night. The coffin was in the front room with the lid off, and everyone filed past and said a prayer. His mother made her go in and touch his face—it was like a stone face and cold like ice and she felt she was going mad. When she was in the funeral car with his mother and father, they passed the lane at the back of Rose Street and she saw Granma with

43

the baby in its pusher and started to cry. They stood round the grave while a priest gave a talk, then everyone threw a flower on the coffin when it was lowered into the ground. Trim's, the second-hand clothes people, read his death notice in the *Advertiser* and sent a card to see if she had anything to sell.

After the funeral, his mother shut herself in a room for a week and wouldn't talk to anyone. His father said he'd finish paying the kitchen dresser off and have it for himself. She went back to the house in Rose Street with the bedroom suite, and they put it in the top room for Granma and Granpa. She slept in the next room with her mother and her mongol aunty; and the baby slept there, too, in its cot.

Granma got up one day and suddenly grabbed her by the throat, and she thought she was going to be choked; she cried out to her mother and had to fight to get away. Granpa wasn't very well, he just sat round in a chair. There was a fire down the shed, and he got hit on the head when he went to open the gate for the firemen; it caused a blood clot and he went sort of funny and died, and then Granma died in the hospital by the railway line.

Her mother made a fuss of the baby and said, 'Poor little thing, who knows what's ahead of it?' and made it dresses and shawls and took it to the pictures, where it'd cry and she'd have to take it out.

Her mongol aunty touched its face and hands with little pats, and nursed it on her lap—she couldn't walk round nursing the baby, her feet were small and she was a bit unsteady on them; she'd tuck it in its pusher very tight, though it hated that and kicked everything off; and all the old ladies watched over their front fences as she took it for a walk in its pusher up the street.

READING THE SIGNS

Michael Wilding

AUTHOR'S NOTE

I wrote 'Reading the Signs' in 1978 at 24 Wharf Road, Balmain, towards the end of my year on an Australia Council Literature Board fellowship. I had revisited England and the United States and 'Reading the Signs' drew on the experiences of these two worlds. It marked a return in my fiction to the materials of childhood and adolescence. It meant a return to a past period but this was not in intention a nostalgic evasion of the present. Rather, those concerns that were seen as distinctively contemporary, indeed Californian, in contrast to that past, were rediscovered as having always inhabited that past. It began a project of rediscovering what had been forgotten or ignored or repressed. Much of what was distinctively contemporary then has now become the mark of a particular historical moment itself. But the other issues that the story recalls, the experience of class society, remain persistently present and have refused to be relegated to history. It is because this story draws on all these various issues and themes, because it has the intention of saying something, that I include it in this personal selection.

It has proved a popular story. First published in the *New Yorker*, it was reprinted by Geoffrey Dutton in the *Bulletin* literary supplement and in the *Illustrated Treasury of Australian Stories*, and by the Filipino writer Antonio Reyes Enriquez in *The Barangsay Voice*. Frank Moorhouse included it in his *State of the Art* anthology. It was broadcast by the ABC and Radio Australia and issued on cassette in a selection from that anthology. One of the developments between my earlier stories and later stories was a developed sense of writing for readings, with the spoken voice as present as the vision of the printed page. I have read 'Reading the Signs' at readings in Australia, Germany and the United States, and on television on Channel 7 in Sydney and on Central in England.

Michael Wilding

READING THE SIGNS

It grew under the apple tree. It got a start because nothing much else ever grew there. We did try potatoes occasionally, but you caught your fork in the tree roots trying to dig them up. So that from the apple tree to the fence at the right was my garden, and from the apple tree to the path at the left was my sister's. She put in rocks and moss and things for the fairies.

It grew there with its stubby wooden stem and its bushy branches of leaves and then this amazing pinkish-purplish bugle of a flower. We let it grow because we had never seen anything like it; even before the flower, it had this presence, this numinousness. But the flower was a clarion of mystery. Then the seedpod formed, green and spiky at first, and then it darkened and became rounded and leathery.

We asked everybody what it was, and no one knew. Even Dad must have accepted some of its mystery, because he never pulled it up. Even though under the apple tree was not productive and even though he didn't believe in stripping off all unplanted vegetation like some of the people in the avenue, the bigger weeds got pulled up and put on the compost heap.

So nobody knew, and we picked the seedpod and kept it in a little fishpaste jar in the kitchen window, sitting in the fishpaste jar like an egg in an eggcup on the windowsill above the sink, among the rubber rings that sealed the fruit we bottled in jars, and the hairpins, and the used razor blades, and countless other things. Sometimes the robin would hop in through the open window and peck around. Year after year the windowsill was in the robin's territory.

The seedpod cracked open, and we kept the dark-brown seeds in the bottom of the fishpaste jar through the winter, and they stayed on the windowsill with all the other accreted things and got forgotten. The plant died beneath the apple tree, and the dried stem was tossed onto a bonfire.

The next year, it came again. But the next year it had come

all over the rest of England, too. Neighbours had them. The newspapers reported its mysterious appearance throughout the country. The Californian thorn apple, they called it. Jimsonweed. *Datura stramonium*. Said to be deadly poisonous.

'Wonder you didn't poison the lot of us,' Dad said. Poisonous, they all said. No one said it was a hallucinogen. But they stamped them out and burned them just the same.

Once the plant was everywhere and had been named, we didn't know what else to do. We knew there was a mystery, but the naming and the reported spread of it were made to do service for the revelation. We never did take any of it, boiled or brewed or powdered or smoked or rubbed into the skin. The newspapers never suggested you could do that. That sort of knowledge hadn't survived. It was about this time Mum had her fortune read at the village fête and was told that in a few years she'd be doing the same herself: reading fortunes. She was always able to read the signs. If she dropped a big knife it would be a tall visitor coming, and a little knife a short visitor. The magpies would fly over the fields, one for sorrow, two for joy. But the uses of the thorn apple had been stamped out in the witch burnings. Everything comes in threes was another of Mum's sayings. But the third year the thorn apple didn't come back. And the seeds had got thrown on the fire because of everyone's saying how poisonous it was. I think that was a mistake, not keeping the seeds.

'That flying saucer you saw,' I asked Mum.

'Oh, Michael, did we?' she said. 'I can't remember now.'

It was like this when I needed my precise time of birth for the astrological chart. 'Here we are. Five. One. Or was that the date? Wait until I find my specs.'

'When we were living up the avenue. You remember.'

The avenue was a row of twenty-seven houses, with fields in front of us—because they hadn't built on the other side of the road—and fields behind. They stopped building when the war started. The prisoners of war used to hoe in the fields at the back.

'We were in the back garden talking one evening and it just came across,' Mum said. 'I can't remember if it was our back garden, even.'

'And it just came over the garden?'

'I think so,' Mum said. 'It wasn't very high. It was just like a bright light. It had a sort of tail, I think.'

'And where did it go?'

'It just vanished. It just went. It wasn't there any more.'

'No,' said Dad. 'No, no, no, it was in the front of the houses. We were standing in the road. It was going up the river. It was a meteorite. It was going up the river.'

'What, following it along?'

'That's what it looked like.'

Dad wrote to the paper. 'As an iron-moulder, it seemed to me like a glowing red ball of molten iron.'

Sometimes he would be at home with burns on his hands or feet from molten iron that had spilled. Now he is at home dying of emphysema from the foundry dust.

'It was just like the molten iron when it comes out of the furnace.'

Mum was furious, embarrassed. She went red.

'I never expected them to print it,' Dad said. 'I just wrote it as information for them.'

Other people in town had sighted it. There were other letters.

'You might have known they'd print it.'

'No, I didn't, so that's that,' said Dad.

Mum was mortified. On the forms at school we wrote 'Engineer', not 'Iron-moulder'. Filling in the forms for university, I went off to a private place and my stomach wrenched for a long time and for 'Father's Profession or Occupation' I crossed out 'Profession' and wrote 'Iron-moulder'.

The man at the appointments board, just before I left, congratulated me. 'Well, well,' he said, 'you're tipped for a first, you edited the university paper, you've done very well for an iron-moulder's son.'

Dad said, 'It went along up the river glowing like molten

iron and then it exploded. It was a meteorite.'

'There wasn't any noise,' Mum said.

'I didn't say there was any noise,' Dad said. 'It exploded in a big flash.'

'But explosions usually make a noise,' Mum said.

I don't know whether Dad clipped the letter or not. I've had letters in print that were not intended for print. I think I kept them but kept them beneath dark stacks of things.

'People who've seen them don't seem to talk about them much,' I said.

'That's right,' Mum said. 'We didn't talk about it much, did we?' she said to Dad.

What they talked about was the letter. The shame of being a manual worker and the ridicule for having seen a flying saucer and the breaking of the taboo in revealing these things in print.

A SNAKE DOWN UNDER

Glenda Adams

AUTHOR'S NOTE

In 1971 I was living on the sixth floor of a walk-up on the west side of Manhattan. The world was changing in fundamental ways before our eyes. There had been the civil rights movement of the sixties; the Viet Nam protests and student activism were continuing; Lyndon Johnson had stepped down as president; and the women's movement was emerging. At the time it seemed possible for ordinary people to bring about change.

I had been away from Australia for seven years, five in New York City, two in Europe. The few Australians in New York at the time did not seek one another out, perhaps trying to avoid the shudder of recognition of the self, which young people travelling abroad are often eager to change in fundamental ways, too.

Then I saw Nicholas Roeg's film *Walkabout* and was pitched back into the past, which at first seemed remote from the events of the day. Those Australian voices, that girl's school uniform, the colours of the land and trees, the tensions between the schoolgirl's refined vowels and the vigour of the indigenous life affected me deeply. And there was John Meillon up there on the screen as the crazed father, shooting at his children in the outback and then dying in the blaze of his Volkswagen, John Meillon whose autograph I had asked for back in 1950, when I was a child of Hamelin and he, a young man, played the lame boy in Heather Gell's production of *The Pied Piper*. Leonard Teale, who was Superman on the radio, was the Pied Piper. He drew Superman's chest insignia in my autograph book, and Dennis Glenny, who played the mayor of Hamelin, wrote: 'Naughty little cuss words, such as "dash" and "blow", often lead to worse words, which lead to down below.' I even remembered the cheesecloth hoods and tunics and the homemade stockinette tights we wore, stitched and dyed by our hard-working mothers, and I remembered the hole that developed in one leg, clearly visible to the audience, which I never bothered to mend. I was reeling with recognitions and recollections, which led me far from the triggering film, producing a kind of exhilaration rather than a shudder.

After *Walkabout* I wrote down everything I knew about snakes, all the rules given to us as children: if you meet a snake break its back with a stick; but don't pick up sticks because they might well be sleeping snakes; don't jump over logs in case there's a snake sleeping on the other side. Those rules led me to remember others: if a shark approaches stay perfectly still; if a shark approaches splash and shout; if a shark attacks, poke its eyes out; pour boiling water over redback spiders; shake your shoes before you put your feet in to make sure there are no funnel-web spiders in them; don't leave your car if you break down in the outback; put out a hubcap to collect dew; look both ways when you cross the road; don't talk to strangers; keep your dignity. They were all warnings, suggesting imminent violence, inevitable danger and uneasy relationships with the natural environment and with other humans.

I accumulated dozens of pages, extremely unwieldy, with no shape. I knew there was a story there somewhere, so I started cutting everything out: the sharks, spiders, hubcaps, road crossings, until I was left with the stories about snakes and keeping your dignity, which seemed to go quite nicely together. There emerged, empirically, so to speak, a story and symbols that have been in our culture since Adam and Eve. But I was not aware of that as I wrote it. The pleasure for me was capturing the tone of voice and feeling connected to characters and incidents I had dismissed years before—the gym teacher, for instance, and that scripture teacher. (We were so fed up with Church of England scripture taught by that madman, who promised hellfire if we wavered from the straight and narrow, that once we went instead to the library where the atheists were allowed to read, but the sudden increase in atheists made the librarian suspicious, and we were caught and of course reprimanded by the headmistress, in that same tone of voice.) The story brought forth in me a great fury at some of our narrowness, and then beyond that a certain humour and affection for the folly of us all.

I added a preamble about *Walkabout* and sent the whole thing to *The Village Voice*, a lively paper at the time, ready to defy certain conventions in keeping with the spirit of the times, and so 'A Snake Down Under' passed as a review of Roeg's film.

As a writer, I thought I had found a way to tackle every new story: just list everything about anything. But that was a foolish vanity. I had to learn what every writer has to learn, that there is no formula for writing stories. Structure, content and meaning have to be discovered, unearthed, each time the writer sits down to write a story.

Glenda Adams

A SNAKE DOWN UNDER

We sat in our navy-blue serge tunics with white blouses. We sat without moving, our hands on our heads, our feet squarely on the floor under our desks.

The teacher read us a story: A girl got lost in the bush. She wandered all day looking for the way back home. When night fell she took refuge in a cave and fell asleep on the rocky floor. When she awoke she saw to her dismay that a snake had come while she slept and had coiled itself on her warm lap, where it now rested peacefully. The girl did not scream or move lest the snake be aroused and bite her. She stayed still without budging the whole day and the following night, until at last the snake slid away of its own accord. The girl was shocked but unharmed.

We sat on the floor of the gym in our uniforms: brown shirts and old-fashioned flared shorts no higher than six inches above the knee, beige ankle socks and brown sneakers. Our mothers had embroidered our initials in gold on the shirt pocket. We sat cross-legged in rows, our backs straight, our hands resting on our knees.

The gym mistress, in ballet slippers, stood before us, her hands clasped before her, her back straight, her stomach muscles firm. She said: If ever a snake should bite you, do not panic. Take a belt or a piece of string and tie a tourniquet around the affected limb between the bite and the heart. Take a sharp knife or razor blade. Make a series of cuts, crisscross, over the bite. Then, suck at the cuts to remove the poison. Do not swallow. Spit out the blood and the poison. If you have a cut on your gum or lip, get a friend to suck out the poison instead. Then go to the nearest doctor. Try to kill the snake and take it with you. Otherwise, note carefully its distinguishing features.

My friend at school was caught with a copy of *East of Eden*.

The headmistress called a special assembly. We stood in rows, at attention, eyes front, half an arm's distance from each other.

The headmistress said: One girl, and I shan't name names, has been reading a book that is highly unsuitable for high school pupils. I shan't name the book, but you know which book I mean. If I find that book inside the school gates again, I will take serious measures. It is hard for some of you to know what is right and what is wrong. Just remember this. If you are thinking of doing something, ask yourself: could I tell my mother about this? If the answer is no, then you can be sure you are doing something wrong.

I know of a girl who went bushwalking and sat on a snake curled up on a rock in the sun. The snake bit her. But since she was with a group that included boys, she was too embarrassed to say anything. So she kept on walking, until the poison overcame her. She fell ill and only then did she admit that a snake had bitten her on a very private part. But it was too late to help her. She died.

When I was sixteen my mother encouraged me to telephone a boy and ask him to be my partner for the school dance. She said: You are old enough to decide who you want to go out with and who you don't want to go out with. I trust you completely.

After that I went out with a Roman Catholic, then an immigrant Dutchman, then an Indonesian.

My mother asked me what I thought I was doing. She said: You can go out with anyone you like as long as it's someone nice.

In the museum were two photographs. In the first, a snake had bitten and killed a young goat. In the second, the snake's jaws were stretched open and the goat was half inside the snake. The outline of the goat's body was visible within the body of the snake. The caption read: Snake trying to eat goat. Once snake begins to eat, it cannot stop. Jaws work like conveyor belt.

A girl on our street suddenly left and went to Queensland for six months. My mother said it was because she had gone too far. She said to me: You know, don't you, that if anything ever happens to you, you can come to me for help. But of course I know you won't ever have to, because you wouldn't ever do anything like that.

Forty minutes of scripture a week was compulsory in all state schools. The Church of England girls sat with hands flat on the desk to preclude fidgeting and note passing. A lay-preacher stood before us, his arms upstretched to heaven, his hands and voice shaking. He said: Fornication is a sin, and evil. I kissed only one woman, once, before I married. And that was the woman who became my wife. The day I asked her to marry me and she said yes, we sealed our vow with a kiss. I have looked upon no other woman.

I encountered my first snake when I went for an early morning walk beside a wheat field in France. I walked gazing at the sky. When I felt a movement on my leg I looked down. Across my instep rested the tail of a tweedy-skinned snake. The rest of its body was inside the leg of my jeans, resting against my own bare leg. The head was at my knee.

I broke the rules. I screamed and kicked and stamped. The snake fell out of my jeans in a heap and fled into the wheat. I ran back to the house crying.

My friend said, 'Did it offer you an apple?'

AMERICAN DREAMS

Peter Carey

AUTHOR'S NOTE

I am, of course, no longer the same person who wrote of *The Fat Man in History*, but this story by that other person is one that I still feel comfortable with—provided I am permitted to fiddle with it a little when I read it in public, to alter a sentence here, to delete a whole paragraph there (a mistake, I know, but I can't help myself).

The original manuscript of 'American Dreams' had one final paragraph which had been cut by the time the story went to print. In this excised paragraph I had the two boys saving the dollars the tourists gave them. And why? Because, in spite of everything that had happened to them, they *still* wanted to go to America.

Craig Munroe at UQP suggested that this was one ending too many and so I cut it. I thought he was right at the time. Indeed, I still think he was right. But I wish I had had the wit and the skill to include this thought in the fabric of the story somehow, and whenever I think about the story the thought is there, somehow, but in a better, truer way.

I am sure it is this amputated paragraph in 'American Dreams' that makes me so fond of the story. It's always a bit of a shock to realize that I am the only person who remembers it was ever there.

Peter Carey

AMERICAN DREAMS

No one can, to this day, remember what it was we did to offend him. Dyer the butcher remembers a day when he gave him the wrong meat and another day when he served someone else first by mistake. Often when Dyer gets drunk he recalls this day and curses himself for his foolishness. But no one seriously believes that it was Dyer who offended him.

But one of us did something. We slighted him terribly in some way, this small meek man with the rimless glasses and neat suit who used to smile so nicely at us all. We thought, I suppose, he was a bit of a fool and sometimes he was so quiet and grey that we ignored him, forgetting he was there at all.

When I was a boy I often stole apples from the trees at his house up in Mason's Lane. He often saw me. No, that's not correct. Let me say I often sensed that he saw me. I sensed him peering out from behind the lace curtains of his house. And I was not the only one. Many of us came to take his apples, alone and in groups, and it is possible that he chose to exact payment for all these apples in his own peculiar way.

Yet I am sure it wasn't the apples.

What has happened is that we all, all eight hundred of us, have come to remember small transgressions against Mr Gleason who once lived amongst us.

My father, who has never borne malice against a single living creature, still believes that Gleason meant to do us well, that he loved the town more than any of us. My father says we have treated the town badly in our minds. We have used it, this little valley, as nothing more than a stopping place. Somewhere on the way to somewhere else. Even those of us who have been here many years have never taken the town seriously. Oh yes, the place is pretty. The hills are green and the woods thick. The stream is full of fish. But it is not where we would rather be.

For years we have watched the films at the Roxy and dreamed, if not of America, then at least of our capital city. For our own town, my father says, we have nothing but contempt. We have treated it badly, like a whore. We have cut down the giant shady trees in the main street to make doors for the school house and seats for the football pavilion. We have left big holes all over the countryside from which we have taken brown coal and given back nothing.

The commercial travellers who buy fish and chips at George the Greek's care for us more than we do, because we all have dreams of the big city, of wealth, of modern houses, of big motor cars: American dreams, my father has called them.

Although my father ran a petrol station he was also an inventor. He sat in his office all day drawing strange pieces of equipment on the back of delivery dockets. Every spare piece of paper in the house was covered with these little drawings and my mother would always be very careful about throwing away any piece of paper no matter how small. She would look on both sides of any piece of paper very carefully and always preserved any that had so much as a pencil mark.

I think it was because of this that my father felt that he understood Gleason. He never said as much, but he inferred that he understood Gleason because he, too, was concerned with similar problems. My father was working on plans for a giant gravel crusher, but occasionally he would become distracted and become interested in something else.

There was, for instance, the time when Dyer the butcher bought a new bicycle with gears, and for a while my father talked of nothing else but the gears. Often I would see him across the road squatting down beside Dyer's bicycle as if he were talking to it.

We all rode bicycles because we didn't have the money for anything better. My father did have an old Chev truck, but he rarely used it and it occurs to me now that it might have had some mechanical problem that was impossible to solve, or perhaps it was just that he was saving it, not wishing to wear it out all at once. Normally, he went everywhere on his bicycle and, when I was younger, he carried me on the cross bar, both of us dismounting to trudge up the hills that led into and out of the main street. It was a common sight in our town to see people pushing bicycles. They were as much a burden as a means of transport.

Gleason also had his bicycle and every lunchtime he pushed and pedalled it home from the shire offices to his little weatherboard house out at Mason's Lane. It was a three-mile ride and people said that he went home for lunch because he was fussy and wouldn't eat either his wife's sandwiches or the hot meal available at Mrs Lessing's café.

But while Gleason pedalled and pushed his bicycle to and from the shire offices everything in our town proceeded as normal. It was only when he retired that things began to go wrong.

Because it was then that Mr Gleason started supervising the building of the wall around the two-acre plot up on Bald Hill. He paid too much for this land. He bought it from Johnny Weeks, who now, I am sure, believes the whole episode was his fault, firstly for cheating Gleason, secondly for selling him the land at all. But Gleason hired some Chinese and set to work to build his wall. It was then that we knew we'd offended him. My father rode all the way out to Bald Hill and tried to talk Mr Gleason out of his wall. He said there was no need for us to build walls. That no one wished to spy on Mr Gleason or whatever he wished to do on Bald Hill. He said no one was in the least bit interested in Mr Gleason. Mr Gleason, neat in a new sportscoat, polished his glasses and smiled vaguely at his feet. Bicycling back, my father thought that he had gone too far. Of course we had an interest in Mr Gleason. He pedalled back and asked him to attend a dance that was to be held on the next Friday, but Mr Gleason said he didn't dance.

'Oh, well,' my father said, 'any time, just drop over.'

Mr Gleason went back to supervising his family of Chinese labourers on his wall.

Bald Hill towered high above the town and from my father's small filling station you could sit and watch the wall going up. It was an interesting sight. I watched it for two years, while I waited for customers who rarely came. After school and on Saturdays I had all the time in the world to watch the agonizing progress of Mr Gleason's wall. It was as painful as a clock. Sometimes I could see the Chinese labourers running at a jog-trot carrying bricks on long wooden planks. The hill was bare, and on this bareness Mr Gleason was, for some reason, building a wall.

In the beginning people thought it peculiar that someone would build such a big wall on Bald Hill. The only thing to recommend Bald Hill was the view of the town, and Mr Gleason was building a wall that denied that view. The topsoil was thin and bare clay showed through in places. Nothing would ever grow there. Everyone assumed that Gleason had simply gone mad and after the initial interest they accepted his madness as they accepted his wall and as they accepted Bald Hill itself.

Occasionally someone would pull in for petrol at my father's filling station and ask about the wall and my father would shrug and I would see, once more, the strangeness of it.

'A house?' the stranger would ask. 'Up on that hill?'

'No,' my father would say, 'chap named Gleason is building a wall.'

And the strangers would want to know why, and my father would shrug and look up at Bald Hill once more. 'Damned if I know,' he'd say.

Gleason still lived in his old house at Mason's Lane. It was a plain weatherboard house with a rose garden at the front, a vegetable garden down the side, and an orchard at the back.

At night we kids would sometimes ride out to Bald Hill on our bicycles. It was an agonizing, muscle-twitching ride, the worst part of which was a steep, unmade road up which we finally pushed our bikes, our lungs rasping in the night air. When we arrived we found nothing but walls. Once we broke down some of the brickwork and another time we threw stones at the tents where the Chinese labourers slept. Thus we expressed our frustration at this inexplicable thing.

The wall must have been finished on the day before my twelfth birthday. I remember going on a picnic birthday party up to Eleven Mile Creek and we lit a fire and cooked chops at a bend in the river from where it was possible to see the walls on Bald Hill. I remember standing with a hot chop in my hand and someone saying, 'Look, they're leaving!'

We stood on the creek bed and watched the Chinese labourers walking their bicycles slowly down the hill. Someone said they were going to build a chimney up at the mine at A.1 and certainly there is a large brick chimney there now, so I suppose they built it.

When the word spread that the walls were finished most of the town went up to look. They walked around the four walls which were as interesting as any other brick walls. They stood in front of the big wooden gates and tried to peer through, but all they could see was a small blind wall that had obviously been constructed for this special purpose. The walls themselves were ten feet high and topped with broken glass and barbed wire. When it became obvious that we were not going to discover the contents of the enclosure, we all gave up and went home.

Mr Gleason had long since stopped coming into town. His wife came instead, wheeling a pram down Mason's Lane to Main Street and filling it with groceries and meat (they never bought vegetables, they grew their own) and wheeling it back to Mason's Lane. Sometimes you would see her standing with the pram halfway up the Gell Street hill. Just standing there, catching her breath. No one asked her about the wall. They knew she wasn't responsible for the wall and they felt sorry for her, having to bear the burden of the pram and her husband's madness. Even when she began to visit Dixon's hardware and buy plaster of paris and tins of paint and waterproofing compound, no one asked her what these things were for. She had a way of averting her eyes that indicated her terror of questions. Old Dixon carried the plaster of paris and the tins of paint out to her pram for her and watched her push them away. 'Poor woman,' he said, 'poor bloody woman.'

From the filling station where I sat dreaming in the sun, or from the enclosed office where I gazed mournfully at the rain, I would see, occasionally, Gleason entering or leaving his walled compound, a tiny figure way up on Bald Hill. And I'd think 'Gleason', but not much more.

Occasionally strangers drove up there to see what was going on, often egged on by locals who told them it was a Chinese temple or some other silly thing. Once a group of Italians had a picnic outside the walls and took photographs of each other standing in front of the closed door. God knows what they thought it was.

But for five years between my twelfth and seventeenth birthdays there was nothing to interest me in Gleason's walls. Those years seem lost to me now and I can remember very little of them. I developed a crush on Susy Markin and followed her back from the swimming pool on my bicycle. I sat behind her in the pictures and wandered past her house. Then her parents moved to another town and I sat in the sun and waited for them to come back.

We became very keen on modernization. When coloured paints became available the whole town went berserk and brightly coloured houses blossomed overnight. But the paints were not of good quality and quickly faded and peeled, so that the town looked like a garden of dead flowers. Thinking of those years, the only real thing I recall is the soft hiss of bicycle tyres on the main street. When I think of it now it seems very peaceful, but I remember then that the sound induced in me a feeling of melancholy, a feeling somehow mixed with the early afternoons when the sun went down behind Bald Hill and the town felt as sad as an empty dance hall on a Sunday afternoon.

And then, during my seventeenth year, Mr Gleason died. We found out when we saw Mrs Gleason's pram parked out in front of Phonsey Joy's Funeral Parlour. It looked very sad, that pram, standing by itself in the windswept street. We came and looked at the pram and felt sad for Mrs Gleason. She hadn't had much of a life.

Phonsey Joy carried old Mr Gleason out to the cemetery by

the Parwan Railway Station and Mrs Gleason rode behind in a taxi. People watched the old hearse go by and thought, 'Gleason', but not much else.

And then, less than a month after Gleason had been buried out at the lonely cemetery by the Parwan Railway Station, the Chinese labourers came back. We saw them push their bicycles up the hill. I stood with my father and Phonsey Joy and wondered what was going on.

And then I saw Mrs Gleason trudging up the hill. I nearly didn't recognize her, because she didn't have her pram. She carried a black umbrella and walked slowly up Bald Hill and it wasn't until she stopped for breath and leant forward that I recognized her.

'It's Mrs Gleason,' I said, 'with the Chinese.'

But it wasn't until the next morning that it became obvious what was happening. People lined the main street in the way they do for a big funeral but, instead of gazing towards the Grant Street corner, they all looked up at Bald Hill.

All that day and all the next people gathered to watch the destruction of the walls. They saw the Chinese labourers darting to and fro, but it wasn't until they knocked down a large section of the wall facing the town that we realized there really was something inside. It was impossible to see what it was, but there was something there. People stood and wondered and pointed out Mrs Gleason to each other as she went to and fro supervising the work.

And finally, in ones and twos, on bicycles and on foot, the whole town moved up to Bald Hill. Mr Dyer closed up his butcher shop and my father got out the old Chev truck and we finally arrived up at Bald Hill with twenty people on board. They crowded into the back tray and hung onto the running boards and my father grimly steered his way through the crowds of bicycles and parked just where the dirt track gets really steep. We trudged up this last steep track, never for a moment suspecting what we would find at the top.

It was very quiet up there. The Chinese labourers worked

diligently, removing the third and fourth walls and cleaning the bricks which they stacked neatly in big piles. Mrs Gleason said nothing either. She stood in the only remaining corner of the walls and looked defiantly at the townspeople who stood open mouthed where another corner had been.

And between us and Mrs Gleason was the most incredibly beautiful thing I had ever seen in my life. For one moment I didn't recognize it. I stood open mouthed, and breathed the surprising beauty of it. And then I realized it was our town. The buildings were two feet high and they were a little rough but very correct. I saw Mr Dyer nudge my father and whisper that Gleason had got the faded 'U' in the BUTCHER sign of his shop.

I think at that moment everyone was overcome with a feeling of simple joy. I can't remember ever having felt so uplifted and happy. It was perhaps a childish emotion but I looked up at my father and saw a smile of such warmth spread across his face that I knew he felt just as I did. Later he told me that he thought Gleason had built the model of our town just for this moment, to let us see the beauty of our own town, to make us proud of ourselves and to stop the American Dreams we were so prone to. For the rest, my father said, was not Gleason's plan and he could not have foreseen the things that happened afterwards.

I have come to think that this view of my father's is a little sentimental and also, perhaps, insulting to Gleason. I personally believe that he knew everything that would happen. One day the proof of my theory may be discovered. Certainly there are in existence some personal papers, and I firmly believe that these papers will show that Gleason knew exactly what would happen.

We had been so overcome by the model of the town that we hadn't noticed what was the most remarkable thing of all. Not only had Gleason built the houses and the shops of our town, he had also peopled it. As we tiptoed into the town we suddenly found ourselves. 'Look,' I said to Mr Dyer, 'there you are.'

And there he was, standing in front of his shop in his apron.

As I bent down to examine the tiny figure I was staggered by the look on its face. The modelling was crude, the paintwork was sloppy, and the face a little too white, but the expression was absolutely perfect: those pursed, quizzical lips and the eyebrows lifted high. It was Mr Dyer and no one else on earth.

And there beside Mr Dyer was my father, squatting on the footpath and gazing lovingly at Mr Dyer's bicycle's gears, his face marked with grease and hope.

And there was I, back at the filling station, leaning against a petrol pump in an American pose and talking to Brian Sparrow who was amusing me with his clownish antics.

Phonsey Joy standing beside his hearse. Mr Dixon sitting inside his hardware store. Everyone I knew was there in that tiny town. If they were not in the streets or in their backyards they were inside their houses, and it didn't take very long to discover that you could lift off the roofs and peer inside.

We tiptoed around the streets peeping into each other's windows, lifting off each other's roofs, admiring each other's gardens, and, while we did it, Mrs Gleason slipped silently away down the hill towards Mason's Lane. She spoke to nobody and nobody spoke to her.

I confess that I was the one who took the roof from Cavanagh's house. So I was the one who found Mrs Cavanagh in bed with young Craigie Evans.

I stood there for a long time, hardly knowing what I was seeing. I stared at the pair of them for a long, long time. And when I finally knew what I was seeing I felt such an incredible mixture of jealousy and guilt and wonder that I didn't know what to do with the roof.

Eventually it was Phonsey Joy who took the roof from my hands and placed it carefully back on the house, much, I imagine, as he would have placed the lid on a coffin. By then other people had seen what I had seen and the word passed around very quickly.

And then we all stood around in little groups and regarded the model town with what could only have been fear. If Gleason knew about Mrs Cavanagh and Craigie Evans (and no one else had), what other things might he know? Those who hadn't seen themselves yet in the town began to look a little nervous and were unsure of whether to look for themselves or not. We gazed silently at the roofs and felt mistrustful and guilty.

We all walked down the hill then, very quietly, the way people walk away from a funeral, listening only to the crunch of the gravel under our feet while the women had trouble with their high-heeled shoes.

The next day a special meeting of the shire council passed a motion calling on Mrs Gleason to destroy the model town on the grounds that it contravened building regulations.

It is unfortunate that this order wasn't carried out before the city newspapers found out. Before another day had gone by the government had stepped in.

The model town and its model occupants were to be preserved. The minister for tourism came in a large black car and made a speech to us in the football pavilion. We sat on the high, tiered seats eating potato chips while he stood against the fence and talked to us. We couldn't hear him very well, but we heard enough. He called the model town a work of art and we stared at him grimly. He said it would be an invaluable tourist attraction. He said tourists would come from everywhere to see the model town. We would be famous. Our businesses would flourish. There would be work for guides and interpreters and caretakers and taxi drivers and people selling soft drinks and ice-creams.

The Americans would come, he said. They would visit our town in buses and in cars and on the train. They would take photographs and bring wallets bulging with dollars. American dollars.

We looked at the minister mistrustfully, wondering if he knew about Mrs Cavanagh, and he must have seen the look because he said that certain controversial items would be removed, had already been removed. We shifted in our seats, like you do when a particularly tense part of a film has come to its climax, and then we relaxed and listened to what the minister had to say. And we all began, once more, to dream our American dreams.

We saw our big smooth cars cruising through cities with bright lights. We entered expensive night clubs and danced till dawn. We made love to women like Kim Novak and men like Rock Hudson. We drank cocktails. We gazed lazily into refrigerators filled with food and prepared ourselves lavish midnight snacks which we ate while we watched huge television sets on which we would be able to see American movies free of charge and forever.

The minister, like someone from our American dreams, re-entered his large black car and cruised slowly from our humble sportsground, and the newspaper men arrived and swarmed over the pavilion with their cameras and notebooks. They took photographs of us and photographs of the models up on Bald Hill. And the next day we were all over the newspapers. The photographs of the model people side by side with photographs of the real people. And our names and ages and what we did were all printed there in black and white.

They interviewed Mrs Gleason but she said nothing of interest. She said the model town had been her husband's hobby.

We all felt good now. It was very pleasant to have your photograph in the paper. And, once more, we changed our opinion of Gleason. The shire council held another meeting and named the dirt track up Bald Hill, 'Gleason Avenue'. Then we all went home and waited for the Americans we had been promised.

It didn't take long for them to come, although at the time it seemed an eternity, and we spent six long months doing nothing more with our lives than waiting for the Americans.

Well, they did come. And let me tell you how it has all worked out for us.

The Americans arrive every day in buses and cars and sometimes the younger ones come on the train. There is now a small airstrip out near the Parwan cemetery and they also arrive there, in small aeroplanes. Phonsey Joy drives them to the cemetery where they look at Gleason's grave and then up to Bald Hill and then down to the town. He is doing very well from it all. It is good to see someone doing well from it. Phonsey is becoming a big man in town and is on the shire council.

On Bald Hill there are half a dozen telescopes through which the Americans can spy on the town and reassure themselves that it is the same down there as it is on Bald Hill. Herb Gravney sells them ice-creams and soft drinks and extra film for their cameras. He is another one who is doing well. He bought the whole model from Mrs Gleason and charges five American dollars admission. Herb is on the council now too. He's doing very well for himself. He sells them the film so they can take photographs of the houses and the model people and so they can come down to the town with their special maps and hunt out the real people.

To tell the truth most of us are pretty sick of the game. They come looking for my father and ask him to stare at the gears of Dyer's bicycle. I watch my father cross the street slowly, his head hung low. He doesn't greet the Americans any more. He doesn't ask them questions about colour television or Washington DC. He kneels on the footpath in front of Dyer's bike. They stand around him. Often they remember the model incorrectly and try to get my father to pose in the wrong way. Originally he argued with them, but now he argues no more. He does what they ask. They push him this way and that and worry about the expression on his face which is no longer what it was.

Then I know they will come to find me. I am next on the map. I am very popular for some reason. They come in search of me and my petrol pump as they have done for four years now. I do not await them eagerly because I know, before they reach me, that they will be disappointed.

'But this is not the boy.'

'Yes,' says Phonsey, 'this is him all right.' And he gets me to show them my certificate.

They examine the certificate suspiciously, feeling the paper as if it might be a clever forgery. 'No,' they declare. (Americans are so confident.) 'No,' they shake their heads, 'this is not the real boy. The real boy is younger.'

'He's older now. He used to be younger.' Phonsey looks weary when he tells them. He can afford to look weary.

The Americans peer at my face closely. 'It's a different boy.'

But finally they get their cameras out. I stand sullenly and try to look amused as I did once. Gleason saw me looking amused but I can no longer remember how it felt. I was looking at Brian Sparrow. But Brian is also tired. He finds it difficult to do his clownish antics and to the Americans his little act isn't funny. They prefer the model. I watch him sadly, sorry that he must perform for such an unsympathetic audience.

The Americans pay one dollar for the right to take our photographs. Having paid the money they are worried about being cheated. They spend their time being disappointed and I spend my time feeling guilty, that I have somehow let them down by growing older and sadder.

THE BRUSH BRONZEWING

James McQueen

AUTHOR'S NOTE

In the past twelve years I have written about 150 short stories; at first sight it should be difficult to choose a favourite. But it isn't. There are perhaps half a dozen stories among the 150 that I might choose, yet, when I list them, I come back always to this one. Although it is probably no better—or worse—a story than the others. Still, it remains my true favourite.

A writer who has retained some touch with reality is always aware, when a story is finished, whether or not it has worked. Sometimes we like a story that no one else does simply because we can see something special about it that may be less visible to others—maybe the pacing is just right, maybe there were special technical problems that had to be worked out.

But that is not enough, of course. Technique is only the prerequisite for good writing. A good story must ring bells, and mere technique never did that.

I have very few recollections of the actual writing of this piece. It was one of twelve stories that were written in a ten-week period during one of those fertile patches when the work has an imperative of its own, and one story seems to merge into the next. But on re-reading it I can see that it exemplifies one of those truths well known to short story writers—that often a single idea is not enough to constitute a story. Often two ideas are necessary, and we may carry them round in our heads for years until one day they fall into natural juxtaposition—and suddenly the story comes alive.

Like the boy in the story, my first job during school holidays was cleaning out a picture theatre. And I did spend some holidays on a farm where I first learned how to handle firearms. Putting these two bits together, finding the conflict—easy enough to do in one of those patches when writing is going well.

But of course there must be more than that in this story to make it my favourite.

Although it was something that I am sure never struck me at the time, there is an element in this piece that rings a bell for me now, years later, when I re-read it. Because I think the story is really all about choices; the fact that we all have choices, that our lives are a procession of choices, choices that may shape our future in quite drastic ways. In this sense, the story has certain echoes of Theravada Buddhism (with which I wasn't acquainted at the time I wrote it) which suggests that we create our own future hour by hour throughout our lives. The boy in the story, in his split-second of choice, shapes or reshapes his whole life.

One of the most pleasant things that can happen to a writer is to find in something he has written a little more than he has consciously put into it. Fiction at its best is invented truth; but the invention is seldom a conscious process. Perhaps when we look back and see what we have made, and find unexpected things, then that is when we find our favourites . . .

James McQueen

THE BRUSH BRONZEWING

With the passing of the years he had ceased almost to think about it; and at last the sporadic moments of recollection struck at him, when they occasionally did, with a shock of alien discord. And with the thirty-year-old memory would come the questions: what would I have been, what nightmares would have claimed me, if my childhood had lasted a hundredth of a second longer?

There was no question, in the days of his childhood, of the use to which school holidays must be put. Economic exigency dictated that a job must be found, and the wages put to the family account. By the time he was twelve his two older brothers were already at work; one an apprentice butcher, the other in a sawmill. So that year, the beginning of his thirteenth, he found himself on the threshold of labour.

At the beginning of the summer holidays his eldest brother told him: Eddie Harris is looking for a cleaner . . .

And so he had presented himself next day at the office of the picture theatre. In the clutter of old posters, faded stills, ticket rolls, film cans, he made his nervous application. Harris—thin, stooped, as grey and insubstantial as the images on his patched screen, his greasy felt hat tipped back—greeted him with dignity. All right, he said, rolling a spittled cigarette to the corner of his mouth, start on Monday. And then: I'd thought fifteen bob a week, but it's worth a quid of any man's money . . .

And the boy went away with a straighter back, feeling the new weight of employment solid on his shoulders. A pound a week: his father earned only five.

The work was neither hard nor demanding. He cleaned the stalls three times a week, after each performance; folding back the rows of wooden seats, sweeping away the tidewrack of lolly papers, ice-cream wrappers and torn ticket stubs, hardly nervous at all at the scrabbling of the rats beyond his vision. The great

73

vault of the theatre was lit only dimly by half a dozen small bulbs, but darkness had never worried him. All the same, sometimes, stopping to free his soles of the wads of chewing gum, he would listen with some small apprehension; not to the silence, but to the faint sounds of movement from the circle, high above, behind the long curved balustrade.

For up there, Bummer Bill was at work.

And the boy nursed a small kernel of secret fear—held in check, mentioned to no one—since his brother had told him of the job; had carried in his mind each day the image of the tall shambling figure with its strong sloping shoulders, its lank dark hair and sly spaniel eyes. That image was coupled indissolubly in his mind with the stories—told in low voices caught halfway between horror and fascination—of the things done to boys caught alone by Bill in the sandhills, in the shelter sheds, under the bridge, in the deserted recreation ground. It was true that he had never been charged, even arrested. But, with the knowledge that children carry—below the threshold of adult wisdom—they knew that in the shambling gait and yellow leer there lay a menace as real as the clash of buffers in the railway yards where they played.

No one called him Bummer Bill to his face, of course; only behind his back, or shouted from a safe anonymous distance.

And now the boy was trapped with the menace for long hours in the vast darkened theatre. For Bill was assistant projectionist, upstairs cleaner, maintenance man; shuffling quietly and unpredictably about the narrow stairways, the rat-ridden aisles and dim storage rooms.

The boy comforted himself with the thought that Eddie wouldn't let anything happen, wouldn't permit Bill's presence if there were really any risk . . .

But—Eddie was an adult, beyond the reach of children's truths.

The weeks passed, though, and Bill did no more than leer a little, grin knowingly as they passed.

All the same, it was a relief to leave the theatre for two days each week; days in the sun with ladder, pastepot, rolls of posters. There were hoardings scattered through the town, and he would make his rounds, the paste and posters an honourable badge; he had a place, however temporary, in the world of adults. He savoured the thick smell of flour paste, the brightness of the garish inks, the vicarious glory of the names: Roy Rogers, Gregory Peck, Spencer Tracy, John Garfield, James Cagney . . .

But always there was the dark theatre waiting, the thought of it casting a small shadow on the summer's brightness.

With the coming of February, though, the shadow began to lighten. The end of the job, the holidays, was in sight, and still Bill kept his distance.

Eddie sent him, one afternoon, to clean out a room under the stage against the coming winter repertory season. It was bare and musty; dust and rat droppings were thick on the floor, the kalsomine was powdery on the old brick walls, the bulb dangling from its frayed flex was dim and clouded.

It was there that Bill, slouching through the doorway, found him. 'Keepin' you busy, then?' he said, his voice low and sly.

The boy said nothing, stood quite still in the far corner, the stink of old dirt and mould a sudden stifling threat.

Then Bill smiled at him.

And the boy knew then that the stories *were* true. With no avenue for retreat, he stood his ground as Bill sidled closer. He thought once of darting past to the door.

But then it was too late. He was seized, wedged into the angle of the corner, kalsomine flouring his back, his arms, his hair. He looked up into the wide brown eyes, saw the lurking blank worms of strange lusts. Opened his mouth to shout, to scream.

Bill shook his head slowly, and the boy closed his mouth again.

He felt a hand reach down and slowly unbutton his fly, a crooked forefinger winkle out his small limp penis. Then suddenly a pair of pliers was in the hand, nipping his foreskin, holding him imprisoned by the threat of greater pain. His jaw began to tremble, and he feared that he was going to cry.

Frozen into immobility by the grip of the pliers, he felt the fingers of the other hand slip into the fly, squeeze his testicles, invading, violating, their obscene curling explorations triggering in him a deep loathing; and the first great hot blooming of a murderous hate. Staring up into the dark empty eyes, his own—wide, blue, shocked—began slowly to kindle with rage of violence so deep that its power frightened him.

Then, dropping into the hot silence like blessings, came the salvation of footsteps in the aisles above; and the thin echoes of Eddie's voice. 'Bill? Bill? You there, Bill?'

The obscenely caressing hands were gone, the pliers' grip released. He looked down at the angry pinchmarks on his foreskin, fumbled at his buttons, concealing his shame.

'Comin', Mr Harris . . .' Bill paused in the doorway, looked back at the boy, shook his head slowly, meaningfully. Then, in sardonic arrogance, raising his voice: 'Just givin' the lad a bit of a hand . . .'

That evening he had thrown in his job, offering no explanations. His father had grumbled. But after all, school was only days away.

In the next weeks he saw Bill occasionally; in the street, at the cricket, on the beach. Gave him a wide berth, evading the knowing leers, the hints of obscene complicity in the man's sallow grimaces. And lay awake for many nights, flushed with the memory of his shame; but afraid too, and able to exorcise the fear only by contemplating the violent extinction of his enemy. The warming thought of death was all that could bring him peace.

But as winter began to crisp the land, and as his life slowly resumed its natural shape, the fears and shames faded a little. What was left, and what hung to him as the months passed, was a cold implacable hate.

In the May holidays he was summoned by his grandfather—his mother's father—to the farm sixty miles away. Both of his brothers had made the visit, singly and in their turn, and had never gone back again.

He went, if not with enthusiasm, at least willingly, and with his mother's encouragement.

His father said nothing. It was years since he and the old

man had spoken. It rankled with his father that the two-hundred-acre farm was running slowly to ruin. It would one day come to his wife, and he seemed already to think of it as his own.

The boy caught the bus on the first day of the school holidays.

The old man met him at the door of the old sagging farmhouse; looked at him keenly, carefully, said little, led him away to a small bedroom. From the window the boy could see the gnarled and lichened trees of a neglected orchard, a few blighted fruit clinging to the stark branches. The rank grass was spotted with fallen apples, rotting slowly, and spiked with high rusty docks and grey thistles. The old man, thin, slow, and knotted with arthritis, had limped off, leaving the boy to unpack.

At dusk they sat down in the kitchen to a meal of barley soup, mutton and potatoes, cold custard. The old man ate little. Across the scrubbed table the boy watched him surreptitiously: the blunt forehead, the beak of his roman nose rising like a ship's prow from the furrows of his cheeks, the hard pale eyes in their deep sockets. After the meal the boy sat by the fire, listening to the crackling radio and the harsh rattling of the old man's breathing. Later, in his own hard narrow bed, he could hear the old man groaning softly as he prepared himself for the night.

In the morning, after porridge, the old man laboured to his feet. The frosty light silvered his skin to the colour of a weathered fence-post.

'Take down the gun,' said the old man, clapping a worn felt hat on his head, picking up his sticks.

The boy had seen the shotgun on its pegs by the dresser. He took it down gingerly. He had never fired so much as a pea rifle, and the weight of the gun, the gleaming metallic solidity, the menace of the long barrels, daunted him.

'In the crook of your arm,' said the old man. 'Fingers off the metal, you'll leave rustmarks.'

Outside, across the stretch of mud and weeds, stood the cowshed. The man who came in twice a day to milk was at work, and the air was filled with the lowing of the beasts, the rattle of cans, the warm yeasty smell of fresh dung. The old

77

man watched for a moment or two then turned, uninterested, away.

They set out along the paths of the farm; the old man with his twin props, the boy with the lethal grace of the gun; up to the edge of the hills, along the high hedges, across the sodden pastures to the edge of the river's great reed beds. The old man paused often, his breath rattling, his lungs bubbling. Watching him, the boy thought that his eyes were the colour of the pale sky, the stubble on his cheeks as icy as the frost.

The boy wondered aloud at the impotent burden of the unloaded gun.

'Just carry it,' said the old man. 'Get used to the feel of it . . . that's all.'

Curiously, the boy looked at the knotted arthritic claws that clamped the two sticks; could not imagine them holding the delicate curve of the gun's stock, stroking the smooth curves of the twin triggers.

'That's right,' said the old man, catching the glance, the wisp of a smile creasing his thin lips. 'Past it, I am. Never mind . . .' He paused. 'Your brothers are bloody useless.'

Later, sitting on a log, the old man said: 'Just so you know, it's a twelve-bore, thirty-inch barrels, side locks. The trigger pull's light, two and a half pounds. Right barrel scatter, left barrel three-quarter choke.' He stopped then, eyeing the boy with something like malicious mockery. 'I had it made for me in England, a long time ago . . . It's worth a lot of money, maybe a thousand pounds . . .'

The boy looked carefully, with some awe, at the smooth oiled walnut stock, the blue sheen of the metal, the delicate chasing about the breech. It seemed impossible that anything could be worth so much money. And yet already its presence, balanced almost weightless in his crooked elbow, was beginning to work some small magic in him, a magic that hinted at the beginnings of some commitment.

A little later he turned to ask a question, the gun swinging with him. And felt the weighted lightning of the old man's stick on his shoulder.

'Never point it at anyone . . .'

He rubbed his shoulder.

The old man laughed, almost happily. 'That's the first rule. There are only three.'

'What are the others?'

'All guns are loaded, until you find out otherwise.'

'You said there were three.'

'Don't miss,' said the old man, limping along the track towards the house. By the time they reached the door the old man was gasping, choking, and seemed almost on the point of collapse.

The woman who came in to cook and clean the house hustled him off to his room to rest. But at the doorway he paused, looked back at the boy. 'I'm sorry,' he said. 'About the stick. But there isn't much time . . .'

Without quite knowing why, the boy searched until he found oil and rags, cleaned the gun carefully before setting it back on its pegs.

Sitting alone by the fire the boy was suddenly aware that quite soon the old man was going to die.

In the morning, though, the old man seemed to have recruited a certain fragile strength. And, while the boy again carried the gun, he had, slung across his shoulders, an old haversack. Across the tidal flats of the broad grey river a chill wind blew from the sea, salt and sour. The old man reached into the haversack, drew out a handful of red cartridges. 'Break the gun . . .'

He showed the boy how. Showed him how the ejector spun the shells from the breech. Showed him how to thumb back the hatched hammers.

'No one can teach you to shoot,' said the old man, his voice as thin as the wind's edge. 'Either you can or you can't.' He paused. 'Your brothers can't.' He took a slow breath, mustering terminal energy, clenching back the convulsions of his lungs. He spoke steadily, slowly, each word planted like an exhausted runner's footfall. 'Books tell you where to put your feet. How

79

to stand, how to move, how to swing. Everything. It's all shit. Everything's too quick, there's never time. Balance, if you've got balance you're right.' He paused, sucking air. 'Just two things. Squeeze the trigger, squeeze it, gentle as if it were a girl's tit. And don't hold on a target. Swing, sight, squeeze, it's all in one movement, don't wait, let your arm go with the gun . . .'

The boy felt quick apprehension, the sense of approaching a test of some kind that might mean more to the old man even than his tenuous hold on life.

They plodded on another hundred yards, the gun now charged with its lethal red capsules.

And the boy knew that soon he would have to fire it.

Remembered the old man's words. Your brothers are bloody useless . . .

'Past the next clump of reeds,' said the old man, 'there'll be native hens. They run fast, low to the ground. Take a close one with the right barrel, then another with the choke.'

Stepping from behind a wall of headhigh reeds the boy saw them. Five big dun birds scattered, feeding, in the clearing thirty yards away.

The boy was never quite sure what happened to him at that moment.

Except that something strange and new was born in him; a kind of calmness, a certainty. The world about him seemed to move with great slowness, and his mind functioned with an enormous clear precision. The birds scattered—in comic slow-motion, it seemed to him—one of them to the left, the others fanning to the right. The gun swung up, and he snagged back the hammers as it rose. Motion, time, seemed almost frozen. The butt nestled sweetly to his shoulder and the focus of the world narrowed to the bright bead of the foresight. As it reached the first bird he squeezed gently, felt the recoil firm and reassuring as a hand's pressure on his shoulder. The sound of the shot was no more than a distant echo as the twin barrels swung, traversed, his fingers slipping smoothly to the rear trigger. Two more birds were converging rapidly, heads down, racing, necks to the ground.

He let the barrels drop a little, waiting. Then, as their shapes merged for an instant forty yards away, swung up, squeezed again. Saw both bodies tossed, blown, dropped lifeless in the thin grass. Smelling the burnt pungency of the charges, he broke the gun, and the twin red cylinders of the empty cartridges curved over his shoulder.

And the world resumed suddenly its normal aspect; sound and movement caught again their accustomed pace, and he felt himself shivering in the cold wind. He turned a little uncertainly to look up at the old man.

Watching the ancient harsh-boned face, he was appalled to see two small tears form in the corners of the cold eyes, runnel slowly down beside the pinched beak of the nose.

'Oh, holy Christ,' said the old man. And to the boy the familiar oath sounded more like some kind of grateful prayer. Then the old man turned away, stood motionless, looking off into the distance where clouds were gathering over the mounded hills.

In the days that followed they tramped the farm, the scrub, the hill together. He shot more native hen; and baldcoot, rabbit, hare, pigeon, plover. The boy protested at the plover. 'Aren't they protected?'

The old man was curt. 'They're on my land.' And, seeing a hare break cover: 'There!'

As his visit drew to a close he noticed that the old man took longer each day to recover; his feet dragged, his breathing laboured more, and his face grew more drawn. But as the flesh fell away the cold blue spark in his eyes burned keener and brighter. He watched the boy as avidly as a lover might.

On the last evening the boy cleaned the gun for the final time and hung it on its pegs. They sat in front of the fire, and outside the rain beat on the rusting iron roof.

'When I'm gone,' said the old man, looking into the flames, 'you'll get the gun.'

The boy said nothing in the face of such a manifest improbability. Yet the yearning was now burned into him like a deep scar, and every few minutes his eyes slid away to the dull gleam of blued metal on the wall. The prospect of abandoning it in the morning seemed like the threat of an amputation.

'You're a good boy,' said the old man, eyes lost in the shadows of his heavy eyebrows.

At home again, preparing for school, for winter, he did not speak of the gun. His brothers asked him: Did he make you go shooting?

'He didn't make me,' he answered equivocally.

At the beginning of September, with the first daffodils, the old man died. The boy's father preserved a discreet silence; his mother wept a little, departed for the funeral.

'There's no money,' she told his father later. 'The farm's mortgaged, there'll be nothing left after the debts are paid.' His father's face set in grim cheated lines that faded only slowly, leaving a residue of querulous irritation.

No one mentioned the gun, and the boy could not ask, could not hope.

But a month later the solicitors sent a letter, a letter addressed to him, written in a crabbed and painful script. 'You will have the gun,' it read. 'I have taken steps to see that no one can take it away from you, a good friend owns it now and will not ask for it back and you will get it legally when she dies. This is to protect you. Show this letter to your father. Your loving grandfather . . .'

His father snarled half-heartedly. 'Don't blame me if you blow your foot off. And don't expect me to buy you cartridges . . .'

His brothers laughed; but a trifle enviously, remembering its possible value. Each one thinking, it could have been mine . . .

But he cared nothing for what they thought, any of them. And one day a parcel arrived. Inside was a mahogany case, baize-lined, the gun—broken down, oiled and shining—nestled into the recesses. He had no money for cartridges, but it did not matter; for the present the gun was enough. It seemed to him that in some new way he was complete, a missing part slipped neatly into place. And he waited, with comfortable expectation, for the summer.

Strangely, the death of the old man touched him little; it was simply as if a natural messenger had visited then departed.

He had grown in the year, his frame taking a new wiriness, a hardening of muscles. So he found a summer job at the cannery, forking peas from trucks into the viner. It was grinding, aching work. But he did not mind. Because it was well-paid, and he could buy cartridges. Those were the years when the sight of a boy with a gun brought no comment, and in the evenings he would walk along the disused railway line and into the bush. There, fatigue dropping away, he would become a different animal: quiet, untiring, predatory. Each night he returned at dark with game; rabbits, a hare, pigeon, quail even.

His father sneered at the gun, but ate the game.

Yet, for all this, he was still a boy, intent on boyish things: Sunday afternoons spying on lovers in the dunes; small vandalisms on the golfcourse; swimming by the long breakwater; and postman's knock, played with giggling girls in the green thickets of german ivy.

It was a good time; yet memories of the previous summer, of the rat-ridden theatre, of his terror in the small dim room, slipped at times unbidden and unwelcomed, into his mind. And frightened him a little. Because, still, at the outskirts of his life, slunk the half-threatening figure of Bummer Bill: distant glimpses in the dunes; fleeting glances behind the toilets at cricket matches and in the low scrub by the creek. Always in the smooth sallow features the boy seemed to sense the threat of some final culmination of what had begun in the theatre cellar. And at those times he felt a sharp chill.

He had even, once or twice, caught sight of the familiar overalled figure in the evenings; the man slinking a long way behind, dodging into a stand of wattle by the rusted tracks, or simply waiting, silent and still, by the factory gate.

What surprised him most was that the man seemed still to seek him out, not realizing that what had been, at a certain time, a feeling of strange fear, mystery, terrible fascination even, had passed not only through the fear but beyond it into a cold rage.

But the boy felt a certain new control now, unfamiliar and pleasing, and contented himself with avoiding Bill, sensing that another year or two would remove him forever from the small ambits of those strange lusts. That Bill seemed not to accept his rejection puzzled and angered him; for the dissipation of his fear was almost complete, its infrequent onslaughts always drowned out quickly by his controlled and icy hate.

Towards the end of the summer he moved in the evenings into the deeper bush, the dense thickets of eucalypt regrowth, seeking wood-pigeon—the brush bronzewing that were seldom seen closer to cultivated land. He sought them out because the pursuit taxed his new skills; and he rejoiced at the sight of the birds bursting from thick coppices, bulleting through the low branches between narrow crowded trunks, their feathers gleaming penny-bright, the pale shields of their breasts catching the late flat light.

One evening, moving slowly and carefully over the dry crackling leaf-floor—tense, intent only on the prospect of birds bursting from scrub pockets, the outside world eclipsed, its realities suspended—he was struck, stunned, frozen into immobility by the sudden sight of Bill standing motionless, fifty feet away, at the edge of a clearing.

The boy's entrails seemed to shrivel, and a sick trembling shivered in his belly at the familiar figure in its overalls; the strong sloping shoulders, the dark oily hair, the slight and knowing leer. He gaped, the gun suddenly heavy and awkward in his hands; it was no longer a charm, a talisman that might protect the confused and frightened boy he had suddenly become again from the dark and obscene fears that invaded him.

'Been a while, eh?' said the man, grinning slyly. 'Came out all this way just to see you, thought you might want a bit of a hand . . .'

And with the words the boy felt the last remnants of his courage drain away. Hate grew thin and unlikely, rage failed him. He knew then that in spite of his new prides and prowess he was alone, abandoned, vulnerable as any other paltry victim.

Tremors in his calves rose and puttied his knees.

Then, suddenly, the miracle of a small brown explosion shattered the stillness, and a wood-pigeon broke over to Bill's left, swooping across the clearing. And with a volition that seemed its own the gun in the boy's hand took its old life, rose, imparting the calm familiar sureness to his arms as they swung to follow the bird. The barrels led the pigeon's flight, flight that took it past the back of the man's head. Then, as the bird sped on, the boy found with some little surprise that the gun had not followed it, that the bead of the foresight was steady on the junction of the man's dark brows. He had heard his grandfather say it so many times: squeeze, don't wait. . . And as his right hand tightened on the stock the old rage flowed back, and life rose again redly in him; and death was only a matter of skill.

And then, in the millisecond before the sear tripped and the hammer fell, he seemed to see the world change shape; old patterns found new and wonderful perspectives, and his hate was only the single side of a spinning coin. He knew, in that moment, that the man before him had no place in his new world, in any world, and his rage was extinguished, his fear dissolved; pity even was born. His left hand tipped the fore-end of the gun and the shot rattled and tore through the leaves above the man's head.

Without thought or decision the gun swung in his hands, the foresight overtaking the receding bird. Now it sped through the thick maze of saplings, its shape half lost in shadow. As it burst past a tree trunk he squeezed the trigger and took it cleanly with the choke barrel at forty yards. It dropped, a sudden puff of bronze feathers catching the low sunlight like a shattered mirror.

He broke the gun, not bothering to reload, not looking at the man. Walked through crackling twigs, picked up the body of the bird. Turned back again.

The man had not moved. But now the sallow face was wax-pale, with light sudden sweat beading his upper lip. His mouth hung a little open, discoloured teeth exposed, one lip corner twitching in a kind of unspoken supplication. The boy stopped a pace or two away, tossed the dead pigeon at the man's feet. It struck his shoe, and bright blood splashed the scuffed leather, speckled the dirty trouser cuffs.

The boy said nothing. But he smiled, and found with pleased surprise that it was not a smile of triumph, but of release. He shook his head lightly once, almost impatiently, then turned and trudged off, gameless, into the deepening dusk.

As the years passed he still shot regularly. But some urgency had passed. The gun was always kept as pristine and immaculate as ever. But by the time he had seen his own sons approach their bridgeheads to manhood it was only once or twice a season, he found, that he took it down, went off alone into the hills and scrub patches. And it was only ever the most difficult of shots that he essayed, shots that demanded the subtlest of his skills.

But he knew that, although his ventures might diminish in frequency, they would never cease entirely. Not, at least, until the need arose to pass on certain privileges; for the occasional exercise of his skill had become not only the celebration of a release, the preservation of some nebulous trust, but the confirmation of a gift. And, being a man without sentimentality, he knew that a few small deaths was a price that weighed lightly against his debt.

LITTLE HELEN'S SUNDAY AFTERNOON

Helen Garner

AUTHOR'S NOTE: IN DEFENCE OF THE BUCKET

For good or ill I know most of my stories practically by heart, through having read them publicly as part of the fragmented living I make as a writer. If I weren't such a slow writer, I'd have more to read and thus would be less painfully familiar with the faults of each story. My opinions about all of them change constantly, according to who else I've been reading and what progress I'm making on my current work. I haven't got a *best story*, therefore, and if I did I don't think this would be it, but today, as I am writing this, 'Little Helen's Sunday Afternoon' means something to me: I mean, it's less awkward to contemplate than it might have been on a different day.

I wrote it in 1985 when I was putting *Postcards from Surfers* together. It's a slow starter. The early dialogue embarrasses me with its tentative tone and lack of forward movement: all that plod, just to establish the family relationships, and the father as a surgeon! I wish I'd done it in a couple of short stabs or a direct statement. Little Helen's inner states, thoughts and memories in the first half have a static effect. I like them, but I was indulging myself: I should have been briefer. The story doesn't kick off till she gets to the shed, realizes there's something going on inside, and pulls out the bucket. Now this bucket was dismissed by one good critic as *a crude device*. Maybe so—but I had more fun with that bucket than with anything else I've written. I love the way it is a *savage* bucket and claws blood into her neat cotton sock, that symbol of self-righteous little-girlhood. I enjoyed having to remember that the bucket was attached to her, and having to alter her gait, her postures and the sound of her steps to accommodate its stubborn presence:

it wouldn't let me let it go. This bucket is an *emblematic* bucket. It makes me laugh almost as much as the idea that Little Helen's ridiculous visions, inspired by boredom and then by panic, are the faintest echo of the poorest man's Flannery O'Connor.

It's an old-fashioned story. Nothing here for the theoreticians to get their teeth into. It's about the deathly paralysis of a suburban Sunday in Melbourne, and about someone prim, vain, clever, lonely and innocent being dragged into a confrontation with real horror. I like the way things look in it, I think it's funny and, best of all, nothing in it 'actually happened' to me or to anyone I know or have heard of. Except for the surgeon's slide-box, of which I have unfortunately seen an example, I *made it all up.*

Helen Garner

LITTLE HELEN'S SUNDAY AFTERNOON

Late on a winter Sunday afternoon, Little Helen stood behind her mother on the verandah of Noah's house. Her mother raised her finger to the buzzer but the door opened from the inside and Noah's father came hurrying out.

'Bad luck, girls,' he said. He was pulling on his jacket. 'Just got a call from Northern General. Some kid's cut his finger off.'

'His whole finger?' said Little Helen. 'Right off?'

'I hope someone slung it in the icebox,' said Little Helen's mother. 'What a time to make you work.'

'*Unpaid* work,' said Noah's mother. 'Will I save you some soup, Jim?'

'Let's see,' said Noah's father. 'Four-thirty. I'll have to do a graft. Five-thirty, six, six-thirty. Yeah. Save me some.'

As he talked he walked, and was already in the car. The drive was full of coloured leaves.

Little Helen's mother and Noah's were sisters and liked to shriek a lot when visiting.

'Little Helen!' said Noah's mother. 'Jump up! Let me have a hold of you!'

Little Helen stepped out from behind her mother, bent her knees, raised her arms and sprang. Noah's mother caught her, but staggered and gave a cry. 'Ark! You used to be such a fairy little thing. Last time you were here you sat on my knee and do you know what you said? You said, "I *love* being small!"'

Little Helen went red and dropped her eyes. She saw her own foot, in its large, strapped blue shoe, swinging awkwardly near her aunt's hip.

'Come on, Meg,' said Little Helen's mother. 'Let's pop into the bedroom. I've got some business to conduct. It's in this bag.'

Noah's mother unclasped her hands under Little Helen's bottom and let her slide to the ground.

'Another hair shirt, is it,' she said to Little Helen's mother.

'I suppose I'll be left holding the baby.'

'What are you going to call it if it's a boy?' said Little Helen.

The women looked at each other. Their cheeks puffed out and their lips went tight. They went into the bedroom and closed the door without answering her question. Little Helen could hear them screeching and crashing round in front of the mirror. She knew that it was not a hair shirt at all, but a pair of shoes her mother had paid a lot of money for and worn once then discovered they were too big, and which she hoped that Noah's mother would buy from her. Little Helen brushed the back of her tartan skirt down flat and stood in the hallway. She saw her own feet parallel. She thought of a waitress. It was a long time ago, in the dining room of the Bull and Mouth Hotel in Stawell. The waitress was quite old and she stood patiently, holding her order pad and pencil, while Little Helen's father took a long time to make up his mind what to have. Little Helen, who always had roast lamb, tried to stop looking at the waitress's feet, but could not. There was nothing special about the feet. But the neatness of their position, two inches apart and perfectly parallel on the carpet's green and orange flowers, caused Little Helen to experience a painful sadness. She decided to have chicken instead.

'Chicken's pretty risky,' said her father.

'I want chicken, though,' said Little Helen.

She got chicken. It was all right but rather dry. She ate more of it than she wanted.

'How's the chicken?' said her father.

'A bit risky,' said Little Helen.

Her father laughed so much that everyone at the other tables turned to stare.

Little Helen knew she was clever but she noticed that words did not always bear the same simple, serious meaning that they had at school when she copied them into her exercise book. On her spelling list she had the word 'capacious' to put into a sentence. 'The elephant is a capacious beast,' she wrote. Her mother's mouth trembled when Little Helen showed her the twenty finished sentences, in best writing and ruled off. She explained why 'capacious' was not quite right. Her polite kindness and her trembling mouth made Little Helen blush until tears filled her eyes.

Little Helen stood outside her aunt's bedroom and waited for something to happen. Time became elastic, and sagged. She hated visiting. She had to be dragged away from her wooden table, her full set of Derwents, her different inks and textas, her special paper-cutting scissors, her rulers and sharpeners and rubbers. The teacher never gave her enough homework. She could have worked all weekend.

She did not like the feeling of other people's houses. There was nothing to do. Pieces of furniture stood sparsely in chilly rooms. The long stretches of skirting board were empty of meaning, and the kitchen smells were mournful, as if the saucepans on the stove contained nothing but grey bones boiling for a stew.

The bedroom door opened and Little Helen's mother poked her head out. She had been laughing. Her face was pink and she was wearing nothing but a bra and pants and a black hat like a box with a bit of net hanging over her eyes.

'We're having dress-ups,' she said. 'Want to come in and play?'

Little Helen was embarrassed and shook her head. They didn't know how to play properly. They were much too tall and had real bosoms, and they talked all the time about how much they had paid for the clothes and where they would go to wear them, instead of being serious and thoughtful about what the clothes meant in the game.

'Oh, don't be so unsociable!' said her mother. 'Go and see Noah.'

'He won't want to see me,' said Little Helen. 'Anyway I don't know where he is.'

'He's out the back,' shouted his mother from inside the bedroom. 'Probably making something. Some white elephant or other.'

They started to laugh again, and Little Helen's mother went back into the bedroom and slammed the door.

Little Helen plodded down the hall and entered the kitchen.

The lunch dishes were all over the sink. Between the stacked plates she found quite a lot of tinned sweet corn, crusted with cold butter. She put her mouth down to the china and sucked up the scrapings. Her palate took on a coating of grease. She moved over to the pantry cupboard and helped herself to five Marie biscuits, some peeled almonds, four squares of cooking chocolate and a handful of crystallised ginger. Eating fast and furtively, bolting the food inside the big dark cupboard, she started to get that rude and secret feeling of wanting to do a shit. She crossed her legs and squeezed her bum shut, and went on guzzling. A little salvo of farts escaped into her pants and if something funny had occurred to her at that moment she would not have been able to hang on; but she kept her mind on that poor boy who had cut his finger off, and gradually she felt the lump go back up inside her for later.

If she ate any more she would spoil her tea. She hitched up her skirt, wiped her palms on her pants, and set out across the kitchen towards the wide glass door.

Noah's yard was long and sloped steeply down to the back fence. The trees had no leaves, and from the porch steps Little Helen could see for miles and miles, as far as the centre of the city. She paused to stare at the tiny bunch of skyscrapers, like a city in a film, and at the long curved bridge beyond them with its chain of lights already flicking on. The afternoon was nearly over. It was not raining now. Water lay in puddles on the sky-blue plastic cover of the swimming pool. The branches of bare bushes were a glossy black, like a licked pencil lead.

Little Helen's feet sank into the spongy grass. Her shoes looked very large and blue on the greenness. The grass was so green that it made her feel sick. The sky was low. An unnatural light leaked out of the clouds, and the chords the light played were in the same dull, complicated key as the grass-sickness. The air did not move. It was cold. Her legs felt white and thin under the pleated skirt.

Grass grew right up to the shed door, which was shut. Noah must be in there. She stood outside it and paid attention. There was a noise like somebody using sandpaper on a piece of wood, but softer; like two people using sandpaper, two rhythms not quite hitting the same beat. Someone laughed.

Little Helen saw a red plastic bucket half under the shed. She pulled it out and turned it upside down. Its bottom was cracked and it was almost too weak to hold her, but by keeping her shoes on the very outside of its rim she could balance on it and get her head up to the window. Rags had been hooked across it on the inside, and only one small corner was uncovered. She put her eye to it. It was even darker inside. In there the night had already begun. How could he see what he was doing?

She shifted her left foot on the bucket and missed the rim. The toe of her shoe pierced the split base. Her fingers lost their hold on the windowsill. A fierce sharpness scraped through her sock and raked its claws up her shin. She swivelled sideways with a grunt, lurched against the shed wall, and stumbled out onto the lawn. Shocked and gasping, she found herself still upright, but with the red bucket clamped round her left leg just below the knee.

In the upper part of the sky, above the bunch of skyscrapers, the clouds split like rotten cloth and let a flat blade of light through. It leaned between sky and earth, a crooked pillar. Little Helen took a breath. She clenched her fists. She opened her mouth and bellowed.

'Noah!'

There was a silence, then a harsh scrabbling inside the shed.

'Come out!' bawled Little Helen. 'Come out and see me! It's not fair! I'm tired of waiting!'

Her shin was stinging very hard, as if her mother had already pressed onto the broken skin the Listerine-soaked cottonwool. Her invisible left sock felt wet. Little Helen thought, 'I could easily be crying.' The shed door was wrenched open and a huge boy with red hair and skin like boiled custard burst through. He was croaking.

'You were spying! Who said you could spy on me?'

Something strange had happened to Noah, and not only to

93

his voice. The whole shape of his head had changed. He didn't look like a boy any more. He looked like a dog, or a fish. His eyes were like slits, and had moved higher up his face and outwards into his temples.

'Look, Noah,' whispered Little Helen. She was not sure whether she meant the drunken pillar of light or the bucket on her leg. He took three steps towards her and grabbed her by the arm. She jerked her face away from the smell of him: not just sweaty but raw, like steak.

'If you tell what you saw,' he choked. Red patches flared low on his speckled cheeks.

'It was dark,' said Little Helen. She could feel blood running down into her cotton sock. 'I couldn't even see in. I couldn't see anything. I only heard the noise. I promise.'

He dragged her towards the shed door. The grass squelched under his thick-soled jogging shoes. She had to stagger with her legs apart because of the bucket, but he did not notice it, and pushed her up the step. Another boy was standing just inside. Their great bodies, panting and stinking, filled the shed.

'Don't bring her in here, you fuckwit!' said the other boy. His shoelaces were undone and he was doing up his trousers. 'I'm going home.'

The shed smelt of cigarettes. They must have smoked a whole packet. They would get lung cancer. They would get into really bad trouble. The other boy bent to tie his lace and Little Helen saw that there was a third person in the shed. A girl was sitting on a sleeping bag that was spread out on the floor. She was pulling on her boots. As she scrambled to her feet she spotted Little Helen's bucket. She stopped on all fours in dog position and looked up into Little Helen's face. Her eyes were caked with black stuff and her hair was stiff, like burnt grass. She laughed; Little Helen could see all her back teeth.

'Ha!' said the girl. 'Now you know what happens to people who snoop. Come on, Justin. Let's go.'

She stood up and buckled her belt. The two of them barged out the door. Little Helen heard their feet thumping on the grass and then crunching on the gravel drive.

'I know what *you've* been doing,' said Little Helen. The butts were everywhere. Some had lipstick on the yellow end.

'Shut your face,' said Noah. In the grey light from the open door his head with its short orange hair and flat temples was as smooth and savage as a bull terrier's. He gave a high snigger. 'You look stupid with that bucket on your leg.'

The moment for crying was long gone. She would have had to fake it, though she knew she had the right. 'It hurts,' said Little Helen. 'I can feel blood still coming out. It hurts quite a lot, actually. It might be serious.'

'You want to know about blood?' said Noah. His small, high, dog's eyes began to glow, as if a weak torch battery had flicked on inside his head. 'I'll show you what can happen to people.'

'I think I'd better speak to my mother,' said Little Helen. 'I need to ask her about something very important.'

'First I'll show you something,' said Noah.

'I can't walk,' said Little Helen. She folded her arms and stood square, with her knees apart to accommodate the bucket, but he scooped her off the ground in one round movement and ran out of the shed and across the garden.

From her sideways and horizontal position Little Helen saw the grassy world bounce and swing. She kept her left leg stuck out straight so the bucket would not be interfered with. His big hip and thigh worked under her waist like a horse's. He took the back steps in a couple of bounds. At the top he swung her across his front while he fumbled with the glass door, and in its broad pane she saw reflected her own white underpants, twisted half off her bottom, and down in its lower corner, half obscured by the image of her faithful bucket, the bunch of skyscrapers flaming with light. She writhed to cover her pants and his hard fingers gripped her tighter. He forged through the kitchen, along the passage and into a small dim room that smelt of leather and Finepoint pens with their caps off.

Dumped, she staggered for the door, but he got past her and kicked it shut.

'Mum!' said Little Helen, without conviction.

'Look,' said Noah. He kept one foot against the door and reached behind her to a large, low, wooden cupboard that stood on legs against one wall. He slid open its front panel and switched on a light inside it.

It was not a cupboard. It was a box. It was deep, and it was full of pictures, tiny square ones, suspended in space, arranged in neat horizontal rows and lit gently from behind so that they glowed in many colours, jewel-like, but mostly yellow, brown and red. The magical idea, the bright orderliness of it, took Little Helen's breath away. She limped forward, smiling, favouring her bucketed leg. Noah left the door and crouched beside her. He must have forgiven her: he was panting from his run, from his haste to bring her to this wonder.

The pictures were slides. They seemed to be of children's faces. But there was something unusual about them. Were they children in face paint? Were they dressed in Costumes of Other Lands, or at a Hat Competition? Were they disguised as angels, or fairies? Little Helen tried to kneel, but her bucket bothered her. She spread her legs wide and bent them, and opened her arms to keep her balance. In this Balinese posture she lowered herself to contemplate the mystery.

The children were horrible. Their heads were bloodied. Their hair had been torn out by the roots, their scalps were raw and crisscrossed with black railway lines. Their lips were blue and swollen and bulged outwards, barely contained by stitches. Their eyes had burst like pickled onions, their foreheads were stove in, their chins were crushed to pink pulp. One baby, too new to sit up, had a huge purple furry thing growing from its temple to its chin. Another had two dark holes instead of a nose and its top lip was not there at all.

But the worst thing was that not a single one of them was crying. The ones whose eyes still worked looked straight at Little Helen with a patient, sober gaze. They were not surprised that these terrible things had happened to them, that their mothers had turned away at the wrong moment, that the war had come, that men with guns and knives had got into the house and found them. Little Helen's hackles went lumpy and her stomach rose into her throat. She shut her eyes and tried to straighten up, but Noah put his hand down hard on her shoulder and croaked.

'See that kid there? A power line fell on him. His brain woulda blown right out of his skull.'

Little Helen squirmed out from under his hand and crawled away. He did not follow her, but watched her drag her bucket to the door and stand up and reach the high handle. She got her good foot out into the hall and looked back. He was crouching before the picture box. The soft white light from inside it polished his furry hair. Little Helen saw that he could not stop looking at the pictures. He turned to her.

'See?' he said. 'See what can happen to little kids?'

She nodded.

'Don't you like it?' The dim torch battery went on behind his eyes. He was smiling. 'You don't, do you. Piss weak. Look at this equipment. Best that money can buy.'

'What—' She cleared her throat. 'Did they all die?'

'Die? Course they didn't die. My dad sewed 'em up. But they were very sick. And afterwards they were always ugly. For the rest of their lives.'

Little Helen let go the door handle and slid out into the hallway. Her palms were sticky and the backs of her hands had shrunk and gone hard, but she was not going to be sick. She stumped away down the passage towards the front of the house. The bucket made a soft clunk with every second step.

Her mother and Noah's were sitting quietly on the edge of the big double bed. They were dressed in their ordinary clothes and sat with their hands folded in their laps as if waiting for something. Little Helen clumped into the doorway and stopped. They looked up. She saw their two white faces, round and flat as dinner plates, shining above their dark dresses in what remained of the light.

SISTER SHIPS

Joan London

AUTHOR'S NOTE

For a long time I tried to write a story about three girls travelling together. Two of the girls had sprung to mind fully named, and I thought they were the focus of my interest. I could never find a name for the third. Originally I conceived her as a victim, the over-protected middle-class girl, trapped in a vision of 'the nice'. She was to crack up at the end, or at least be last seen limping home.

It wasn't until I shifted the action to a ship, and the point of view to this third girl, that the story started to move. It was as if my initial vision of her had been too stereotyped, and as if the other two girls, already known to me, could only have a freshness of interest for me when presented through her eyes. It turned out that, in fact, she was the one I knew the best. Her name became Hull—I thought of her as the sort of girl at school who is known, not altogether affectionately, by her surname— but the 'symbolic' nature of this name had to be pointed out to me.

After this the story was comparatively easy to write, perhaps because of the naïvety of the observer, and the double-edge this allows, and because shipboard life is a given image, in which the action could be built up around certain universal situations. The progress of the voyage seemed to carry the narrative along and allowed many unplanned things to flow through. The German man, for instance, at first included for shipboard colour: on a real sea voyage I once made there was a German man who would appear at your elbow and talk very fast and knowledgeably about the waters we were travelling through, and then disappear again. He was so elusive, yet intense, that we nicknamed him the 'White

Rabbit'. I was well into the story before the idea of the German man's metamorphosis into his nickname, and the role he would play for Hull, occurred to me.

I think this final scene is why I'm fond of this story, not only because it was enjoyable to write—I laughed a lot as I wrote it, though I've learnt this isn't always a good sign—but because it shaped itself, like a dream, and breaking away from the 'real', even in a small way, was something that at the time I'd been wanting to do.

Joan London

SISTER SHIPS

1

Kaye Garrett is late again. She has rushed into the cabin in her bikini and thrown her wet towel on my bunk.

'Have I got time for a ciggie?' she asks, lighting up anyway though she knows we are First Sitting. Then she gets down to work. She circles her eyes with a sort of white lipstick and dots biscuit-coloured lotion onto the compass points of her face. I take this opportunity to slip her towel onto the floor.

'I don't know why you go to all this trouble,' Bar Holland calls down from the top bunk. 'The people on this ship are only interested in food and sexual intercourse.'

'Oh?' says Kaye Garrett. 'Why do you say that?' Her eyes are open very wide in the mirror but she's not looking at us. With a little black brush she is grooming the wing of her lashes. Does she know that as she does this her mouth springs open like a fish?

'Observation,' Bar Holland says. I hear her yawning. 'I haven't put it to the test.'

The dinner chimes crackle over the PA. Doors slam up and down the corridor and a great wave of people calling out and jingling keys seems to rush past our cabin. I stand up. I have been ready for ages.

Kaye rips off her bikini and reaches into the wardrobe. 'Oh Hull.' She's turning to me, she's holding my pink shirt, 'Oh Hully, would you mind, could I please . . .?'

I take a breath. I've practised this. I was going to say, in a light, pleasant voice, 'Actually Kaye, I'd thought of wearing that myself tomorrow.' But when she stands in front of me like this, naked, watching me, as if she's testing me, I don't know where to look . . .

There is a quick knock and the door swings open. Kaye screams and clutches my shirt to her.

'Sorry ladeez, so sorry ladeez.' It is Taki, our cabin steward, with an armful of towels. He backs out, groping to close the door behind him.

'Bloody Taki,' Kaye says. She's buttoning up my shirt.

'Hot Greek blood,' calls down Bar.

'He must have thought we'd gone to dinner,' I say. 'We *are* late.' In the mornings I find him waiting outside the door with his mop and duster. I say, 'I'm sorry. The other girls are still slee-ping.' I put my head on my hands to mime a pillow. He nods and smiles. He understands.

'Oh yeah?' says Kaye. 'He's always barging in.' She's pulling on a black skirt, tucking in my shirt. The pink shirt is part of an ensemble my mother and I bought after my last day at school. 'For deck games,' my mother said. Sometimes I think about the Trip as my mother planned it. It is like another ship travelling alongside this one, with all its passengers on deck waving in a friendly sort of way. There are bound to be some awfully nice types amongst them, my parents had a ball on their Trip Out, they are waving but getting hard to see now, the animal throb and grind of this ship is leaving them behind.

The lights flicker in the narrow corridors. We stagger a little as the ship sways. Voices are rising in the bars, 'Aloha' and 'Chelsea', where the early drinkers have settled in. As our heels clatter up the stairs two stewards hiss from a doorway: 'Psst! I love you!' We look straight ahead but we giggle. Don't they know that with us their case is hopeless?

We part at the doors of the dining room. Kaye Garrett sort of glides in past us, gone for the night.

'I'll meet you here afterwards,' I say to Bar Holland. If I don't say this she is quite likely to wander off in her absent-minded way, and then I am alone for the whole evening. '*Here*, okay?'

'Okay,' she says. She brings her book with her. She sits at a table with a big family. Quite often they are seasick and only the father is there. He is glad of a bit of peace and quiet, Bar says. He's quite happy if she reads between courses.

My table is for four, on the far side of the dining room. I take my usual seat, next to the German man. I say Good Evening to him, I have never caught his name. He wears a white suit to dinner and has a short white beard. He's about my father's age: it is his eleventh sea voyage. This is all I know about him.

'We thought you were going to miss out on the soup,' Marie says from across the table. She is a secretary from Wollongong. 'Still, not to worry, we've only just got ours as usual.' Marie is frustrated by the service on this ship, especially at the table. 'It's the same old story,' she told me, 'the quiet ones get over-looked.'

'Hi,' says Eric, who sits next to her.

'Try and catch the waiter's eye,' Marie advises me, 'when he goes to that big table.'

But I don't want any soup. I am trying to think of something to say to Eric.

'How did you go at deck-tennis this afternoon?'

He laughs. 'I got a thrashing. I'm out of the tournament. I think I'm going to have to invent deck-cricket. Maybe I'd make a better fist of that.'

I laugh, understandingly. I know that Eric plays cricket in summer, swims all year round, likes early Blues and opera, grew up on a farm in northern New South Wales, has just finished his second year of Law. I know because over two weeks' meals I have asked him. The trouble is, I'm running out of questions. He asks me questions too sometimes, often the same questions. I've told him three times now that I've just done my matric, that I'm going to stay with relatives in England.

'Get a load of that would you,' Marie says. 'That big table. On to the main course already and we haven't even ordered the entrée!'

'I met another girl from Perth today,' Eric says to me. His nose is sunburnt, a big nose, he isn't really good-looking. But the first time he came to our table and smiled and pulled Marie's chair out for her, I thought: He's *nice*. 'A blonde girl, Barbara.'

'Oh, Bar Holland. She went to school with me. She shares my cabin.'

'She seems like quite an original.'

'Yes. Well I didn't really get to know her before this trip. We were in different classes . . .'

'You can't have any secrets when you share a cabin, I can tell you,' Marie says.

'Do you share a cabin?' I ask the German man after a while. It seems so terribly rude not to say anything to him for the whole meal.

'I am alone,' the German man replies. 'I prefer.'

'I think I would too.' I give a little laugh. 'Not that I've got any secrets.'

'Ah,' says the German man. 'Without secrets nothing is possible.'

'What *is* your cabin number by the way?' Eric asks me.

'There she is,' I say to Bar Holland. We are taking our after-dinner stroll around A Deck.

'Who?'

'*Kaye*. It looks like it's Officers' Night tonight.'

'Chelsea' is dimly lit, but the pink shirt, the white uniforms around it, glow in the light from behind the bar.

'I suppose it's a good way to learn Greek,' I say, climbing up the ladder onto Boat Deck behind Bar Holland. There is a railing at the front of Boat Deck, past the funnels, where we always stand. It is as high and far as you can go.

I want to talk about Kaye Garrett with Bar, but something holds me back. 'All that make-up,' I want to say, 'do you think she looks *hard*? Do you think she looks older than seventeen? I think swearing is unfeminine. Does she swear in front of men? What is sex-appeal anyway? She's got lots of nice clothes herself, I don't know why she . . .'

It is quieter up here, we are further away from the engine, you can even hear the crisp breaking of the wake, white in the black sea. The wind blows back Bar Holland's beach-white hair from her long, stern chin. Her eyelashes are white too, so that her stare beyond the ship seems unblinking. I wish that I was like Bar Holland, my mind on higher things.

'Think I'll go down and read,' she says.

'Yes,' I say, 'I *must* finish my letter.'

Music has started up in the ballroom. The soft thud of the drum, the even ripple of the piano. '*Leesten*,' the singer's voice crackles as he adjusts the microphone, '*do you want to know a see-gret?*'

Corridor by corridor we descend the ship.

We went to the ballroom once, on our first night aboard. Kaye was with us then. We sat at a table by the dancefloor and ordered drinks. 'To us,' Kaye said. The band, in midnight-blue tuxedos, winked and bowed at us. There was a solo on the electric guitar, the theme song from 'Bonanza'. A middle-aged couple danced a professional tango under the swirling gold hexagons of the dome in the middle of the ceiling.

'Oh my God,' Kaye Garrett said. 'This is *dire*.'

But after a while the ballroom filled with people. Second Sitting people. The band took off their coats. The dance floor thronged, lights dimmed, shadows raced around the walls. A white uniform bowed before Kaye. She got up slowly, her face was severe over his shoulder as they circled the floor. Bar Holland and I sipped our drinks, islanded amongst empty tables and chairs. Bar Holland stood up.

'I'm going,' she said. 'I'm bored.'

We made a great show of fanning ourselves on the deck, of gasping for fresh air.

'Who do you write all these letters to?' Bar Holland's bunk creaks above me as she changes position, sighs, flicks pages. I look at my watch. Nine-thirty. We have made our descent too early. But there's no going back. That would be against our code, our anti-ship stance. And I've already rollered up my hair.

'Oh—my parents mainly,' I say.

'S'pose I ought to drop the folks a line,' says Bar. 'But what do you say? "I am eating, sleeping and reading. Fondest regards."'

'I'm sure they'd like to know how you are.'

The bunk thumps, Bar Holland's legs wave past me. She crouch-lands on the floor. 'They know I'm alive,' she says. 'The rest is just—role play.'

'But your parents—well, they feel for you,' I say from the shadows of my bunk.

'Do they?' She is walking up and down the cabin breast-stroking the air. 'How do you know what you feel if you just keep on spouting off your lines?' Her voice trails off, she yawns. 'Anyway,' she mutters, 'I don't seem to go in for *feelings.*'

There's a knock at the door. I shrink back clutching my rollers. Bar Holland opens it an inch. Her blouse at the back is hanging out of her skirt. Her hair is fizzed into a little crown from lying down.

'Oh, it's you,' she says. She sounds almost angry. 'Oh, all right, why not.' She reaches for her key on the dressing-table.

It's Eric.

2

You should see me now, I write, *lying back next to the swimming pool!* I pause. This is more or less the case. It was a relief to see this empty deckchair as I picked my way through all those brown oily bodies. 'Yes dear, come and join me,' the old lady in the next chair said. She's asleep now. We're not all that far from the pool. *The weather is perfect, everybody is here.* I waved to Kaye Garrett but she didn't see me. She's amongst a very lively crowd of people. Marie waves though, from under her big sunhat, while another girl rubs cream into her shoulders. Even the German man is standing by the railing, looking at something through binoculars. *Bar Holland's in the pool, having a swimming lesson!* Eric kneels by the side of the pool while Bar thrashes her way up and back to him. When she emerges, spouting water, hair plastered over her eyes, Eric leans right down to her to demonstrate a stroke. *Luckily I have the cabin to myself a lot*

*these days. I am teaching English to our steward. He brings me
his photos and I point and say 'brother-in-law', 'grandmother' etc.
He is very grateful.* His knock is so gentle it might be just another
note in the rattle and hum of the cabin. The cool dark cabin.
I shut my eyes against the white glare of the deck. *Actually it's
getting very hot out here, I can't last much longer. I don't think
I'm ever going to finish this letter!*

The funny thing is, I can't see my parents any more. I mean
I can't see their faces. I see them as silhouettes moving round
the rooms at home, dark figures against light coming through
doors and windows. I see light coming onto the kitchen table,
onto the knives and forks in their set places, but the room is
empty. I see the pool of light under their bedroom door. Voices
*. . . join in . . . people of her own age . . . the Garrett girl has
got a berth . . .*

I see my father's big frame blocking the light of the hall
as he comes in from checking the letterbox. The jingle of small
change in his pockets has a disappointed sound.

'Do *you* speak French too?' Eric asks me at lunch.

'No.'

'That's a pity. We could have put in a bit of practice over
déjeuner.' He is buttering his roll lavishly, smiling to himself.

'Bar Holland got the French prize at school,' I say. It is cold
cuts for lunch again today. I choose a small slice of luncheon
meat. 'And then of course this scholarship to Paris.'

'Well, she's got a real challenge on her hands now,' Eric says.
'She's going to have me speaking French by the time we get
to Southampton.'

'Ah ha,' says the German man, his voice cracking out, crusty.
We all turn to him. 'That is the best way to learn a language.
The language off love.' His head shakes up and down over his
plate. I can't tell if he's laughing. We all bend back over our
plates.

'Bar will do it if anyone can,' I say. I reach for the
Worcestershire sauce and shake it over my meat. 'Not only is

107

she terribly intelligent, she is a very hard worker.' I take my time, making a little package for my fork. 'At school she had no time for anything else. No sport, no social life. It was work work work.' The ship dips, the bright water in the porthole behind Eric flashes on, flashes off. The words keep coming. 'She was sort of famous for it.'

'My cabin mate Nan and I,' Marie begins, 'we can't understand a word our steward says to us. Speaka da English *please*, I say to him . . .' I can hear Eric scraping back his chair, but Marie has caught my eye and won't let go. 'Wouldn't you think they'd try and get an English-speaking crew?'

'If you'll excuse me,' Eric says.

I put down my knife and fork. I can't eat the cold cuts. They taste of the ship's refrigerator, they taste as if they have soaked up all the smells of the ship. The ship itself is like a giant refrigerator. If you turned it off you would smell its staleness, its collective odours from a thousand lives in cold storage.

That the knock does come, at the same time as yesterday, makes it seem like an appointment. I too have my rendezvous. I don't leave him to use his key, but open the door myself.

His eyes are waiting for me. No mop, no towels. He's not pretending this time that he has work to do. I recognize the red plastic cover of his photo album.

More photos? That cheerful teaching voice. But it helps to get me to the bunk, turn on the little spotlight over the pillow, pat a place for him.

Seester, nephew, brudder-in-lo. It is touching to see this manly hand, black hair crawling from the cuff over the fingers, stabbing so patiently.

Very good. Pounding blood seems to fill up my eyes. I peer at stoic faces clustered up the front steps of a house. A bare twiggy tree by the balcony. I point. *Brr. Cold.*

Cold? He slides an arm around me. *You are cold?*

No no. The photo. Must be winter. His thighs nudge mine, narrow and hard, like gateposts. *When it's winter in Greece, it's summer in Aus* . . . I am falling back.

You good girl. His breath is warm in my ear. *The most good girl on the sheep.*

Best. The best girl. But I . . . But my voice is small again as he covers my face with little popping kisses. Our knees rise as the bunk creaks. He lurches on top of me and flicks his tongue wetly into my ear, kisses my neck, squeezes my breasts. All this is, I know, to be expected. He is quite systematic, in a hasty way. He seems to be in a hurry.

So this is what it's like. A full close-up of a scalp. He's heavy. My legs are flattened off the edge of the bunk. There's saliva on my chin, but my arms are pinned to the elbow. I roll my eyes and catch sight of Bar Holland's big bottle-green school bloomers slung to dry over the towel-rail. It is rather clinical, I decide, like being in a dentist's chair. The same helplessness, the same need to remind yourself there is no reason to feel embarrassed. His hand is steadily ruching up my skirt. *You should see me now* . . .

'No.' I push at his shoulder. 'Please.'

He lifts his head. 'No?'

He is up like a shot, tucking in his shirt, looking round for his photo album.

'I'm sorry. I didn't mean . . .' I have broken a rule, I know. I have *led him on.*

He smiles down at me. He shrugs.

'Leetle girl.'

He ducks for a moment at the mirror on his way out and, using two hands, smooths back his hair.

3

We are getting into colder waters now. The swimming pool is covered with a net. There are whole decks where the wind sweeps down and the spray leaps up to startle only empty deckchairs. The sea and sky have joined forces, huge, murky and untrustworthy.

'Dirty old day,' the old lady from the deckchair mutters as we pass. Her head is bandaged in a scarf as if she has the mumps. We seldom pass without a nod or comment, we fellow deck-bravers, who have taken over now the brown bodies have deserted, the blind man and his wife, the mad boy counting his steps, the Indian couple, her peacock skirts brushing against wet railings, the tired-looking father from Bar Holland's table, the German man in a black, high-shouldered coat.

Inside it's different too. The rattle and sway of the ship fighting its way seems to diminish the music and the voices. The bars are cosy and crowded, all day people huddle by salt-misted windows, shrieking as their glasses slide and slop across the tables. There is a sense of closing-in, an end coming.

I see Bar Holland and Eric everywhere. If I pop my head into the Lounge, looking for a private corner, they will be there, frowning over chess. In the Writing Room, where I might sit, but never write, they are sharing a desk, whispering. I see them emerging from the Cinema, Greek Dancing Classes, the Purser's Office. Will they think I'm spying on them? They do not see me, they are too involved in a sort of permanent private debate. Bar Holland's bumpy suitcase, her pile of dog-eared paperbacks, remain untouched in the cabin. Her bunk with its virgin turned-down sheet is a still-life. She is more tousled than ever, but exercise has given a sheen to the pale planes of her chin and forehead. She wears, day and night, a big sweater of Eric's.

Now that I spend so much time out of the cabin, I see a lot. I leave the cabin early, well before breakfast. I see girls with set faces weaving their way in evening clothes up dark corridors. During one of my long mornings on the deck, I see two husbands start a fight between the funnels, with little puffs of punches, stumbling feet. One night I see Kaye Garrett bent over the railing, being sick. I recognize her by the luminous fuzz of my pale blue angora sweater. She tucks strings of hair behind her ears and zigzags haughtily back to the bar.

If I see a uniform coming, I have my escape routes. I know my way around the secrets of the ship. I skirt roped-off passages, fortress doors, steep metal stairways marked STRICTLY CREW ONLY. I pass clattering kitchens, doors sucked closed on blackness, tiny decks just above the water where dark men smoke and laugh.

Sometimes it's unavoidable. I have to keep walking. I drop my eyes and watch my feet pass theirs. There is always a whisper, a hiss, a laugh. Once I heard it. *Leetle girl.*

I say it over and over to myself through sucked teeth. I suppose I'm hoping that, like an orange, humiliation can be sucked dry.

One night Eric is late for dinner.

'Will I order the soup for him anyway so as not to hold us up?' Marie asks me and the German man.

'This is not like Eric,' she says a little later.

We eat our soup. We order and munch away silently at our Fried Schnapper à la Saint-Germaine. We are about to tackle our Bon Fillet à l'Anglais with Ribbon Potatoes when Marie spots him. By turning in my chair and following the direction of her faintly shaking finger I can see him too, wedged in next to a pillar far across the dining room. A fork stabs the air in front of him. A blonde head subsides behind the pillar.

'We've been deserted!' says Marie. She leans over and takes Eric's bread roll, pops it in her bag. 'Aren't I awful?' she says to me. 'Nan and I get starving after Bingo.'

Like Marie and the German man, I eat steadily, right through to the Sherry Trifle and Selected Cheeses, and leave my plate bare.

When the PA announces that at twenty-one hours and ten minutes precisely we will be passing our Sister Ship, I climb the ladder to the old place on Boat Deck. The sky is star-dazzled. Nobody else seems to be around.

A row of lights comes suddenly out of darkness and rushes towards us. I can feel our own pace now as the Sister Ship takes shape, slides her long glittering flank beside us. The two ships snort at one another like animals from the same litter, mournful bellows across the frothing wakes. Rockets spray out from between the answering sets of funnels. I glimpse long shelves of decks under swinging lights, hear scraps of frantic music. Tiny figures lift their hands: I have lifted mine, like a salute. Then they are gone.

I sleep a great deal. I dream. I dream I am sitting at the table with Marie and the German man. The waiter puts before me a big plate of bones. Large, angular bones, freshly butchered, tufted with meat and cold white fat. I am unable to stop myself attacking the bones. I gnaw, dribble and crunch: as I throw one over my shoulder I reach for another. I shut my eyes and groan with satisfaction. Marie and the German man watch me. Marie shakes her head, sorrowful. 'You are very greedy,' she says.

One morning the wild black decks are forbidden to the passengers. But it's the dangerous hour below, when stewards come out with sheets and keys. I slip through Reading Rooms, Cocktail Lounges, the deserted bars. I come to the ballroom. On the stage the piano is open and the German man is playing. I take a seat at one of the empty tables across the floor.

At first I watch the German man. He has gathered his long private face together as if he is regretful about something. He makes mistakes, stumbles, only just makes it over a hill of notes, but he never stops, his fingers push on, bite down.

Then I pick up a pattern in the notes. Just as I wait for it again it breaks up, scatters, comes together differently. It seems to me the music has a voice that knows more than I ever will, that leads me on, further, further, and at the last minute shows me where it is the pattern really lies.

The German man throws his hands into his lap and swivels on his stool. He shows no surprise at seeing me.

'I play very badly,' he says, shaking his head, though to me he seems flushed and exhilarated. 'I do not practise for a long time.'

'I wish I could play like that.'

'The Hammerklavier. First and second movements.' He gets out a handkerchief and slowly wipes his face. 'It is just like anything else. At first it is technical and then the meaning starts to come as you learn the piece.'

As I get up to go he says, 'You should hear it played—right—one day.'

'Yes, I will try,' I say.

'I've put on that much weight,' Marie sighs over soup. 'Still, not to worry, I'll probably have to starve in London.'

Our destination is very close now. Suitcases block the corridors. There are flustered queues outside the Purser's Office. Addresses are exchanged in bars rowdy with farewell. The waiters slap down our plates. The menus are stained and repetitive. I take two sips of my Creme Milanese, crumble my roll.

'You're not pregnant are you?' Marie says with a wink at the German man. 'I bet you wouldn't be the only one.'

The German man eats on as if he hasn't heard.

'The trouble with you is,' she says a little later, leaning over to me, 'you're a worrier. You mightn't think it, but I'm a worrier too.'

I have noticed that lines spray out from Marie's eyes and mouth and tendons strain in her neck when she peers at other tables.

'That's why I'm on this trip. You've got to get out of yourself, mix in.'

I don't dare look at the German man.

'I tell you what,' Marie goes on, 'Nan and I are going to the Fancy Dress Ball tonight. It's the farewell do. Why don't you come along, make it a three?'

'I will think up a cozzie for us,' she says with a wink. 'Leave it to me.'

'Tonight at eight-thirty then, my cabin,' she says.

The German man looks at his watch, stands up, nods to us.

'I'll be glad to see the end of him,' Marie says, as we watch his square white back leave the dining room. 'There's something

113

about him . . . you know?'

She reaches over and takes his orange.

Kaye Garrett is sitting cross-legged on her bunk, writing. I have not seen her for days. I ask her if she's going to the Fancy Dress Ball.

'You've got to be joking.'

She doesn't look as if she's going anywhere. She is wearing just a T-shirt, bending through her bare knees to an exercise book and ashtray on the coverlet.

I sit down on my bunk. 'What are you writing?'

'My diary.' She doesn't stop. Her hair is scraped back into a pony-tail. She is left-handed. She writes very fast, her hand looping like a child's.

After a while she looks up. Her face is scrubbed of make-up, her skin looks damp and porous, there are dark circles under her eyes. This is how she used to look, last year. Her house was right near the school, by the river. She would stalk into the classroom late, breathing morning steam. While she stuffed her beret into her pocket, her eyes travelled the desks, as if she was counting something up. Or looking for something.

'I'm trying to sort out where I stand,' she says. 'I'm in the shit all over the ship. Greek men are terribly possessive, Hull.'

She bends to write. I can just hear the scratch of her pen. It has a companionable sound.

'Maybe I won't go to that ball,' I say.

'You've got to do what you want, *I* think.'

She is still writing when I get up to go.

'Bye Hully,' she says, quite gently.

It is strange to leave Kaye Garrett behind me. Through the corridors I think of her bent head against the shadows of the cabin, and the scratch of her pen, writing.

I can hear the rustling even as I knock on Marie's door.

'Oh, there you are,' she says, pulling me inside. She is wrapped neck to foot in white crêpe paper. 'Put your arms up! Come on! We're going to miss the Grand Parade.' She starts to wind white paper around me too, so that we both crackle like bonfires. 'Pins Nan!' she calls. 'This is the little lass I've been telling you about, the one from Perth.'

Nan is not in costume. I recognize her as the girl who's often with Marie, the one with the long neck and the red-rimmed eyes as if she's just been crying. She smiles at me through little childish teeth.

'Don't move,' Marie hisses through pins.

'What are we?'

'Guess!' She waves two cylinders of black crêpe paper at me. Each has an uneven white cross glued to it. 'Our crowning glory,' she says. 'Oh, what a hoot!'

Nan wedges one onto my head while Marie adjusts hers in the mirror. They press down over our eyebrows. We look at one another with pained, spaniel-hooded eyes.

'Sister Ships,' says Marie. 'These are our funnels. Aren't I clever?'

She slings a whistle on a string around my neck. 'Your foghorn. The idea is, in the Grand Parade we sort of run past each other blowing our whistles.'

'Come on,' she says, looking at my face, 'don't go and chicken out on me like Nan. It's only for laughs. You can reimburse me for the paper and pins et cetera tomorrow.'

We totter up the stairs. The wind catches us as we cross the deck to the ballroom and we rustle like an army of bats. We clutch our funnels. 'They're going to die when they see us,' Marie whispers.

We enter the ballroom to a burst of cheering and wolf-whistles. But the crowd have their backs to us. As we crane, funnels lurching, the band strikes up, the lights dim, the crowd moves off onto the floor. Marie does not waste time on regrets.

'Now is our chance,' she says over her shoulder, swerving a course through dancing couples. She piles bags and coats onto a vacated table, drags the chairs right to the edge of the floor.

'Excuse me, excuse me,' she says, pulling a third chair from

115

under a flailing hand, and sitting down on it.

'I learnt the hard way on this ship, believe me,' she says, as Nan and I slide down next to her. 'Nobody's going to lift a finger for you.' She hails a waiter. 'What'll be your pleasure, girls? Going to join me in an Athens' Special?'

I am glad Marie is not too disappointed about missing the Grand Parade. She seems to be thoroughly enjoying herself, peering at the costumes as they pass on the dance floor. There are a lot of men dressed up as women, even pregnant women, with signs like SUZY WENT WONG and I SHOULD HAVE DANCED ALL NIGHT pinned on their backs. 'Oh, get a load of this one,' Marie cries, slapping my knee. It is a man in a nightie and a necklace of gin bottles. He is called OFFICERS MESS. 'Oh there'll be some red faces here tonight.' She has to wipe her eyes.

The band launches into 'I Did It My Way'. For this the lead singer undoes the buttons of his shirt. It is very hot and stuffy. We have drunk our Athens' Specials. Marie sends Nan off to get some more.

An Arab headdress bows before me.

'Go on,' Marie nudges me. 'It Dennis from Bingo.'

Dennis and I sway together for a while with linked, clammy hands.

'The band is very *thing* tonight, isn't it?' he says.

'Yes.' I can't see his face, he's wearing dark glasses, like a sheikh.

'I got this Arab outfit in Aden. What are you supposed to be? Nurses? The Ku Klux Klan?'

'Sister Ships.'

'What?' The band is very loud.

'*Sister Ships.*'

'Oh, ha ha, well don't let it worry you,' he says. I don't think he can hear me. He takes me back to my seat and asks Nan to dance. As they bump past I hear him say to her, 'The band is very *thing* tonight, isn't it?'

The band plays 'The Girl From Ipanema' and people start

to clap and move to the edge of the dance floor. Marie and I sip our drinks and peer through the crowd. The professional dance couple are at it again, under the swirling gold dome. Up and down they pass one another, back and forward, flashing smiles over their shoulders, they turn at the same moment, up and down again, it's a sort of prowl, back and forward . . . it makes me dizzy.

I blink and blink at the couple and it is suddenly clear to me that they are my parents. They are in disguise, of course, like all of us: they have been on board all the time! It's their movements that give them away. The way they hold their backs so straight and know their steps so well, everything's planned . . . though there's something rather fixed about their smiles, they're not quite real, the way their arms flare out from the elbow at the same time reminds me of puppets . . .

'Your shout,' Marie is saying, pushing her glass at me. Her funnel has slipped over one eye.

I stand up with the glasses, keeping an eye on my parents. I edge around the dance floor towards the bar. It is very important that they don't see me. I'm afraid that if they did they might call out to me, make me join in. I have come this far without them now.

The ship lurches. I have to watch my steps very carefully, but I keep the gold dome swirling in the corner of my eye.

I look up and I see him. The German man, standing by the ballroom door. He is wearing not only his white suit, but also white gloves with which he holds his drink. On his head are fixed two large white ears.

I come and stand before him.

He bows. I see that his ears are two ship serviettes, like the ones that sit on our table, stiff white cones pulled into peaks. I glimpse the thin wire to which they are attached, circling his head.

The ship lurches the other way. He puts down his drink. He inclines his head very slightly towards the door.

'Ready?' he says. I could swear his ears twitch.

I am rustling down a long corridor. My funnel has fallen off, my crêpe paper rips and drags behind me.

I am sure I saw something white flash around that corner.

AMATEUR HOUR

Garry Disher

AUTHOR'S NOTE

This story was once a novel but, as many novels should have been short stories, perhaps it's a good thing that I distilled ten pages from two hundred. It's a little burdened by the cast-off material (all that establishing at the start instead of getting on with it), but in its present form it won a major award, was published here and overseas, and achieves, I think, my intention: to tell the story of a local tragedy as a way of revealing a greater one.

I might still write the novel. The material is there. When I was twenty-one I left Australia and, after two years of travelling and working, arrived in South Africa broke and with no ticket out. I found a job, and for the first and only time in my life I kept a diary. When I re-read it years later I found myself wanting to explore the things I had only half sensed at the time.

The job I had was much like the narrator's, and I was once shown some handguns between courses at a dinner party, but the rest is fiction. I moved the action to the present and got my story by asking: What if there had been a shooting? And what if the witness were somehow found wanting?

Garry Disher

AMATEUR HOUR

Sometimes they sounded like poets. I was new there, and they wanted me to understand, and sometimes their words lodged in my head like songs.

On the morning of the tragedy, Evert took me to map a slope of Black Mountain. Tobias followed us, carrying our equipment upon his shoulder and collecting wood for his fire. We worked through the day, and late in the afternoon we climbed to the top of the mountain to see the view, to see how tiny our camp was at the base, and, while Tobias squatted and smoked a cigarette at a seemly distance from us, Evert explained things to me, because I was new there, and an *Engelsman*.

A lucky soaking of spring rain in that part of the desert always brought on a brief, famed crop of wildflowers, he said. They grew almost overnight; along the dunes, between the claypans, around the eroded hills. People came from everywhere to see them. Last year a BBC television crew filmed them, he said. *National Geographic* did a story. He motioned with his hand and said, 'Picture it.'

I looked out, to the edges of the desert. In Springbok and Pofadder the tourists stop the mail drivers and shopping farmers and ask, 'Is this the best time?' They drive ninety kilometres for a Sunday picnic at the favoured spot, the veldt near Black Mountain, skimming over the corrugations that otherwise would rattle their bones, speeding back at the end of the day in time for Evening Prayers.

'Those TV boys got bogged in the sand,' said Evert.

Had they been covering the necklace killings, the evictions, the bulldozings? They have time to spare and fly to Springbok and hire a car. They joke with the farmer, who has given them permission to use his access road, that they are after a bit of local colour. They speak slowly, clearly, for the fellow is an Afrikaner. English tangles his tongue. Families snug at home turn on their TV sets. A reporter is gesturing at Black Mountain and the wildflower carpet behind him. Sunlight glints on the strap of his wristwatch. He announces that this is a land of great beauty and . . . But what can he say next? And great extremes, he says.

'Everyone gets hayfever then,' said Evert.

In the mornings the geologists and field hands lie in bed, tapping their knuckles against the fibro-cement walls of their huts, waiting for the first aching sneeze. They walk to the mess and kick the petals unfolding in the sun.

'Mr Weeramantry sells hayfever pills,' said Evert, and he told me the story of Wikkie Roux, the man who had this job before me. Wikkie Roux races in from the veldt at knock-off time on Saturday afternoons, sneezing his head off in the dust and pollen swirling around in the Land Rover's cabin. He pauses at the Coloureds' Compound just long enough for Tobias to jump out, and then whooh! man, flat out to Weeramantry's trading store to buy six bottles of Carling beer and a packet of hayfever pills. The combination is fatal. He tilts back his chair in the mess, thumps his fist, roars out sentimental songs of the Republic, a bit touchy, a little violent, on the subjects of kaffirs, wildflowers and low camp morale, and then, more than likely, he passes out, and some poor bloody coloured, like our cook boy, Willem Pretorius, has to drag him out.

'Good story, ay?' Evert said.

The wind blew in from the South Atlantic. It was very cold. I watched Tobias draw on the cigarette cupped between his palms. He had pulled his woollen cap down over his ears, and he wore his coat inside out to show the satin lining. I drew my coat closed at the neck. Only Evert seemed unaffected. He was in a mood to be sentimental, in his shorts and thin shirt and unbuttoned anorak, as though his flanks were not veined and bumpy in the wind, his skin not stretched tight to tearing point over his shin bones.

'Hell of a cold, ay?' he said. He grinned and told me to wait a few weeks, for the sunshine and the spring rains, when the red and yellow and blue wildflowers would spill along the canyons

121

and spread over the veldt and gather at the base of the stony peaks.

His words were like a song, but the cold wind blew and the desert looked endless, wrung out and inconvenient. Here and there wheel tracks scribbled over the sand. Clouds scudded across the sky, their shadows creeping like stains over the dunes and the camp huts. Someone had tied down the helicopter. The windsock pointed in the wind like a finger. Sand drifts were obscuring the black letters on the laboratory roof: 'Zuurwater' and 'Kendell Copper Tucson'. No one was walking around down there.

I identified my hut among the other tiny corrugated iron roofs on the far side of the airstrip. I knew it was mine because it had no garden and I would have to plant one soon. Our engineer and his wife lived in the hut next to me. They had two extra rooms, a carport for their station wagon, a garden and a trellis vine. Every day two maids came up from the Coloureds' Compound, a hessian and tin town never seen by any Tucson executive. After lunch Marion Reed liked to open the tailgate of the station wagon, bundle the maids in and drive the one kilometre to Mr Weeramantry's to do the shopping, in the manner of a housewife in a suburb.

Then I remembered. Nothing ever happened here, the trouble was elsewhere, but I had heard a man's resolute shout in the darkness one night as I lay trying to sleep: 'Get away from here, you black bugger.'

There was a moment of heatless sunlight. It flared on the red dunes and brightened the distant hills. We were drenched in it. Evert stood up and swept round in a circle, stretching his arms, suddenly on top of the world. 'London,' he shouted, offering his left hand, 'Antarctica,' unfolding his right. And the border where he had been a conscript halting the terrorists, the blind gully where Boers had trapped British soldiers, the Orange River and baboons and crocodiles and diamonds. And Cape Town, the Sea Point guesthouses, compared and dreamed over in the mess hut every evening.

'Time to go back,' Evert said. '*Kom*, Tobias.'

Tobias stubbed out his cigarette on a rock and put the butt into a paper bag in his pocket.

'*Yirra*,' said Evert.

Far below us a police Land Rover was pitching about on the track leading out of the wadi by the Coloureds' Compound. It reached the Springbok road and gained speed, sliding on the corners and raising a dust cloud.

'Tobias,' said Evert. 'What is the trouble, hey?'

'I don't know, my boss.'

He was climbing down ahead of us, a tripod upon his shoulder, firewood under his arm. Evert muttered, '*Ag*, I don't like it, man.' He nodded at Tobias clambering over the treacherous round stones. 'Your coloured out here is a peaceful fellow, isn't it. He hasn't got his head filled with ideas.' He clicked his tongue.

We hurried down. At the bottom of the mountain Tobias loaded the Land Rover and Evert took him back to the Compound. I walked through the camp and across the airstrip to my hut. There was a note under the door: 'Pop in for a drink after work, before the *braaivleis*. Marion Reed.'

Marion handed me a clay mug and said, 'This will warm you up.'

I held the mug with both hands, feeling the heat coming through from the fluid inside it. I put my nose to the rising steam. A rush of hot, spiced claret fumes filled my head. My eyes watered.

Everyone laughed. '*Gluhwein*,' said Don Reed. 'Marion made it to take to the *braaivleis* tonight.'

They smiled at me. Two small girls, home from their boarding school, sprawled on a hide rug at my feet. I looked around the room. The Reeds had moved from continent to continent, mining camp to mining camp. They had ricepaper fans, jade idols, Texan hats, boomerangs, shields, ivory elephants. We sipped our drinks and I had the sensation that the Reed family was waiting for a moment when they might declare me theirs.

'Something I wanted to ask you,' Marion said. 'I edit the camp newspaper. Would you like to write something for us? About your travels, first impressions, anything like that.'

She handed me a sheaf of roneod pages stapled together along one edge. 'You see, camp morale's at an all time low, and we're trying to do something about it.'

'The men are depressed by the food and the early starts and the cold weather,' Don said. 'Arguments, fights. You probably haven't noticed it yet.'

'It's sad,' said Marion. 'They just live for their next week off at Sea Point and don't care about anything else.'

'Hence the newspaper and the *braaivleis*. And we're having an Amateur Hour concert soon.'

The two little girls sat on the arms of my chair and turned the roneod pages with me while their parents talked. They stopped me at *Don's Diary*: 'Last month's film was the best we've had in a long time. It must have been; the coloureds enjoyed it— pow! boof! crash!'

'If there's anything you're good at,' Don said, 'any special interest, just let us know. Can you shoot?'

I looked at him. He leaned forward and said, 'I thought I'd start a gun club.'

He stood up and walked out of the room. Marion said, 'The police were at the Compound today. I suppose you heard.'

Don returned carrying a small wooden case. Inside it were two handguns resting in moulded foam. 'I'll use these,' he said. 'I'll use them if I have to, make no mistake about that. If they want to creep around here at night they can learn what to expect.'

Marion laughed. She steadied him with her hand on his arm and she gave me a look as if to say: What am I going to do with this man?

'A wife and two daughters,' Don said.

The kitchen staff had set the mess chairs upon the blighted patch of lawn near the main office. Willem Pretorius cooked steaks and chops for us on iron grilling plates and we leaned towards the burning logs, paper plates on our knees. We talked. They drank to my health.

Clouds blocked the stars and the moon, the fire lost its heat and the firelight was meagre, but the plan had worked, Marion and Don had a right to beam. They nodded to Willem and his men, thank you, go home now, threw logs onto the coals, and called us to bring our chairs closer. Marion's *gluhwein* kept us warm and crack-brained, we stamped our feet, we sang 'Zulu Warrior, Zulu Chief'.

Later, when the generator was turned off, we could hear the wind between the huts. People drifted off to bed, but some of us remained, staring into the coals. Evert produced a bottle of brandy. Sunday tomorrow, we said.

At one point we saw headlights and heard a vehicle, far out on the black veldt. It approached the camp but turned away and disappeared behind Black Mountain. The passengers were singing, whoever they were. Evert laughed. 'Sunday tomorrow.'

I said, 'Did you find out what the police wanted?'

'Just a patrol,' he said. Then he slapped his thigh. 'Tobias is hell of a lucky he was with us today. They saw his bakkie in the Compound and told his wife to get it registered. Did she give him hell. Whooh!'

There were five of us left. We looked into the coals, nursing the last of the brandy, telling each other that we had stamina. We dreamed. 'Stay at the Carnaby,' Evert said, 'for your week off. Ay, kaffir,' he said, 'what do you want in this place?'

Tobias came shyly into the light of the fire, grinning, holding his woollen cap, looking around at someone behind him and back at Evert again, unable to suppress a little snorting laugh.

'Please, the boss he is give me a drink?'

Evert waved him away. 'Cheeky kaffir. I gave you five rands last week and now you want me to give you a drink.'

Tobias giggled again and moved back into the dark with his friends.

The incident woke us up. We climbed onto the back of a Land Rover and Evert drove us to the Reeds' house, where we parked and roared: 'We love you Marion, oh yes we do.' The Reeds ignored us yet they were awake, I think; I could feel them listening. But it was late and too cold and we soon fell silent. I jumped out and said goodnight.

I walked across to my hut, where I lit a lantern, feeling too alert to sleep. I sat and thought, re-read a love letter, moved things around. Tobias knocked on my door.

'Please boss, you are give me a drink?' he said. 'I must have a drink for my head.'

'Go home to bed, Tobias,' I said, 'It's late. It's cold.'

'Tomorrow we are not working, isn't it?' he said. 'Tonight I am have a party, my boss, same like always. You are give me a drink please?'

'I haven't got any,' I said.

'Oh.' He drew back. He looked at my room, at my rucksack in the corner by the rickety wardrobe.

'The boss he is come from America?'

'No,' I said.

He said 'Oh' again, but then he whirled round and crouched, his feet wide apart, his hand quick-drawing a gun from the holster on his hip, his smoking finger drilling me through the heart. I jumped in fright and laughed.

'John Wayne,' said Tobias, delighted. He put his thumb behind his satin lapel as though there were a badge pinned to it. 'Sheriff,' he said.

He shrugged off the role and looked moodily at the walls, the spindly furniture, his shadow swooping in the lamplight. 'The boss is give me five rands?' he said. 'For to buy petrol for my bakkie to go to church tomorrow.'

I gave him the money. He said, 'You is believe in Jesus Christ, my boss?'

I thought, and replied, 'No.'

I could have said yes. In that little room, in the dislocating darkness of the hour, I had distressed him. He held his hands together. He said that he would pray for me.

He left and I went to bed.

It is clear to me now that Tobias set off to see who else might be awake, and that his head would not let him alone. He negotiated the precise rows of white-painted stones that defined the Reeds' yard, and he passed among the wires and stakes in their garden beds, but he was snarled by two new garbage bins, specials from Weeramantry's, and I heard, almost at once, Don Reed cry out and then shoot him.

He shot twice more while I was running from my hut, and he was still shooting when I came upon him, firing shot after shot into the ground as though he could not make the gun stop, crying out, 'Oh don't, oh don't.' He threw the gun away, aghast.

Marion stepped out of the house, a gas lantern in her hand. She put her arm around her husband and led him inside. 'Poor old boy,' she said. 'Poor old boy.'

In the mornings I walked along the beach at Sea Point, returning in time for lunch in the Carnaby's dining room, and in the afternoons I went into the centre of Cape Town, where I saw films or paid to join the half-day bus tours of the area. I had my ticket home and I was waiting for the day. I went in to pick up my pay cheque from the company's Cape Town office. The man there frowned: over the years he had grown sick and tired of fellows who wouldn't stay on—didn't we get paid top rates? They had photographs hanging on their walls: the camp, springbok and bat-eared foxes among the wildflowers, secretary birds, Black Mountain, all in gaudy colours and with the company logo in one corner. Once, I saw our technician on the beach; in Sea Point to begin his week off, I suppose. He stared at me and I at him, and, at the moment we drew alongside one another, he looked up at the guesthouses on the beach front and I looked out at the sea.

But the thing is, one afternoon when the days were dragging I happened to stand by my window at the Carnaby and look down at a woman lying drunk on her side in the alley across the street, lying with her head on her arm, her feet in men's shoes neatly together, and as I watched her she rolled on her hip and put her hand under her dress, she pulled down her pants until they stretched like a web across her knees, and she fell back slowly in relief as her urine poured along the ground. I thought how sharp it would smell, and how her thighs would rub together and irritate the damp skin, and as I watched a maid from the Carnaby ran across the street to her. The maid leaned down and tugged at the woman's arm. The woman was too heavy. The maid looked around helplessly, sensed me, and looked up. The thing is, I didn't move from the window, I continued to watch, even as the maid stood holding her dress out to shield the woman from me, her face turned away from me, overcome by shame, and it was only when two policemen threw the woman into a van and drove away that I turned away from the window. It was that look on the maid's face that dislodged anything else I might have been thinking.

A, B, C, D, E, F, G, H, I, J, K, L, M, N, O, P, Q, R, S, T, U, V, W, X, Y, Z

Murray Bail

AUTHOR'S NOTE

'A,B,C,D . . .' was either the first or the second story I wrote in London. After two years in Bombay I had arrived early in 1970 with a fat novel under my arm: so highly did I think of it I carried it on the plane as hand-luggage. The first six months were spent at various addresses trying to revise the novel, until, in a basement flat in Langham Street, a stone's throw from the BBC, I realized there was nothing for it but to dismantle the manuscript and toss it out with the rubbish. Living in the basement I was surrounded by other people's rubbish bins. They were outside the window which looked up to the footpath, often with their lids off. That was where the novel belonged, I decided. I should cut my losses and turn to short stories. To do otherwise, I said, was the sign of an *amateur*.

Unfortunately, the very moment I tossed out the novel coincided with the beginning of the longest-running dustmen's strike in the history of London. I became surrounded even more than usual by the stench of rubbish (the fish I remember clearly), and, as the garbage mounted higher on the footpath above me, blocking out the light like a plastic mountain, with pages of my novel somehow always fluttering on top to remind of my incompetence, it began to rot and leak, and although London was grey I was transported back via my nostrils to Bombay. I remember thinking a lot about India; I could never get it out of my mind. Even today I often see parts of that complex city, Bombay, and its peculiar rotting smell which seemed to coat all sensations. And so in that basement flat the subject of 'A,B,C,D . . .' was activated by a rich tropical stench and mixed with my reflections on the appearance and meaning of words—although it is set in Pakistan, where I have never set foot, except for a few yards at an army post near Amritsar. (It was set in Pakistan to make it more imagined.) It was written in four or five days, revised a few weeks later, and sent off. The editor of the distinguished literary magazine thought it was okay but wondered if I could remove the meditations—'distractions' I think was his word—on language and just stick to the business between the man and the woman. It was accepted by *Transatlantic Review*, and of course I never again sent a story to the first magazine, which I believe is still functioning.

Aside from proofs for the collection *Contemporary Portraits* (published in 1975) I haven't re-read the story; for all I know it may be embarrassingly pretentious or quite unconvincing. I doubt whether it is my best work, but it is a favourite and offered here for the unsatisfactory reasons mentioned: sentimentality for India, a basement room in London, and the pages of a lost novel.

Murray Bail

A, B, C, D, E, F, G, H, I, J, K, L, M, N, O, P, Q, R, S, T, U, V, W, X, Y, Z

I select from these letters, pressing my fingers down. The letter (or an image of it) appears on the sheet of paper. It signifies little or nothing, I have to add more. Other letters are placed alongside until a 'word' is formed. And it is not always the word WORD.

The word matches either my memory of its appearance, or a picture of the object the word denotes. TREE: I see the shape of a tree at mid-distance, and green.

I am writing a story.

Here, the trouble begins.

The word 'dog', as William James pointed out, does not bite; and my story begins with a weeping woman. She sat at the kitchen table one afternoon and wept uncontrollably. How can words, particularly 'wept uncontrollably', convey her sadness (her self-pity)? Philosophers other than myself have discussed the inadequacy of words. 'Woman' covers women of every shape and size, whereas the one I have in mind is red-haired, has soft arms, plain face, high-heeled shoes with shining straps.

And she was weeping.

Her name, let us say, is Kathy Pridham.

For the past two years she has worked as a librarian for the British Council in Karachi. She, of all the British community there, was one of the few who took the trouble to learn Urdu, the local language. She could speak it, not read it: those calligraphic loops and dots meant nothing to her, except that 'it was a language'. Speaking it was enough. The local staff at the Council, shopkeepers, and even the cream of Karachi society (who cultivated European manners), felt that she knew them as they themselves did.

At this point, consider the word 'Karachi'. Not having been

there myself I see clusters of white-cube buildings with the edge of a port to the left, a general slowness, a shaded verandahed suburb for the Burra-sahibs. Perhaps, eventually, boredom—or disgust with noises and smells not understood. Kathy, who was at first lonely and disturbed, quickly settled in. She became fully occupied and happy; insofar as that word has any meaning. There was a surplus of men in Karachi: young English bachelors sent out from head office, and pale appraising types who work at the embassies; but the ones who fell over themselves to be near her were Pakistanis. They were young and lazy. With her they were ardent and gay.

Already the words Kathy and Karachi are becoming inextricably linked.

It was not long before she too was rolling her head in slow motion during conversations, and clicking her tongue, as they did, to signify 'no'. Her bungalow in the European quarter with its lawn, verandah, two archaic servants, became a sort of *salon*, especially at the Sunday lunches where Kathy reigned, supervising, flitting from one group to the next. Those afternoons never seemed to end. No one wanted to leave. Sometimes she had musicians perform. And there was always plenty of liquor (imported), with wide dishes of hot food. Kathy spoke instantly and volubly on the country's problems, its complicated politics, yet in London if she had an opinion she had rarely expressed it.

When Kathy thought of London she often saw 'London'— the six letters arranged in recognizable order. Then parts of an endless construction appeared, much of it badly blurred. There was the thick stone. Concentrating, she could recall a familiar bus stop, the interior of a building where she had last worked. Her street invariably appeared, strangely dead. Some men in overcoats. It was all so far away she sometimes thought it existed only when she was there. Her best friends had been two women, one a schoolteacher, the other married to a taciturn engineer. With them she went to Scotland for holidays, to the concerts at the Albert Hall. Karachi was different. The word stands for something else.

The woman weeping at the kitchen table is Kathy Pridham. It is somewhere in London (there are virtually no kitchen tables in Karachi).

After a year or so Kathy noticed at a party a man standing apart from the others, watching her. His face was bony and fierce, and he had a thin moustache. Kathy, of course, turned away, yet at the same time tilted her chin and began acting over-earnest in conversation. For she pictured her appearance: seeing it (she thought) from his eyes.

She noticed him at other parties, and at one where she knew the host well enough, casually asked, 'Tell me. Who is that over there?'

They both looked at the man watching her.

'If you mean him, that's Syed Masood. Not your cup of tea, Kathy. What you would call a wild man.' The host was a successful journalist and drew in on his cigarette. 'Perhaps he is our best painter. I don't know; I have my doubts.'

Kathy lowered her eyes, confused.

When she looked up, the man called Syed Masood had gone.

Over the next few days, she went to the galleries around town and asked to see the paintings of Syed Masood. She was interested in local arts and crafts, and had decided that if she saw something of his she liked she would buy it. These gallery owners threw up their hands. 'He has released nothing for two years now. What has got into him I don't know.'

Somehow this made Kathy smile.

Ten or eleven days pass—in words that take only seconds to put down, even less to absorb (the discrepancy between Time and Language). It is one of her Sunday lunches. Kathy is only half listening to conversations and when she breaks into laughter it is a fraction too loud. She has invited this man Masood and has one eye on the door. He arrives late. Perhaps he too is nervous.

Their opening conversation (aural) went something like this (visual).

'Do come in. I don't think we've met. My name is Kathy Pridham.'

'Why do you mix with these shits?' he replied, looking around the room.

Just then an alarm wristlet watch on one of the young men began ringing. Everyone laughed, slapping each other, except Masood.

'I'll get you something,' said Kathy quietly. 'You're probably hungry.'

She felt hot and awkward, although now that they were together he seemed to take no notice of her. Several of the European men came over, but Masood didn't say much and they drifted back. She watched him eat and drink: the bones of his face working.

He finally turned to her. 'You come from—where?'

'London.'

'Then why have you come here?'

She told him.

'And these?' he asked, meaning the crowd reclining on cushions.

'My friends. They're people I've met here.'

Suddenly she felt like crying.

But he took her by the shoulders. 'What is this? You speak Urdu? And not at all bad? Say something more, please.'

Before she could think of anything he said in a voice that disturbed her, 'You are something extraordinary.' He was so close she could feel his breath. 'Do you know that? Of course. But do you know how extraordinary? Let me tell you something, although another man might put it differently. It begins here'— for a second one of his many hands touched her breasts; Kathy jumped—'and it *emanates*. Your volume fills the room. Certainly! So you are quite vast, but beautiful.'

Then he added, watching her, 'If you see what I mean.'

He was standing close to her, but when he spoke again she saw him grinning. 'Now repeat what I have just said in Urdu.'

He made her laugh.

Here—now—an interruption. While considering the change in Kathy's personality I remember an incident from last Thursday, the 12th. This is an intrusion but from 'real life'. The words in the following paragraph reconstruct the event as remembered. As accurately as possible, of course.

A beggar came up to me in a Soho bar and asked (a hoarse whisper) if I wished to see photographs of funerals. I immediately pictured a rectangular hole, sky, men and women in coats. Without waiting for my reply he fished out from an inside pocket the wad of photographs, postcard size, each one of a burial. They were dog-eared and he had dirty fingernails. 'Did you know these dead people?' He shook his head. 'Not even their names?' He shook his head. 'That one,' he said, not taking his eyes off the photographs, 'was dug yesterday. That one, in 1969.' There was little difference. Both showed men and women standing around a dark rectangle, perplexed. I felt a sharp tap on my wrist. The beggar had his hand out. Yes, I gave him a shilling. The barman spoke: 'Odd way to earn a living. He's been doing that for—'

Kathy soon saw Masood again. He arrived one night with his shirt hanging out while she was entertaining the senior British Council representative, Mr L, and his wife. They were a cautious experienced pair, years in the service, yet Mrs L began talking loudly and hastily, a sign of indignation, when Masood sat away from the table, silently watching them. Mr L cleared his throat several times—another sign. It was a hot night with both ceiling fans hardly altering the sedentary air. Masood suddenly spoke to Kathy in his own language. She nodded and poured him another coffee. Mrs L caught her husband's eye, and when they left shortly afterwards, Kathy and Masood leaned back and laughed.

'You can spell my name four different ways,' Masood declared in the morning, 'but I am still the one person! Ah,' he said laughing, 'I am in a good mood. This is an auspicious day.'

'I have to go to work,' said Kathy.

'Look up "auspicious" when you get to the library. See what it says in one of your English dictionaries.'

She bent over to fit her brassiere. Her body was marmoreal, the opposite to his: bony and nervy.

'Instead of thinking of me during the day,' he went on, 'think of an exclamation mark! It amounts to the same thing. I would see you, I think, as a colour. Yes, I think more than likely pink, or something soft like yellow.'

'You can talk,' said Kathy laughing.

But she liked hearing him talk. Perhaps there'll be further examples of why she enjoyed hearing him talk.

That night Masood took her to his studio. It was in the inner part of the city where Europeans rarely ventured, and as Masood strode ahead Kathy avoided, but not always successfully, the stares of women in doorways, the fingers of beggars, and rows of sleeping bodies. She noticed how some men deliberately dawdled or bumped into her; striding ahead, Masood seemed to enjoy having her there. In an alleyway he unbolted a powder-blue door as a curious crowd gathered. He suddenly clapped his hands to move them. Then Kathy was inside: a fluorescent room, dirty white-washed walls. In the corner was a wooden bed called a 'charpoy', some clothes over a chair. There were brushes in jars, and tins of paint.

'Syed, are these your pictures?'

'Leave them,' he said sharply. 'Come here. I would like to see you.'

Through the door she could feel the crowd in the alleyway. She was perspiring still and now he was undoing her blouse.

'Syed, let's go?'

He stepped back.

'What is the matter? The natives are too dirty tonight. Is that it? Yes, the walls; the disgusting size of the place. All this stench. It must be affecting your nostrils? Rub your nose in it. Lie in my shit and muck. If you wait around you might see a rat. You could dirty your Mem-sahib's hands for a change.' Then he kicked his foot through one of the canvases by the door. 'The pretty paintings you came to see.'

As she began crying she wondered why. (He was only a person who used certain words.)

I will continue with further words.

Kathy made room for Masood in her house, in her bed as

well as the spare room which she made his studio. Her friends noticed a change. At work, they heard the pronoun 'we' constantly. She told them of parties they went to, the trips they planned to take, how she supervised his meals; she even confessed (laughing) he snored and possessed a violent temper. At parties, she took to sitting on the floor. She began wearing 'kurtas' instead of 'blouses', 'lungis' rather than 'dresses', even though with her large body she looked clumsy. To the Europeans she somehow became, or seemed, untidy. They no longer understood her, and so they felt sorry for her. It was about then that Kathy's luncheon parties stopped, and she and Masood, who were always together, went out less frequently. Most people saw Masood behind this— he had never disguised his contempt for her friends—but others connected it with an incident at the office. Kathy arrived one morning wearing a sari and was told by the chief librarian it was inappropriate; she couldn't serve at the counter wearing that. Then Mr L himself, rapidly consulting his wife, spoke to her. He spelt out the *British* Council's function in Karachi, underlining the word British. 'Kathy, are you happy?' he suddenly asked. Like others, he was concerned. He wanted to say, 'Do you know what you are doing?' 'Oh, yes,' Kathy replied. 'With this chap, I mean,' he said, waving his hand. And Kathy left the room.

People's distrust of Masood seemed to centre around his unconventional appearance and (perhaps more than anything) his rude silences. Nobody could say they knew him, although just about everybody said he drank too much. Stories began circulating. 'A surly bugger,' he was called behind his back. That was common now. There were times when he cursed Kathy in public. Strange, though, the wives and other women were more ready to accept the affair. There was something about Masood, his face and manner. And they recognized the tenacity with which Kathy kept living with him. They understood her quick defence of him, often silent but always there, even when she came late to work, puff-eyed from crying and, once, her cheek bruised.

Here, the life of Kathy draws rapidly to a close.

It was now obvious to everyone that Masood was drinking

too much. At the few parties they attended he usually made a scene of some sort; and Kathy would take him home. Think of swear words. She was arriving late for work and missed whole days. Then she disappeared for a week. They had argued one night and Kathy screamed at him to leave. He replied by hitting her across the mouth. She moved into a cheap hotel, but within the week he found her. 'Syed spent all day, every day, looking for me,' was how she later put it. 'He needs someone.' When she was reprimanded for her disappearance and general conduct, she burst into tears.

In London, the woman with elbows on the table is Kathy Pridham. She has unwrapped a parcel from Karachi. Imagine: coarse screwed-up paper and string lie on the table. Masood has sent a self-portrait, oil on canvas, quite a striking resemblance. His vanity, pride and troubles are enormous. His face, leaning against the teapot, stares across at Kathy weeping.

She cannot help thinking of him; of his appearance.

Words. These marks on paper, and so on.

PRECIOUS BANE

Gerald Murnane

AUTHOR'S NOTE

On 27 April 1985 I sat down to write a short piece for an anthology of speculative fiction. I did not know then any more than I know today what speculative fiction is or how it differs from other sorts of fiction. I had first found myself regarded as a writer of speculative fiction in 1982, when my third book, *The Plains*, was published by Norstrilia Press, a publisher with a number of science fiction titles on its list. When Damien Broderick asked me early in 1985 for a piece of speculative fiction, I set out to write in my own way. I trusted that Damien would regard it as speculative. At the same time, I trusted that my story would be acceptable to readers who had never thought of me as a writer of speculative fiction.

As a result of circumstances too complicated to explain here, I had only three weeks to write my piece. For a full-time writer this would have been no trouble, but I am a full-time teacher of writing with only a few hours each week for my own fiction. I had only about twenty hours of writing time for what became 'Precious Bane'. Even this might have been no trouble for many another writer, but I am usually a slow writer. I sometimes scribble for twenty minutes trying to produce a sentence that seems to me faultless.

I know the date was 27 April 1985 when I began 'Precious Bane' because I wrote the date in a corner of the first page of my first draft. That first page and the other thirty-six pages of the early drafts of 'Precious Bane' (some handwritten and some typed) are beside me now. When I've finished with those pages today I'll put them back where they belong— in one of the three 4-door steel filing cabinets where I store all the notes and drafts of all the prose fiction that I've written since 1962 together with all the letters that I've received and most of the letters that I've written since 1958, cuttings from old newspapers, the six volumes of the journal that I kept from 1958 to 1978, the typescripts of the poems that I wrote before I gave up writing poetry when my first book of fiction was published in 1974, the sketches of dream-racecourses that I made thirty-five years ago, the holy cards that I collected forty years ago . . .

On 20 June 1986 two persons wrote to me from an institute of higher learning in New South Wales offering to buy some of the papers in my three filing cabinets. I lifted out from my files just now the letter of 9 July 1986 that I wrote in reply to the two persons. Here is part of it:

> I am not about to part with any of my precious hoard of paper . . . I find myself quite often having to dip into it and splash about in it; I need these spiritual baths and showers as much as I need the other sort.

If I were a snail I would be always stopping to admire the silvery twistings and turnings behind me. As a writer of fiction I'm always leafing through the stacks of paper that I've thrown up behind me. I would hate to have to wander around the world looking for what some people call 'ideas for stories'. I only have to look into my filing cabinets and I know I could write another ten books of fiction with the material I have already.

The material that I use for my writing consists of much more than the events of my uneventful life. Fiction is not autobiography—although the reverse may be true. The material that I use for fiction is the contents of my mind. And, as far as I can see, the contents of my mind are images.

When I look today at the page of my notes headed 27 April 1985, I remember some of the earliest of the images that gave rise to 'Precious Bane'. I remember seeing in my mind the amber of beer and the orange-brown of whisky together with the grey of rain and of unhealthy skin. I remember seeing also the gold or yellow of the cloth cover of a certain second-hand book. In the published text the book is the narrator's copy of *Precious Bane*. I, the author of the story 'Precious Bane', walked just now to my shelves and looked at my own copy of *Precious Bane*, which I have never read. The cloth cover is green.

My notes told me today that the title 'Precious Bane' did not occur to me until I had scribbled three pages of rough drafts of the first few paragraphs. This surprises me. I am hardly ever able to begin a piece of fiction of any length unless I have a title in my mind. A title seems to me not something attached to the writing but part of the writing itself—something lifted out from deep inside the writing. My notes do not tell me so, but I believe I must have felt a surge of energy as soon as I had found that the title of my piece of fiction was made up of two words rich in allusions.

In the margin of my first page of notes is the entry 'My ideas of atomic theory'. From this I understood that my writing about alcohol and grey skin and forgotten books had caused me to think about the human brain. While I was writing pages 1-10 of my notes I was seeing in my mind brain cells shaped like the blobs that I had first seen in sketches in my science book in the junior forms of secondary school. (In the same way, I have always thought of all atomic particles as being shaped like the planet Saturn in drawings in comic strips.) However, on page 10 of my notes I wrote for the first time about the cells of a Carthusian monastery. At this point in the notes my handwriting becomes a rapid scrawl. I was hurrying to get on paper all the images crowding into my mind.

During the two weeks after my discovering that the narrator's brain was a monastery, I wrote one handwritten draft of the whole of 'Precious Bane' and then I typed what became the final draft. This makes 'Precious Bane' one of the most swiftly and cleanly written of all my pieces of fiction, whether short story length or book length.

Nearly every piece of fiction that I've written has had at its heart an image of some simple object linking two previously separate clusters of images. I made notes for several years about the themes of my first novel, but I was not able to write the text until I had discovered the image of the glass marble named Tamarisk Row. In 1987 I had almost given up trying to write *Inland* when I discovered the image of the fishpond in Pascoe Vale, which contained the image of the well in Hungary. These images, like the image of the monastery in 'Precious Bane', have revealed to me truths more profound than anything I have learned from priests or scientists or philosophers. When I discover one of these images I am reassured that the writing of fiction is the most satisfying of all vocations.

Gerald Murnane

PRECIOUS BANE

I first thought of this story on a day of drizzling rain in a second-hand bookshop in Prahran. I was the only customer in the shop. The owner sat near the door and stared out at the rain and the endless traffic. This was all he seemed to do all day. I had passed the shop often and walked through the man's gaze; and during the moment when I intersected that gaze I felt what it might be like to be invisible.

On the day of drizzle I was inside the man's shop for the first time. (I buy many second-hand books, but I buy them from catalogues. Second-hand bookshops make me unhappy. Even reading the catalogues is bad enough. But the second-hand books that I buy do not sadden me. Taking them out of their parcels and putting them on my shelves, I tell them they have found a good home at last. And I warn my children often that they must not sell my books after I have died. My children need not read the books, but they must keep them on shelves in rooms where people might glance at them sometimes or even handle them a little and wonder about them.) The man had glanced at me when I came into his shop, but then he had looked away and gone on gazing. And all the while I poked among his books he never looked back at me.

The books were badly arranged, dusty, neglected. Some were heaped on tables, or even on the floor, when they could easily have been shelved if the man had cared to put his shop in order. I looked over the section marked LITERATURE. I had in my hand one of what I called my book-buying notebooks. It was the notebook labelled: *1900–1940 . . . Unjustly Neglected.* The forty years covered by the notebook were not only the first forty of the century. Written backwards—'1940–1900'—they were the first forty years from the year of my birth to a time that I thought of as the Age of Books. If my life had been pointed in that direction I would have been, just then, not sheltering from rain in a graveyard of books but inspecting wall after wall of leather-bound volumes in my mansion in a city of books. Or I would have been at my desk, a writer in the fullness of his powers, looking through tall windows at a park-like scene in the countryside of books while I waited for my next sentence to come to me.

I put together four or five titles and took them to the gazing man. While he checked the prices pencilled in the front leaves I looked at him from under my eyebrows. He was not so old as I had thought. But his skin had a greyness that made me think of alcohol. The bookseller's liver is almost rotted away, I told myself. The poor bastard is an alcoholic.

I believed, in those days, that I was on the way myself to becoming an alcoholic, and I was always noticing signs of what I might look like in twenty or ten years or even sooner. If the bookseller had pickled his liver, then I understood why he sat and gazed so often. He suffered all day from the mood that came over me every Sunday afternoon when I had been sipping for forty-eight hours and had finally stopped and tried to sober up and to begin the four pages of fiction I was supposed to finish each weekend.

In my Sunday afternoon mood I usually gave up trying to write and looked over my bookshelves. Before nightfall I had usually decided there was no point in writing my sort of fiction in 1980. Even if my work was published at last, and a few people read it for a few years, what would be the end of it all? Where would my book be in, say, forty years' time? Its author by then would no longer be around to investigate the matter. He would have poisoned the last of his brain cells and died long before. Of the few copies that had actually been bought, fewer still would be stacked on shelves. Of these few even fewer would be opened, or even glanced at, as weeks and months passed. And of the few people still alive who had actually read the book, how many would remember any part of it?

At this point in my wondering I used to devise a scene from around the year 2020. It was Sunday afternoon (or, if the working week had shrunk as forecast, a Monday or even a Tuesday afternoon). Someone vaguely like myself, a man who had failed at what he most wanted to do, was standing in gloomy twilight before a wall of bookshelves. The man did not know it, but he happened to be the last person on the planet who still owned a copy of a certain book that had been composed on grey Sunday afternoons forty years before. The same man had once actually read the book, many years before the afternoon when he searched for it on his shelves. And more than this, he still remembered vaguely a certain something about the book.

There is no word for what this man remembers—it is so faint, so hardly perceptible among his other thoughts. But I stop (in my own thinking, on many a Sunday afternoon) to ask myself what it is exactly that the man still posssesses of my book. I reassure myself that the something he half remembers must be just a little different from all the other vague somethings in his memory. And then I think about the man's brain.

I know very little about the human brain. In all my three thousand books there is probably no description of a brain. If someone counted in my books the occurrence of nouns referring to parts of the body, 'brain' would probably have a very low score. And yet I have bought all those books and read nearly half of them and defended my reading of them because I believe my books can teach me all I need to know about how people think and feel.

I think freely about the brain of the man standing in front of his bookshelves and trying to remember: trying (although he does not know it) to rescue the last trace of my own writing— to save my thought from extinction. I know that this thinking of mine is, in a way, false. But I trust my thinking just the same, because I am sure my own brain is helping me to think; and I cannot believe that one brain could be quite mistaken about another of its kind.

I think of the man's brain as made up of many cells. Each cell is like a Carthusian monastery, with high walls around it and a little garden between the front wall and the front door. (The Carthusians are almost hermits; each monk belongs to the monastery, but he spends most of his day reading in his cell

145

or tending the vegetables in his walled garden.) And each cell is a storehouse of information; each cell is crammed with books.

A few books are cloth-bound with paper jackets, but most are leather-bound. And far outnumbering the books are the manuscripts. (I have trouble envisaging the manuscripts. One of my own books—in my room, on the grey Sunday afternoon—has photographs of pages from an illuminated manuscript. But I wonder what a collection of such pages would look like and how it would be bound. And I have no idea how a collection of such bound manuscripts would be stored—lying flat, on top of one another? sideways? upright in ranks like cloth-bound books on my own shelves? I wonder too what sort of furniture would store or display the manuscripts. So, although I can see each monk in his cell reaching up to his shelf of books from more recent times, when I want to think of him searching among the bulk of his library I see only a greyness: the grey of the monk's robe, of the stone walls of his cell, of the afternoon sky at his little window, and the greyness of blurred and incomprehensible texts.)

There are very few Carthusian monks in the world—I mean, the world outside my window and under the grey sky on Sunday afternoon. But when I say that, I am only repeating what a priest told me at secondary school nearly thirty years ago, when I was dreaming of becoming a monk and living in a library with a little garden and a wall around me. Apart from the priest's vague answer, the only information I have about the Carthusian Order comes from an article in the English *Geographical Magazine*. But that article was published in the 1930s, at about the time when I was learning to read in my other lifetime that leads back towards the Age of Books. I cannot check the article now because all of my old magazines are wrapped in grey plastic garbage bags and stored above the ceiling of my house. I stored them there three years ago with four hundred books that I will never read again—I needed more space on my shelves for the latest books I was buying.

What I mainly remember about that article was that it was

all text with no photographs. Nowadays the *Geographical Magazine* is half filled with coloured photographs. I sometimes skip the brief, jargonized texts of the articles and find all I need to know in the captions under the photographs. But the 1930s magazines (in the grey plastic bag, in the twilight above the ceiling over my head) included many an article with not one illustration. I imagine the authors of those articles as bookish chaps in tweeds, returning from strolls among hedgerows to sit at desks in their libraries and write (with fountain pens and few crossings-out) splendid essays and admirable articles and pleasant memoirs. I see those writers clearly. I knew them well in the years of my teens, as the 1920s passed and the Great War loomed ahead. When those gentlemen-writers post their *belles-lettres* to editors, they include no illustrations. The gentlemen actually boast of not knowing how to use cameras or gramophones or other modern gadgets, and their readers love the gentlemen for their charming dottiness. (I have never learned to use a camera or a tape recorder, but when I tell this to people they think I am striking a pose to draw attention to myself.)

I do not think the Carthusians would have objected to a gentleman-writer's taking a few photographs of their monastery so I assume that the author of the article trusted his words and sentences to describe clearly what he saw. The monastery was in Surrey, or it might have been Kent. This had disappointed me. When I first read the article I no longer dreamed of becoming a monk, but I liked to dream of monks living like hermits in remote landscapes; and Surrey or Kent was too populous for dreams about peaceful libraries. The only placename I remember from the article is Parkminster. I looked into my *Times Atlas of the World* just now and found no Parkminster in the index. (While I looked I vaguely remembered having looked for the same word more than once in the past with the same result.) Parkminster is therefore a hamlet too small to be marked on maps; or perhaps the monastery itself is called Parkminster, and the monks asked the writer not to mention any placenames in his article because they wanted no curious sightseers trying to peep into their cells.

But, in any case, the article was published in the 1930s, and, for all I know, the Carthusians and their cells and the word 'Parkminster' may have drifted off towards the Age of Monasteries and I may be the only one who remembers them, or at least what was once written about them.

Yet, when I think of the man reaching up to his bookshelves, on a grey afternoon in the year 2020, I see broad gravel paths with trees above them: whole districts of paths with cells beside the paths and in every cell a monk surrounded by books and manuscripts.

The man at his bookshelves—the last rememberer of my book—not only fails to remember what he once read in my book but cannot remember where he last saw my book on his shelves. He stands there and tries to remember.

A lay-brother walks along an avenue of his monastery. Lay-brothers are bound by solemn vows to their monastery, like other monks, but their duties and privileges are somewhat different. A lay-brother is not so much confined to his cell. Each day while the priest-monks are in their cells reading, or reciting the divine office, or tending their gardens, the lay-brothers are working for the monastery as a whole: taking messages and instructions and even dealing, in a limited way, with the world outside the monastery. Each lay-brother knows his way around some suburb of the monastery; he knows which monk lives behind which wall in his particular district. The lay-brother even gets to know, in a general sense, what the hermit-monks keep in their libraries: what books and manuscripts they spend their days reading. A lay-brother, having only a few books himself, thinks of books and libraries in a convenient, summary way. He learns to quote in full the titles of books he has never opened or never seen, whereas a monk in his cell might spend a year reading a certain book or copying and embellishing a certain manuscript and thinking of it for the rest of his life as an enormous pattern of rainbow pages of capital letters spiralling inwards and long laneways of words like the streets of other monasteries inviting him to dream about their cells of books and manuscripts.

A lay-brother walks along an avenue of the monastery. He has an errand to undertake but he is in no hurry. This is not easy to explain to people ignorant of monasteries. Monks behind their walls observe time differently from the people in the world outside. While only a few moments seem to pass on an uneventful, grey afternoon outside the monastery, a monk on the other side of the wall might have turned, at long intervals, page after page of a manuscript. The mystery can never be explained because no one has been able to be at once both outside and inside a monastery.

So, the lay-brother is in no hurry. He stands admiring the vegetables and herbs in each of the gardens of the cells he has been instructed to visit. When each monk has come to the door, the lay-brother asks him a certain question or questions but with no show of urgency. The lay-brother will call again, he says, on the next day or, perhaps, on the day after. In the meanwhile, if the monk could consult his books or his manuscripts for the needed information . . .

There is more than one lay-brother, of course. There may be hundreds, thousands, all striding or ambling through the leafy streets of the monastery while the last of my readers runs a finger along the spines of his books and tries to remember something of my book. And although I think of the lay-brothers as walking mostly through a particular quarter or district of the monastery, I know there are districts and more districts beyond them. In one of those districts, I decide on the grey Sunday afternoon when I have to decide whether to begin my writing or to go on sipping—in one of those districts, in a cell with grey walls no different from all the grey walls in all the streets in all the districts around it, in a collection of manuscripts that has lain undisturbed during many quiet afternoons, is a page where a monk once read or wrote what the man in the year 2020 would like to recall. The monk himself has forgotten most of what he once read or wrote. He could, perhaps, find the passage again— if he were asked to search for it among all the other pages he has read and written in all the years he has been reading and writing in his cell. But no lay-brother comes to ask the monk to look for any such page. Outside the monk's grey walls, no footstep sounds on many a grey afternoon.

The man cannot remember what he once read in my book. He cannot remember where among his shelves he once put away my thin volume. The man fills his glass again and goes on sipping some costly poison of the twenty-first century. He does not understand the importance of his forgetfulness, but I understand it. I know that no one now remembers anything of my writing.

So, on many a Sunday afternoon I leave my writing in its folder. I cannot bring myself to write what will become at last a greyness in a heap of manuscripts I can hardly imagine.

In the bookshop, I paid for my books and pocketed my change. The books were still on the table where the man had stacked them while he checked their prices. The man waited for me to take away the books so he could go on with his gazing, but I wanted to say something to the man. I wanted to reassure him that the books would be safe in their new home. I wanted to tell him that some of them were books I had wanted for a long time—unjustly neglected books that would now be read and remembered.

The topmost book was *Precious Bane* by Mary Webb. I touched the faded yellow cloth cover and I told the man that I had been searching for a long time for *Precious Bane*; that I intended to read it very soon.

The man looked not at the book or at me but out at the rain. With his face towards the greyness at his window, he said that he knew *Precious Bane* well. Or rather, he corrected himself, he had once known the book well. It had been a well-known book in its time. He had read it, but he hardly remembered it, he said, especially since his health was not what it had been. But it didn't matter, he said. It didn't matter if you couldn't remember anything about a book. The important thing was to read a book; to store it up inside you. It was all there inside somewhere, he said. It was all safely preserved. He lifted a hand, as though he might have pointed to some precise point on his skull, but then he let the hand fall again into the position where it normally rested while he gazed.

I took my books home. I entered the titles and the authors' names in my catalogue, and then I put each book in its correct place in my library, which is arranged in alphabetical order according to authors' surnames.

On the following Sunday, when it was time to stop sipping and to begin writing, I thought as usual of the man in the year 2020. He still tried and failed to remember a certain book, the book that I had written forty years before. But after he had walked away from his shelves and had sat down again to sip, I thought of him as knowing that my book was still safely preserved after all.

Then I thought of the monastery, and I saw that the sky above it had been changed. A golden glow was in the air; it was not so much the yellow of sunlight; more the dark gold of the cover of Mary Webb's unjustly neglected book or the amber of beer or the autumn colour of whisky. The light in the sky made the avenues of the monastery seem even more tranquil. The lay-brothers on their way from cell to cell sauntered rather than walked. Each monk in his cell, when he reached for a certain book or manuscript, was utterly calm and deliberate. And when he held up a page to inspect it, the light from his window lay faintly gold on the intricate pen-strokes or the tinted initials, and he found with ease what he had been asked to find.

On that afternoon, and on many Sundays afterwards, I wrote while I sipped. When I next called at the bookshop I had been writing for six months of Sundays.

After I had paid the man for my books, I told him I was a writer. I told him I had been writing on every Sunday since I had last seen him. By the following winter I would have finished what I was writing. And by the winter after that, my writing would have been preserved in a book. I wanted the cover of my book to be a rich, gold colour, I told the man, although he seemed hardly interested. I did not care about the colour of my dust-jacket, but when forty years had passed and the jacket had been torn away or lost and my book had been stored in a far corner of a shop like his, I wanted the gold colour of its spine to stand out among the greys and greens and dark blues of all the almost-forgotten books.

I told all this to the man while he went on gazing out into the sunlight as though it was still the same grey that he had gazed at when he told me about the books he could never forget. But this time the man would not reassure me. He was the last of a dying race, he told me. There would be no more shops like his in forty years. If people in those days wanted to preserve the stuff that had once been in books, they would preserve it in computers: in millions of tiny circuits in silicon chips in computers.

The man lifted his hand. His thumb and his index fingers made the shape of pincers, with a tiny gap between the pads of the two fingers. He held his fingers for a moment against the light from outside and stared at the crack between them. Then he let his hand fall, and he went back to gazing in his usual way.

On the following Sunday I did not go on with the writing that I had wanted to become a book with dark gold covers. I sat and sipped and thought about circuits and silicon chips. I thought of silicon as grey, the grey of granite when it was wet from rain under a grey sky. And I thought of a circuit as a grid of gold tracks in the grey. I saw that the tracks of a circuit would have a pattern hardly different from the paths of a monastery. The circuits I thought of seemed rather more remote from me than any monastery. But the pattern was the same. I could see only thin trails of gold across the grey, but I supposed the gold came from close-set treetops on either side of the long avenues of the circuit. The weather over the circuits would have been an endless calm autumn afternoon, the best weather for remembering.

I still could not imagine what sort of people would walk beneath the overspreading autumn-gold. But a few Sundays after

I had first thought about circuits, I began to write about a monastery where a page of writing might have been buried deep beneath a stack of manuscripts in a grey room but that page would never be lost or forgotten. As I wrote, I believed that my writing itself, my account of the monastery, would rest safely forever in some unimaginable room of books under gold foliage in a city of circuits. That monastery, I wrote, was only a monastery in a story, but the story was safe and so, therefore, was the monastery and everything in it. I saw story, monastery, circuit, story, monastery, circuit ... receding endlessly in the same direction as the lifetime that would have taken me towards the Golden Age of Books.

But as I wrote I came to see that the monastery was not, of course, endless. Somewhere, on the far side of the monastery wall, another greyness began: the greyness of the land of the barbarians, the streetless steppes where people lived without books.

Those people would not always stay on their steppes: the Age of Books would not go on forever. One day the barbarians would mount their horses and ride towards the monastery and turn backwards the history I had so often dreamed of.

I stopped writing. I poured another drink and looked far into the deep colour in my glass. Then I read aloud what I had written of my story, pausing now and then to sip, and after each sip to gaze at the red-gold sunset in the sky over all that I could remember.

THROUGH ROAD

Jean Bedford

AUTHOR'S NOTE

I think this is my best story because:

a) Rose Creswell says it is, and I'm a sucker for peer-group pressure;

b) I wrote it one afternoon in California on cocaine for a workshop class at Stanford (NB Drug Squad—I no longer use it);

c) I wanted to experiment with the present tense, having come under the influence of contemporary American writers, and it's present as well as tense;

d) although it's not my favourite story, I think its shape is the most satisfactory of anything I've written.

Jean Bedford

THROUGH ROAD

It starts the minute we get into the car. The kids are in the back seat complaining because they're missing 'Laverne and Shirley' or some shit and I can tell Robert's wishing he could have stayed at home himself.

Then the car won't go. I yank on the key and push the accelerator as hard as I can and it just moans a bit and won't catch at all.

'Have you tried the choke?' he says.

'No, I haven't tried the choke. It's automatic.'

'Did you give it some revs when you turned the key then?'

'Yes, I gave it revs. Just leave it a minute.' I think I've flooded it and want to give it time to settle. I can smell petrol.

'You've probably flooded it.'

'Mmmm . . .'

We sit and wait a few minutes. The kids are getting on our nerves but neither of us is going to be the first to yell at them. Finally I sit up again and reach for the key. This time the motor catches and starts. We grin at each other and Robert tells the kids he'll whack them both if they don't shut up. We're already ten minutes late and we're still in the parking lot.

I drive off, concentrating on staying on the right side of the road, with all the bulk of the car on *my* right side, which disturbs the habit reactions of twenty years. The roads are very dark, and narrow, and I get a surprise every time a car passes me from the other direction. At the first intersection we have to turn up a slight hill and the car dies as soon as I take my foot off the accelerator.

'What's the matter?' he says anxiously.

'It's okay. I just don't want to roll backwards when the lights change.'

The lights do change and I manage to let go the handbrake, turn the ignition key and put the semi-automatic shift into first, then quickly shove my foot on the gas pedal. I'm sitting hunched

156

forward holding the wheel tightly, trying to work out the shape of the road ahead. I know we've got another two or three intersections, one where I have to cut across the traffic and make a left turn, something I haven't done here yet. The first part is easy, just bends in the road and no traffic coming, but then we get to the major crossing and, I hope, the road my friend lives on. I don't know which way to go and the street numbers aren't indicated. The kids are quarrelling in low voices and Robert's starting to tell me about some book review he read in the *TLS*.

'You've got a green light,' he says.

'Yes, I know. But I don't know which way to turn.'

'Are you sure this is the road?'

'Well, it says so on the sign. Unless they're lying.' I know I'm being unfair—his poor night vision precludes him from reading the signs.

'Who's fucking this duck?' I say, and he laughs.

'Didn't what's her name? Ellis? Didn't she tell you which way to turn?'

'She *said* right. But on the map her road doesn't go to the right here—it's called something else entirely.' While I'm talking the light has turned amber and I decide to take the left turn.

'Shit! Look out!'

He grabs the wheel just as I start to turn into three lanes of oncoming cars. I make a wobbly recovery and somehow get to the correct side of the road. I pull into the next byway and study the map again. The house numbers here are nothing like the one written on my scrap of paper.

This goes on for another half an hour. We do U-turns and end up back at Palo Alto. We look at the map again in the grounds of an Old People's Home. We go up and down the road, and every time I take my foot off the gas the motor dies and I have to do my no-hands, four-feet juggling act with the brake and gears and accelerator. We get back to the original crossing and I turn right.

'Are you okay now?'

'No. I'm heading home. At least I know where that is.' The

oil light has begun to flicker on and off. 'We'll have an omelette at home, kids, and visit Ellis some other day. All right?'

They don't care, they're just mad they've missed their TV show.

'Oh, bugger it.' I pull over to the side of the road about a mile from home. 'I can't bear to admit defeat. What if we have one more go? We'll ignore the map and believe Ellis. What do you reckon?'

'Sure, mom.' The kids' accents are so good now I don't know whether they're still putting them on or if they've really acquired a California voice. I know Robert would rather go home, but he agrees too.

We go back, make a new turn and end up outside I. Magnin's in a shopping complex. We approach from a different angle and I spot a house number very close to the one Ellis has given me and I pull up immediately. We're almost there. An hour and a half late, and we still have to walk a hundred yards or so along a dark road, throwing ourselves into the hedge with each passing car, but we are really there. Even the children are silent and grateful by now. We see lights in the windows, I recognize Jolly's bike, we stumble across the unlit lawn and ring the bell.

The party is okay. Everyone has given us up and started eating but as soon as I have a couple of fast beers and a bowl of spaghetti I feel fine. I serve Robert his pasta, making sure I give him plenty, knowing that that sort of car tension can lower his sugar radically. I intend to remind him to have an extra serving of fruit or ice-cream, but I get talking and I forget. It's the first time he has met these people, my fellow post-doctoral students, and I don't want to nag him in front of them.

I look over at him from time to time; he seems to be getting on well, talking about Australia and Barry Humphries with Joe, who has spent some time in England. The kids are a great hit, Sally shimmying away to the music and Rosa curling up on an oversize cushion, sleeping like a rosy cherub through all the noise and people stumbling over her. I smoke a lot and Robert makes smartarsed remarks about it, but good-humouredly.

For the last half hour we sit together in the big rocking chair and stroke each other's arms. When we leave, the kids sleep-stunned in the back seat under a quilt, we get home without any problems at all. Ellis turns out to live about seven minutes away.

We put the kids to bed and come downstairs to drink tea. We gossip a while, aimlessly, about the other people at the party, sorting them into who we really like, don't mind, who reminds us of friends back home. Robert admits he's had a good time. Then we go to bed. After he puts out the lights I turn to him. Things are not always this relaxed between us.

'I'm sorry,' he says. 'I'm too tired. Is that okay?'

'Sure,' I say in a broad American voice. 'It'll keep.'

Then I lie awake for a while thinking about everything: what we are doing here, thousands of miles from home, what we are still doing together; sorting out all the things that make life worth going on with. Apart from the children there don't seem to be many . . .

. . . When I was still living in New Guinea, Annie Minsen warned me, at a cricket match. It was a blue, pellucid day during the Dry and we were playing on a pitch set into a grassy promontory— if the ball fell into the sea it was automatically a six.

'I've nursed diabetics,' Annie said. 'Really, you don't want to get involved with one. He's okay now, maybe, but with age comes complications. It's hard on their families.'

We were sitting in the shade of a gnarled, creamily flowering frangipani, eating sweet orange quarters. I was thinking of *goin pinis*, going finish. Home for good. I wondered if Annie was getting her revenge for my asking if she was Eurasian when we first met. She was angrily proud of her pure Chinese lineage. I thought idly that she might have ideas of racial purity, or euthanasia for the genetically unsound.

'Of course,' she said, as if hearing my thoughts, 'there would be some danger in having children too. It could be hereditary,

159

no one knows.'

Later, Robert and I often referred, joking, to this conversation. 'Perhaps you should have listened,' he always said. 'Can't say I wasn't warned,' I always replied.

But warnings often come too late. It was not possible, then, for me to weigh potential failure against the languid joy of those early months; the hot Port Moresby nights; the seeming cornucopia of mango, pawpaw, avocado; gin-and-tonics so cold and strong they shone blue in their frosted glasses. It was a sexual love then, of frantic, earnest experiment, our two bodies seeming to share the one parameter of skin. There were the dawn walks along the grey-sand beach with small crabs plopping dirty holes at our feet; there were the late-night, early-morning, sweaty lovemakings, in my narrow bed, Creedence Clearwater blaring from the stereo bought cheap from the strange Russian in Engineering. There were my arrivals at morning classes still trembling in the aftermath of orgasm, sure that my language students could smell him on me, understood my shaking hands. So that sex became irretrievably associated with the diagrams of Transformational Grammar, which I never thought to apply to my own life as Chomsky might have advised. The deep meaning of any sentence always there, programmed into our synapses, discoverable under the most convoluted spider-web of syntax: the most sophisticated, intricate, evolving, cunningly-spun love affair reducible, perhaps, to girl meets boy.

And so, tonight, in another foreign country, thinking all this, I fall asleep, waking before dawn with the familiar apprehension already prickling at my skin, the old coldness in the bowels. I put my hand out, tentatively, to feel the soaked sheets, his cool, clammy flesh.

'Bobby. Are you okay?' If he can answer it's not too bad.

'Love. Are you all right?' My voice is soft, friendly, I keep it steady. I don't want to startle him awake. That can trigger deep shock, leads to ambulances, straitjackets, the messy jabbing at veins with syringes like horse-needles.

I touch him gently on the shoulder. His eyes open but his whole body is stiff, extended. I know the cramps have started. He is awake but he cannot speak. Sweat is still breaking out all over him, even his feet are covered in tiny droplets.

'Bobby? It's okay. I'll get some sugar milk. It's okay.'

I tremble, going down the stairs, and my palms are moist, but I am fast and efficient, spooning sugar into milk until it is barely liquid. My body does not panic, but my mind is racing, racing. Back in the bedroom it is clear that he cannot take the milk himself. I run downstairs again for more sugar until the glass is full of a sweet paste. This has happened before, I tell myself repeatedly as I go back up, it will be all right. I dip my finger into the mixture and place it on his tongue. I do this many times. I know it will be absorbed eventually but I hope it will be before he goes into real insulin shock. His eyes roll, but he is swallowing. Now I can put my arm behind the pillow to prop his head and spoon the sugar into his mouth. Finally he begins to lick it from the spoon himself. When that glass is finished I go quietly down for more, this time drinkable. I wait beside the stove for five minutes exactly by the clock, to give the first sugar time to work a little. I don't want to go back upstairs until he is out of it but I can't risk waiting longer.

He is muttering when I come in, about boxing. He is counting himself out '. . . One . . . two . . . three . . . you bastard . . . I can get up . . . four . . . five . . . you rotten cunt . . . all right . . . six . . . seven . . . I'm getting up . . .' I know this is the tricky stage, when he is conscious but not really aware of where he is. I have to become part of the delirium myself if I want him to drink.

'Here's your milk, champ,' I say. I keep my voice light and dry. He refuses it. He begins to recite dirty verse and reaches for my breast.

'Only if you have some of this first,' I say.

He laughs, and I laugh too. He goes on with Abdul el Bulbul Emir . . . 'The harlots turned green, the men shouted "Quean!" It was laughed at for years by the Tsar. For Abdul the fool,

161

left half of his tool, Up Ivan Skivinsky Skivar . . .'

He laughs again, softly. I try to hand him the milk but he knocks it away and some spills on the bed.

'I haven't finished,' he says. 'There are ten more verses at least.'

'No,' I say. 'That was the last verse, now you must drink the milk.'

He raises his head and looks at me and then he groans.

'Oh Jesus, Jesus. My love, I'm sorry. Oh Christ you bastard.'

'It's okay,' I say and I try to smile. 'Here, drink this.'

'I hate it. What is it?'

'Just finish it, there's not much more.'

When he has drunk it all I put the glass down in a puddle of sticky syrup and then I get my dressing gown on and sit on the bed. This is the time when I must not recriminate, as I have too often before, must not ask how or why or whether he over-injected or had too little carbohydrate at dinner. This is the time when he is remorseful, apologetic, sometimes begs to die. I stroke his damp hair, gently, holding in my anger. He has stopped sweating, he is out of it. His eyes close and I let him sleep for a little while. When I am sure his breathing is normal I wake him up so that we can change the sheets. He goes to shower and then makes a pot of tea which we drink, sitting up, in the fresh bed. The sky is grey outside the window, it is morning. Suddenly the digital alarm sounds and I switch it off.

'You're not going to run this morning are you?' I ask. I can't help it.

'Not now. Perhaps later.' His voice is obstinate, he knows what I think about running after a bad reaction. He puts his hand on my thigh. 'I'm sorry. I don't know how you put up with me.'

'Well,' I say, 'I was warned, and I took no notice.'

I take the cups downstairs, with the sticky glass, and I wash them at the sink. I stand with my hands in the warm water trying to fight down my anger, and the tears come. I think that I hate him but that I can't leave him because he needs me. I think that it is his fault I was not with my mother when she died and that I might not forgive that. I think about how we drank and smoked dope and went to parties and Chinese restaurants when we first lived together, about how if I met him now, teetotal, non-smoking, jogging ascetic, I would not be attracted. I think that I would like a word-processor and about his contempt for technology. I think about how he never acts on the notes the children bring home from school, that it is always me who arranges the cakes for the fête, the presents for birthdays and Christmas. I think that I always buy his underwear and socks. Then I find myself laughing, at the sink, the water turning cold around my wrists. I am reminded of my mother, rouged, permed, the cigarette tongued to the corner of her mouth, who always said when things were at their worst, 'Well, you have to laugh, don't you? If you don't laugh, you cry.'

When I go back to bed he is getting up. He dresses in his running gear, turns the light off and pulls down the blind against the morning noise. I can hear the children stirring in the next room.

'Hey,' I say, 'come here.'

We kiss, affectionately, like a very old couple. He tucks the blankets around me, closes the bedroom door and goes to organize the kids' breakfast, dressing, school, as he usually does.

I know that he won't wake me until he gets back from running. I think of him, pushing himself panting round and round the track until he has done his five miles, while I sleep. I hope, closing my eyes, that I am smiling.

GATES

Barry Hill

AUTHOR'S NOTE

'Gates' is the third in a set of stories ('Making the Island'). These stories were composed about eighteen months apart—written with two full gestations of time between them, thus allowing for due contemplation of genetic determinants. That's one reward from writing, writing anything actually: a time lapse can make the drift of some meanings clearer.

The stories are set in Bali, and deal with a youngish couple, Andrew and Sally, on holiday with their new baby. She is caught up with the baby rather than him, or so he thinks. He is perhaps too academic, or vainly self-conscious, to know. In the first story, 'Sluts', he gets a kind of comeuppance when he is cornered (or he corners himself) into taking nude photographs of another traveller, a man, a stud perhaps uncomfortably akin to him. In the second story, 'Sandshoes', the identity stakes are raised somewhat when Andrew goes into the mountains alone, crosses a lake, and finds himself in a native burial ground. Then, in 'Gates', down from the mountain he comes.

After bearing witness to Andrew's pitiable contortions with respect to the forces of life and death within him, a friend once said to me, 'Something needs to happen to that man.' Too right, I thought, and a few months after that I came to write 'Gates'.

Previously, and for quite a few years, I hoped I'd been writing under the stylistic mantle of Pound, Eliot, early Joyce, Flaubert, Chekhov—reticence, the impersonal, objective correlatives all over the place, any autobiography to be firmly framed. But writing 'Gates' made me feel the constriction of that 'model'—not because I was compelled to set down all my own domestic details (I didn't, that would have been another story), but because, after

Andrew's visit to the burial ground, the mythic narrative structure that I'd found myself using, combined with the pressure of recounting what would happen to him next, made me think it much more important to write towards the object rather than away from it; to write, if necessary, at it. This was a liberation. While working on 'Gates' I realized that once a certain kind of momentum is established in the telling, and once the drift of a story's structure coheres, almost independently of the author, a lyric can have a force that transcends aesthetically determined autobiographical qualms.

And the object, what *was* the object exactly? (I still like the story for forcing such bluntness. I like its defiance of the unspoken.) Well, an older, wiser, friend of mine exclaimed, 'The horror, the horror,' when he finished with the childbirth passages. With the arrogance of the younger man, I was pleased at his disapproval: maybe I'd gone further into the cave than before, written something that hadn't quite been written before. At the same time, no, later, after reading the warm light-soaked treatment of the subject by William Carlos Williams in *White Mule*, I wished my friend had acknowledged the tender awe and the trepidation with which even Andrew approached the sacred. In essaying upon the genesis of myth—that which makes the truth of facts—Robert Duncan reminds us that the term comes from the Greek to murmur, mutter, moan, to drink with closed lips, to suck in. There is an open-eyed howl forced out in 'Gates', but beneath it there is also an affirmative murmuring, an in-breath, despite the last three words of the story, the *'no no no'* (which were, horrifyingly, somehow lopped off when it was first published).

Barry Hill

166

GATES

Down from the mountain he came. The bus tunnelled shadows. He'd made decisions. In and out of dark, the driver after each turn speeded up, rushing the jungle past. The horn wailed ahead. He would tell Sally. He'd confess, or, if not confess, declare, since where these days was authority deserving of confession? She could do what she liked with that Kurt. Even if the bloke had left the island, that was not the point; she could do what she liked with the next man. Because he, Andrew, was not—'I, your husband, am not'—any longer jealous. He'd cut it out, overcome that pathetic, self-defeating infantile 'mode of possession', ah, yes.

That was one thing. The bus lurched, and the horn, temporarily, ceased, and in the speeding silence he nursed his other statement of intent. He found himself . . . attracted; he desired, he *wanted* that sloppy slut, and he wanted Sal to know it. For he was inclined to 'follow the woman up'. There, he had the words already. He'd say that. She had a right to know. We all have rights to see the cards on the table. And all of a sudden he felt . . . well, he felt contemporary, with the bus still roaring down, out of gear.

They were going down the mountain very fast now. Just in case he tried himself out. He looked out the window. There was the jungle. But the picture in his mind was of a man coming over the dune with Sal, while he sat there on the beach. He kept looking at the blur of trees, but that's what he saw, another man rising into view with his wife, their faces baking in the sun. Then he let go, and the film ran backwards: instead of coming towards him as they had a week ago, the couple reversed into the dunes. He went after them. There was a hut. He entered the hut with them. The driver was leaning in panic or passion or both on the horn and yet Andrew knew that the cause for concern was not outside but inside, that the racket was within. Down on the floor of the hut he went, with them. There she was on the man, underneath him, going at it like mad. Image after image ripped into him, he let it, he stayed, he stopped right there beside the

167

couple, his face low on the mat, and at one stage reached out and found her hand, and his own lust.

The bus swayed, lurched, he was still in his seat, it had worked, though they were careering now, down. By stopping, taking the pain in, going into it, he'd killed it off, and now he could (as soon as the bus stopped) rise again, rise up, re-emerging from his own grave, so to speak. He thought of the Tantric expression, *chöd*, where one faced horror in order later to live well. Would he tell her that? Maybe not, it would grant her too much. Yet he would however declare that she be free, he would say that. 'You should be free and so should I, we should be free, at least for a while'—yes, that was the way to put it, that sounded right, it felt right, it fitted, and the thought of it lightened him; he felt, now, lightened himself; that was the line of argument (not quite the right expression, argument, but still) that one could share with anyone, everyone, ah! The bus had taken a wide turn and come out into a valley. A wide valley with paddies incredibly green, absolutely green, God had someone ripped the covers off! Then they were out on a wide arc of terrace, fold after fold of descent then, to him, unbearably, almost, lush.

In their next fast run, where they listed savagely, one couple up front fell out of their seats. The man broke his fall with his fat little mitts, while the woman, presumably his wife, tumbled onto his hip, all arms and pantihose, though how she managed in the heat was anybody's guess. A bark went up. She turned. The bark was, Andrew realized, his own. And then they were roaring between embankments again, and the woman had to recover her seat. He stood up and swung by the strap. Ha! Ha! No one heard above the horn. Ha! Ha! Ha! Ha! And he could see the lot—the river emerald spotted white (oxen), chrome splatterings (duck, ducklings) and up on the bank, a line of tattered flames (rags on the farmer's pole) and then with one more turn, they descended again, and were among the low paddies on the long run home towards the sea, and the villagers, the humidity gaining weight as they ran at dogs, children, bikes, carts blocking the way. An old woman, squatting by her golden mat of rice, waved. She had the face of a warrior, and her arms went up—ecstasy or alarm?—when a bike skidded on grain. And they did have to slow. The big red, belching Mercedes, holding the centre, farting oil, unyielding still, cruised on down, the horn still going, they descended, finally, with heavy, ruthless calm that called for a celebration, didn't it? Of course it did!

He'd got off at the place he started out from that morning. Outside the café that sold those cheap and world-famous and illegal magic omelettes—where couples sat; unflickering and comatose but privately blissed no doubt, even if they did look—what did he say later?—even if they looked hopelessly fucked: he got off there and started to run. Down through the stalls. He ran, no, he jogged, steadily and calmly jogged; a man at one with himself, surely, and still with a decent pair of legs; he jogged past carvings paintings ice-creams shirts umbrellas paintings—hell, did people spend their lives smearing those psychedelic and pastel tints? He jogged, at one with himself, past huts cafés temples bars hotels, through the settlement by the sea where the evil spirits lived because the good ones occupied the mountain, until he came to the duty free shop where he bought the gin, a large bottle of the best because it would have no scent it would be so pure. Sally loved gin.

And they had their first drinks on the porch, with Tommo wandering between them, uniting and then dividing his parents with the entrails of mango, creating mess under both chairs. The boy had been on the porch when his father burst through the bamboo, from the lane that was a short cut through the settlement. One son with ten red and blue blocks. 'Hey Tommo,' he called, and the boy looked up at the trees with their huge, overprotective fronds edging the last light, and he stood up and went inside: he came out riding his mother's hip as Andrew reached the porch. Dad hugged them both, and the boy piped, 'Kissing House,' and so the parents sustained, for a few seconds, his bower, stuck at their closed circuit until Sally, finally, pulled out: 'Phew,' she said, 'just let me do this.' 'If you insist,' Andrew said.

For the boy she set out fruit salad. Its sweetness and her

frangipani oil, the thickness of scent, he remembered; and the nape of her neck was clean cut too, with her hair tied back and no strand loose; it was as if she had just prepared herself for him; so he was as he waited a little pleased with his patience, for at another time he might have poured the drinks straightaway as a bait for her to sit down and rest then and there with him. In due course she'd come, he realized; and of course she did. She put her feet, nut brown, up on the rail. A slack sheen of thigh lolled on its long bone. Her glass saluted his—cheers. The child ate, night fell, husband and wife sat together; a dewy, accepting air rose between them and he felt then that they were for a moment sipping the sheer fluid of sustained promise and safety we call trust. He could tell her anything.

But it didn't last. Nothing lasts—he'd be saying that, as well, as we all do in an effort to get our stories straight or at least their genre right—it didn't last because after he had eaten Tommo wandered between them for a time and then slipped: he skidded on the mess of uterine pink pips beneath him, smacking his head on the tiles. And in the howl that went up Andrew let himself ask: 'Did you miss me?' and he heard her laugh: 'Of course, silly. You were gone for at least twelve hours. It was *hard work*.'

He did his best with the joke but it was not good enough. He said, 'I almost didn't get back.' And she replied: 'That would have been okay. I half expected you to stay the night up there. We'd have been all right. I hope you didn't rush back for our sakes.' No, he said, he hadn't rushed back for their sakes. Then he was compelled to go on; he had to explain: he told her that the ascent had taken *ages*, that it had been an *expedition* to the village, and once there an *ordeal* to get out, time seemed to stand still or go backwards, he rediscovered *reality*, he said, only on the way down, which was when he thought vividly of her. He had missed her, he wanted her to know that, even if she hadn't missed him much ... He managed a grin. Anyway, what had she been up to? 'Tell me about your day,' he said, 'you're looking terrific.'

Tommo said, 'Where dadda go?' 'Dad's been on a little trip

to the hills and now he's happy to be home with us.'

'Why don't we put him to bed?'

'Because I'd like to finish this, if you don't mind.'

'Yes, yes, you finish that,' he said, 'that's what I want you to do, you hop into it, mate'—and he carried the boy inside— 'Dadda read to you tonight, hey?' On the bed the boy was happy enough with his head in the crook of his father's arm, making it itch; the book Andrew turned towards the anaemic bulb which lit the room, and he let the boy turn every second page. 'The wild things roared their terrible roars and gnashed their terrible teeth'—a tale that pursued itself ruthlessly, like a beast that had never bitten its own tongue. 'And rolled their terrible eyes and showed their terrible claws.' The boy did not notice her come in at first, nor did he: he glanced up and there she was at the basin, going on with another job. If he spoke she'd say 'someone' had to do it, so he read on. She scrubbed, worried suds, pressed and leaned at the basin. She bent to a bucket. She came up for more. When she turned a gash appeared on the belly of her apple green shorts: the imprint of the basin, but it cut across her like the Caesarean she'd not had, that nightmare missed, thank goodness, leaving her belly like the rest of her, an immaculate, firm surface. The hot work oiled her skin, and when she bent down again with her back to him, that slackness of thigh had gone; it was a sinew as taut as any body squatting by a golden mat of rice, hands feathering the grain; her limbs from knee to recess were one unflawed promise. 'Love you,' he whispered, between terrible cries.

Tommo looked up; Dadda talk to him? Dadda was not, and Andrew's cupped palm guided the boy's skull back down into the book as the woman stood up, crossed the room without— evidently—hearing, going out with her arms full of strangled washing. The bucket she left for him to carry. 'Shoosh,' he said, when their woman had gone.

'Wad?'

'Hear mum?' Andrew heard her step from the porch.

'Hear her?'

'Nup.'

'No, I think you're right. It's the breeze in the ceiling. Bloody draughty huts.' His wife sometimes hummed as she worked.

'Wad's dwaughty?'

'Lets the wind in. Wind through holes, that's draughty. Say draughty.'

'Dwaughty.'

'Draughty.'

Tommo lay there.

'Draughty. Say it.'

'Don't wanna.'

'Drr-aughty. Or no story.'

'Wan mum to read me story,' Tommo said.

'Four more pages.'

The boy heard him out, let him stand and move away from the bed after the last kiss. He said, 'Wanna kiss mum goodnight.'

'You did that before, Sonny Jim.'

'Kiss momma.'

'You there, Sal?'

Yes, she was there; she came in, all dry; she returned to them with the solicitude and warmth of the necessary medium, a smile for each. She nuzzled the child, and offered, once again, unwitting loins to her man: apple green and oil and sweetness of recess—he took his chance. He reached out. Feathered. A soft, golden wedge with the best of intentions, which a lad on his back would find it impossible to see, detect—unless of course she backed up out of it like some panicky mare, *which she did*, didn't she? 'Sorry,' she snapped. 'So am I,' he said, and left her to it.

But she came out after him quick enough. 'I wasn't *quite* ready for you.' She put her cool hand on a troubled forehead.

'It wasn't rape.'

'I'm sorry, pet,' she said, and she sounded too sorry for his liking. Any minute he'd have the ledge of resentment from which to launch his declarations. Except that she added, 'And you won't get anywhere by sulking, you know that.'

'Oh, I'm not sulking.'

'Good,' she said. He drank, and waited some more, there was loads of time. They'd get stuck into the drinking together. The night out there beyond his reach, with its animal presence, it made the water shimmer, and the bamboo rustle; you could if you wanted step out into its arms, and—maybe, tango, that's the kind of night it was, he thought, taking another sip of his drink: A man should invite his wife to dance, he should get up and go to her and offer his arm because she was still a fine-looking woman and he was feeling—still he felt . . . light, lightened; and she was, though prone to weariness like all young mums, indeed a fine-looking woman. A glance, yes, proved it; though sometimes she doubted his word. He had a mind then to pay her no compliment at all. Once he told her, 'You'd perk up if someone else said it,' and she went quiet, which he read as guilt until she piped up, 'I've seen you get a kick out of other people'—which was too true to deny, too silly to refute, since no couple can expect to mirror each other exclusively, especially after the first child. Oh, having Tommo was a step forward, a positive thing for them both, there was no doubt about that: the conception, gestation and arrival was an affirmation, a confirmation, yes, yes, *yes*; and if ever he doubted it he might as well doubt the animality of the night, for the power of good it would do him—whenever he was dumb enough to doubt it. Flagging as he might as a father or even a husband, he cast himself back to the birth, and was replenished. Gratitude. Gratitude and reverence, or, if not reverence, awe. His debt, that occasion. Honour. His debt, honour and horror—he *should* ask her to dance. Reach out and touch, lightly caress, his debt— which is what he'd done, back inside, eh? Fingered his honour, ha! And horror ha ha ha and debt, ha ha ha ha ha.

'What's so funny?'

'Nothing,' he said, unaware of letting anything out, just yet.

'Come on, tell me what was in your head.'

'Well, my dear,' he said, 'I was thinking, adoringly, about your unutterably edible, terrifically fecund cunt.'

God, gin was a wonderful drink!

'My cunt,' he added, conclusively.

'Ours,' he said, thinking better of it.

'I thought you wanted to hear about my day,' she said. 'Oh I do I do I do,' he said, 'tell me all. What did you do with young Tommo, did he have a nice time in the pig shit?' But of course his son had not played in the pig shit; he had played with the son of the manageress, a boy his own age called Wyan, yet another first born. Andrew thought, 'Everyman a first born.' He said, 'Tell me about your day, my love, the night is young, how did it start and how did it end up, let us live for the dreams that are told, and retold.' He waved an arm at the palm tree. Light was not the word—he had never felt so aerated, so affirmative, optimistic. A bloke had better watch himself. Any tick and he'd go under.

So he made an effort to listen to the details of her day. It was not easy. She had a special interest in gates, of all things. That day she'd managed to see a lot of them. She got away early. Each compound that took her fancy she went into. She sat, observing, until she felt like moving on to the next one. From compound to compound she wandered, meditating on the gates, the crumbling entrances, and then on to the next one when the mood took her. It had been a good day, a truly instructive day, she said: all that time alone; the time, and the space of those gates—her face lit up when she said that. He said he was pleased for her. (That's what she failed most to realize, he'd say later; what power I had within me to be pleased *for* her . . .)

The point is this: Sally was finishing off her degree in anthropology, and the gates were to her structures that expressed certain philosophies of living. From the moment she arrived on the island, she'd been captivated by those crumbling, derelict pylons marking the entrance to the compounds: so open, casual— they were no more than remnants, most of them, of ancient gates. Archways, if they had been, had long gone. And so the entrances remained, and became increasingly abstract as well as tacit, ceremonial and indirect: she loved for instance the way one was deflected to the side, and had to approach at an angle, off-centre— which showed a bold understanding of movement, a grace of passage, a command of the physical, a capacity for being properly at home in the physical realm.

'You're laying it on a bit,' he said.

But now she was in her full flight of ex-po-sition. (Ex-po-sition—was his pronunciation whenever anyone enquired about their holiday, or their life together; he held on to the word and swirled it about in his mouth like a full-bodied claret.) For she thought very passionately about these representations, just as he, at that point, had a pang of concern for the falling level of the gin; and she went on at length about these people's confidence in the abstractness of their physical life, so that he was moved to demand: okay, what is it exactly to be at home in the physical realm? She said: Having the right degree of detachment, being able to look on as if the movements of your body are not your own—and that, he was prepared to admit afterwards (he was to develop a thesis, you might say, around it), that unsettled him most. It reminded him of the time he'd made a dreadful mistake.

Soon after their boy was born, Andrew confessed to shame. He felt shame at a certain tendency within himself to focus exclusively on that one part of her, as if he cared obsessively about that part, as if perhaps it was all that he loved in her. An obscenity, was it not, this sexist (he knew the terms) splitting of her, his one-eyed objectification, when in reality he had a larger, wholer love? He fell silent at that point and she spoke to him in the collected tone she now employed on the gates: he worried too much. He should not fret. Instead he should develop ways of being in and out of the body at the same time, if he couldn't do it already? And he'd never forgiven the super-ciliousness, just as it still frightened him that he might have done something to deserve it. So when she had finished her ex-po-sition, he said, 'Darls, you talk a lot of crap but you're beautiful and I love you.'

'Thank you, Andy.'

'You don't have to be a bitch, either.'

All she had to do now was goad him a little bit more.

She said, 'I was just telling you about my day. You asked.

I went for a swim, too. And I had a massage.'

'So I gathered. I can taste the frangipani, just about.'

'Can you? I showered.'

'Who gave you the massage? What's-her-name?' If it had been the sloppy slut, he'd have said he wished he'd been in on the act.

'No. One of the boys gave me the massage.'

'On the beach?'

'No.'

'One of the boys, eh.'

'I had the massage, and I fucked him.' . . . Just like that . . .

She said, 'I had the massage, and I fucked him.' Her announcement. A simple statement of fact. History . . .

He sat there.

He heard his son cough—a thin clearing of the throat as the head turned on the hot pillow.

He sat there, aware of his own breathing. He was breathing through his nostrils, and for some reason thought of the prickly hairs that protruded from them, which had to be snipped with the bathroom scissors. He thought of this, and then carried on with his breathing; it was amazing.

Amazing, there was no other word for it. It is a much abused word these days, he knew that; like trauma, which is also tossed about at dinner tables. But he was amazed at his calm, his forbearance. Finally, he was able to say: 'How did it happen? Do you want to tell me more?'

Reasonable.

She spoke very quietly. 'I don't know. But I did want to tell you that.'

'Are you drunk?'

'I might be, a bit.'

'Were you drunk, or anything, then?'

'No, I was not drunk or anything then.'

'You're woozy though,' he observed.

'I feel,' she was suddenly vague, 'I actually feel . . . good, I feel . . . loose.' She laughed. 'I feel pretty terrific, as a matter of fact. I'm sorry.'

'I imagine.'

'What do you imagine?'

'That you feel . . . loose.'

'Don't be a bastard.'

(It was incredible, he would say later, she called *me* a bastard.)

She was watching him; he was on his mettle. He said, 'I'm serious, I'm pleased for you, I don't want to sound stupid. I'm pleased for us. I wish you'd tell me more.'

'Tell you more?'

'Yes, you've said this much.'

'He offered. I said yes. It was good then, fine. It's unimportant now. Is there more gin?'

'Where were you?'

'His hut.'

'At least you didn't bring him here.'

'We were here, for a while.'

'Did he have a big one?'

'Here we go,' she said.

'Come on. Did he have a whopper? I bet he did.'

She got up and poured her own drink.

'I'm sorry,' he said, 'do you want ice?'

She did not want ice.

'You're pissed as a newt,' he said. 'You ought to fucking stop.'

They concentrated on their drinks, not speaking. A thought crossed his mind—'Maybe I had this coming to me?'—and then it was gone again. He said, 'I said I was sorry.'

'Okay.'

After a while, he said, 'So it was okay, yes, at the time?'

'Yes, at the time.'

'But unimportant.'

'Yes.'

'Just a fuck, eh.'

'Just a fuck, yes.'

'Just a fucking fuck,' he said. He threw his glass—into dark. With a hopeless thud it hit the palm tree, and didn't break.

He heard her going on. 'If you want me to say I'm sorry and plead forgiveness, I will. I mean it when I say I don't want it to hurt us. But it happened. We can face that, can't we? We can face that together, and go on. I want to go on, there is no doubt about that in my mind, it does not even come up as an *issue*.'

Now he could feel the cunning rising in him; a certain return of strength. (Subsequently he'd say, 'There *are* legitimate claims; we can make legitimate claims on each other, and in this lies our dignity and strength . . .')

He said, 'I can hear you. Just let me get adjusted a bit, will you. I'm shocked, I'm shocked to the core, do you realize that?'

'I can see you're upset, yes.'

'You'd be upset, I bet you'd be upset, for Chrissake.'

'I suppose so.'

'You suppose so! So help me Christ you suppose so!' He rose.

'I don't know for sure,' she said. 'I'm not you, remember.'

'You're not me all right, I'll say you're not.'

(Who was she then?)

He sat down again. 'Tell me then, how much did it cost?'

She sighed. 'You mean the massage?'

'You mean you paid for the fuck, for the bloke?'

'He was a boy. Yes, I paid.'

'O me O my,' he said, 'O me O my'—an expression he had never in his life used before. 'And how much, tell me how much?'

'Fifteen bucks.'

'Fifteen bucks, well well well, O me O my. Then we had better be careful with the housekeeping this week, hadn't we. What do we do, take it off the meat bill?'

For a second there she laughed too; she took up what she thought to be his joke, his transcendent wit; that's what it might have been. Except that he had the bottle in his hand. He pitched it, it hit the same tree, there was another dull thud in the dark, and no breakage—'Oh you slut you dumb bitch you fucking moll you dumb cunt'—and he was running at her . . .

But she was on her feet too; she went towards him; in an

instinctive, silent move, she was in his arms before he could strike her (if that's what he was going to do). 'She fell into my arms,' he'd say later, 'begging for it.'

Begging? Come on mate, No one begs for it these days. I kid you not, she was begging for it. I'm here to tell you that she dragged me off, she dragged me down to the beach, and it was when we got there that I slapped her because that in my judgment was what she wanted; that's right, she wanted it right there on the sand, wet sand it was as well, with the tide out, right down there on the ribs of sand running all the way out to the shallows, with no scum on the beach either, it was washed clean, you couldn't even see a soldier crab, they must have taken nosedives, I can tell you, those crabs, or they were way down beneath her, under her head, or in her hair, or under or up her bum, who knows, ha ha ha ha . . . Begged for it, yes—

And his friends had not finished dessert before he said—I'm here to tell you that the birth was the most important event of my life.

Good one, Andy.

Listen, you arseholes.

And listen they did. And here was yet another story of a woman on her back. Begging for it, Andy? No, no, no, not begging for it, but heaving, he'd say that. For twenty hours. A day and a night . . . his wife, yes, that's what she was, his wife, damnit, was laid out for all that time and mostly he was alone with her: a nurse might come in to look, and there she was breathing gently, easily, patiently while her husband was at the bed beside her. The whole day and the early part of that night, it seemed, were peaceful with nothing perceptibly moving, either inside or out. He was with her, that was all, and it was enough. Sometimes she moved from one hip to another, or sat up on her elbow, leaning her belly like a great wet sandbag—it looked wet, it glistened because he had earlier rubbed it with baby oil, had soothed and scented it with the neutral scent of baby oil, leaving the sheet over her lower belly which had at her request remained unshaved; intact still. And so sometimes she heaved herself about, repositioning her great plumb weight, while he was with her waiting with equal patience, holding her hand. And when he could sit still no longer he got up and walked around the bed and looked out the window, into the car park of the hospital, across the fence to the pub at the back where he'd buy her a drink as soon as it was all over, he promised—because still there was no sign of the pain, just the upbeat of her pulse, occasionally, and the increasing discomfort, whenever she tried to sit up. He plumped pillows. He sat down again. He plumped the soft down inside himself, it was so sweet waiting there; he was astonished at his tenderness, his solicitude, when he was by nature, she'd say, tetchy, impatient, intolerant. Yet here he was anticipating the first grimace—which came, finally, in the early evening, as the car park emptied, and the lights went on in the pub; it came and she went into her deeper, cyclic breathing and he prepared to join her in that. It came, and then it went away again. She lay smiling in anticipation.

Her cries began as murmurs. He murmured with her, his head on her pillow. He held her hand and the pain went away again. He could tell from the tensing of her fingers, her electronic sweat, when she began to call the pain back. Deeply he breathed with her, and tried to send it away again. Or must he wish it upon her? for her next cry deepened and then rose in a tidal swell. He grabbed at the oxygen mask. She waved it off. He took her hand again, and the pain went away. Water? Yes, she took some water, but the next wave was upon her, and he had no choice then; it ran through in one steady, sharpening swell that screwed her face up before breaking it open, her smile ran back into her temples and every vein in her neck puffed like a squid shot through with its own ink. And her breathing, its rhythm, then, slipped all of a sudden, too, she cried out: 'Oh, hell, oh,' her hand doing a mad dance along the bed, snatching for his. Then he was with her; he started out in the pain too—the waiting no longer delicate and tedious—when the next wave came he was able, to some extent, to rise with her, to be buoyed up in the pain, and this pleased and relieved him too, this exultation.

She was opening, he knew that. He only had to look. He was at the bed head, while everyone else—the room had populated as she heaved, the more she abandoned herself, the more bustle went on about her feet. But he could imagine well enough, he thought. And when he did look, she was all there, he found that wet sopping welcome, a man might reach out, or put his face to rest, or to work, or ... But he saw too, the film over the eye, the great eye. And a swimming in a slit of winey fluid, oh yes, yes. That look took him; after that he forced himself to catch her gaze. Held on to his smile. It is okay, he said, it is good, it looks good (Oh, Christ how did he manage to utter that word, good); and yet there she was, there it was, coming; it was coming: 'Oh oh, it's coming,' she cried with the next wave, 'Oh love, love, I'm coming, I'm making a baby.'

And here, at the dinner table, he'd pause. Was everybody happy? Did everyone have what they wanted. Booze, fags? Who wanted a cigar?

No one wanted a cigar just yet, thank you, Andrew.

Swimming in the slit, shadow pulsing in the gap.

What's that, mate?

The shadow pulsing in the gap, continued our vulgarian, pulsing in the gap, yes, a filmy dark, looming there; and it did not bleed, no, that was the other thing, the lack of blood. A slow, milky trickle at one point, translucence, and a winey gloss at other times, but no blood; a pale diaphanous jelly instead, when all the time you might have expected from that everyday miracle, that swampy site, that dark diurnal lunar love nest— call it what you like, fellas, I'll leave you to fill in the gap— he laughed—no blood, no, that was the point, just the uncoloured swelling, and her bone-dry lips, a mouth that kept on and kept on swelling. So wide it was not going to be wide enough. It was not going to stretch that far, was it? It would split. It would burst. All of her, it, would break open. Yet still the shadow pulsed there, in the gap.

Then it split some more. It did, she did, but how the hell could she? A man did not know what to do with himself, eh:

it split more, the shadow slid . . . forward . . . and then back. Gone. There for a moment at the mouth, then gone. And how dry the lips were. Monstrously puffed, even in repose. And the splitting again then, pulse bulging, a form now, not a fluid, a solid protruding; it was firm, furry, like a nut, now with its dark sheen. Then gone again. But the next time, when it came after that, it was advanced firmly, and of course it stuck, it had to be. Could she split more? She must not. She'd burst. It was stuck in that gap. It was stuck in his throat. It would have to be cut. They would cut her, cut him, he could feel erupting in his gullet membranes, his loss of voice, oh no, even less human now— Oh yes yes yes yes, she cried, she screamed for the first time at the lava, bluish grey, and the sister called, good girl, good girl, good girl, push—calling girl to this ecstatic, exploding, alien woman!—and he heard himself, good good good, push good push, and then for a time there was a pause, and enduring equipoise in that crowning: Shrieking, she offered the head; for a long moment you could see the skull cupped, fully cupped with the face of the boy still buried in the woman, only the top of his skull, all slime, showing, a perfect brown egg: a moment then of this last dark agonized gift, before the propulsion, its ejection— out on to the mat, a rubber mat—splat. God. A whole baby placed upon the belly still ballooned, while the rest of her is limp, mutilated, is a wound she is oblivious to, is one untroubled, unholy ooze and sag, with the free bleeding finally. Show me the man now, Andrew said, the man then, he demanded, who does *not* know what to do with himself, who does not turn away in the knowledge that he must love her, or it—her *and* it, all right then— that he *will* love her forever . . .

So. He'd stopped. But had he finished? That's what they wanted to know . . .

What was Andy waiting for now?

. . . Soon they would go home.

And it was clear, wasn't it; he was still feeling—what do we say these days?—vulnerable. The man was still—hurt. Witness romanticisms. The sentimentality. He could not open his mouth without bleeding, or finish a sentence without it curling into self-justification, or proud, self-pitying spiel. But he was not too proud to report Sally's observation after the delivery. She said that *he* was totally grey. He looked like sky trying hard to rain.

Actually, those at the table who also knew Sally had quite likely also heard another version of, if not the birth, then what happened with that trip to the beach, or rather what happened when they came back from the beach. Sally was no great talker, but there are a few things that, with close women friends, it does not pay to bottle up. After all, her self-disgust lay not in the possibility she had betrayed him; it was her conviction and still is that the trust we extend to each other is in its carnality both more pedestrian and elevated, and the pity was that Andrew with his capacity for self-torture and ambivalence and inability to do what he really wanted could not see it. (She saw it now, soon after their split; the rabbit slept in as many burrows as was geometrically possible in one city without losing fatal track of his own address). Of course Sally did some work on herself about the degree to which she had in fact submitted, there on the wet sand. There was a certain lingering self-disgust that she had seen fit to indulge, if not solicit, the man's—pathos, rage, lust; not to mention the pleasure she had momentarily extracted from her own submission at the time. Guilt—maybe guilt was relevant after all, we are so deeply conditioned, all of us, women particularly—guilt plays nasty tricks. But she was getting over that.

What she did not so easily get over, and what no friend encouraged her to forget, was the man's behaviour when they came back from the beach. While they were away the boy had woken up. Tommo stood on the porch. There he was knuckling his sleepy eyes, his pants down, as if he had walked like an overheated cub out into the night to cool off—a picture of animal self-containment, except that as soon as he saw them, he wept, and it was his father who swept him up, took him in on the run, then turned him around to face Sally. He held the boy. The child stood at attention, arms rammed in. And although, from Sally's point of view, they had walked back from the beach hand in hand, like new lovers, one might have thought at a distance, or even close up, if one passed without noticing their woodiness, the balsa flesh of faces lightened with exhaustion, although that was the prelude, what she heard was the father shouting in his son's ear: 'Take a look at this boy, this is your mother, okay, have a good look at the bitch, what you've got here sonny is a proper slut, I said slut, here we have the prime little cunt of a bitch who hardly knows her back from her front, her arse from her tit, see her, step forward son, and get a better look, go on, get a load of her, get a whiff, that's right, put your nose in there, good one, that's the way . . .' And he shoved the boy's head back at it.

A light went on in the manager's office. On the porch opposite, someone appeared in the unlit doorway, then retreated. And what Sally could not bear or understand or properly assimilate for a long time was herself sitting there on the step of the porch, her face in her hands.

But she was working on that, too. The split was a necessary thing, no one doubts. Within weeks of their final separation, she gained weight: Why, she could each day feel the muscles in her neck softening. She and Tom moved into a large house with two of her women friends, and the arrangement was, which Andrew agreed to (he was reasonable in lots of ways), that he would take Tommo on weekends. During the week Sally would have him. Omens for the future were good. And the boy was fine. Both parents were amazed at the way he went from strength to strength. Don't let anyone tell you kids are damaged, necessarily, by separations, no no no.

LADIES NEED ONLY APPLY

Thea Astley

AUTHOR'S NOTE

The idea for 'Ladies Need Only Apply' came from an advertisement in the Personal column of a country newspaper. I was amused by the misplaced adverb and what could be the unfortunate connotations if the placement were taken literally.

Some years before I had written a story for Hal Porter's edition of *Coast to Coast*. This story was called 'The Scenery Never Changes'. It dealt with a woman schoolteacher who seemed to be prone to unfortunate and disastrous relationships with men. I often wondered what happened to her. So I took Sadie on long service leave to northern Queensland, put her at a beach resort, had her read that advertisement and meet her nemesis. 'Ladies Need Only Apply' is the result.

Thea Astley

LADIES NEED ONLY APPLY

I hear about Leo, Leo who worked for me once at the motel: body-built, sang vilely, and vanished without trace.

Tripp drops by with a coral trout he has hooked somewhere up the coast and shoves its heroic bulk generously into my deep-freeze, artistically withholding his predicate until I produce the whisky. He's a great noser-out and trundles his made-over jeep into all parts of the country, stacking his boot with stories.

'Gone to earth.' He's picking over a crab claw with the scientific lust he brings to eating. 'I stumbled on him quite by accident holed up about fifty miles from here. A very odd set-up. Very. You ought to drop by.'

Tripp understands my disenchantment, but he wants me to accept it, all cheer and giggles. 'You'll never see the whole of it,' he warns. 'Never. The versions are infinite.'

Well, I'll accept that as I accept my little handicap, but as the evening thins and the whisky level drops I persuade him all the same to draw me a little map.

I'll draw it for you.

'It's both too long and too short,' he uttered sententiously.

'What is?'

'Life.'

Inwardly she yawned, flapping an I've-heard-it-all-before hand over her mouth. Any minute now he'd trot out that old cliché about Tahiti: how did it go? A week is too long and a year isn't long enough. But he was threatening her with a fugue— *that* fugue—his only one, she estimated sourly, and she rose abruptly and, turning her back on him, padded out to the verandah. In his day he would have got more emotional mileage out of the Appassionata (played badly) than any man living and (by fifty-six, was it? -seven?) had declined the verb to lie in every mood and every tense of those moods, had slipped into an adroitness of supines and gerundives: in order to love, to be about to be loved, requiring to be loved.

He showered a few opening bars on her but she refused to succumb, sucking noisily at the last seeds in the passionfruit, making kid noises, denying his nicely organized nostalgia at the teeth of his tinny grand. But there were the two of them, no denying it, hanging perilously together on an escarpment in the range in his dinge of a shack whose walls he had pansied with arrogant arrangements of dried fan-palm frond. '*Trachycarpus fortunei*,' he had said to her, botanically whimsical. 'Nature is the true artist.' And she had snorted inwardly again, 'Ah, crap!' But then they had been together only two hours and already, she assessed, drawing on her serial of calamities, she could calculate him to infinity.

Leaning her insolence back on the railing, she surveyed the inside of the room, repressing her list to interest, her eyes scuttling like sand-crabs over the adze-hewn benches, the dried grasses in bottles, his few books and a pile of music manuscript the hue of disappointment. And him. His looming bulk, his hairiness, the sweet-and-sour line of his mouth and a certain twitchiness (the nerves are where the heart is!), seemed themselves to reject the meditative calm jargon he had been peddling like some yoga rep. who hit the roads with his sample bag crammed to the brim with transcendental hogwash.

This is Thursday, she reminded herself. And that was when? Last Thursday? And now here? The hows of it were remarkable even for her, for whom time had done nothing but reposition the factors of error. Take the aimlessness of leave (too much of it) and middle-age (too much of that) and multiply. The product is bravado loneliness in a postcard tropadise (the greens are too green! the blues too blue!), another snappy set of casual wear expensively commenting on the thickening body beneath, and an eye, increasingly less casual, flicking, mock-flicking over the personal columns.

At first she kept telling herself she was only pretending, a joky research; but at the back of it all operated that mumbo-jumbo nerve that made her devour her stars for the morrow, pass over her tea-slops in cafés, hold out her palm, wear lucky dangles, drop coins in wishing-wells. Although she discounted the sexual adventure promised in trendier magazine columns ('I am not into leather and bondage!' she would assure her women pals with a giggle), she still ran her tired but hopeful eye down the more homespun cries in parish-pump journals where, she imagined, a more genuine anguish might be at work. There's nothing quite like recognizing buddies in misfortune. My God, were some of them for laughs!

One particular notice should have halted her laughter.

Did, in fact, for a little, so that she re-read. And again. 'Companion housekeeper required for macrobiotic musician. Keep plus some wage. Interest in an alternative lifestyle, willingness to share musical and gardening interests essential. Genuine ladies need only apply.'

Rolling back on her beach towel, she had trilled with delight. Was she a genuine lady? Or genuine and a lady? The essential abstract? she wondered, viewing her carefully enamelled nails, the over-plump lurch of thigh. The misplaced adverb coupled with the pretentiousness of the demand pleased her enormously. 'Boy, could I handle him! I have only—no, merely—to apply!' she kept amusedly telling herself. 'And I get it. We get it. There'll be dozens and dozens of us.' And even as she rolled over again and nuzzled her face into her arm in a self-mocking attempt to stifle her mirth, she knew she would write.

The sun shouted at the sea and the sea kept repeating its answer, insidiously gentle, on the long beach north of town where, for a pointless month already, she had baited herself and lain unhooked beside a motel pool stuffed with ockers from the south. In a bleached way she had thought occasionally of the classrooms as a nightmare sequence on whose blackboard episodes she had stabbed sticks of chalk to death. The din of playground traffic rolled over the sand and the trimmed tourist grass with its heavy luncheon breath, and a word formed and kept re-forming in her mind against the sunny blood of her eyelids: no. No to that. Most definitely no.

And perhaps yes, microscopic but possible yes to this.

How estimate the stunning propositions of that advertisement's despair?

There were palms behind her and behind those palms there were overripe bracts of bougainvillea and behind that again the thundery blues of the tableland. Cracks between palm-frond were awash with sky so lucid, so resistless in its emptily spaced intentions, she knew she didn't have a hope.

She wrote. 'I must be,' she said to herself as she scrabbled for suitable words, 'crazy.' 'I must be,' she said to herself as she gummed down the envelope, 'out of my mind.' She licked the stamp. 'Mad,' she said to herself. And her mind stopped to catch its breath.

Stock-taking wasn't too good in the motel evenings, alone with the cold cream and the replays on telly. She felt, at times, despairingly, that she was one of those desperate women who infest reef waters from March to October. 'The stingers move out,' the locals used to say, 'and the birds move in. You get bitten either way.'

She wasn't conservative. She wasn't really dull. She was simply—well, let's put it this way—forty-two. And too often lately her nights had been a chop ('Got to keep that strength up!'— but for what?) or two poached eggs, or a concert series ticket when she cut a safe dash in something long and shapeless and her earlobes killed her with unaccustomed trinkets. Once, midway, she had been married, but only for half an hour as it were. At the end of a year he had gone with such flatness of purpose she had barely noticed. One night he had said, 'Darling, I'm just going to put the garbage out,' and had never come back.

For a week after she had written and was finally beginning to forget she had, she lay by the pool revving up her tan or wandered disconsolate along the sand front where sometimes she stopped for a bit and built rather lopsided little sandcastles. When she dug doors in them, the sand wept briefly and collapsed. Everything was like that for her. Some humble erection. The totter. The rupture. The flattened surface.

That she received a reply to her monstrously coy note surprised her. She read it trying not to feel eager, and the old pulse, the old excitation, began its idiot pounding. She let the letter dangle from her fingers and waved it delicately against the fact of five months more of leave. The perimeters of that time became space and the edges of space melted and broke, desert-fashion. 'Naughty!' she chipped herself. 'You are a naughty, foolish thing.'

Nevertheless she thrust back her self-queryings and dressed with extra care for the meeting. Ah! all those other meetings, dressing, extra care. The dabs of something not quite innocuous at vital spots, the straining muscle torture for the rear and profile glimpse which mirrored nothing of the inner suspense yet caught her in a dangerous hall of mirrors with herself still straining, turning, dabbing in an unending colonnade of doppel-gangers.

He was much older than she had expected.

So was she.

He sported a bushwhacker beard of streaked white and his bald skull had a leathery and repulsive tan to it. She gave him an extra point for height but subtracted two for a something in the eyes she could not read. There had been a shouting silence while her fingers dabbled about in her curls. Then he waded in.

'Miss Klein?'

'Mr Stringer?'

It was a relief to shake hands, establish formality while ferociously her mind tossed around negations: I've never . . . you mustn't think . . . don't imagine . . . this is not really like. . . . She said none of those things and he watched her saying none of it. He appeared, in fact, indifferent to the situation and asked carelessly would she like to sit in the restaurant attached to the motel. Would he care for tea? she asked. He didn't drink it. Coffee perhaps? Never. Well, something a little—she hesitated.

'I eat natural foods only,' he said. 'Actually I just thought you might like to have a bit of a talk first.'

She was about to agree when he went on, 'But if you prefer we'll take the run straight back and have a look at the place.'

'Whatever you—' She became firm. 'I think I will have tea.'

So they sat and inspected each other and he sipped water while she messed around with her tea and he repeated his remark, 'I eat natural foods only,' tempering it with a smile this time. She responded understandingly. Natural foods need only apply. 'Nuts. Fruit. Never meat, you understand. Lots of vegetables, raw. And I rarely cook. Cooking destroys essentials.' His hands emptied out something useless and she wondered if that last dab of blusher had destroyed her own. Hating herself—and she didn't know this was to be a pattern—she found she was clucking phrases like 'You're right, of course', 'There's a lot to be said for it.'

'There is everything to be said for it.' There was only the merest adumbration of menace. 'Everything.'

His blatant belief in his rightness was affecting her like sunstroke. She knew, oh, she knew already, she had made a mistake. It all seemed like a bad joke, one gone wrong, whose only redemption would be the later jocular recounting, the wacky thrill of the send-up; but then the very thought of later was a stopper in itself, so it was inevitable when once more he suggested they drive up the plateau that she should groggily accept.

The floor of the panel van was scattered with empty grain sacks. She wedged her smashing new sandals between two drums of honey and cranked down the window clumsily. My God! she thought. Madness!

He had watched her expressionlessly for a moment and then gave a smile of such warmth she was charmed.

'Easy. Easy does it.' He leant across her and finished the winding.

This was the point, she decided, for a loud and firm announcement that never, not ever, had she resorted to the dubiousness of advertised friendship, and she half opened her mouth for confession when he anticipated her.

'I get the feeling you're a bit of a newcomer to this.'

'This what?'

'Well, this sort of thing. Ring up a pal.' He switched on the ignition.

'You're an old hand?'

'I didn't say that.'

They drove steadily north in silence, reef waters to the right and hills pressing hard on the left.

'Mr Stringer—'

'The name is Leo.'

'Leo, then. Tell me—'

'And yours is Sadie, isn't it? I think we might as well skip the formal bits.'

This was the point where she always played it wrong. She decided on smiling silence.

'Is Klein your married name?'

That jolted her. 'I don't recall saying I was.'

'But you were.' His emphasis hardly needed an answer and anyway he was smiling again, tricking curves on the road as well.

'Well, yes. For a while.'

'What was it?'

'What was what?'

'Your married name.'

'I don't remember,' she replied. 'Were you? Married I mean?'

'Now and then,' he said and roared with laughter.

She was unable to inspect the random creases of his amusement but recalled the rinsed quality of his eyes and her bleakness returned. On the steering wheel his hands observed a blunt competence and, watching the careless strength of them, her folly appalled her, erupted into misgiving made positive by the loneliness of the coast road where, by now, they had lost sight of the sea. That movement of water-light had bolstered her but the taciturn quality of the hill scrub into which the car had turned made her belly twitch.

It remained taciturn for miles. Occasionally the man beside her put a question, made a comment, but each question or statement was strangely tangential. There she was, a woman of non-radiant years bashing away into distance now midfield with a stranger in a game whose rules, this time, she didn't know.

Even the soft-edge warnings were gone.

They'd left the bitumen and some of the heat as well as the road lumbered up into the hills between rainforest so chancelled with trees that the mid-morning took on the dreamy airless implications of late afternoon. There was only the car's panting.

'You must be pretty isolated,' she suggested, partly to challenge the thwack in the blood.

He glanced at her and knew she was regretting her stupidity.

'Pretty much. It's the way I like it. Cities are filth.'

Funnily enough the violence of his last emphasis reassured her, was a pattern-part of what his appearance seemed to claim. The stickiness under her fingers dried on the dilly-bag straps she had been clutching like a lifebelt.

A down-slope now. After the climb west from the coast the van took a set of ruts along an old snigging trail heading east again and there came a sense of half-tone as the trees panned out, demobilized finally by a broad clearing on the remote side of which, through groined intervals in the plateau scrub, the sea cried its permanent name.

It was a blueprint for a slovenly Eden.

An intransigent fecundity dominated two shacks which were cringing beneath banana clumps, passion-vines, granadillas. One was a patchy timber affair of cedar planking, and across from it, connected by a log bridge that spanned a steeply banked creek, was a smaller building plastered with mud and pebbles. And everywhere flowers and leaves exploded with tropic swagger.

She tried to repress her gasp, but it was too much for her and she said so.

'Is it?' He seemed amused and then he was out of the car, slamming the door behind him and leaving her to fight the stiff handle on her own side. He watched her till she made it and for a moment she hated him, blindly, as she cracked her knuckles and felt the pain shiver right up her arm. 'Christ!' she said under her breath, and then the door gave, almost flinging her out, and she had to chew up the yelp she wanted to give and offer instead a smile, bluffing but askew.

It was wasted. He'd turned already and she could only follow his indifferent back as he stepped high and light down the track between the papaw trees to the front of the bigger shack where he stood waiting ('Tapping his bloody foot!' she would tell them later), a meaty bulk of a man, cross-hatched by stratagems of light and shadow that made the him of the fellow even more elusive. But pain had damped down her fright.

The house was instantly knowable. There were only three walls, the front merely a verandah'd extension of the inner room, unenclosed but so massed with plants and streamers of vine it seemed stubbornly to be the bush itself.

She'd hardly begun to say 'Why?' when he thumped in an explanation.

'The heat. We do it this way for the heat. If you position it right it doesn't catch the weather. Not much, that is. And it's a hell of a lot cooler.'

She nodded, still rubbing her knuckles. 'Yes. Yes, of course. But your things? How do you lock up?'

'You must be from town, Miss Klein!' he said, mocking. 'I don't have many—what you call *things*. Anyone after my few scraps'd have to come a damn long way. They'd have to be really looking, wouldn't they?'

The more he out-manoeuvred her, the more the dislike settled in, became familiar. Why, we could almost be friends, she thought angrily, regaining her irony. Her hand throbbed but reassured her like a known part of her track workout. Oh, God! she thought bitterly and said, 'It's enchanting.'

It was true that in her sense he hadn't many things. The shack was one yawning room about twenty feet square, bullied by a very large piano set well back but still dominating a bed, a couple of cane chairs and some kitchen still-life. The walls bristled with fan-palm and on a table near the piano were some lumpish carvings, animal–human hybrids of lustreless black. Her eyes were drawn to their unpleasantness first.

'Genuine,' he offered almost contemptuously. 'None of your tourist gallery trash.'

She could sense him wanting her to bleat phrases of adulatory rubbish and when she did, inspired by her dislike, she achieved an unwanted victory, for suddenly he became more talkative. He picked up one carving after another, perhaps trying to throw her with their sexual hyperbole, but by now she felt in control and only half listened as he told her where he'd got it, what it meant. But she fractured the mood by wandering away from him to the piano, and he offered her a drink.

'Only herbal, I'm afraid.' He challenged her with a shine of teeth through beard. 'No concessions, not even for visitors.'

She struck a note. The sound was plangent, distorted by age and years of damp, and the pretentiousness of the piano's bulk alongside its quality again pleased her sense of irony. Why, swinging round to observe his idiot seriousness watching her, she felt better already. Better better better.

'Please,' she said. 'Straight.'

As she sat sipping at the cloudy, faintly acrid mixture he'd poured her, he began looking her over more closely, charting her quality. She was big boned and probably strong and, despite the enamelled properties of her, he was thinking, not the fool he might have wanted or the incompetent he would reject. He'd learnt during a lifetime spent poking around in odd corners to assess malleability to the last submissive quiver. The volatility of her nature and a certain melting flesh he observed within the opening of her shirt challenged his creativity. He began to talk about himself, opening with king's pawn, about his private theories, his dogmatisms, unapologetic and absorbed.

Miss Klein, playing along, tried to throw herself into the spirit of it, looking for amusement; but there was too much of it. In for a brisk plunge, and there you were dog-paddling desperately through glue. When at last he had gone to the pensioner piano, trying another gambit, she'd headed for the verandah and tried listening to the view; but he was beside her within minutes and to her shock she found that without turning she was conscious of his body.

'Well, now,' he asked, looking hard at her above his glass

rim, above the herbal trickle that ran yellow into his beard, 'what do you think of the place?'

Her hesitation amplified and echoed in the big dim barn. It was almost scrupulously clean, she had noticed, and in its exotic way disturbingly neat. That note she had struck—had it pulled apart regimens of permitted sound? For its aftermath still seemed to rock the air despite the fugue. She regretted that note.

She looked back inside. Sun was clouting the room with light through a western window. There was a smell of soap and leaves.

Gush seemed to have seeped away with her newly found indifference.

'It's very different.'

'Compared with what?' He didn't want her to reply but drummed out a few bars with his fingers on the rail beside her. 'You're wondering,' he went on, not looking at her but at his practising fingers, 'just why I advertised. Aren't you?'

'You could ask me the same.'

'I know why *you* did.' He paused to let it reach home. Check. Rightly, he estimated, she would understand all the elements of affront. 'I've tried to explain to you why I'm here. I've some income, not much, but some. I don't need the cities any more. I haven't needed them for a long time. I need a hand, not just for town trips—I do hate the bloody place—to pick up essentials but with the garden. You won't believe it, but I can't keep up to the watering in summer. It takes a good two or three hours every day. And there are other things.' He raised his eyebrows comically and won her for a moment. 'I need someone to moan to. I wanted,' he said practising a diminuendo, 'to have someone to share it with.'

'You mean you get lonely?'

'Sometimes.' She couldn't believe it.

'Why a woman?' she asked with the faintest touch of tartness.

'Why not? They can be—or so I've found—less difficult.'

And before she could negotiate that he'd steered her back into the room again to have another go at the herbal stuff and a dish of cheese and fruit he'd put on the table. Harmonics still hung in the air.

The hows of it. And now there were the two of them dangling perilously together and heat-impressed like flowers in some book to wilt in each other's pages.

'There's another thing,' he said.

'What?'

He regarded her hands with the too-long nails on the too-plump fingers. Something checked him.

'I'll let you know as we go. If we go.'

'I hate mysteries,' she said. 'What should I say?'

'You don't say anything.' Her antagonism became an instant goad. 'Not yet, eh? Would you like to see the rest of the place? Your part of it. If you're interested.'

It was much like his, only smaller, barer; but at the rear and awash with papaw light there was a tiny shower room under the water tank.

'It's spartan,' she commented.

'You did say,' he challenged her, 'you were after something different.'

They paused on the centre of the bridge and she mopped at some of the afternoon which was running down her face.

'I did, didn't I?'

Her irony showed and he felt she was slipping away from him. He gave her a marvellous smile. 'You could give it a try, you know. Both of us. Testing. It will be a help, especially now I have pupils.'

'Pupils?' The merest pucker on her face, but he caught it.

'Only a couple. I'm really too far out. And then I'm not interested in numbers, you understand. Only quality.'

He managed to make the prerequisite sound like a compliment to her.

She looked back at the shacks. She looked down at the garden and the barbaric leaf shape and sheen with its succulent pulpy cannibal gobbling of heat and moisture. Impossible. She looked back at him and he loomed across a landscape of crowded playgrounds and empty rooms and the brutality of the sameness that

197

had leached her out. It was still impossible.

Overhead, a small Beechcraft droned in from the north, swinging in closer, low, too close, dipped one saluting wing and swung away again down the coast.

Mr Stringer was waving a casual arm. The gesture was attractively *dégagé* as if some divine prompter was hooting at her from the wings.

The first of it for her was both easy and hard.

A week softened their wariness and when he found her to be more competent than he had hoped he would surprise himself pausing to observe her slogging away in some corner of the garden. The utter difference in lifestyle gave her much inward amusement and she hummed 'If my friends could see me now,' dragging hoses round the lower acre. Stripped to shirt and shorts, the muck off her face, she revealed a sturdy handsomeness that interested the watching man, who conceded a blooming he might some time desire to control.

The days for her stretched into an endurance of muscle and became one enlarged aching scar on an endless calendar of surprising dawns and exhausted evenings. The tropic blaze, of course, did not diminish, and the week or so of trial she had secretly allowed herself for laughs extended as she discovered he was tolerable simply as a present chunk of male whose remoter coastline she found herself wanting to chart. Although he knew she had taught, she refrained from telling him she was on leave and allowed him to believe her retired and independent. As well, she refused wages, and kept one economic jump ahead.

The second mandate came within a week.

He was a singer, an achromatic baritone, despite the thick-set chest, and had once grubbed out an undignified living for a short time singing ballad spots round clubs in the south. He had little talent, even Miss Klein could see; but like most singers remained unaware. As she spaded and mulched and watered, unending skeins of arpeggios and scales, ravelled phrases and dangerously sustained top notes, blew through the garden clearing and out to sea. When he learnt she played a little, he set her to work with him, rostering practice hours for her to work on song accompaniments while he was out of the shack and doing the heavier work on a section he was clearing. His voice, she thought amusedly, and the piano were a perfect match. Sometimes she had a vision of herself in this improbable situation, and the folly of it set her teeth on edge until she reminded herself it was only for giggles, my God, it was—and in any case, in *any* case, she was waiting for something. What that something was she refused to examine.

Sometimes, bluffed by the distances he set between them, she found herself deliberately seeking his approval, and felt he was turning her into one of her own pupils, eager to be noticed.

Lately, on her way back from the lower clearing where she had been deep-watering the younger trees, she came upon him stripped and showering lustily beneath the tank-stand. Anyone could see he was in splendid shape. If this were the awaited moment it confused her, and during her hesitation he swung round to face her and slowly, deliberately, not taking his eyes off her, raised one arm and began lathering an armpit. Awkwardly she jerked away.

The second time it happened he simply stood still; and there were the two of them staring at each other until he gave her a scant smile that lost itself in hair.

Now and again a visitor (pupils, he said) shoved a battered Kombi down the by-road, and as she wilted in the afternoon siesta she would hear from the other shack across the creek talk and interrupted musical clauses that flowed as part of the heat: both stunned her. There was a singer (softly young and large-eyed with a voice like a flute) and a pianist who played with greater bombast than the master. Should Sadie surprise the singer's arrival when she was on one of her compost-lugging missions in the top section, she would be given a flitter smile (eyes shifting shyly from their own morsel of goodwill) and endure an odour of resentment like part of the weather.

The piano pupil didn't speak at all. His sombre, good-looking face inspected hers briefly, made some quick calculation, then turned away. He would drive up, park, play savagely for an hour as if he wanted to kill the piano, then leave.

Leo was vague about his students as he was about his own musical background. She felt, from the few facts he tossed her like placatory biscuits ('The boy? Galipo—some lawyer's kid. Bit of a smartarse who needs sitting on hard') . . . that he'd always been one for the fantasy of living rather than the actuality. In her resenting moments (My God! Why do I stay?), she wanted to open up on him with acid truths.

'You can't sing,' she longed to say, 'and your playing isn't much better. You're a bag of wind.' But then he would charm her with a sudden warmth or enthusiasm, so that she was kept swinging in a maddening emotional suspension through which the vision of him beneath the shower ballooned and retreated.

After a month she noticed he was managing to manipulate her absence on student afternoons.

'Need a bit more kero,' he'd say. 'How about trotting down to town for it?' Or, 'We're running light on flour. And there's a couple of other things while you're about it. There's a part for the generator. I'll write it down.'

As she banged away sulkily over the dirt road she pondered on the girl, Flute, speculated irritably as to what they did when she was not there, how Flute comported herself in that Rousseau landscape, the tiger in the leaves. But it was Sadie who was tiger.

Reduced to mere clippings of dialogue over the evening chess-board. Lack of detail was beginning to make her prowl while frustration made her want to eat him whole.

In the fifth week, as they were sitting together after tea and just as she had decided once more that she must leave, he deposited on the back of her hand one of the rare pats that so whetted her. Mosquito-coils smoked all round them. The distant sea had become slate. Leo crushed a couple of March flies to death on his splendid mahogany thigh and looked at her speculatively.

'I think you're getting to like it here now.'

'Why, yes. I think I do. At least I'm getting used to it.'

'Are you getting used to me?'

She chewed her answer. Was this the point where grace ran out of the soul? There was menace in his jocular question, but the hand still lay like an oblation on her own.

'You're a man of many parts,' she said. 'They take some getting used to.'

He was pleased with that. He rose and stood above her with a curious inspecting gaze she resented, and she sullenly dropped her eyes to find them on a level with his thighs. She had never seen so much hair. She swerved, bending back in the cane lounger, to be assaulted again by weather-stained and bulging shorts, the shining breasts, and the stink of sweat that came with him: blocking out thought now till she found his face and saw nothing but the white of teeth behind beard. Suddenly she resented his smile, his continual unsmiling smile; and suspecting mockery she sat up and pettishly looked down at herself. He was nudging her bare ribs with his knee.

'You're fining down, Sadie. Looks a lot better. A very lot better.'

The knee stayed.

It was true. Six weeks had removed the blubber. There was a deal of tan. The lumpish excitement that grabbed her took her fingers to her face and she tracked its planes vaguely, dragged at her unbarbered hair that hung freer, oilier, in sweaty elf-locks about her shoulders.

'You think?'

He watched closely as her hands moving humbly down her hips recognized this and stirred by her diffidence, for it was diffidence he wanted, he bent over and seized her. His mouth seemed to be biting into her neck, but she could hear words being mumbled and she dragged herself back from him to hear him say, 'You've lost the patent-leather look, Sadie. You look like a woman.' His eyes were insolent and then his mouth was back again, biting that smile into her throat.

Her vanity revolted. She tensed and shoved at him.

'You mean I wasn't before?'

'Not much.'

Her fury wrestled and his arms seemed to be everywhere, hands, mouth: the settee overturned into a silent and massive struggle that writhed across the floor of the shack until she bit him savagely and he let her go with a cry.

'That wasn't in the agreement,' she gasped.

He glared at her, panting. 'Maybe not. Sorry.'

The ripe stink of them yowled; but he was shrivelled and furiously bounced up to take his rage down the steps into the dark garden.

Of course he punished her after that in a variety of ways, but he didn't suggest she leave and, contrarily, she didn't offer. There were earlier and earlier risings, brutally hearty and notched out on the pearl of the mornings with walloping wakey cries: 'Upski, Sadie! Outski! Water gir-hir-hirl! [sung badly] Where are you hi-yi-ding?' Caught in mid-note by her while his eyes stayed hard.

As well, he stopped sending her on fake errands when Flute came sauntering into the jungle.

'Hullo, Sadie!' Flute would trill these days, dawdling deliberately as Sadie savaged pest on the soursops. The girl would twist long strands of hair round a thoughtful finger then give her neat peasant-wrapped bottom a little shake before turning to Leo who always stood waiting for her on the verandah, stripped to the waist, smiling as he watched the two of them.

He was making Miss Klein (and lately, now, he called her that) aware that it was not only voice he moulded.

For he had, not long after their angry struggle, stationed her (with geographic cunning) to set out some silver beet in a patch he had dug just below the window of the bigger shack. She was halfway through her task when she became aware that the singing had stopped and they could now be heard working at pleasure of another kind. Their penultimate groans slammed her hand-fork into the damp soil and propelled her nauseated lust into a run—tripping, stumbling, over the footbridge to her room where perplexity and desire spreadeagled her across the seething quilt.

It was still close enough to hear Flute's final gasp. 'Sod you!' Sadie whispered into the quilt. Over and over: 'Oh, sod you, sod you, sod you.'

I would go, she kept telling herself now, if I had any pride. But had she ever gone, ever dodged the ignominy of dismissal? Genuine and luscious tears of indulgence washed twenty years of dismissal down her streaked cheeks. It was as if she were frozen into patterns of martyrdom that insisted she had no pride at all as her last Max-Factored-skin was peeled away. There was only Sadie Klein of riper—let's still not quibble about numbers—years pared down to the sore parts and lugging a need that was always charged overweight.

Tea was silent that night as she sulked to his triumphant crunching, crumbs stuck arrogantly all through his beard.

He was paddling about in his soup.

'Could have been colder!' he criticized, chucking a gob of cream into the bowl and stirring. Cheap beatitudes sang through his body as he squatted half naked in the heavy vine-dark of the verandah eating noisily and smacking the moths that kept rushing to die in lamplight. The night outside was bulky with unbroken rains and noisy with tree and creek.

'It's you,' she said bitterly. 'You'd warm anything.' And she snatched her plate up and went back to her shack and finished eating alone. But he still intruded, for after she'd gone he started singing as he clashed plates together in the sink and his voice seemed to bore right into the marrow of her solitariness.

These days as he worked he sang a great deal with a challenging insolence that appeared in his swinging walk. His voice seemed to be thickening as phlegmily as the cloud-piles massing up and moving over before the wet. Dragging hoses down the far end of the clearing she would hear and wonder why it ate at the pith of her, and she checked off again the days left—but for what? Perhaps she dreaded an end to hatred. Yet it all seemed an exercise in paradox. Now it was she who, filled with eager dislike, put the chess-board away after tea and suggested a song or two; who blundered into muddles of small talk, abhorring the vacuum; who began once more, but delicately, to make up her mouth.

He listened to this and he looked at this. And he smiled.

He began digging easements for the wet and he went on singing in his clogged voice.

One day, the day Flute was expected for her lesson, Sadie set herself to work by the entrance gates where they were trying to establish an arcade of sorts sculptured out of guinea vine. Ripe for assault of a spiritual kind, she leant her lipsticked insolvency on an impudent spade and watched as the van pulled in. She smiled. Learning, she smiled.

Flute came round the front of the van.

'Hullo,' she said, curious, hugging her tattered alibi of sheet-music to a chest which, Sadie noticed with malice, was less emphatic than her own.

Sadie didn't answer. Oh, the power of it! But she smiled. She smiled and smiled and went on spading the dirt with an abstracted unawareness. She smiled again when Flute went past an hour later; but this time the girl kept her eyes down and pretended not to see.

The defiance tasted of love as well.

When she went back to the shack to prepare the evening meal, she was most aware of him in her eye's oblique and sensitive corner that kept seeing him fifty yards off working beneath the trees. His sun-blackened shoulders shone wet, his body, she understood with corrupting pleasure, bent, straightened, bent, straightened with the rhythm of verse. Should she practise the indifference of the smile upon him? Their problem was, of course, her refusal to be humbled.

That night, as he took his place at the table, her resolution failed. She could not offer the smile. She was too consumed and, instead, her hand, impelled by sexual gloom, hovered then rested on his. He watched it with some amusement, then pushed it delicately aside.

'That isn't quite enough,' he said.

'What do you mean?'

'Oh, not the what of it,' he replied, reaching over for the bread. 'The how. The how.'

'I don't understand.' She was dying inwardly again.

'Oh, you will. You most certainly will.'

Back in her own shack, she examined and re-examined the remark, her mind refusing whole octaves of possibility as she heard him crack his way up a scale. She lay down, trying to munch away at a book; but it was hopeless, and as she slammed it down she heard his car roar away across its pages.

Still insomniac when he returned hours later, she saw the headlamps cutting slices into the dark of the unlined walls and it was only after she heard his feet creak lightly up the stairs and across his verandah that she let go the fear she had been hugging in the thick darkness of the rainforest and fell asleep.

'Aren't you going to ask?' he nagged next morning.

She stared past him at the glutinous green.

'Ask what?'

'Where I went last night.'

Her confidence had returned. 'No. Did you go somewhere?'

'Oh, come on, Sadie. You're dying to.' He swallowed a raw egg oyster-fashion.

Her rage was so athletic with bile she swayed.

'All right,' she conceded, her eyes pasted on him. 'Where?'

'To get a bit of tail.' He shouted with laughter at the sight of her face.

She began, 'I think I must tell you—'

'What must you tell me, Sadie? What must you bloody tell me? What did you expect me to say? Look, I'll tell you something, you member of a virgin breed screwed up with your wants and your don't wants. Oh, yes, I know you're not a virgin in the literal sense. Don't wince. You don't like words like virgin, do you? Virgin virgin virgin virgin.' He sang it, scale-form. 'But in the real sense you are a puking bloody-minded product of every bloody-minded piece of published magazine garbage that ever was. Giant tips humming with green bottle flies. And the flies all have their big compound eyes beautifully made up. And while they lay their little corrupt eggs, that make-up mustn't be disturbed. My God, it mustn't.'

'Mustn't be disturbed!' he sang and cracked another egg into his hand and swallowed it.

'You sing flat,' she said.

He flinched as if she'd hit him. They stared at each other in a terrible silence and her words kept echoing round the room.

'I think I'd better leave.' She waited.

He seemed to recover his humour all of a sudden. 'Leave?' he said. 'Leave? Just because I've told you a few good-humoured home truths? We both have. Where's that logic of yours, eh? The very thing that attracted me about you. Where's that genuine search for another lifestyle? You didn't like the one you had, you've told me often enough. No, Sadie, my dear, you won't leave. Because I won't help you to and more fundamentally than that— you don't want to. And I like,' he added with cunning and wanting to gain the upper hand, 'to have you around.'

'Oh, my God!' she cried, flummoxed.

The day moved into its pattern.

In the new clearing by the creek where he had felled most of the big stuff, she attacked the landscape with anger, grubbing out the wait-a-while and bush-sword that was still guzzling round the stumps. Fifty yards off he worked with a hand axe. Clump clump, persistent, driving. The mail flight north went overhead and dipped its wing to his wave, and the small circle created by his circling arm widened, expanded, and flowed out to break on the mild timeless edges of the grove. She was slipping into infinity, she thought, unable to reason beyond this moment of the cracking back, the shoulder tug, the sweat drench between the breasts.

That afternoon she went down to the creek where it entered the forest, stripped, and floated in the waterhole. She wanted silence so she could think it out; but as she floated under the forest canopy she found there was nothing to think about or salvage in the coolness that reduplicated whatever it was he was playing up at the shack; so that the run of notes brothered the creek, moved into it, into the white blur she had become.

After, as she dried herself, there were leeches, blood, tears.

Humbled, she asked that night, 'What was it you were playing this afternoon?'

'You liked it, Sadie?'

She was afraid of tricks. After all, she was trying to atone.

'Yes. Yes, I did. Very much.'

'And what did you like about it?' His glinting eye challenged her. The tea-towel dangled from her hand, hopeless. There was a trick.

'I'm not sure,' she said. 'I just liked. Something. The creek in it.'

'The creek in it?' He made her sound foolish. Wait, she told herself. Wait for the smile.

'Yes.' It sounded stupid now, not beautiful as she had intended. And he was smiling again. 'I wouldn't mind hearing it once more.'

'Wouldn't you?' he said, enjoying her penance. 'To tell the truth, I don't feel much like playing this evening. It's been a heavy day. I think I'll turn in early. And you'd better catch up on some sleep, too.'

'Oh, my God!' she cried. 'We're getting nowhere at all, are we?' He was silent. 'Do you hear? It's simply getting nowhere. Nowhere. It's a waste of time. To tell the truth'—it was unconscious parody—'a total goddamn waste of time and we both know it. Have known for weeks.'

'I thought you'd never notice,' he replied, not bothering with the whack her mouth showed but becoming, despite the lighted room, part of the dark outside it.

Even Sadie marvelled at her capacity for punishment as she shone her torch back across the footbridge. Even when spoken goodnights had failed her they still wanted to be uttered.

The papaw trees clustered with fruit now smelled thickly in air still and loud with the held-back water of the wet. As again she lay sleepless on the tumbled bed, the night was so motionless she could hear the crackle of turned pages of the week-old paper he was reading. She became all ear in the weighty dark, a tightened membrane against which the stir of his hair, his lips, the unbent muscles of his fingers, lost their silence and made monstrous drumming.

Later that evening the clouds broke.

Into further days. Into further nights. They were all latticed with water.

There could be no question of her leaving now, for the next morning his crackling radio told them they were cut off at the bottom of the range road. In the short sun-dazzles that came between the striding rain, Leo would dig the easement run-offs deeper, splaying out the storm-water drains that ran from both shacks to the creek. Flute and the pianist stopped coming and there were the two of them still hanging perilously together on this escarpment in the range, forced to share the same bitter herbal quaffs and chess games she was no longer careful to lose. Monsoon clouds kept hauling their freight from the north as the sticky heat of the day glued the landscape into a ripening circle that sprouted more trees, more fruit. Pulp. Pulp and mould.

The heaviest rain seemed to come at night. Sadie would sprawl naked on her bed deafened by the crash of water on tin, watching the incessant silver of it in the lamp-glow, cut off, she knew now, from the world. The din of playground traffic no longer rolled across the clearing; the luncheon breath could not penetrate this grille, this mesh, so tough it became a caul. At times, in the heart of a downpour, the small sweating room was like an air-bubble trapped undersea and to move into the outer world would be to drown.

Between one fall and the next, landscape was sponge, aching with wet.

On the fourth morning in, under the gust of it, she found that the creek was only a few inches below the straplog of the bridge.

He was inclined to grunt when she first told him, but later commented almost genially as they had breakfast, 'Quite an adventure for you!' Full of nods and becks and bloody wreathed smiles, she thought sourly. 'Don't you like all this?' Gesturing at the weeping landscape. 'It makes me feel marvellous.'

She stared out at climate-shock. 'It's too much. Too hard. Too sudden.'

'But it's always like this. Every year. We're in for weeks of it now,' he said maliciously. 'Surely you're not frightened by the prospect! You're like all southerners, and when I say southerners I mean anyone below the tropic. They throw a mickey the first time they cop it. The Noah syndrome.'

'Did you say weeks?'

'Weeks. Ten. Twelve. Not much we can do about the garden for a bit, but that's the beauty of it. Enforced contemplation—for you, Sadie, anyway. It'll do you good. By God, it's doing me good.'

And it was. Each sodden dawn he did elaborately detailed flexing exercises until his body ran with the sweat the garden once gave him, displaying his body as he might one of his carvings. She watched until his fitness savaged her and she could watch no longer.

'Join in! You'll get the old flab back if you don't.'

'The mind's got it already,' she commented softly. Not aggressively. Just commented. But he didn't hear, was away on body presses which he performed with the dedication of a revivalist. Was he scourging the flesh, she wondered, or perfecting it?

During the second week of rain an electric storm clattered in from the sea and spent itself on the ridges. Lightning sabred the open side of her shack with primitive switches of high white dazzle that cut the dark wide open. She rigged up a blanket from a cross-beam as a sort of screen and lay sleepless before these summer movies and tried not to think about Leo. This can't keep up, she told herself. A couple of weeks and I'll be gone. She had a vision of the glade as some Druidic circle, herself spreadeagled in the centre of her humiliation, the permanent, the undying victim for whom the factors of error had now become the ever-raised, the never-falling knife. The sudden shock of the thought that perhaps this was her final destiny shot her upright, fully alert; and despite the rattle of water and the biblical thunder she caught the sound of tinny patches of music blowing across and through, contrapuntally, not in twin frenzy but in a kind of ironic—My God, could he really be playing Mozart at a time like this?—comment: the sort of opponent in debate who quibbles about your grammar or pronunciation.

'You bastard,' she breathed into her clammy hands. 'You arrogant bastard. I hate you.'

The footbridge was under by morning and the creek a thirty-foot spasm of sulky brown, biting at the roots of the first papaw planting up by the other shack. She called Leo's name once, twice; then she saw him come sauntering onto his verandah naked and polished once more with sweat as if he'd just finished a workout. He waved a casual hand and shouted something.

Wind smothered his words.

'What?' She had to yell twice.

She could see him cup his hands about his mouth to call.

'I said you'll have to sit it out for a bit. Don't try to get across.' She could tell he was smiling. 'It'll probably go down in a few hours if the weather eases.' He appeared to be inspecting her reactions with interest. 'Got any tucker?'

'Not much. There's a bit of fruit here and I can make tea,' she called.

He yelled back, 'You do that.'

'What if it gets worse?' Her words blew out to sea. She called out again, but he only waved and went back inside.

The whole sky was rioting.

Throughout the day she glimpsed him throughout the blotching green of the shifting trees as he moved the chairs on his verandah back in from the galing wet. Every surface absorbed and sucked the sky down into it. She measured hours by pots of tea—that and the constant checking of the flood levels and trying to catch something on her battery radio. Its static exhausted her, and as the lead of the day-rain became the slippery black-silver of night she submitted, went out to the furthest edge of the verandah, and cried his name over and over against the hurlings of the wind.

Nothing. His name boomeranged back into her mouth, was tasted and flung out again. Still nothing.

The water was racing eagerly about the piles of the shack and she gave what seemed to be a scream for him; but although there was no answering shout it seemed for a moment that she glimpsed him, a flitter of shadow, across the path of his light.

Later she went to press down the switch of her own lamp but the room remained dark. Shaken, she flicked it again. Again. The power was gone; and as she recalled the rackety generator he housed behind the main shack she knew it was hopeless to expect anything before morning. Wondering if there would be a morning.

Stock-taking wasn't any too good on this night of brawling trees and she could have sobbed in the shaken dark for the emptiness of the motel room and the cold cream and the replays on telly. Joke's over, Miss Klein, she told herself. Joke's way way over. And after one more delaying cigarette she went back into the top-heavy shadows of the verandah to check the water level. Lamplight was still showing from the other shack between the scrimmaging branches, and faintly she could hear the pulse of transistor radio expanding and narrowing its fur of static that became, as she listened, the diastole–systole placental force linking her to the only other human within this egg of water.

Her bare toes on the verandah planking became aware of their balancing tensions; the skin on the sole of each poised foot tingled and a current of apprehension shook her whole body as she bent shuddering across the rail to flash her torch on the water below. It was biting the top step. The rain became teeth.

'Leo!' she bawled, quite uselessly against symphonies of squall. 'Leo!' The radio replied in breathy bursts of static and violins. Her third and fourth cries were slashed off the tip of her tongue and drenched, whatever she meant to tell him. And through the hatred of him, through this last evidence of his soft brutality, unexpected, the wanting sprang contrarily. It made her gulp, wetted her eyes with anger.

Her decision stopped the rocking in her blood.

He had become the desired coefficient, the necessary factor of disaster she craved and detested. Almost calmly now she walked back into the room and by torchlight inspected her face in the small wall-mirror. Doubled, though not what she really hoped for; rather what she dreaded: the face carved more sharply into definiteness in which the eyes, the eyebrows, even the darker stain of her blurred mouth, appeared to be awaiting an answer. She swung her hair forward across those parts of her face which she found harshest and in its loose shadow confidence rose. Slowly, watching her face, she removed her clothes. Her hands touched shoulders, breasts, testing his indifference; and her feelings were mostly hate. I hate him, she insisted aloud. Hate him. Running the heels of her hands down each slow thigh. Hate.

By the verandah edge the torrent was cold and muddy.

One step and she was in to her waist, and then the current grabbed her and flung her towards the bridge. In a minute she had crashed against it and felt the skin above her ribs rip as she hung there just keeping her head gruntingly above water. Inch after inch, using the logs as lever, she shoved her way through a force that delighted her perversely until pummelled, gulping, under the slamming drench of rain, she was snatching at slimy weeds on the far slope, grasping, slipping, losing, dragging, and at last hauling herself through mud and banana ooze onto higher ground.

She took a couple of falls in the beating dark and was filthy with turned earth and plasters of leaves and blood. But the sky streamed over her naked body, a terrible effluence, slapping the hair-licks back from her face as she leant gasping against one of the fruit trees.

His lamp shone through the movement all about her with the steadiness of truth, of honour. But then she couldn't think for rain.

Out of shelter again and up through the squelch towards light and music. Hatred and wanting were intertwined, had become that moment towards which everything else had built.

A blown passion vine caught her before she reached his stairs and plunged her once more on her face into slush. Something hot zipped in a tendon behind her knee, and when she tried to pull herself up pain shouted her down.

Again she had a vision of herself, an animal vision, as slowly, on all fours now, she crawled up the higher ground the last thirty paces to his shack, unaware of water, pain, or blood; and she laughed, crawling towards that other face in the mirror, knowing nothing most beautifully, her purpose the empty kernel of lit music.

At the foot of his stairs she cried furiously and briefly for her shame, grief and rain becoming one.

Ponderously she dragged herself onto the first step, then the second, before she called out to him.

She heard the movement of his chair shoved back, heard his bare feet pad across board; and not until she felt the frightful quality of him did she look up, forcing herself into the one word, 'Please?': into one smile—the whole body and want of her into one doubtful, querying smile as he looked down at her on all fours, naked, glistening silver with lust and rain.

'That's better,' he said. 'That's more like it. Come on in.'

THE ARCHBISHOP OR THE LADY

Gerard Windsor

AUTHOR'S NOTE

Even otherwise respectable writers are sometimes reduced to clichés. Mine, for the moment, is that stories are like children, and no wise or even self-interested parent will own up to favourites. Penelope Leach, purveyor of the gospel for us modern mothers, lays it down that such admissions as 'Percy is my best child' or 'Gwen is the one I have most affection for' are just not on. What self-respecting parent is going to own up to a least best or a minimally affected offspring? Look at the anarchy it leads to. Isn't the very first line of the greatest tragedy of all a dire warning against this sort of ranking? 'I thought the King had more affected the Duke of Albany than Cornwall.' And to think that some people say that remark ranks very low and flat on the scale of opening lines! It's as pregnant with the germ of human tactlessness and misery as you could wish.

No, Leach and Lear have warned me to keep my preferences to myself. And even to myself to admit only a greater, if gratuitous, preference, and not greater virtue. My guiding principle is fairness to all the children. If you find that some are getting all the treats, then you look to compensate the others. If outsiders persist in praising selected children, you naturally push the others forward. Which is not to say that the objects of your affirmative action mightn't also be the apples of the eye. But you don't let on.

It's time to give an outing to 'The Archbishop or the Lady'. It's a good child and a credit to its parent. And probably even more in his image than most of its siblings. I'll explain. When I first began writing, at the advanced age of twenty, it was verse, nostalgic and religious verse. In 1968 when I got to ANU I showed an example of this genre to Rodney Hall, who was Creative Arts

Fellow. The poem was about the Council of Chalcedon in 451 and its definition of the dual nature of Christ. Rodney Hall was not encouraging. He said the poem had too many adjectives. I gave verse away. I couldn't escape myself as subject, I had no sense of irony, and I found the only way I could get a new perspective was via prose. Two volumes of short stories later, I felt I was able to cope with someone very roughly like myself as subject. 'The Archbishop or the Lady' was the transition story. I had the Mannix experience in the story. I did not have the sexual experience in the story.

The Mannix experience—like much other 'religious' experience—composted away in me for years. How to use it? What significance was there in this particular kind of brush with fame? What, if any, organic relationship could there be between such an exotic experience and mundanity? What continuity could there be in the life of someone—like myself—once celibate and of the elect, later yet another sexual being in a mass secular world? Such questions naturally started to suggest a content for the story, and they meshed with questions of technique (not of course starkly differentiated like that). How to get a perspective on my Mannix story while keeping the immediacy of the Mannix character? Ah, a female narrator to break down the masculine fellowship character of the source material.

I like to believe I ended up with a story on the only worthwhile themes—love/sex (maybe life) and death. But, O guardian angel of stories set adrift, save me from crude identifications along the line of her/now/life and Mannix/then/death. Religion is sensuous, sex is celestial . . . I like it when one reader tells me the story is very erotic, and another that it is very funny. I'm not sure about my intentions, but I'll cop those readings, and others. They seem plausible.

And Judy Brett published it in *Meanjin* (after suggesting, with great sureness of touch, a change in the ending). She was a great editor. For range of academic interest and expertise, an anchor on the everyday earth, commonsense, forceful and ever accessible prose, she has no peer among Australian intellectuals. Lucky

Meanjin contributors. Some parturient writers have good hospital experiences.

Gerard Windsor

THE ARCHBISHOP OR THE LADY

Twenty-one years later he came to my bed. I'm not just being archaic or coy or romantic. It is a precise description of what he did. Late one Friday night, when the children were all asleep, but I still had the light on and was reading. I'm not casting any slur if I say that ever since I had once more become legally single he had been aware of me, in contact with me, in a way that had not been true before. He certainly always knew when I was attached or between attachments—not least because I always told him; it was that sort of intimacy. And now too it was the dying days of his own marriage. So when he turned up, unannounced, I had to restrain myself from some such operatic greeting as 'I was expecting you'. True as it might have been, it would have suggested a self-possession and control of the situation that I certainly did not feel. I had envisaged his initiative, but I had not decided on any response.

So I let him in, and the natural reaction to his apologies and protestations was to hop straight back into bed and to let him look after himself. He came and sat on the side of the bed. It served no one's purpose for him to stay there. He would have done so, at least for some time, and then only have made his moves tentatively and ambiguously. Too much the gentleman, too much the adolescent. I'm too old for that. He had played his cards quite openly by coming in the first place, and I saw no point in prevarication now.

'Why don't you hop in? You'll be much more comfortable.' I laughed and tried to give it a reassuring tone. 'And so will I.'

He undressed, to his briefs, but without any trace of emotion. No sign of haste, no sign of resignation. But as he went to the far side of the bed and got in, back to me, he said, 'Actually I feel I want to have a good talk to you.'

'Fine,' I assured him, 'make yourself comfortable.' I patted him on the hand, but otherwise made no move to change my position. It was a November night, with just enough of the fresh warmth of summer in the air to key me up.

'I don't really know where to begin,' he said. 'Somehow I feel it is a season of anniversaries.'

'Ours certainly,' I admitted, thinking back to teenage courtesies, and an aesthetic restraint, and a lemon shared silently in the garden while the unrestrained children of nature moved to the chords of Buddy Holly and Duane Eddy.

'Yes, that too,' he agreed, and I could see that it had not been on his mind, or at least that he had not been allowing it any prominence.

'Do you ever get a sense of your place in history?'

'No,' I said. 'Never.' It was true. History and my life are total strangers. But it was more to the point that he wanted to talk about himself, not hear about me.

'You haven't started to grow old, that's why,' he said, and he stretched out a vague, blind hand in my direction. For the first time since his arrival there was a light touch to his voice, and so, in spite of the rather tired gallantry of his remark, I responded by finding his hand and giving it a squeeze of encouragement.

'Well . . .' I said. It was enough of the dumurral against any assumption that I had only the bright, forward face of the child. 'Besides, I'm not even an attendant lady. I've never so much as waited on the great. And I very much doubt whether that's been a loss at all.'

'No, of course not,' he hurried to assure me. 'Except in rare cases. Just occasionally, very occasionally I suppose, it helps you to take bearings, to get a perspective. An eminence from which measurements can be taken. Mundanity is just not a platform.'

He does nudge away in the direction of pomposity a great deal of the time. But he was getting around to whatever he wanted to say, and there was no point in pulling him up short. I felt no fatigue or unwillingness to listen. His very distance from me, his leisurely, unselfconfident preamble, were atypical enough to stimulate me. I found myself putting my book away, sinking slightly into the bed, and pulling up the covers a fraction—all a gesture of settling in. But I knew that if he couldn't be bumped around he could be led. 'What is the anniversary?' I asked.

'The death of Archbishop Mannix.'

For the first time since he'd arrived I felt a twinge of relief that there was no third party eavesdropping. People who keep historical anniversaries are a tiresome, earnest, simple-minded lot. Amongst people I associate with the only anniversary commemorated is the overthrow of Whitlam—and even that illustrates all the worst features of the habit. But this midnight memory, welling up in someone I thought had a healthy scepticism about the cloth and all its works and pomps, sounded like recidivism of a most embarrassing kind. And in any case such a choice seemed so bizarre, so meaningless to me. 'Fill me in,' I asked. 'When did that happen?'

'I know, I know,' he answered, and he actually unloosened himself and turned towards me. 'It's all very idiosyncratic, but you, if anyone, would understand.'

It was not flattery. I could feel the affection, and although there was a spurt of cosy emotion behind the sudden kiss he gave me, there was certainly no planning. I put my arm around his shoulders and drew his head towards me.

'I feel . . . illuminated,' he began. 'And you know I'm not a mystical type, not even a religious type very much. It's just that the round figure of twenty years seems to be working like some kind of gong in my mind. Twenty years since I left school, twenty years since I became a novice. The year, 1963, hangs over me now. 1963 and all the promise I had. You know I had promise. Everyone knows it. That just makes the post-mortem all the more dicey. Maybe I've been trying to distract myself by asking if the year really was so significant. And the one event consistently recurs. The death of Mannix. It seems terribly significant, but I'm not sure how. I really seem to have had some sort of a revelation. In fact what convinces me it's the case is that the interpretation does not come easy. That's revelation running true to form. It's a phenomenon of my old age. I had the experience all right back then in '63, but I never seem to have made anything of it until now.' He paused. 'You must get a lot of this sort of crap.' Then he tried to be jocular. 'But this is a mid-life crisis with a difference.'

'Stop it. It's nothing of the kind, either kind. You don't have to interpolate for me. Let's take all that as unsaid.'

For a moment I could feel the tension in his shoulders as he considered taking me up on my admonition. But he let it pass. 'No, all right,' he said, 'I'll be intimately theological. My revelation had all the classical ingredients. The circumstances were highly unusual, so that my memory was able to make special provision. I took in the detail at the time, and my imagination and brain have been able to work on it for years since. "And Mary came down from the Temple and pondered all this in her heart."'

I jabbed him lightly in the cheek with my knuckles. 'Go on, stop the drivel. Which of the saints did you see, or was it God himself?'

'They took me to meet Mannix. As part of the novices' training, we spent a month in the hospice for the dying—wiping the brows of those in their agony, laying out the dead, falling in love with the nursing aides, reciting the rosary over the PR system, gathering the wisdom and bawdry of the old. Not the common and garden routine of the eighteen-year-old male, but ordinary enough for all that. What made it different was that Mannix lived next door. To a Sydney boy he was a distant luminary who really belonged among the fabled dead. Suddenly he was there, next door. Every month the two novices on duty were granted half an hour with him. It was late October 1963.'

'And I was still, and always, among ordinary mortals,' I reflected. 'In the last years of leisure when final school exams were still a token obstacle and before the world got too much with us.'

He looked across at me. 'Yes,' he said, 'and who else is getting romantic? The Indian summer before the storms came. The more conventional pattern, but harder, I admit.' He reached up and

221

stretched the skin where the crows' feet stood. 'He shall wipe away every line from their eyes.'

I half brushed, half slapped his hand away. 'Leave them,' I said. 'They'll be useful credentials when I go to judgment.' But I didn't want to discourage or distract the expansive mood. 'Mannix and the turning spring of '63.'

He stared ahead for a moment, apparently composing himself. 'The house . . . Raheen . . . was what came to mind years later when I first read Yeats—peacocks on the cultivated lawns. Otherwise the building was irrelevant. We were taken up to his bedroom, a slight, earnest primary school teacher from Ipswich and myself. The archbishop sat close to the grate of his fireplace, fully dressed, biretta in place, and a red tartan rug around his legs. I was awed and nervous. Of course I'd never met a dignitary, and here my very first was this eminence from the past, half in uniform, half in motley, and with the inscrutable expression and elaborately slow speech and gestures of the immensely old. He was ninety-nine as every Catholic child knew. I remember only one moment in our conversation. It was as much as I remembered at that instant, twenty years ago, when I left the mansion. Cricket must have been mentioned. The previous summer Ted Dexter's Englishmen had toured, and their manager had been the Duke of Norfolk.'

'The premier Catholic earl,' I chimed in, sensing a direction to this anecdote.

'Exactly. The premier Catholic earl,' he repeated. 'The archbishop made much the same point. He said he had met several Dukes of Norfolk in his time, and the first had been in Rome, when he was a young priest, just newly ordained. It must have been about 1890. Nearly a century ago.'

I shifted across in the bed, and snuggled, with my head on his shoulder and under his chin. He stroked my arm, but I think it was a reflex of his charm, and the rhythm of his story never changed.

'Another young Irish priest and himself had missed out on a papal audience that had been arranged. "But," said the archbishop, "in Rome at the time there happened to be a group of English Catholic pilgrims, and they were led by the then Duke of Norfolk. They themselves had a private audience arranged with His Holiness, and somehow the Duke got to hear of the plight of the two young Irish priests. He asked us if we would like to join his group." At which point the old actor paused, and exercised the decayed jaw and rolled his lips in and out on the gums. Then he said, with clearly satisfied pride, "We refused." There was a hiatus, filled only by a mild panic, as we both fought for the correct response. It was the barely vestigial Irish in us, we both decided, that was supposed to be reacting, and so we laughed, the Ipswich teacher more fulsomely, but both of us were forced and tense. We were, I suspect, just a little disedified at this tale of churlishness and Catholic fragmentation. Maybe our discomfort betrayed itself. Or maybe it was wholly predictable, and its occurrence counted on by the archbishop's strategy. Two Jesuit novices were nothing to him: he had been playing with the reaction of crowds when our grandfathers were young men. Two priggish youths were but clay. At any rate, at some carefully judged moment, Mannix leaned forward to us, to me, and his expression gave nothing away, except that I saw, or was it I imagined, or simply that I now imagine, a twinkle or perhaps a glitter in his eyes. "Ah, but you must understand," he said, with the most attentive articulation, "that the English and the Irish were not such good friends then as they are now." He hung forward an instant, then subsided into his chair, and made a minute readjustment to his biretta. The half hour was up.'

The narration stopped. But there remained a distance and solemnity about him, as though he had not really been talking to me, but had been intoning to himself, and was still listening to the last echoes die away. I lightly tugged the lobe of his ear. 'Come away, come away,' I called. 'It's a nice story, but you're in the real world now.'

'Hang on,' he said. 'I haven't made my point yet. As we walked off across the gravel towards the gate, the Ipswich teacher said, "Funny old codger. Bright as a button." I suppose I grunted some

223

sort of assent being a well-bred young novice, but even then I had an irritated sense that he had demeaned the man and the moment. Not that I expected him to rise to the moment: he was a colourless unimaginative youth, and it was a pity the occasion had to be wasted on him.'

'Why are you so angry still?' I asked him.

'I'm not,' he said with tired calm. 'A bit sad perhaps.'

'Angry, sad, whatever you are, you shouldn't still be emotionally subject to all that. Heavens, it was virtually your childhood.' I raised myself from his shoulder, and settled back on my pillow.

'Maybe, maybe, but you miss my point. Yes, I'm mildly sad at the Ipswich teacher, but, God, he wasn't responsible for his limitations—and they were circumstantial limitations too. He didn't get the point that I got, but maybe only because it was the end of his dealings with the man. But it wasn't the end for me. I'm talking about what I got out of it. In that story-telling I had seen achievement as an artifact. I had witnessed the honed perfection of a human action. There he was at ninety-nine, crafting his life, and each segment of it, with total control, each cluster of gestures and speech and tone a lyric breaking free from him, like a detached balloon from a cartoon character, except that it always had dignity and nobility.'

He was straining just a little too hard, and I was roused. But I reined myself in from too sharp a tone. 'Are you sure you weren't taken in by experienced posing?'

'No! What I'm saying is that that's my feeling now.'

He seemed to me to be going round in a circle. I wasn't sure what he really wanted of me, but I imagined he didn't know that himself. I was an atmosphere—somehow the appropriate one—in which he could think aloud. That feeling was reinforced by the sheer oddity of our situation. In spite of the intimacy of it, we weren't even facing one another. There was contact, even some warmth, but the words were going out across the foot of the bed, and bouncing back to us from the white wall. We were acting out some domestic parody of Plato's Cave, and the sheer artificiality of it made me laugh.

'Go on,' I said in answer to his disturbed movement of query. I reached out, and with the back of my fingers I stroked his hair and the prickly side of his face. It was cajoling, but it was not wholly calculated.

'My point is,' he began, 'that what I had which the Ipswich teacher missed was a balancing experience. The following Sunday he went back to the novitiate and was replaced by another chap somewhat older than I was, a New Zealand dairy farmer, a rangy ironic bloke with a gentle contempt for Australia and a determination to keep his spirituality to himself. We laboured and laughed together over the dying; Mr Portelli, blind and barely articulate in English, lay in his cot and sucked on Kool Mints; Mr Hodgkinson, the father of two nuns, bellowed constantly for the pan and swore to the ward after every ordeal that all he could get was fucking wind; Mr Rayner scratched savagely at himself with nails he would let no one cut, and whimpered about his twin afflictions of dandruff and itchy balls, and all the while his cancer moved outwards.

'And one mid-afternoon, spreading the gospel of the Melbourne Cup—Gatum Gatum is the only winner I could name from that year to this—we got an urgent request to go next door. Did we go in through the back, through a kitchen? I can't even remember. Simply that we went upstairs with seemly religious haste. The archbishop was in the same chair, in the same spot, but the picture had been smudged violently. His biretta was on the floor beside him, and the still thick hair had been not merely displaced but blasted into rigid, misshapen tufts, and cowlicks slewed across the eyes and nose. The face was the first really grey one I had ever seen. The teeth had been removed and the head lolled and the dribble ran down onto the loosened purple stock and black soutane. We were there simply to get him into bed. The dairy farmer hardly needed me. He slid his arms around the back of the faintly panting figure and hoisted him. I was hesitant about touching this flesh, but the prospect of its being dragged must have struck me as a worse indignity. I bent and lifted each of the black-shrouded shanks up around my hips, and we shuffled towards the bed. Up went the burden, buttocks first, onto the princely expanse. Up we went after it, crawling across the first double bed other than my parents' I had ever experienced, heaving and yanking the occupant with us, till we had positioned him somewhere near the centre. The covers had not even been turned; our task had nothing to do with the restoration of life, everything to do with the restoration of dignity. We were placing him in the sanctified attitude of death. We were thanked and dismissed.'

He was silent. All the time I had not taken my hand away from the side of his face. I moved it with uneven strokes and in an irregular rhythm, determined to keep him alive to something outside his own engrossing memories. But I couldn't ignore this focus of his concentration. 'Something to tell your grandchildren,' I said. 'Or the likes of me in the meantime.'

'Come on,' he turned to me, and propped himself on his elbow. 'You can do better than that.' And, for the first time since he had arrived, I felt an engagement about him, the initial movements of a hardening towards passion. There was anger present all right, but it was the kind of spark that ran out igniting a whole web of feelings.

'Glib, insensitive responses are too much the order of most days,' he continued. 'The dairy farmer was at it too. "All in a day's work," was his only, laughing remark. And behind that, at the most, was the hackneyed convention of archbishop and Italian greengrocer coming to the same end.'

'What more did you want?'

'Silence, I suppose. I had seen the glory, and the glory had departed. In a moment, almost while my back was turned. It wasn't just life that was gone, or a known personality that had been obliterated. It was that consummation of wit and self-knowledge and irony and tone and universal understanding. It was achieved humanity that had been taken away.'

'Look,' I said. 'In fact, look at me.' He had been talking at my throat, but now he raised his eyes, and his right hand came round and rested on my shoulder. 'Why are you telling me this?'

'Isn't it obvious?'

'No, it's not. We've known one another for ages, we can take a whole world of religion and mores for granted . . . but that doesn't explain what I'm supposed to do with these memories.'

'What do you do with any work of art,' he told me, but he did have to make an effort to stop his mouth opening in a smile. 'Contemplate it. If you get any ravishing insights, pass them on to me. But please spare me criticism.' The smile was released, and the slide into skittishness, even carefreeness, carried him on to kiss me, lightly but several times across my shoulder and my neck. And he drew himself closer, and I felt that the balance of his interest had shifted. But if he had to cast his pearls in front of me, I wanted to see them all: he no longer seemed in danger of being mesmerized by his own alleged treasures.

'Was that the end of your dealings with the great?'

For a moment I thought he was going to waive the chance to continue. He wasn't, but his tone had altered. 'No, no, the work is a triptych. Decide the order of the panels yourself.' He tapped his finger three times across my breast bone. 'The old nuns in the hospital prayed in frenzy that Dr Mannix would live to see one hundred. He didn't. I finished my stint and went home, and the same night we were all herded into a bus to go and wake the body in St Patrick's Cathedral by singing something or other, Vespers I think, from the Office for the Dead.'

'Can you sing?'

'No, of course not. I couldn't even find my place, in the book, in the procession, anything.'

'Sing me something.'

'Careful, or I'll break into psalms and spiritual songs. We got very lugubrious on them that night.'

'Let me shut my eyes a minute, and see if I can conjure up the choir boy . . . Ah, he's coming, he's coming . . . No, he refuses to appear. All I can see is a beast in my bed.'

He took it as cue, and snarled, and let his fingers beat a swift tattoo on my breast, and then he withdrew as though nothing

227

had happened, and took up his story again. 'The whole affair was a pageant, a fancy dress ball, monks and friars of every skin and persuasion, purple episcopal flashes here and there, choirmasters and masters of ceremonies scuttling up and down like sheepdogs, piping inaudible notes on their discreet reeds, calling out page references.'

'But you were being very pious and uncynical at the time, weren't you?'

'I was doing my best to be decorous, but I knew it was a fair fiasco. Jesuits were an unharmonious rabble when it came to monastic preserves such as the public antiphonal chanting of the Office. We processed in pairs—an unvarying clerical habit— the mating instinct asserting itself no doubt—and I was beside a some-time QC from Sydney, a larrikin and great fun. He was there under sufferance. He had even less voice than I, he felt a fool in a surplice, but most of all a Federal election was on and he thought of Mannix merely as a political opponent.'

'Spare me,' I pleaded.

'You are in a vulnerable mood tonight.' He lunged in, his jaw open, towards my throat, and then transformed the bite so that all I felt were the lips grazing softly and closing and opening, and the light, slowmotion prancing of his tongue. I held him by the back of the head and let my hands swing to the motion of his mouth.

'You're right,' he whispered as he caressed. 'Politics were irrelevant. There we were, in this great dim cave, shouting out to one another all sorts of crazy things across the thrilling eminence of this corpse.'

'Go on,' I told him, 'what sorts of crazy things?'

'Mad things, mad things when you stop and think.'

'Don't stop and think, just tell me.'

'Over the great patrician showman, cadaverously on show, I bellowed that I would please God in the country of the living.'

'And you did?'

'I said I would stake out the land of the living, and be pleasing in it.'

'Hold me.'

'I wailed that the time of my exile had been prolonged.'

'And I answered that my soul was in deep exile.'

'You have snatched my soul from death.'

'And my eyes from tears.'

'Free my soul from evil lips.'

'And from deceitful tongues.' And then I laughed. 'Come on,' I said, 'that doesn't feel deceitful to me.' And I rolled myself around him.

'We said other things,' he tried to mumble. 'Or we should have. In all the chaos. As the notes jangled, off-key and off-tempo, in the bleating of that great mob of lost sheep.'

'Come on now.'

'And irregularly, ecstatic escapees of sound, flashing, in trajectory, across the vault. Conceived in the muddle and the discord.'

'Blowing kisses to death.'

'And our hearts rising in the dark.'

'Brimming.'

'Swelling, in the glory of death.'

'And our eyes wide at the sight.'

'Seeing the littered earth we had risen from, the sad mess we were returning to.'

Outside, dogs barked, and nearby a child stirred and cried out, and reaching through the rain of tears I took him by the hand.

THE COMMUNE DOES NOT WANT YOU

Frank Moorhouse

AUTHOR'S NOTE

The story evolved from a painful loss of a friend, a going of
different ways. I wrote another story about that lost friendship
called 'Loss of a Friend by Cablegram' (also in the book *Tales
of Mystery and Romance*, in fact the whole book was very much
about parting of ways). It was pain turned to humour.

I did not 'choose' to turn the pain to humour, nor did I do
it for 'therapy'. I felt pain and it chose its own way of expression.

Although the story is out of my life, in the sense that it
expresses, in an inverted way, a condition of my being at a certain
time, it is not autobiographical. My friend did not go into a
commune. I did not answer an advertisement to join a commune.
They were comic representations of 'going in different ways'.

The house described existed. Other friends of mine owned
it and were changing it into a polyfunctional endospace. I visited
it often and watched this transformation.

It was written at the time when some students, nature lovers,
and bohemians, were introducing rural life into the city as a way
of keeping in touch with nature. Some of my friends had sheep,
some had goats, a donkey. None of them had a pig.

I had a cat which disappeared around the time that my
friendship broke down. This saddened me. The cat got into the
story too. In one version the pig the narrator sits upon was my
cat.

The commune is a site of the times in which the story was
written, and represents the alien, cult-urally superior world where
my friend was fantasised, by me, to now reside.

I did visit a commune in Arizona and the American Indian
incident happened. The discussion of fried rice versus boiled rice

is from the *Financial Review*.

One day while visiting the house which was being transformed into a polyfunctional endospace a baby fell through the communication hole they had cut into the ceiling. The baby fell onto an armchair, unhurt, before my eyes. I had that in the story for a while but it seemed unbelievable. The baby became a note wrapped around a stone—another version of the 'cablegram' in the other lost friend story.

The story now appears to me also to be about the anxiety of not belonging to fashionable movements of the times, the anxiety of not being of the consciousness of your times, or at least of your sub-group. It is also about moving on, of not belonging to the younger generation.

The dialogues of the story as I now see them and which I probably didn't consciously see at the time of writing, are, a quarrel with my times, expressed as satire of self and the cult ideologies, a dialogue about styles of being.

I landscape the story with homage to other writers: Milton, Pushkin, Schreiner, Buckminster Fuller, Simone de Beauvoir, F. Scott Fitzgerald, 'Papa' Hemingway. 'Milton' was chosen as the central character's name because my lost friend had written a book on Milton. My story 'The Girl Who Met Simone de Beauvoir in Paris' is mentioned. It appeared in an earlier book. My friend and I are both therefore 'in' the story in a coded way.

'Adrian' is a real person mentioned as homage. Sheena and Lance were names of the times.

The story might have been an act of retaliation against my lost friend too.

I see the story as being a comic presentation of the discomfort of myself, unease of self.

Frank Moorhouse

THE COMMUNE DOES NOT WANT YOU

At the door of the commune I hesitated. What ectoplasmic shapes and indistinguishable bearded denim and mumbling cabalism throbbed here, Oh Lord.

I knocked. Do you knock at a commune door? (too unflowing? does it pre-empt their attention?) Do you just go in, affectionately, pacifically? Or is it by initiation?

A young man as fresh as a constable, no beard, came to the door, opened it and went back in.

'Hey,' I called, 'is this Milton's commune?'

'It's not *Milton's* commune, but he lives here, yes,' he said, over his shoulder.

'Is he in?' I asked the receding back but the man disappeared into a dark hole at the end of the hall.

Don't they have caution? I could be the enemy of the commune.

Any manners, residue of their middle class?

Any guidelines for the handling of callers?

I groped my way into the commune.

There appeared in the dim light, amid the raga music, to be a person in every room or the shape of a person. Were they the residents or were they callers? Or were they too answering the advertisement for the room? In a commune there is always this group sitting around the kitchen table reading or picking at themselves, toes or noses, drinking tea, and you don't know if any of them live there or whether you can sit in that chair or is that Big Paddy's chair or is that where Papa Milton always sits.

I'm too dressed. I reprimand my bow tie with a twist, a yank.

No one looks up when I come in. Nose picking leads to brain damage.

'Hullo there.'

Someone dragged snot a mile along their nasal passage.

They have their heads down, reading upside down newspaper

wrapping or the labels on packets, drinking tea from enamel army mugs.

'Is Milton in?'

'I think he's in his room.'

I could not see who said this. I could not, for the life of me, see their lips move.

'Which is his room?'

'Just bang on the wall and shout.'

I was not going to bang on the wall and shout.

'I think he's with some chick,' someone else said, although again I saw no lips move.

I moved into the other room. It was not so much that I moved, more that the unreceptivity poked me out through a huge circular hole in the wall into yet another even darker room. They had knocked this huge circular hole in the wall, leaving rubble. I sat down on a lopsided bean bag chair, keeping one of my legs outriggered so that I wouldn't fall over. The beans always move away from me. A pig squealed out from somewhere in the chair. A pig. From under me.

In the dimness I saw a girl with long suffocating hair about her face—personality concealment—who said, 'Come here Pushkin, did the nasty man sit upon you.'

'It wasn't my intention,' I told her, 'I like . . . animals . . . pigs.'

'Do you have a pig?' she asked.

'I did have a cat but it decamped. It went away. Greener pastures.'

'Cats only do that to people who ill-treat them.'

'Oh no—it just went away.'

'You must have ill-treated it.'

'No, cats just go sometimes—for personal reasons.'

'That's the only reason they run away—ill-treatment.'

'No, I like animals. I used to talk to the cat. Shaw said cats like a good conversation but you must speak slowly.'

'You hurt Pushkin.'

'I didn't mean to hurt Pushkin. I want to see Milton. About

the vacant room. Is he with a chick?'

'Don't use the word "chick" with me if you want a reply.'

But. I was going to say to her that I never use the word but that it had hopped onto my tongue from the other room, from the Kitchen Klatsch, but, oh well, I let it go.

'The herbs look good—the watercress is growing well.'

'Anyone can grow watercress.'

I was going to tell her that in the story 'The Girl Who Met Simone de Beauvoir in Paris' the male in the story is based on me. That I have, despite my use of the word chick, agonized on the questions of liberation. I am imperfectly liberated, that's true, I wanted to reconstruct but parts were missing. Maybe they could be imported.

I told her instead that I went to a commune once in Phoenix, Arizona, where everyone was smoking dope and I was drinking Lone Star beer and they had a pet Red Indian who noticed this and came over to me and said, Wow man, you drinking Lone Star beer, give me some man, I love beer, I can't smoke this shit, where you from. I told him from Australia and he said he'd heard great things about Australia, like everyone drinks. I said yes everyone drinks, almost everyone. He said that sounded like the place for him.

At first she made no comment.

Then she said, 'Do you always talk so much—you're not a very "still" person are you? And I suppose that was meant to be a put-down of dope.'

How long, I thought, how long should I give Milton if he's with a girl.

'How is the commune coming along?' I asked, ploughing on with courtesy.

'Look, man, this is a house we all share, if you want to call it a commune you call it a commune, but for us it is a simple experiment in shared living with a polyfunctional endospace.'

Ah!! So that explains the knocked down walls, the huge circular holes.

I had been told that, as for sharing, it was Milton who paid.

235

'Why do you wear a bow tie?'

'Oh that,' I looked down, as if it had grown there unnoticed by me, 'Oh . . . a bit of a lark . . . a bit of a giggle . . . a bit of a scream . . . a sort of a joke.'

She seemed to be staring at me severely.

I stumbled on, 'Oh, about clothes—I don't give a damn. A lark. Dress never worries me. I've got some jeans at home, actually.'

'Pity,' she said, 'I thought for a moment we'd have one male here who presented himself. Men think that caring about clothing is female. And therefore beneath consideration. See, sloppiness is another put-down of women. Dress for me is a way of speaking.'

'I like the idea of a sharing experience,' I said, 'learning to share Milton's money.'

'I find that offensive,' she said.

'Oh come now,' I said, 'it was a joke. I lived with Milton before—in the Gatsby House and he paid then. He paid for the jazz bands on the lawn, everything. I mean it wasn't a moral statement. Far be it from me . . .'

'I didn't know Milton then,' she said. She was, I could tell, not interested in knowing about anything which happened before her existence. She was not interested.

I don't blame her.

I began to stare at my hands, which an interviewer once said were 'nervous'.

Then I thought of something chatty to say, knowing about brown rice and communes and such, 'In Chinese restaurants it was always sophisticated to order boiled rice instead of fried rice. I always liked fried rice best but ordered boiled to be correct. Now I read Ted Moloney and he says ordering fried rice is quite acceptable and doesn't offend Chinese chefs.'

Again she made no comment. I think she was being 'still'.

She spoke, 'I don't find that in any way interesting—getting hung-up about sophistication and all that.'

'But I thought it showed . . . never mind . . . have you read the latest *Rolling Stone*?' I asked.

'I don't read newspapers,' she said.

'Oh, I read every newspaper.'

'You must have a very messed up head.'

'I read the manifest content and I read the non-manifest content. I read the archetypes, osmotypes and the leadertypes. I see the ideological meaning and the unintended information.'

'I don't read any newspapers,' she repeated.

'Oh, I guess I really just read the manifest content. I've pretty much given up classifying news into Merry Tales, Fairy Tales, Animals Tales, Migratory Legends, Cosmogonic Legends and such. I don't do that much now.'

'I'm a dancer.'

'Oh yes?'

'I'm learning Theatre of the Noh.'

'It's a rich world—I'm learning Theatre of the Maybe Not.'

'Is that some sort of put-down?'

'I wonder if he's finished yet,' I said, nodding upwards, leaning across and stroking the . . . pig.

'Do you know Lance Ferguson?' she asked.

'No.'

'Do you know Sheena Petrie?'

'No.'

'Are you Australian?'

'Of course, from Sydney.'

'Strange that you don't know anyone.'

'I know *some* people.'

'Where do you live?'

'Here, here in Balmain.'

'No . . . !!'

'Yep—for ten years or more.'

'Incredible, and you don't know Lance Ferguson or Sheena Petrie?'

'Never heard of them.'

'Wow,' she shook her head to herself and made a coughing laugh, 'oh wow—you must live in a hole in the ground or something.'

'I guess,' I said glumly, 'they're Milton's new scene—I'm from his first scene.'

'And you say you know Milton?'

'Yes, of course.'

'You mustn't know him very well if you don't know Lance Ferguson or Sheena Petrie.'

'Ten years—I've known him for ten years. He was my closet friend, I mean closest friend. I haven't seen him for a few months.'

'Are you part of the Balmain Bourgeoisie?'

'No. Not part of the Balmain Bourgeoisie.'

'Who do you know?'

'Adrian Heber.'

'He's a spy. Everyone knows Adrian Heber.'

'He's not a spy.'

'Sheena won't believe this when I tell her.'

'I wonder if Milton's finished yet.'

I heard a lavatory flush, 'Maybe that's him,' I said.

'No, that's Harvey.'

'How do you know?'

'He has a weak bladder.'

I stare at my nervous hands again.

'I have no problems like that,' I reassure her.

Then I said, 'Perhaps I should go up or something.'

She then left the room, without saying where she was going, but she took the pig with her—as if I couldn't be trusted with it.

I fancied that I could still hear the bed squeaking above me.

I looked through the huge circular hole in the wall at the people still sitting around the kitchen table, picking at themselves. Nose picking can lead to brain damage.

I gave up. I went to the wall and banged and shouted, 'Milton!' No one answered.

I went back into the dim endospace and fought my way onto the bean bag chair.

'You!!' an imperious voice came from the ceiling and, looking up, I saw a hitherto unnoticed manhole-sized hole. A girl, not the girl with the pig, but a girl dressed as far as I could see in only a man's shirt was crouched there.

It occurred to me that I may have been watched the whole time—by the Commune Committee.

'Here's a note from Milton and your book back,' she called, and dropped a note wrapped around a stone, and a book.

The note read: 'Go away. The commune does not want you.'

The book he returned was Olive Schreiner's *Stories, Dreams and Allegories*.

'Did he like it?' I asked, trying to point attention away from the wounding note.

'He said he didn't open it. If you gave it to him he said, it must have had a malign intent. A way of spooking his equilibrium.'

Scratching his duco.

'He said that applying for the room under the name Buck Fuller was not considered a good joke by the commune and the commune was not fooled.'

And the commune did not laugh.

'Are you Sheena Petrie?'

'No.'

'Do you know her?'

'Of course. Everyone knows Sheena. She's Milton's best friend.'

'Is there a commune for people who do not fit very well into communes? Could you advise me?'

'I was instructed not to talk with you any further. You must go now.'

JUNCTION

Kate Grenville

AUTHOR'S NOTE

'Junction' was the first story I wrote and, unlike almost everything else I've written, I've changed it very little since the first version.

I wrote it when I was living in Paris in 1977, and the original version was set there. I'd been reading the newspaper *Libération*, which has a lonely-hearts section at the back, and I noticed an advertisement similar to Doug's. For the first time my imagination was fired by something other than my own experiences (I had just written a terrible novel grandiosely called *Memoirs*), and I wrote the story in an exhilarating burst of invention. It was a real breakthrough for me to emerge from the claustrophobia of my novel-gazing to join the rest of the human race.

As well as being the first story I wrote, it was also the first one I had published, within weeks of writing it (I should explain that I didn't get another story published for nearly two years after that, however). I took it in to the editor of *Paris-Metro*, an English-language weekly, and sat opposite her at her desk while she read it. That was another breakthrough: I had a most liberating feeling that it didn't matter what she thought of me personally, all that mattered was whether she liked the story. I felt free to be myself in a way I never had before.

As well as these rather sentimental reasons for choosing 'Junction', I think it's interesting on a formal, technical level. American friends in Paris were introducing me to the world of fiction beyond the dreary old well-made story that I'd been brought up on. I'd been reading, with amazement and some hostility, the work of some contemporary 'experimental' writers and as well as being outraged at the lack of commas and full stops I was hugely excited by it and wanted to give it a go. The rather toneless hysteria of what came out seemed to match the subject well in this story. It seemed, too, to offer a way out of the terribly prosaic quality of prose—a way of letting it steal some of the energy and light-footedness of poetry.

In some ways 'Junction' is about the things that continue to preoccupy me in fiction. I seem to keep returning to the sordid physical facts of living (I'd always said that books should have toilets in them, and I lost no time in practising what I preached). Doug is the first of many characters I've explored in fiction who are isolated, feeling themselves to be out of step with their society. And I'm interested in characters who are story-tellers: characters who use words to invent their own lives, as Doug's sequence of advertisements tells his version of what is happening.

Kate Grenville

JUNCTION

Will the girl with brown hair on the 4:15 from Gayton last Thursday who smiled at the man on the platform please call Doug on 467 3241.

He stays in all day all night. He leaves his door ajar to listen for the phone. He cleans his teeth very quietly and he doesn't play the radio.

The haggle-faced old onion of a woman who runs the rooming house thinks he's a good tenant but he makes a lot of noise these days leaping up the stairs tripping every time on the cracked lino to be the first to get to the phone.

—Yes yes yes hello hello.

—Oh. I'll see if he's in.

It's never for him. He puts off going to the toilet she might phone. He doesn't linger there over *Playboy* like he used to ignoring the rattling door handle. The landlady thinks it's a good sign maybe he's looking for a job at last.

He's in there and the phone rings. He leaps up grabs for the chain in a frenzy misses and gets the light-string instead, flails in the dark for the chain scrabbles at the lock and leaps up the stairs holding his pants up with one hand one shoe comes off when he trips on the lino but he's first to the phone.

—Hello hello yes yes yes

—No this is 467 3241 that's okay bye.

His pants are slipping down and the landlady's staring at him through her aura of old cooking fat.

—Expecting a call are you?

—No yes not really sort of

He makes it back to his room and sits on the side of the bed feeling constipated. The light struggling in through his window lies listlessly on the gritty mat. The corners of the room are very square and the walls stand drearily on guard.

It's three o'clock so he starts to get dressed. He wears the same clothes every day when he goes to meet the 4:15 from Gayton otherwise she won't remember him. He shaves very carefully avoiding the pimples and cuts himself only once on the rusty blade. The cold water makes his face blue but he wets his hair and combs it flat. Then he thinks that makes him look too young so he rubs it dry and tries to make it look casual.

Each day he buys a bunch of violets from the ancient woman who sits like a toad among her flowers.

Something told me I'd see you today so I bought these.

Or perhaps:

I bought these they go with your eyes.

But what if her eyes are brown?

They should be forget-me-nots because I remembered you.

He races up and down the train looking in every carriage it only stops for seven minutes. He stumbles along tripping over the straw baskets and grey-faced dribble-nosed kids in the corridor and when he gets to the end of the train and jumps off, the violets are wilted and greasy but he doesn't want to throw them away they remind him of her so he stuffs them in his pocket.

He tries to look indifferent as he passes the toadwoman on the way out but she winks evilly at him and cackles through her gums and he hears the 4:15 pulling away from the station.

By the fourth day the ticket collector is grinning as he takes the platform ticket and on the fifth day as he takes the ticket he says something to the ex-jockey who sells papers and they both guffaw.

Will the girl on the 4:15 from Gayton last Thursday with short brown hair wearing a red raincoat who smiled at the man on the platform call Doug on 467 3241 I think I love you.

In his room he boils an egg and eats it with revulsion he wishes he knew how to cook. Then he sits and burps and stares at the spatters on the tiles behind the cooker and waits. The pus-coloured walls are closing in so he goes for a walk looking carefully at every girl he passes it might be her it might be her.

None of them is her.

He walks slowly back through the old milk cartons and crumbled dog turds and hears the phone ringing inside the house. Lunging his hand in for the keys he rips his pocket drops the keys grabs them they slip his hands are sweaty he rams the key at the lock it won't go in he's using the wrong key he drops them again but snatches them up before they hit the ground jabs the key into the lock can't remember which way to turn it finally gets the door open his nose is running his ears are burning he pounds up the stairs and the phone stops ringing.

He wants to throw his head back and bay savagely at the moon but there's only peeling paint above his head and the landlady in curlers and clotted dressing gown is standing at the foot of the stairs looking up.

—She'll phone again love, nice boy like you, she says with heavy irony.

He worries that he'll miss her so next day he goes down the train twice, once in each direction, to make sure. The flatfaced old women growing out of the seats are staring at him now and he's panting and stumbling and knocking kids out of his way as he gallops up and down the corridor. An old woman with a wrinkled face like the top of a custard mutters crossly at him. A kid cries and rams its knuckles into its eye the man hit me WAAAAAAAAAAAAAAH. The guard comes up.

—Wotcha doin' mister lookin' for someone?

—Yeah that's right.

His eyes are flickering round what if she goes past while this moron's blocking the view.

—Yeah yeah certainly no won't do it again, okay, he mumbles and sidles past while the guard stares suspiciously. She's not on the train.

Next day he gets to the station at three and the toadwoman tells him: You're early love, and makes a noise like a dog barking. He catches a train to the next station back up the line so he can get on the 4:15 from Gayton there. That way there'll be plenty of time to look for her. On the way they pass the earlier train from Gayton. He strains to separate the blur of carriages and there's a flash of red my god his heart leaps: there she is I've missed her. He searches the 4:15 but without hope.

The ticket collector suggests he get a season ticket for the platform. Ha ha.

He dreams of her all night and wakes panting as she eludes him again. He wakes with his hand clutching the corner of her raincoat which turns before his eyes into the corner of the sheet. Wakes breathless and heart thudding after running after her, she's on the back platform of a train which always goes just a little too fast and he keeps stumbling over his pants which have fallen around his ankles. The toadwoman cackles and her face withers like a piece of newspaper about to burst into flames. He sees a red coat on the other side of a crumbling mountain of straw baskets which he desperately climbs to get to her they fall on top of him his feet become wedged in them he's almost on top of them the train jerks into movement and he falls awake sobbing.

He sees her everywhere. Dashes after women in the street but they're never her. He spends a fortune in hamburgers he leaves to harden when he rushes out to chase a red raincoat across the road. Nearly gets arrested: Whereja think ya goin' gotta pay ya know. He nearly gets killed: Why doncha look where ya goin' dummie. Kindly old men creak after him: Hey sonny sonny you forgot your newspaper.

There's a wet spell and red raincoats are everywhere. He's getting a lot of exercise and not much to eat. When he can't sleep he writes poetry.

> Red is the colour of my true love's coat,
> Brown is her hair and short.
> My love's like a small brown bird
> That never will be caught.

This he copies neatly into a special book with a red cover. He buys a red raincoat and hangs it at the foot of his bed and puts the violets in the pockets. He buys a brown wig and the woman winks slyly as he chooses it: Yes dearie that looks real nice on you you take my word for it. He keeps it on his pillow at night but his landlady finds it and lingers in the hall outside talking loudly about deviants.

He searches the 4:15 for the last time. He comes home. He puts the wig on, puts the raincoat on and takes his pants off. He stands in front of the mirror staring at himself with his hand moving faster and faster in the rubbery smell of sweaty raincoat, tears rolling down his face until at last he groans and doubles over holding himself as if shot.

Will the girl with blonde hair and blue ribbons waiting for a 63 bus Friday at noon please call Doug on 467 3241.

WEDNESDAYS AND FRIDAYS

Elizabeth Jolley

AUTHOR'S NOTE

. . . Many a woman—some of the Highest in the Land—have had a Trouble in their time; and why should you Trumpet yours when others do not Trumpet theirs . . .

This is a part of Mrs Durbeyfield's letter to her daughter, Tess, just before her marriage to Angel Clare—in the novel *Tess of the D'Urbervilles* by Thomas Hardy. Contained in the letter is the mother's care for her daughter. The letter, as part of the fiction, is very moving and the reader hopes that Tess will listen to her mother. Tess ignores her mother's advice. If she had taken it the novel would have been very slim.

Stan Parker, writing to his wife Amy in Patrick White's *Tree of Man*, holds his head on one side and writes slowly in the handwriting taught him by his mother and not used very much. Stan is away at the war:

. . . I could tell you a thing or two if only I could write it, but then we have never been the ones for talk, anyway. I have not, you have done the talking, you have been the tongue for both of us, and how I would like to hear that tongue telling . . .

All the quiet yearning for the life on his little farm is packed into the simply written letters. Included too is the terrible helplessness men feel when caught up in events and systems, in this case the war, that they do not understand. The author of the fiction is able, through the use of the letters, to make a sharp comment.

I am not able to choose a story of mine that I would consider my best because then I would have to consider the worst. While looking for best I might, without wanting to, find worst!

I find it quite hard to explain why I wrote 'Wednesdays and Fridays'. Perhaps if I could explain I would never have written the story. I do not as a rule question why I write anything.

When my children were young I wrote notes to them if I had to correct them in some way. The notes seemed a way of avoiding the anger or embarrassment that might accompany the necessary comment or criticism.

This story is about a difficult and painful situation in family life. A mother is having to look on as her son leaves school before he is ready for the world outside school. He is unemployed, inarticulate about the society in which he is growing up, and has a girlfriend who is making use of him and of his mother's house. I suspect that the girlfriend, discovering perhaps too quickly her own sexuality, is floundering too. It is possible to utter phrases like 'coming to terms with sexuality' and 'the standards and values of society' but that is not my way.

In the story I want to show a mother who works hard and who loves her son. She is prepared to make every effort on behalf of her son and hopes to remain respectable in the eyes of 'society'. The son loves his mother and wants to soothe her with presents which he buys with her money. He has no money of his own. I want to show her effort and his complication without making any judgment. I chose to write in letters to bring the mother's feelings close to a reader. Letters are one of the most intimate forms of writing. I made the story funny, building with repetition and a touch of the ridiculous because human life is made in this way. And perhaps to make the whole thing a little less painful.

I think it is important to lift sharp social comment in a story or a novel by putting into the writing 'a little dance'—this can be done with special passages of description and lively dialogue between characters; or perhaps with little touches of tenderness or love or madness or humour. Letterwriting uses the simplest and most direct language. It is possible to *suggest* characters and situations through letters rather than using flat passages of narrative. A truth can be illustrated rather than told and it seems to me that this can add power to a story or a novel.

Elizabeth Jolley

WEDNESDAYS AND FRIDAYS

Wednesday 4 June
Dear Mr Morgan,
   You will be surprised to have a letter from me since we are living in the same house but I should like to remind you that you have not paid me board for last week.

Yours sincerely,
Mabel Doris Morgan
(landlady)

Wednesday 11 June
Dear Mr Morgan,
   This is to remind you that you are now owing two weeks' board and I should like to take the opportunity to ask you to remove the outboard motor from your room. There is an oil stain on the rug already and I'm afraid for my curtains and bedspread.

Yours sincerely,
Mabel Doris Morgan
(landlady)

Friday 13 June
Dear Mr Morgan,
   I know there isn't anything in the 'Rules of the House' to say outboard motors cannot be kept in bedrooms. I didn't think anyone would want to. Since you mention the rules I would like to draw your attention first to rule number nine which refers to empty beer cans, female visitors and cigarette ends, and to point out that rule eleven states quite clearly the hour for breakfast. It is simply not possible, I am sorry, to serve breakfasts after twelve noon.

Yours sincerely,
Mabel D. Morgan
(landlady)

Wednesday 18 June
Dear Mr Morgan,
I am writing to remind you that you now owe three weeks' board and the price of one single bed sheet which is ruined. Please note that bed linen is not to be used for other purposes. Thank you for moving the outboard motor.

Your sincerely,
Mabel Doris Morgan
(landlady)

Friday 20 June
Dear Mr Morgan,
No. Black oil and grease will not wash out of a sheet, furthermore it's torn badly in places. I can't think how it's possible to damage a sheet as much as this one has been damaged.
I am afraid I shall have to ask you to move the outboard motor again as it is impossible for anyone to sit in the lounge room to watch TV the way you have the propeller balanced between the two easy chairs.

Yours sincerely,
Mabel D. Morgan
(landlady)

Wednesday 25 June
Dear Mr Morgan,
Thank you for the two dollars. I should like to remind you that you now owe four weeks' board less two dollars.

Yours sincerely,
Mabel D. Morgan
(landlady)

Friday 27 June
Dear Mr Morgan,
Leaving a note on the mantelpiece does not excuse anyone for taking two dollars which does not belong to them even if you are only borrowing it back as you say till next week. Board

is at four weeks now. I'm sorry to have to tell you that the hall is too narrow for the storage of an outboard motor. And, would you please replace your bedspread and put up your curtains again as I am afraid they will spoil and they do not in any way help to prevent people from falling over the outboard as they go in and out of this house.

Yours sincerely,
Mabel D. Morgan
(landlady)

Wednesday 2 July
Dear Mr Morgan,
    Board is up to five weeks. With respect, Mr Morgan, I'd like to suggest you try to get a job. I'd like to suggest the way to do this is to get up early and get the paper and read the 'Situations Vacant, Men and Boys', and go after something. I'd like to say this has to be done early and quick. Mr Morgan, five weeks' board is five weeks' board. And Mr Morgan what's been going on in the bathroom? I think I am entitled to an explanation.

Yours sincerely,
Mabel Doris Morgan
(landlady)

Friday 4 July
Dear Mr Morgan,
    Thank you for your very kind thought. The chocolates really look very nice though, as you know, I don't eat sweet things as I have to watch my weight but as I said it's the thought that counts. Do you think it's possible you might be smoking a bit too much. Perhaps you could cut it down to say sixty a day for a start.

Yours sincerely,
Mabel Doris Morgan
(landlady)

Wednesday 9 July
Dear Mr Morgan,

I'm still waiting for an explanation about the bathroom. I must remind you that you now owe me six weeks' board and the cost of one single bed sheet ruined plus the cost of one bottle carpet cleaning detergent plus the price of the four pounds of gift-wrapped confectionery charged to my account at the Highway General Store. Early payment would be appreciated.

Yours sincerely,
Mabel Doris Morgan
(landlady)

Friday 11 July
Mr Morgan,

Get a Job. And clean your room. I never saw such a mess of chocolate papers under anyone's bed, ever. In my whole life I never saw such a mess. Never. I must point out too that I do not intend to spend hours in the kitchen over the hot roast and two veg. for someone who is too full up with rubbish to eat what's good for them. I'd like to remind you how to get a job. You get up early to get a job. I see in the paper concrete hands are wanted, this should suit you, so GET UP EARLY as it's a question of being first on site.

Yours sincerely,
Mabel Doris Morgan
(landlady)

And Mr Morgan, Bathroom? Explanation? And Mr Morgan. Smoking!

Wednesday 16 July
Dear Mr Morgan,

I appreciate you have troubles. We all have our troubles and I do see you have yours and it was kind of you to think of sending me flowers when you have so much on your mind. Thank you for the thought.

Miss, I forget, if you said, what you said her name was, had

255

no business to miss her last bus. In future no guests are to stay in this house without me. See that this does not happen again. You seem to have forgotten the outboard motor. There simply is not room for it in the hall and it's all wet. Please see that it is removed immediately. And please Mr Morgan, Board seven weeks.

Yours sincerely,
Mabel D. Morgan
(landlady)

Friday 18 July
Dear Mr Morgan,

First I must ask for an immediate explanation about the bathroom please. And, secondly, I must ask you to ask Miss whatever her name is to leave. I suggest you ask her what her name is if you didn't get it the first time.

I hope you won't feel offended about this but there really is not room for you to sleep in the hall, you know it has always been too narrow. There simply is not room there for you and the outboard motor. One of you will have to go. And see that young Miss leaves at once. And, Donald, always make sure you know what a girl's name is beforehand. You not knowing her name makes me feel I haven't brought you up right.

Yours sincerely,
Mabel Doris Morgan
(landlady)

Wednesday 23 July
Dear Mr Morgan,

I have to remind you Board eight weeks and Board one week for Extra Person. Perhaps you could persuade Pearl to go back to her lovely boarding school? Could you? I'm sure she's a nice girl but I really can't do with the two of you lazing round the house all day using up all my electricity and hot water. And I don't need to tell you that there really isn't enough space in the hall for your bed, her bicycle and her extra cases and the outboard motor.

Donald it's silly blocking up the hall with your bed. The neighbours will talk in any case. They'll think immorality is going on and what about young Mary? What ideas is she going to get? Donald I'm warning you I'm putting my foot down furthermore the outboard motor is not to be used in the bath. Where can it get you? AND what about a Job?

Yours sincerely,
Mabel Doris Morgan
(landlady)

Friday 25 July
Donald, No more roses please. I haven't got vases. Besides how am I going to pay for them? You know me, I'd just as soon see a flower growing in someone's garden. Thank you all the same for your lovely thought.

Your loving landlady,
Mabel Doris Morgan

Wednesday 30 July
Mr Morgan, This is to remind you Board nine weeks and Board two weeks for one Extra Person. I must say young Pearl has a healthy appetite. I wish you would eat properly.

As I was saying. Board as above, also cost of one single bed sheet, one bottle carpet cleaning detergent plus the price of the four-pound box of assorted confectionery and four dozen red roses, two deliveries, long stalks extra, and to dry cleaning and dyeing one chenille bedspread (purple) and two pairs curtains (electric green). With dry cleaning the price it is it would have been better to consult me first and about the extraordinary choice of colours, especially as I don't think the oil and grease stains will be hidden at all.

Donald, I do seriously think a Job is a good thing. Get a Job. Do try to get a Job.

Yours sincerely,
Mabel Doris Morgan
(landlady)

Friday 1 August
Donald, No more presents please. You know I never use lipsticks and certainly never a phosphorescent one. You must be off your brain. Though I suppose there is always a first time.

Your loving landlady,
Mabel Doris Morgan

Wednesday 6 August
Dear Donald,

I'm pushing this note under your door since you won't come out. I'm leaving a tray on the table outside. Do try and eat something. I'm sorry I said what I said. I am sorry too about the outboard motor. I suppose it wasn't fixed on to the boat properly. You say it's about thirty-five feet down? I didn't know the river was so deep there. Of course I'll lend you twenty dollars to hire a boat and a grappling iron. We'll simply add it on to the Board which is at ten weeks now and three weeks for one Extra Person, plus the cost of one single bed sheet, one bottle carpet cleaning detergent, one four-pound box assorted confectionery gift wrapped, and four dozen red roses, two deliveries (long stalks extra) and to the dry cleaning of one chenille bedspread and two pairs of curtains and the dyeing of the above, purple and electric green, respectively, plus the cost of one Midnight Ecstasy lipstick (phosphorescent frosted ice). I do hope we can find the outboard motor. I'm really looking forward to going on the river in a row boat, it's years since I was in a boat. We'll take Pearl and Mary with us and our lunch.

Your loving mother,
Mabel Doris Morgan
(landlady)

THE LIST OF ALL POSSIBLE ANSWERS

Peter Goldsworthy

AUTHOR'S NOTE

Although I don't regard this as my 'best written' story—it's more sparely written, and less psychologically complex than my current disposition would allow—I have a particular affection for the simplicity of the central idea: a list of economical answers to cover every possible question.

It's also a story that has lasted for me, passed my own private test of time. Just as whatever I am reading at the time is usually my 'favourite' book, whatever I am *writing* at the time is temporarily my favourite poem or story. The further those poems or stories recede from me into the past, the more likely they are to come to seem worthless. 'The List of All Possible Answers', however, has kept its place in my heart—along with only a handful of pieces from my first two collections.

How did I come to write it? I'm a parent—enough said. The idea was stolen from my wife, who realized long before me that the use of 'yes' and 'no' was the most energy-efficient way to converse with demanding children, and wondered why *all* conversations could not be handled, or deflected, with monosyllables.

Ironically, after I had written the piece our children themselves adopted the List, and began answering all *our* questions with terse numbers.

After it appeared in my second collection of stories, *Zooing*, I received many letters from readers about it—more letters than I have received about anything else I have written, in prose at any rate. It obviously struck a chord. In my wildest dreams I began to imagine that I had started something Big, something Significant—especially when Angus and Robertson paid me an advance to publish the list alone, as a . . . well, *list*, to be taped to fridges.

The release was planned for Mother's Day, 1987, but—alas—nothing has been heard since.

Peter Goldsworthy

THE LIST OF ALL POSSIBLE ANSWERS

1

Again the child plucked at his mother's sleeve.

'Why do onions make my eyes water?' he demanded to know. 'Why?'

She shook her arm free and continued chopping the slippery, soapish segments, trying to ignore him. But there was to be no escape.

'Mummy, Mummy—why do . . .'

At precisely that moment the idea came to her.

'Three,' she said.

'Three?'

'Three,' she repeated. 'The answer to your question is three.'

Silence descended while the child puzzled at this.

'What's three mean?' he shortly came out with.

'One of Mummy's little jokes,' his father, slicing tomatoes at the other end of the bench, intervened. '*Another* of Mummy's little jokes.'

He was not amused. But how else was she to cope? Battling away in a classroom full of Year Fives all day, then home to this. A second classroom, she was beginning to think it. No, worse: a second *front*.

'The head is like a pressure-cooker,' she began to explain, speaking in the direction of her son, but actually through him to his father. 'It can only hold so much.'

She paused, averted her face from the onions momentarily, screwed up her eyes, then continued: 'If a joke doesn't emerge from the mouth, steam will shoot out the ears . . .'

'Or worse,' her husband added—also talking through the medium of their child. 'Or worse.'

'I still don't get it,' the boy said. 'What's number three?'

'Number three,' she told him. 'On the list.'

'What list?'

'I'll show you after dinner.'

'What's for dinner?'

She bit her tongue. These endless chains of question, response—once begun there was no ending them. From the moment she collected the child from creche to the moment he finally succumbed to sleep some hours later—his chatter ceasing suddenly, his neck muscles giving out, head plopping softly onto the pillow mid-sentence—he never stopped plucking sleeves, turning up that insistent face, repeating his endless interrogations. *Why, Mummy? Why? Why?*

'The list,' he remembered as he helped the two of them clear the table after dinner. 'The list! The list!'

'Yes, the list,' his father echoed, teasing her. 'Show us the list, Mummy!'

She retreated into the study, and tucked a sheet of quarto into the typewriter. The list took some time—it was little more than an idea, after all. And as for her typing—search and destroy, her husband liked to mock it.

The List of All Possible Answers, she typed across the head of the page, patiently seeking out each individual key, and destroying. That accomplished, she began to move down in a vertical column.

#1. No.

#2. Maybe.

#3 . . .

Here she paused. Three? She was tired, the thoughts refused to flow . . . *Because*, she finally improvised, then removed her handiwork from the carriage and returned to the kitchen. As she taped the list to the fridge door, her husband peered over her shoulder.

'Because?' he wondered. 'What kind of answer is that? Because what?'

'Because nothing,' she said. 'Just because.'

'Sounds like a cop-out to me.'

'It's not a definitive list,' she defended herself. 'Feel free to add to it.'

He opened the fridge door, and unzipped a can of beer.

'Because that's the way God made it?' he suggested, sipping.

She laughed out loud: 'Who was accusing whom of a cop-out?'

She pulled open a kitchen drawer, scrabbled among the odds and ends, and emerged with a pen. *Because that's the way things are*, she added to the list, landing the full stop with a definitive thud.

'It's still a cop-out,' he insisted. He opened the fridge door and reached inside again. 'You want a beer?'

'Four,' she said.

'You want *four* beers?'

'The answer to your question is number four.'

He looked at the list.

'I don't see any number four.'

'Ask me tomorrow,' she yawned. 'I'm going to bed.'

2

She watched with interest as he fetched his first can from the fridge the next evening after work.

#4, he paused to read as he opened the door. *Ask me again tomorrow.*

'Your list of all answers,' he told her, 'is beginning to look like a list of all evasions.'

'Congratulations,' she said. 'You just caught on.'

The list grew quite quickly in the days that followed. *#5.— What do* you *think?*—was pencilled in the following night, and *#6.—Because I said so*—added the night after that. Towards the end of the week, however, the rate of increase seemed to slow. After *#7.—You're too young to understand*—there were no further additions for several days.

'Finished, have we?' her husband, who had been pretending

to ignore it all, couldn't prevent himself asking. 'Finished our little joke?'

'No,' she said.

'How many more?'

She paused, considering.

'A finite number,' she guessed. 'Maybe ten. Yes, ten should just about cover everything.'

But there were loopholes still, she discovered.

'What's finite mean, Mummy?'

#8, she wrote. *Look it up in the Britannica.*

'What's the Britannica, Mummy?'

She scanned the seven preceding entries without reward.

'The answer to that could be nine,' her husband intervened—aid from an unexpected quarter.

'Nine?' the child wondered.

'Ask Mummy when she's in a better mood,' he smiled. 'Ask Mummy when she's learnt a little patience.'

He took a red felt-tip pen from the drawer and added the words in inch-high letters at the bottom of the list. *#9. ASK MUMMY WHEN SHE'S IN A BETTER MOOD.*

'Enough is enough,' he said. 'The joke has gone too far.'

3

The blank façade of the fridge struck him the moment he entered the kitchen the following night. Once again, she was watching carefully.

'Where's the list?' he asked.

'Where's the list?' their child, trotting behind, echoed.

'You were right,' she said. 'The joke had gone too far.'

Her husband smiled, but the child's lower lip began to tremble.

'I want my list,' he stammered. 'I want my answer list.'

'The list has gone,' his father bent to tell him. 'It was a silly list.'

But the child would not be comforted.

'No,' he shouted, twisting away. 'No! I want my list.'

As he ran from the room, his mother was already sifting through the kitchen waste-basket. She found the crumpled sheet, smoothed it between hand and bench, and began to tape it back onto the fridge.

'Please,' her husband said. 'No.'

'Yes,' she insisted.

'How much longer?'

'I don't know,' she admitted. 'I honestly don't know.'

He took a pen from his pocket.

#10, he wrote. *I don't know. I honestly don't know.*

He ruled a thick line across the page beneath his words. If nothing else, there would—surely—be no need for further entries.

THE BODYSURFERS

Robert Drewe

AUTHOR'S NOTE

I have chosen 'The Bodysurfers', the story that anchors my story collection of the same name, for several reasons, some bound up in the same sort of nostalgia for harmony, the spiritual and physical search, that the characters are experiencing. There is another reason: the story, and the book, have kept my head above water for the past five years.

Robert Drewe

THE BODYSURFERS

The murders took the gloss off it. Crossing over the Hawkesbury, David began thinking of them, anticipating the bridge over Mooney Mooney Creek they would soon cross, the picnic area below where, he had read in the papers, the lovers had apparently been forced from their car two nights before, ordered to strip and then struck and run over repeatedly by the murderer's car. When David finally drove over the bridge and the station wagon rounded the bend past the murder site, he nudged Lydia and pointed it out but said nothing because of the younger kids. He thought he could see deep savage skid marks in the gravel.

They were heading this Friday evening for the weekend shack David had just bought at Pearl Beach; he, Lydia, and his children Paul, Helena and Tim. Having turned over the house at Mosman to his wife since their separation, David now lived nearer town in a flat with a green view of Cooper Park. He missed the water in his windows, however, the dependable harbour glimpses framed by the voluptuous pink branches of his own plump gum tree, as well as the early morning bird calls, the barbecue, the irresistible nationalistic combination of bush and water, so he decided that at last he would buy a weekend shack on the coast.

'I see no reason why we can't get what we want,' he had remarked to Lydia, his new lover, as romantic in these matters as himself. He knew exactly what he was looking for. It must be the genuine article. It had to put the city at a respectable distance but be close enough for comfortable weekend commuting. However, locale was only part of it. Anyone of his generation would know what he wanted. No transplanted bourgeois surburban brick-and-tile villa would do. The spirit of the shack had to be right, its character set preferably somewhere in the 1950s. It would need a properly casual, even run-down, beach air. It should have a verandah to sleep weekend guests, a working septic system, an open fireplace and somewhere to hang a dartboard. A glimpse at least of the Pacific through the trees was mandatory.

In his head David carried a clear picture of weekends in his shack. For a start there would be no television. He and Lydia would surf and make love in the afternoon to Rolling Stones tapes and read best-sellers and play Scrabble. On the verandah he and his children would strengthen bonds with quoits and table-tennis. Under his gum trees friends would drink in their swimming costumes and eat grilled fish caught at dawn.

On a sunny spring day with a high swell running from the ocean straight into Broken Bay he had eventually found the shack he wanted on the central coast at Pearl Beach. It was built of weatherboard and fibro-cement, painted the colour of pale clay, and it settled on the hillside sheltered from the southerly wind and facing north along the beach. Its ceiling contained a possum's nest or two, and three mature gums, and a jacaranda in bloom filtered the gleam off the sea. The Recession was forcing the owners, a writer and her husband, to rapidly consolidate their assets and their price was reasonable. Apologetically they pointed out an old ceiling stain of possum urine. David laughed. He liked their honesty about the possum pee, the view of the surf from the wooden balcony and the lizards warming on the railing, and, in his new mood of independence and self-assertion, made them an offer. The nostalgic boom of waves had punctuated their negotiations.

An anticipatory air had overlain this weekend. David was looking forward to showing the shack to the children. This was also their first meeting with Lydia and he hoped the shack would break the ice. Along the Newcastle Expressway things looked optimistic. They sang along with the radio and Helena chattered happily to Lydia. Just beyond the Gosford exit warm spring whiffs of eucalypt pollen and the fecund muddy combustion of subtropical undergrowth suddenly filled the car with the scents of holidays.

'Not long to summer,' he pronounced.

'That's a funny name,' Helena said, pointing. 'Mooney Mooney Creek.'

'Mooney Mooney loony,' Tim burbled.

The police hadn't caught the killer, or killers, and according to the news were completely mystified. Both victims had been married to other people, but the spouses had been unaware of the affair and were not under suspicion. *Thrill Killing?* the tabloids wondered. The lovers, both in their thirties, had driven all the way from Sydney's western suburbs for their tryst by the creek. Oyster farmers on the Hawkesbury had seen their car burning at 5.00 a.m. Later people remembered hearing the high-pitched revving of an engine and perhaps some human cries.

'I hope there's some good surf,' Paul said. His board was strapped to the roof-rack. As usual lately he was alternately amiable and taciturn, in the sixteen-year-old fashion, but did not give the impression as he often did that this was a duty weekend.

Lydia was anxious to please and turned back to smile at him, 'I'm sure there will be.'

It was dark when they reached Pearl Beach. For five minutes David fumbled about in the oleander and hibiscus bushes which scraped against the walls, searching for the fuse box where the old owners had left the key. As he stamped around the periphery lighting matches something rustled in a tree above him and a gumnut dropped with a clatter on the tin roof and rolled into the guttering. Possum, he told himself. A mosquito landed noisily on his cheek. From the black shrubbery Helena gave one of the high indignant screams she had affected since her parents separated. Lately she needed soothing and coddling for every slight and injury, real and imaginary. Meanwhile each cry and sulk, no matter how exaggerated, struck him with a hopelessness, produced a hollow despair in him which made him want to simultaneously embrace and shake her and yell, 'I'm sorry my darling, I love you, and my wounds sting too.'

He found the fuse box and the key and opened the front door. Helena burst inside, her sandals clopping on the wooden floor, crying, 'Paul punched me on the arm!'

'Jesus!' Paul said, sidling in with his sleeping bag. 'I just brushed past her. I wouldn't touch her bloody poxy arm.'

'Easy, you two,' their father said.

Lydia struggled in with a carton of groceries. 'Isn't it cute?' she announced.

'Have you seen it already?' Helena asked suspiciously. 'When did you see it?'

Some mosquitoes had followed them inside and soon had Helena whining. Lydia lit a mosquito-coil and hunted up a tube of Stop-Itch. The previous owners had left them a bottle of Chablis in the fridge with a note saying 'Welcome to Marsupial Manor!' David uncorked it immediately and they swigged wine from coffee mugs while he unloaded the car and they settled in.

'What a terrific gesture,' Lydia said.

Making his final trip from the car carrying the Scrabble set, Lydia's handbag and Helena's pillow shaped like a rhinoceros, David saw the others' faces pass across the bright uncurtained windows and he stopped on the path, surprised at how earnest they all appeared, even the younger children, how foreign and intense in their tasks. They were all frowning. He could hear their feet thudding on the bare boards. He heard a low murmur from Paul and then Lydia's face over the sink lit up and she gave a laugh. She put a paper bag on her head like a chef's cap. Tim giggled.

David went inside to join them. From the balcony the night sea was as slick and black as grease in the new-moon light, and fruit bats flapped against the stars.

In the middle of the night David awoke and instantly regretted the cute rusticity of the lavatory and its position some ten metres outside in the bushes. A breezy brick cubicle, it had no electricity and a reasonable prospect of spiders in the darkness. He would have to set something up with extension cords. He took a couple of steps out the back door and pissed into the hibiscus. Back in bed, he was unable to sleep again; these nights if he woke up he always had trouble falling back to sleep. Anxieties churned in his mind until exhaustion eventually took over at dawn.

Funny, the more numerous and wilder his wakeful thoughts, the less imaginative his dreams. Since the breakup his dreams had been uniformly mundane—of buying a loaf of Vogel's sandwich bread, catching the 387 bus into town, reading the television guide—sexless, fact-filled visions in which each action or transaction was conducted with the utmost solemnity and realism. Perhaps, he told himself, they were subliminal exhortations to live a moderate, conservative life. Whatever, they were so boring and accurate in their triviality that he allowed his bladder to wake him.

And then, back in bed, the sleepless turmoil began.

Why hadn't the lovers run away? His heart pounded in sympathy. The killers must have had a weapon to force them out of their car, to make them remove their clothes, to wound or threaten them sufficiently that they didn't try to escape. Perhaps they did try. Were they chased all over the picnic area?

Was she raped? He presumed so but the papers didn't say. Did their bodies have bullet holes? No idea. Were the bodies too flattened and battered to tell? Considering these horrors, David rolled over on the doughy mattress, his hip bumping against Lydia's warm bottom with a sudden heat and pressure that surprised them both. She murmured in her sleep and turned over.

Their clothes had been found lying unburned a distance from the gutted car, so they'd been dressed when first harassed, not nakedly fornicating such as to inflame the crazy passions of murdering yokels. The killers were likely from these parts. Maybe he had stood alongside them tonight in the hotel bottle shop buying his Dimple Haig. Sandy-haired yobbos with a big gas guzzler throbbing in the car park. He had visions of headlights bearing down on Lydia and him, of them being mesmerized like possums struck by the beam of a torch.

Thump, brake and reverse, wheels spinning crazily in the gravel. Skin and hair on the bumpers.

He told himself the shack was meant to be an antidote to all this.

Amazingly on cue, screams, grunts and thuddings, eerie gurgles and whispers erupted just outside the bedroom window. His scalp prickled, Lydia sat up in terror.

'Just a possum fight,' he calmed her, his chest pounding. He got out of bed again and made them cups of warm milk. Like children they whispered in the foreign room. Her upper lip corners wore a small milky moustache. Stroking each other with an urgent solicitude, they made love aware of daily jeopardy and thin walls.

Father and daughter rose first and early on Saturday morning, murmuring and tiptoeing conspiratorially and taking their orange juice out onto the balcony. A flock of parrots exploded from one of their gum trees. The sun rising out of the Pacific slanted obliquely over their domain and brought a new arrangement of parallel shimmers to the surface of the water below. Instantly David saw he had made one mistake—there was no surf and there would rarely be. Freak conditions had no doubt prevailed the day he inspected the shack, a strange pure easterly perhaps instead of the usual southerly or nor'easter or even westerly. Why hadn't it occurred to him that Box Head would block the nor'easters, Lion Island the southerlies? It didn't matter that their beach faced the open Pacific; there would be no surfing; they would have to drive several kilometres north to swim in the surf. His personal stretch of sea was quiescent, bland as bathwater, nice for fishing, sailboarding and swimming up and down. He felt vaguely sick.

As a boy his happiness had been bound up in the ocean, the regular rising and curling of waves over sandbanks and reefs, the baking sun, the cronies lounging against the promenade, the bunches of girls gossiping and flirting on the sand, the violent contrasting physical pleasures of bodysurfing. In his twenties and early thirties he had still never tired of watching the surf. Like flames it had the capacity to induce a calming trance. It held in store everything from a happy domestic weekend, healthy dawn exercise, to a snappy hangover cure. But over the past few years, through work and travel and the particular, strangely inevitable manner in which his marriage had frayed, then unravelled, he'd lost the habit of those peculiarly satiating Australian days.

He'd liked sharing them and Angela had lost interest; or perhaps among their other discarded mutual interests they had just forgotten them.

Lydia was a bodysurfer.

Lydia had become a keen bodysurfer since knowing him. She had a history as an initiator of extreme physical incidents, as an experimenter and a changer of circumstances. She had already tried abseiling, hang-gliding, show-jumping, scuba-diving and their sexual counterparts. From his watchful position ten years further along the track he could detect in her a vulnerability to danger and a risky wilfulness with the potential to carry her, and others, over the edge. But they matched each other perfectly, blended harmoniously, gripped and floated. In the surf her recklessness made him laugh, the way she launched herself into definite dumpers, surfacing shakily in the foam with a breast out of her bathers, her hair in her eyes and a fist raised in mock victory.

Sitting yawning with his ten-year-old daughter in the quiet early sunlight he tried to pin down the exact sensation of those old ocean days. It was a combination of the exhilarating charge of the surf, the plunge on a wave, the currents pummelling and streaming along the body, the skin stretched salty and taut across the shoulders, the pungent sweetness of suntan oil, the sensual anticipation of future summer days and nights. Certainly he had never been as happy since. Therefore he could hardly be blamed for trying for that feeling again—the harmony and boundless optimism. And he had got it only half right.

Helena snuggled up to him in their warm patch in the treetops. Birds squabbled around them but they seemed the only humans awake anywhere. The world of sea and bush was comatose. He thought of Lydia buried in the valley of the saggy double bed; Paul in his sleeping bag, mouth open, hair awry; Tim flushed and cupid-lipped on the night-and-day. And Angela in her shared Mosman bed under the Amish hand-sewn quilt he had bought her in Pennsylvania. In white stitching the old Amish lady had signed her quilt 'Mrs B. Yoder'. They didn't believe in cosmetics, cars or radios but Mrs Yoder took American Express. He did not want Helena and Timmy snuggling under the quilt for early morning cuddles with the occupants. He did not want the quilt *involved*.

Kissing the crown of Helena's head, he inhaled her parting. 'Want a swim before breakfast, my sweet?' he asked.

She was delighted. 'A secret swim,' he told her. Somehow he wanted to bind her in a conspiracy. He wanted to serve her up private soothing information about their present and future. Holding hands they padded barefoot down the road to the beach. Cool clay squashed under their toes as the sun began to slant over their path. Crows and currawongs fluttered clumsily in the bushes. Under the cliff face the sea baths were like glass. Helena was the bolder. Without hesitating she ran to the deep end and dived in. The coldness shocked him when he joined her; he had to swim three lengths of the pool before his circulation adjusted to the temperature. His daughter's body gave no hint of the cold. She had been having swimming coaching and he was surprised at her new neat prowess, the precise arm strokes slicing into the pool, the efficient three-stroke breathing. When they climbed out she flicked water at him, giggling coquettishly, wiggling her chubby backside and smoothing back her wet hair in parody of a hundred women in shampoo commercials. He noticed her breasts were just starting to grow and she flapped her hands over them while she jigged about. It jolted him that she would cease being a child. It was only the other day she'd been born, a month overdue, in the end chemically induced. She hadn't wanted to join the world then. If only he could warn her, 'Stop now while there's still time. You don't want to get into this can of worms.'

As they left the beach he was still phrasing what he wanted to say to her, at the same time hoping that his message was somehow being telepathically understood, absorbed through the pores.

Finally he said, 'I love you, my sweet,' brushing sand from his feet.

'Me too,' she said. 'Daddy, can I play the Space Invaders?'

At the beach store she played a video game while he bought milk and the papers. The picnic ground murders were still page one of the local paper. Tests were proceeding on the woman's body to determine whether she had been 'assaulted' prior to her death. The extent of the 'injuries' made this difficult. Police asked citizens to immediately report any vehicle with suspicious dents or bloodstains.

Hand in hand they walked back to the shack. 'Can I have my ears pierced, Daddy?' she asked.

'Perhaps when you're older. It doesn't look nice on little girls.'

She was still whining as they walked inside. 'I don't want to hear any more about it,' he said.

Their mid-morning procession to the beach gave the impression of a cartoon jungle safari. Balancing his surfboard on his head, Paul amiably led the single file, followed by a talkative Helena with her flippers and swimming goggles, Lydia carrying her big bag of beach paraphernalia—towels, suntan cream, insect repellent, baby oil and magazines; Tim, the youngest, travelling light and scot-free as usual, dragging a stick in the clay, and David, bringing the Esky of sandwiches and drinks. They had decided on a picnic lunch. 'Bonga, bonga,' boomed the father, imitating native drums. 'Bonga, bonga,' repeated Helena and Tim all the way down to the sand.

Now the beach was warm, and, in its most populated section near the baths, relatively noisy. Children splashed in the baths and shrieked in the shallows. Small wavelets plopped on the shore. Paul had already observed from the balcony the sorry state of the waves but had perversely brought his board anyway, as if to indicate to this soft elderly crowd that this was by no means his element. They dropped their things on the sand and the younger children raced into the water. With a superior grin at the sea Paul flopped down in the sand. 'Top waves, Dad.'

'Give us a break,' his father said, collapsing too.

Next to him Lydia was arranging her towel on a level patch of sand, ironing away lumps and wrinkles and placing her beach appurtenances within reach. Then she removed her bikini top and, her breasts quivering, the nipples wide and brown in the sun, she sat down. Reaching for the suntan cream from her bag, she rubbed some briskly into her breasts with a studious circular motion, paying attention to the nipples. More cream was squeezed onto the stomach and legs, even the tops of the feet.

David was slightly unnerved, as usual, by the act of public revelation (there always seemed to be some sort of statement underlying their sudden exposure among other people), but he had never realized how much her naked breasts actually *moved*. They had three definite motions—they were simultaneously bouncing, swinging and shivering. From the prim, diligent way she pursed her lips while she applied the cream she seemed to be either terribly solicitous of them or disapproving of their independent lives.

David avoided looking at them too openly. Ogling was out of the question. He did, however, glance surreptitiously at his elder son, but Paul, though hardly able to miss them, was staring coolly seawards.

Completing this display, still with a frown of concentration, Lydia flicked a grain of sand from one glistening aureole, spread more cream deftly over her face, and then lay back on her towel with a sigh of contentment. 'I wonder what the poor people are doing,' she said.

I wonder if women know what they're doing, David wondered. How did those tits which had been used to sexually tempt him at 3.00 a.m. suddenly at 11.30 become as neutral as elbows? Who's kidding whom? He was too far gone at thirty-eight, especially after the past couple of years, to read the fine print any more, much less try to keep up with the constant changes in the rules. They were amazing, leave it at that. He was awestruck by the grey areas, the skating-over, the 180-degree turns that women made these days. The breakup and his new status, or

277

lack of status, had made him hypersensitive to the female dichotomies—fashion versus politics, the desperate clash between ideals and glands—and their magical sleight of hand which not only hid it all and kept the audience clapping but left you with a coin up your nose or an egg in your ear.

Lying back under the sun he had to smile at the way Lydia pretended she had no exhibitionist's flair, that she didn't love to flaunt what she had, come on strong. He remembered the actual broad-daylight fuck precipitated by those exposed breasts not long ago on Scarborough Beach down south during their search for the perfect shack. They were sunbaking like this after a surf. A nipple brushed his arm accidentally, then insistently. Then began a sly stroking of his thigh, feathery touches over his groin. The sun, the ocean, the whole salty, teasing, teenage delight of it all! They'd got up without a word and strolled determinedly to the end of the beach and, behind a low cairn of rocks barely higher than their horizontal bodies, momentarily hidden from at least fifty beach fishermen, surfers and swimmers, had a most satisfying quickie in the sand.

Their single-mindedness had surprised and amused him later. 'I thought that might work,' she'd said, grinning as they sauntered back to their belongings. 'Was that like your adolescent days? I must say you were very neat—not a drop of sand in me.'

Tim and Helena ran up from the shore, sandy and squabbling.

'He's using bottom words again,' Helena complained. 'He's saying poo and bum and vagina all the time and he keeps throwing sand.'

'I didn't say vagina, I said Virginia.'

'You said vagina!' Abruptly she began to cry, turning away from them and sobbing despairingly.

'I didn't,' Tim screamed. 'You're a liar!' Overcome with rage and emotion, he fell on the sand and kicked and threshed, his yells turning to shrill cries as he kicked sand in his eyes.

'My God!' shouted David, jumping to his feet. 'What's got into you both? Do you want a hiding?'

'Shee-it,' Paul said. 'He does that all the time lately. What that kid needs is some discipline. Come here, stupid, and I'll get the sand out.'

Lydia had her arms round Helena. 'No one will play with us,' Helena sobbed. 'It's boring here.'

Lydia said, 'I feel like a swim. Let's go.'

The father sank back on the sand. Leaning back on his elbows, breathing deeply, he watched the trio race each other down to the water, Tim stopping sharply at the edge, hanging back and then wading in gingerly, the others plunging in recklessly. Lydia and Helena surfaced and pushed back their hair and jumped and splashed like any ten-year-olds. They shared unselfconsciousness; if anything Lydia seemed the wilder and giddier, standing on her hands, somersaulting and gambolling, and all the time her breasts swung and fluttered in the sun and water.

Tim was beginning to grizzle at being excluded. Sighing loudly, Paul sauntered down to him, hoisted him up in his arms and strode into the water, joining the splashing females. Paul tossed his little brother around like a beach-ball while Tim shrieked with excitement.

Squinting against the glare, David was relieved and gladdened to see his children and Lydia frolicking together in the sea. It wasn't a familiar scene from his marriage, more like one from his own early childhood, a link to it, a summer holiday at the seaside, a rare time when adults dropped their guard and pretensions and acted the goat. He was aware of the sting of the sun on his neck and this too made him happy; the clean buff-coloured sand, the fringe of gum trees, the dusty blue labiate hills, the turquoise vista of the Pacific all uplifed him. Buoyant, he looked over his shoulder and through the jacaranda picked out the balcony of the shack where his and Helena's red and blue towels were drying on the railing. A warm haze gave the shack's roof an uncertain wavy outline, and parrots still screeched in his trees.

Oddly drawn to this setting, attracted to it but, perhaps because of its newness, detached from it, he half-expected to see his children, Lydia, even himself, stroll out onto the balcony and wave a jaunty towel. But they were playing in the sea. He was lounging on the sand. Paul was lifting Tim on his shoulders. Paul's tanned back and shoulder muscles were suddenly sharply defined by the weight, and patterns of sinews moved in his arms and shoulders. Among the shrill giggles his deeper laughter rang out. Lydia was similarly hoisting Helena onto her shoulders—with difficulty—and the action threw back her shoulders and pushed out her chest and almost collapsed her in splashes and giggles.

David watched the couples face each other—grinning, dripping knights on horseback—and heard the yells of encouragement, the snorts and laughter, and saw the infection of excitability strike them. He sat in the sun with a cold constriction in his throat as the riders wrestled and the horses alternately collided and retreated, striking and sliding against each other in the shallows, softness against muscle.

If David could have spoken satisfactorily to Lydia next morning he might have described his dream that night thus:

It began with me driving an Avis car fast and north through scrubby country on a hot, dry day. The highway was clear, the air-conditioning cool, and on the radio old favourites kept my fingers tapping on the wheel. Bugs smeared themselves on the windscreen, but I obliterated them with automatic spray and wipers, the wipers stroking as elegantly as conductors' batons. The car's tyres made a satisfying drumming sound on the tarred joins in the highway paving, a repetitive noise of power and resolve. All this registered on me strongly—the sense of purpose was heightened because the car had been freshly cleaned and the hygienic vinyl scent of the upholstery was high in my head.

I drove for a time, for what seemed like an hour, and from the changing vegetation—the trees were becoming even more stunted and sparse, the wild oats and veldt grass fringing the highway ever dryer and barely covering the sandy ground—I gathered that I was nearing the coast. An arrowed sign said *Aurora—10 km* and I followed it, turning left off the highway.

A wind sprang up as the car left the protection of the hills and it whipped sand drifts across the road. The road cut through sand dunes spread patchily with pigface and tumbleweeds and led obliquely to the sea—every now and then I saw a slice of blue between the white dunes before it disappeared again. Another, bigger sign said *Aurora—5 km* below a logotype of a leaping dolphin against the sun, and I followed it, the car planing occasionally through the sand drifts.

Soon I came to an indication of habitation: a gold dome-shaped building, a sort of civic centre, flying a flag carrying the dolphin-and-sun logo. Before its entrance was a statue carved out of limestone, apparently of King Neptune. Surrounding the gold dome was a flat grassy field, which was kept green and free of the sand drifts, I presumed, from the parallel lines of sprinklers and the presence of five or six heavy rollers, only with great municipal perseverance. As I pulled up two children came over one of the adjacent dunes and slid down it on sleds until they came to rest on the grass. I called out to them, wanting to ask further directions, but they grabbed up their sleds and climbed back up the dune as fast as they could struggle in the sand. I tried the gold building next. From a sharp cloudless sky the sun struck its gleaming surface with such a dazzling glare it was impossible to approach it without squinting. Anyway, the front doors were closed—presumably it was some sort of public holiday here—and the only other sign of life was a nervously hissing bobtail goanna which displayed its blue tongue at me from a clump of pigface by the entrance. A thin pungent smell of decaying seaweed was carried to me on the breeze.

The road circled the gold building and continued, so I drove on, still travelling slantingly towards the ocean, and around the next sandhill I saw the first rotary clothes hoist sticking up in the dunes like a lone palm in the desert, and then more of them, some skeletal, others blooming with washing, and, behind them, facing the sea, a scattering of suburban houses straight from the middle-class outskirts of any western city in the world. In this moonscape the range of architectural styles was unusually extreme, even impressive, in its randomness and unfittingness to the arid environment and climate: mock-Tudor nestled hard up against Mediterranean villa, then came three or four bleak, windswept blocks dotted with FOR SALE signs, a Cape Cod or two, some ranch-modern experiments and an Australian-Romanesque edifice. They did, however, have some features in common: two shiny cars and a cabin cruiser on a trailer sat in every driveway. A sprinkler whirred in each front garden; there were no fences but walls had been cleverly erected to shield the grass and the cars from the sea breeze. The backyards had no shelter and, while the sprinklers whirred in the front, the clothes hoists, with a steady grating hum, spun like catherine wheels in the wind. It was easy to see which way it blew—the clothes hoists all leaned like cypresses from the sou'westerly.

Suddenly the sledding children returned: they were Max and Paul. This was no surprise, the appearance together of my brother and my son, both now the same age—about eight or nine—and similarly skinny, brown-skinned and with their freckled and peeling noses and cheeks coated in zinc cream.

'In there, you nong,' Max said, pointing out a pink-brick home with a 1950s skillion roof. Max was right in that it *was* my mother who came to the door in a Liberty print brunch coat over a swimming costume, gave me an amiable kiss on the cheek and led me inside.

I know I must have seemed exasperated. 'God, I've been searching for ages,' I complained. I was actually immensely relieved. Relief flooded over me and intervening time was abruptly concertinaed into days, hours. 'You made it a bit difficult.'

My mother smiled, a little embarrassed, holding her mouth in a constrained way, like the time she had her teeth capped. 'I know, Davey. It took me a while to make adjustments.' There seemed some strain to the left side of her face, a tautness in the skin that she was shy about. Otherwise she looked very well, and I said so.

'Getting there,' she smiled. 'The dolphins keep me young.'

'They would,' I agreed. 'What do you hear from Dad?'

'Ask him yourself,' she said. 'Let's go down to the boatel.'

We drove off down the road, Amphitrite Avenue, I noticed, with me asking inane questions about her new Volvo—was she happy with the safety features, et cetera?—and presently she indicated another limestone statue of King Neptune, with trident, this one about thirty feet high, rising out of the dunes.

'I like it,' she declared firmly. 'Rex thinks it's vulgar, but I like it. The boatel's near here, in Poseidon Place.'

Was this a delicate situation? Separate living quarters? I kept my questions to myself, however, as we drove up to the Triton Boatel, a dun-coloured limestone structure built right on the edge of the ocean like a Moorish fort. Radiating out from it was a long limestone breakwater sheltering hundreds of pleasure craft, their stays and moorings rattling and tinkling in the wind—yachts, launches and power boats of all sizes and varieties, even a Chinese junk—though their owners, or any people at all, were not to be seen.

We sauntered along a sort of fake gangplank into the boatel lobby, Mum tripping very brightly through the foyer, I thought. She had discarded her brunch coat and looked very tanned and fit in her green Lastex swimsuit, just like the old Jantzen girl trademark.

Dad was behind the counter in his neat summer seersucker. He waved off my enthusiastic greeting, smiling apologetically. 'It's the off-season,' he said. 'We're still settling in, David. The last chap ran the place down. An Iraqi or something.'

'It's very presentable,' I told him. He looked a bit fidgety, though happy enough.

'The boatel business has got to expand,' he asserted stoutly. 'I couldn't wait to get here, I can tell you. Best decision I ever made, running my own show.'

'It's certainly an interesting proposition, Dad.' For some reason he was a little skittish in my company.

'All units right on the ocean, waterbeds in every room, colour TV, fully equipped kitchen, mid-week linen change where applicable. It's got to go like a bomb.'

We left Dad adjusting his Diners Club brochures in their little display stand. My mother was anxious to show me over the marine park. 'Don't worry about him,' she said. 'He's really as keen as I am about the whole Aurora concept.'

It was surprisingly not beyond my comprehension to learn that my mother was leading a new life as a vivacious dolphin communicator. She certainly looked the part as she proudly swept me in to the Aurora Marine Park, the sun catching the blonde streaks in her hair and highlighting her brown, slender limbs. She tossed a silver whistle briskly from hand to hand.

'Activity. Activity-plus is the message humming through Aurora,' she said.

What was new to me was my parents' sudden boundless punchy optimism. I felt slack and middle-aged by comparison; pale, short of wind.

Mum knifed into the pool then, and surfaced balanced on the backs of two dolphins, smiling fit for television. Her charges were just as energetic, jumping and squeaking and snorting through those holes in their heads. She had names for them, unapt modern children's names like Jasmine and Trent and Jason and Bree, and conducted some sort of affectionate dialogue using her whistle while they squirmed self-congratulatingly out of the water and bumped up a ramp towards us like sleek blow-up toys, their grey tongues waggling disgustingly at her.

'Do you speak dolphin, David?' she asked me out of the side of her mouth.

'No, I never learned.'

'I'm particularly fascinated in people exploring the intricacies of the dolphin language,' she went on. 'It's taught in the school here, you know.' She gestured vaguely. 'Humans learn it too.' And then she began speaking warmly to Bree, Trent and company in fractured schoolgirl French. They replied similarly, their beaks actually quite well formed for the nasalities and their accents rather better than my mother's. Fishy vowels hung in the air.

'Think you could hack it here?' Mum asked me suddenly, an arm each around Jason and Trent. '*Je t'aime*,' she murmured to Jason, unnecessarily I thought, raking her inch-long red nails down his tongue. He crooned appreciatively.

'I don't know,' I said. Her jargon jolted, also her recently acquired fondness for animals. She didn't even allow us to have a dog.

'You could be an aquarist,' she suggested, 'helping Damian with the makos and hammerheads.'

'What about Dad at the boatel?'

'If you prefer.' *Allez*! she exclaimed suddenly and blew a blast on her whistle. The dolphins bounced back into the pool. 'You know something?' my mother said to me conversationally, and the sunlight on the sheen of her swimsuit was so glaring it hurt my eyes, 'it may be perpetual summer here but I'm against adultery.'

'Who isn't, Mum?' I said.

'So put that in your pipe and smoke it,' she said.

In the Sunday papers there was nothing about the picnic ground murders. David thought it looked as if the police had put the case in their too-hard basket. He spent most of the day reading alone while the others swam or played Scrabble or, in the children's case, the video games at the store. Mid-afternoon he got them packed up and moving early, he said, to avoid the traffic back to the city. Driving fast to get home, and in deep thought, he crossed Mooney Mooney Creek without noticing.

THE HAIR AND THE TEETH

Carmel Bird

AUTHOR'S NOTE

I have a great affection for this story.

One night, a long time ago, I went for a walk in Paris. I came to the lighted window of a shop that sold antique toys. In the window was a very small wax doll. The next day I returned to the shop and bought the doll which I brought back to Melbourne. The doll lived in a drawer where I kept as well some pieces of antique jewellery and such things as my daughter's first tooth and a lock of her baby hair.

When the contents of the drawer were stolen, I lost the tooth and the hair and the doll, as well as the jewellery. However, at the time of the robbery I remembered the contents of the drawer as being only the jewellery. Some time later I remembered the tooth and the hair. Months later I remembered the wax doll.

My memory of the doll, with its associated images of the Paris night and the lighted window of the toyshop, moved me to begin writing an account of the robbery, to begin putting into words my feelings of great sadness, regret and powerlessness— my sense of having been violated.

I worked in this story with my memory of the robbery and of the events that followed it. I worked also with images as I set out to stir in the reader feelings of smallness and helplessness. Such feelings are mine when I am confronted, as I am daily confronted, by the harsh facts of living in a modern city.

I find the task of commenting on my story to be a difficult task because the story is its own comment. When I write of working with the images, I am aware that the images are related to each other in such a way that their juxtaposition will give rise to the response I desire. However, between the pattern of the images and the response of the reader lies a process, perhaps a mystery, that is the province of my fiction rather than of my thoughts about my fiction.

Carmel Bird

THE HAIR AND THE TEETH

People broke into the house one time when we were out at the supermarket. I suppose we were gone for about an hour and a half. The older children were at school, but I had the two little ones with me. They were only three and two when this happened, and so whatever we did, we did it fairly slowly.

You drive to the shopping centre and park the car in the basement. Then you take the children out of their car seats and get to the lift that takes you up to the level where the supermarket is. You have to get the children past the toyshop with the Humphrey Bear that will sing and dance if you put money in the slot, past the pink elephant ride, past the Coke machine. If you put the children in the trolley at the supermarket there won't be enough room for the stuff you have to get, but if you don't put them in the trolley you have to be prepared to move very, very slowly. So you move slowly. You get the music, the lights, the smell of disinfectant, and all the colours. Everything shimmers in the supermarket.

(I find the music and the lights and so on very tiring and I am inclined to be irritable.)

You fill up the trolley and stand in the queue. The queue moves very slowly. Every trolley in front of you has things in it that need to have their prices checked. The music shifts from the Ascot Gavotte to the Easter Parade, and you cannot be soothed. You want to just grab the children and leave the full trolley where it is. But you wait and you pay and you wheel the trolley to the lift, to the car. You pack the car, strap the children in, park the trolley, drive to the exit, pay to get out, drive home. It is dusk now. When you get home you put your key in the back door but the door won't open because the burglars (what is the correct word here? Is it robber, intruder, thief, crook, bugger?) the burglars have bolted it from the inside.

As soon as the door would not open, I knew pretty well what

had happened. I left the children and the shopping in the car and went round to the front of the house. The window was wide open and the curtain was flapping, in fact billowing out, like a miserable bride or a cheerful ghost. One of the children in the car had started to cry. I went back to the car, took two packets of biscuits from the shopping and gave a packet to each child.

'You can eat these,' I said, tearing open the packets and handing them to the children. The crying stopped and both children looked a bit surprised but they obeyed. I locked them in the car and went round to the front door. This door has no bolt. I opened it, put my hand in to turn on the light, and stood for a few moments listening and looking into the hallway. On the floor at the foot of the stairs was an earring, and halfway between the stairs and the front door was the lid of a jewellery box. The phone is on a table near the front door. I rang the police.

People tell me it takes a long time for the police to come to a break-in, break-ins being so common and policemen so rare, but these police seemed to be there by the time I had put down the phone. Possibly, because of the shock of the whole business, my sense of time was distorted. Anyway, the huge (it seemed to be huge) white car with blue writing and blue lights zoomed up the street and slid (really) in beside the kerb and two police, a man and a woman, jumped (true) out and were suddenly standing beside me. The first thing I thought about was how healthy they looked. They looked just very, very healthy. He was big and young and smiling and sweet. And she was little and young and smiling and sweet. They had hats. They looked very clean—in blue, sky blue and navy. They both smelt of nice soap.

They searched the house for hidden people while I got first the shopping then the children from the car. The children had finished the biscuits. I gave them some chips. By this time the ice-cream was beginning to melt and blood was dripping out of a plastic bag in which there was a chicken.

'Can you leave the kids with a neighbour while we get on with things?' asked the policeman. So I took them in next door. Luckily someone was home and the children were quite happy to stay there watching television.

We went all over the house, the police and I, finding evidence of what they said was the 'work of a real professional'. We sat at the kitchen table and made a list of what was missing.

I used to keep jewellery in the top left-hand drawer of a chest of drawers. They must have emptied the drawer onto the bedspread and then rolled up the bedspread and used it as a sack. I imagine two rat-like little men, real professionals, wearing masks, tiptoeing swiftly down the stairs, one with the sack over his shoulder, the other with an armful of leather coats. I start giving the policeman a list of things that have been taken: coral necklace, princess ring. He writes it all down carefully. The kitchen light seems to be too harsh, the paper the man is writing on too white. The clean strong police faces seem sympathetic but as helpless as the babies we have sent next door. I offer them biscuits and coffee but they say no. Jade ring, silver bracelet with lapis lazuli. They have stolen a basket of firewood. The police cannot explain this. Suddenly I remember that among the sentimental treasures in the drawer were the locks of hair and the baby teeth of the older children. Then my voice starts to waver and I think I am going to cry.

(I had wrapped the teeth in a piece of silk and put them in a tin from a machine in the Paris Metro. Snow was falling. The Metro was warm. I put the money in the machine and got an oval tin of lollies with a wreath of violets on the lid. The lollies inside the tin rattled. They were dusted with sugar.)

Will I tell the police about the teeth and hair? Will I say in my litany:

'Two tortoise-shell combs (Spanish), four ivory bangles (African), nine deciduous teeth (human), and two locks of human hair (golden)'?

They look at me kindly as I sit weeping at the kitchen table. I drink coffee and whisky. They keep writing. Periwinkle necklace, gipsy keeper (garnet).

I ask whether they think I will get any of the things back and they say that, in a case of this nature, it is unlikely we will recover any of the missing items.

I put in the insurance claim and a woman from the insurance company came to interview me. She had a briefcase under her arm and a shrewd look in her eye. She was a bit fat but graceful with a black dress and a fur jacket and beauty parlour make-up, hairdo and fingernails. She was wearing Chanel, and her shoes were Italian. She stood on the doormat with the blue sky behind her and she could have been an advertisement for something, probably wine or, now I come to think of it, insurance. Or funerals.

'Mrs Halliwell from Phoenix. I rang,' she said, and I took her into the sitting room. You couldn't discuss the basket of firewood and the jewellery in the bedspread with Mrs Halliwell in the kitchen. I offered her coffee but she didn't want it. The ordinary rules of hospitality do not apply to the police or to women from the insurance company. She had a typed list of all the things that were stolen. As she sat down, the sofa suddenly looked very shabby. A plastic fire-engine lay just near Mrs Halliwell's left foot.

'I will need more detailed descriptions of some of the items reported missing,' she said, looking up at me over her glasses. 'You will have to be more specific. A princess ring means nothing to me. What is a princess ring?' We came to the coral necklace which I said was made from round beads of coral, pale pink and smooth.

'Polished?' said Mrs Halliwell.

I said I supposed they were polished. 'Angel skin,' she wrote without speaking. Then she asked how long the necklace was, and when I told her she wrote, 'Opera length.' Satisfied, she then said aloud, 'Opera length polished angel skin,' and she almost smiled. 'Is there any other item you have omitted to report missing? This is your final opportunity to claim.' I tried to think of something, as if I needed to please her. Then I thought of saying half the things I had just told her were lies. Then I remembered the hair and the teeth, and all I said at last was no. She said we would have to put in an alarm system, arrange for security patrol, get security doors and windows, or else get a reliable watchdog. I asked her for the name of somebody who puts in security doors and windows, but she said I would have to look in the *Yellow Pages*. Then she said 'reliable watchdog' again as she tucked her briefcase under her arm. I showed her out.

'And a peephole and a security phone on the door,' she said as she walked away.

The next day a man came to measure the doors and windows for bars. He handed me his card at the door. On the card was a picture of a shark behind wire mesh.

'Jack McClaren,' he said, 'from Shark.' He looked around the garden and said, 'Nice large block you've got here. Surprising in this postal district.'

When he had finished measuring, and when we had discussed the quality of the optional one-way mesh and the need for the tri-safe locking system with the three-point deadlocking and anti-pick lock, he had a cup of coffee in the kitchen. We had some shortbread and a cigarette and I told him about the robbery. He said I was lucky and told me about people who had been completely cleaned out. 'Nothing left standing except the electric light. Lucky you weren't here when they came. Then they'd have done it with violence. There's a terrible lot of it these days. Armed robbery with violence. It's on the increase. I see all the statistics, of course.'

So then I told him about the hair and the teeth, and he said that was the worst.

'And the mongrels would just chuck those things away, you know. They'd just chuck the babies' curls into the gutter. I went to a lady's place where they'd taken nearly everything. And all these photos of her son that was killed in the war. You know they just let the photos blow away in the street, in the rain. And weeks later the lady was still finding the remains of her photos in the weeds by the side of the road. She never got over it.'

As he talked I remembered something else that must have been in the drawer with the jewellery. Something else that had been stolen. It was a small wax doll. I first saw her one night in the lighted window of a shop. She was a naked little girl with blue glass eyes and a wig made from real hair. The next day I went back to the shop when it was open. I thought the doll was very expensive, but I bought her.

MY FATHER'S AXE

Tim Winton

AUTHOR'S NOTE

'My Father's Axe' had its beginning in a real theft. When I was
not long married, an axe that I'd borrowed from my father was
stolen from my front verandah. I had a load of wood delivered
the day before and I was chopping it before storing it under
the house, so leaving the axe on the verandah didn't seem an
unreasonable thing to do. Besides, battered old axes never seemed
the sort of thing that people stole. I never saw the axe again.
Its disappearance disturbed me and took my mind completely
away from the novel I was writing, so in the end I sat down
for a day and wrote the short story. The writing was easy; I
felt oddly assured in the outcome, even though the only thing
I knew about the story was that someone had his axe stolen.
It ended up a mix of recollection and speculation, the kind of
blend in which I first recognized my own voice and one of the
themes that has always been present in my work—'the father-son
business' as a friend once called it, and what I've always hoped
to be an uncringing contemplation of masculinity. Also, a
combination of what some people call realism and what I call
dreaminess.

The ease with which this story came onto the page is rare
for me. It's happened in only a few stories and one novel, and
I have the suspicion that it's always produced my best work.
It's an annoying thought because I hate the romantic idea of
artistic inspiration.

Apart from the ease with which it was written and the way
it caught things that I'd been hoping for, 'My Father's Axe' remains
my favourite story for commercial reasons too. It won a prize,
was noticed by an agent, was published in a magazine unliterary

enough to think of paying well, and when collected into my first book of stories, was the subject of a few pleasant, thoughtful letters from non-expert readers. It never dazzled the 'critics' and has never been anthologized before.

Tim Winton

MY FATHER'S AXE

1

Just now I discover the axe gone. I look everywhere inside and outside the house, front and back, but it is gone. It has been on my front verandah since the new truckload of wood arrived and was dumped so intelligently over my front lawn. Jamie says he doesn't know where the axe is and I believe him; he won't chop wood any more. Elaine hasn't seen it; it's men's business, she says. No, it's not anywhere. But who would steal an axe in this neighbourhood, this street where I grew up and have lived much of my life? No one steals on this street. Not an axe.

It is my father's axe.

I used to watch him chop with it when we drove the old Morris and the trailer outside the town limits to gather wood. He would tie a thick, short bar of wood to the end of forty feet of rope and swing it about his head like a lasso and the sound it made was the whoop! of the headmaster's cane you heard when you walked past his office. My father sent the piece of wood high into the crown of a dead sheoak and when it snarled in the stark, grey limbs he would wrap the rope around his waist and then around his big freckled arms, and he would pass me his grey hat with bound hands and tell me to stand right back near the Morris with my mother who poured tea from a Thermos flask. And he pulled. I heard his body grunt and saw his red arms whiten, and the tree's crown quivered and rocked and he added to the motion, tugging, jerking, gasping until the whole bush cracked open and birds burst from all the trees around and the dead, grey crown of the sheoak teetered and toppled to the earth, chased by a shower of twigs and bark. My mother and I cheered and my father ambled over, arms glistening, to drink the tea that tasted faintly of coffee and the rubber seal of the Thermos. Rested, he would then dismember the brittle tree with

297

graceful swings of his axe and later I would saw with him on the bowman saw and have my knees showered with white, pulpy dust.

He could swing an axe, my father.

And that axe is gone.

He taught me how to split wood though I could never do it like him, those long, rhythmic, semicircular movements like a ballet dancer's warm-up; I'm a left-hander, a mollydooker he called me, and I chop in short, jabby strokes which do the job but are somehow less graceful.

When my father began to leave us for long periods for his work—he sold things—he left me with the responsibility of fuelling the home. It gave me pride to know that our hot water, my mother's cooking, the living room fire depended upon me, and my mother called me the man of the house, which frightened me a little. Short, winter afternoons I spent up the back splitting pine for kindling, long, fragrant spines with neat grain, and I opened up the heads of mill-ends and sawn blocks of sheoak my father brought home. Sometimes in the trance of movement and exertion I imagined the blocks of wood as teachers' heads. It was pleasurable work when the wood was dry and the grain good and when I kept the old Kelly axe sharp. I learnt to swing single-handed, to fit wedges into stubborn grain, to negotiate knots with resolve, and the chopping warmed me as I stripped to my singlet and worked until I was ankle-deep in split, open wood and my breath steamed out in front of me with each righteous grunt.

Once, a mouse half caught itself in a trap in the laundry beneath the big stone trough and my mother asked me to kill it, to put it out of its misery, she said. Obediently, I carried the threshing mouse in the trap at arm's length right up to the back of the yard. How to kill a mouse? Wring its neck? Too small. Drown it? In what? I put it on the burred block and hit it with the flat of the axe. It made no noise but it left a speck of red on my knee.

Another time my father, leaving again for a long trip, began softly to weep on our front step. My mother did not see because she was inside finding him some fruit. I saw my father ball his handkerchief up and bite on it to muffle his sobs and I left him there and ran through the house and up to the woodpile where I shattered great blocks of sheoak until it was dark and my arms gave out. In the dark I stacked wood into the buckled shed and listened to my mother calling.

I broke the handle of that axe once, on a camping trip; it was good hickory and I was afraid to tell him. I always broke my father's tools, blunted his chisels, bent his nails. I have never been a handyman like my father. He made things and repaired things and I watched but did not see the need to learn because I knew my father would always be. If I needed something built, something done, there was my father and he protected me.

When I was eight or nine he took my mother and me to a beach shack at a rivermouth up north. The shack was infested with rats and I lay awake nights listening to them until dawn when my father came and roused me and we went down to haul the craypots. The onshore reefs at low tide were bare, clicking and bubbling in the early sun, and octopuses gangled across exposed rocks, lolloping from hole to hole. We caught them for bait; my father caught them and I carried them in the bucket with the tight lid and looked at my face in the still tidal pools that bristled with kelp. But it was not so peaceful at high tide when the swells burst on the upper lip of the reef and cascaded walls of foam that rushed in upon us and rocked us with their force. The water reached my waist though it was only knee-deep for my father. He taught me to brace myself side-on to the waves and find footholds in the reef and I hugged his leg and felt his immovable stance and moulded myself to him. At the edge of the reef I coiled the rope that he hauled up and held the hessian bag as he opened the heavy, timber-slatted pots; he dropped the crays in and I heard their tweaking cries and felt them grovelling against my legs.

During the day my mother read *They're a Weird Mob* and ate raisins and cold crayfish dipped in red vinegar. We played Scrabble and it did not bother me that my father lost.

Lost his axe. Who could have stolen such a worthless thing? The handle is split and taped and the head bears the scars of years; why even look at it?

One night on that holiday a rat set off a trap on the rafter above my bed. My father used to tie the traps to the rafters to prevent the rats from carrying them off. It went off in the middle of the night with a snap like a small fire cracker and in the dark I sensed something moving above me and something warm touched my forehead. I lay still and did not scream because I knew my father would come. Perhaps I did scream in the end, I don't know. But he came, and he lit the Tilley lamp and chuckled and, yes, that was when I screamed. The rat, suspended by six feet of cord, swung in an arc across my bed with the long, hairy whip of tail trailing a foot above my nose. The body still flexed and struggled. My father took it down and went outside with its silhouette in the lamplight in front of him. My mother screamed; there was a drop of blood on my forehead. It was just like *The Pit and the Pendulum*, I said. We had recently seen the film and she had found the book in the library and read it to me for a week at bedtime. Yes, she said with a grim smile, wiping my forehead, and I had nightmares about that long, hairy blade above my throat and saw it snatched away by my father's red arms. In the morning I saw outside that the axe head was dull with blood. After that I often had dreams in which my father rescued me. One was a dream about a burning house—our house, the one I still live in with Elaine and Jamie—and I was trapped inside, hair and bedclothes afire and my father splintered the door with an axe blow and fought his way in and carried me out in those red arms.

My father. He said little. He never won at Scrabble, so it seems he never even stored words up for himself. We never spoke much. It was my mother and I who carried on the long conversations; she knew odd facts, quiz shows on television were her texts. I told her my problems. But with my father I just stood, and we watched each other. Sometimes he looked at me with disappointment, and other times I looked at him the same way.

He hammered big nails in straight and kissed me goodnight and goodbye and hello until I was fourteen and learnt to be ashamed of it and evade it.

When his back stiffened with age he chopped wood less and I wielded the axe more. He sat by the woodpile and sometimes stacked, though mostly he just sat with a thoughtful look on his face. As I grew older my time contracted around me like a shrinking shirt and I chopped wood hurriedly, often finishing before the old man had a chance to come out and sit down.

Then I met Elaine and we married and I left home. For years I went back once a week to chop wood for the old man while Elaine and my mother sat at the Laminex table in the kitchen listening to the tick of the stove. I tried to get my parents interested in electric heating and cooking like most people in the city, but my father did not care for it. He was stubborn and so I continued to split wood for him once a week while he became a frail, old man and his arms lost their ruddiness and went pasty and the flesh lost its grip upon the bones of his forearms. He looked at me in disappointment every week like an old man will, but I came over on Sundays, even when we had Jamie to look after, so he didn't have cause to be that way.

Jamie got old enough to use an axe and I taught him how. He was keen at first, though careless, and he blunted the edge quite often which angered me. I got him to chop wood for his grandfather and dropped him there on Sunday afternoons. I had a telephone installed in their house, though they complained about the colour, and I spoke to my mother sometimes on the phone, just to please her. My father never spoke on the phone. Still doesn't.

Then my mother had her stroke and Jamie began demanding to be paid for woodchopping and Elaine went twice a week to cook and clean for them and I decided on the Home. My mother and father moved out and we moved in and sold our own house. I thought about getting the place converted to electricity but the Home was expensive and Elaine came to enjoy cooking on the old combustion stove and it was worth paying Jamie a little to chop wood. Until recently. Now he won't even do it for money. He is lazier than me.

Still, it was only an old axe.

2

Elaine sleeps softly beside me, her big wide buttocks warm against my legs. The house is quiet; it was always quiet, even when my parents and I lived here. No one ever raised their voice at me in this house, except now my wife and son.

It is hard to sleep, hard, so difficult. Black moves about me and in me and is on me, so black. Fresh, bittersweet, the smell of split wood: hard, splintery jarrah, clean, moist sheoak, hard, fibrous white gum, the shick! of sundering pine. All my muscles sing, a chorus of effort, as I chop quickly, throwing chunks aside, wiping flecks and chips from my chin. Sweat sheets across my eyes and I chop harder, opening big round sawn blocks of sheoak like pies in neat wedged sections. Harder. And my feet begin to lift as I swing the axe high over my shoulder. I strike it home and regain equilibrium. As I swing again my feet lift further and I feel as though I might float up, borne away by the axe above my head, as though it is a helium balloon. No, I don't want to lift up! I drag on the hickory handle, downwards, and I win and drag harder and it gains momentum and begins a slow-motion arc of descent towards the porous surface of the wood and then, halfway down, the axe-head shears off the end of the handle so slowly, so painfully slow that I could take a hold of it four or five times to stop it. In a slow, tumbling trajectory it sails across the woodheap and unseats my father's head from his shoulders and travels on out of sight as my father's head rolls onto the heap, eyes towards me, transfixed at the moment of scission in a squint of disappointment.

I feel a warm dob on my forehead; I do not scream, have never needed to.

The sheets are wet and the light is on and Elaine has me

by the shoulder and her left breast points down at my glistening chest.

'What's the matter?' she says, wiping my brow with the back of her hand. 'You were yelling.'

'A dream,' I croak.

3

Morning sun slants across the pickets at me as I fossick about in the long grass beside the shed finding the skeleton of a wren but nothing else. I shuffle around the shed, picking through the chips and splinters and slivers of wood around the chopping block, see the deep welts in the block where the axe has been, but no axe. In the front yard, as neighbours pass, I scrabble in the pile of new wood, digging into its heart, tossing pieces aside until there is nothing but yellowing grass and a few impassive slaters. Out in the backyard again I amble about shaking my head and putting my hands in my pockets and taking them out again. Elaine is at work. Jamie at school. I have rung the office and told them I won't be in. All morning I mope in the yard, waiting for something to happen, absurdly, expecting the axe to show like a prodigal son. Nothing.

Going inside at noon I notice a deep trench in the verandah post by the back door; it is deep and wide as a heavy axe-blow and I feel the inside of it with my fingers—only for a moment— before I hurry inside trying to recall its being there before. Surely.

I sit by the cold stove in the kitchen in the afternoon, quaking. Is someone trying to kill me? My God.

4

Again Elaine has turned her sumptuous buttocks against me and gone to sleep dissatisfied and I lie awake with my shame and the dark around me.

Some nights as a child I crept into my parents' room and wormed my way into the bed between them and slept soundly, protected from the dark by their warm contact.

Now, I press myself against Elaine's sleeping form and cannot sleep with the knowledge that my back is exposed.

After an hour I get up and prowl about the house, investigating each room with quick flicks of light switches and satisfied grunts when everything seems to be in order. Here, the room where my mother read, here, Jamie's room where I slept as a boy, here, where my father drank his hot, milkless tea in the mornings.

I can think of nothing I've done to offend the neighbours— I'm not a dog baiter or anything—though some of them grumbled about my putting my parents into the Home, as though it was any of their business.

I keep thinking of axe murders, things I've read in the papers, horrible things.

In the living room I take out the old Scrabble box and sit with it on my knee for a while. Perhaps I'll play a game with myself . . .

5

This morning when I woke in the big chair in the living room I saw the floor littered with Scrabble tiles like broken, yellowing teeth. Straightening my stiff back I recalled the dream. I dreamt that I saw my body dissected, raggedly sectioned up and battered and crusted black with blood. The axe, the old axe with the taped hickory handle, was embedded in the trunk where once my legs had joined, right through the pelvis. My severed limbs lay about, pink, black, distorted, like stockings full of sand. My head, to one side, faced the black ceiling, teeth bared, eyes firmly shut. Horrible, but even so, peaceful enough, like a photograph. And then a boy came out of the black—it was Jamie—and picked up my head and held it like a bowling ball. Then there was light and my son opened the door and went outside into the searing suddenness of light. He walked out into the backyard and up to the chopping block in which an axe—*the* axe—was poised. I felt nothing when he split my head in two. It was a poor stroke, but effective enough. Then with half in either hand— by the hair—he slowly walked around the front of the house and then out to the road verge and began skidding the half-orbs into the paths of oncoming cars. I used to do that as a boy; skidding half pig-melons under car wheels until nothing was left but a greenish, wet pulp. Pieces of my head ricocheted from chassis to bitumen, tyre to tyre, until there was only pulp and an angry sounding of car horns.

That does it; I'm going down to the local hardware store to buy another axe. It's high time. I have thought of going to the police but it's too ludicrous; I have nothing to tell: someone has stolen my axe that used to be my father's. A new axe is what I need.

It takes a long time in the Saturday morning rush at the hardware and the axes are so expensive and many are shoddy and the sales boy who pretends to be a professional axeman tires me with his patter. Eventually I buy a Kelly; it costs me forty dollars and it bears a resemblance to my father's. Carrying it home I have the feeling that I'm holding a stage property, not a tool; there are no signs of work on it and the head is so clean and smooth and shiny it doesn't seem intended for chopping.

As I open the front gate, axe over my shoulder, my wife is waiting on the verandah with tears on her face.

'The Home called,' she says. 'It's your father . . .'

6

The day after the funeral I am sitting out on the front verandah in the faint yellow sun. My mother will die soon; her life's work is over and she has no reason to continue in her sluggish, crippled frame. It will not be long before her funeral, I think to myself, not long. A tall sunflower sheds its hard, black seeds near me, shaken by the weight of a bird I can't see but sense. The gate squeals on its hinges and at the end of the path stand a man and a boy.

'Yes?' I ask.

The man prompts the boy forward and I see the lad has something in a hessian bag in his arms that he is offering me. Stepping off the verandah I take it, not heeding the man's apologies and the stutterings of his son. I open the bag and see the hickory handle with its gummy black tape and nicks and burrs and I groan aloud.

'He's sorry he took it,' the man says, 'aren't you, Alan? He—'

'Wait,' I say, turning, bounding back up the verandah, through the house, out onto the back verandah where Elaine and Jamie sit talking. They look startled but I have no time to explain. I grab the shiny, new axe which is yet to be used, and race back through the house with it. Elaine calls out to me, fright in her voice.

In the front yard, the father and son still wait uneasily and they look at me with apprehension as I run towards them with the axe.

'What—' The man tries to shield his son whose mouth begins to open as I come closer.

I hold the axe out before me, my body tingling, and I hold it horizontal with the handle against the boy's heaving chest.

'Here,' I say. 'This is yours.'

SANDCASTLES

Archie Weller

AUTHOR'S NOTE

The story I chose for this anthology is not necessarily my best as it is very hard for me to say just what exactly is my best story and why it is so. I am, by tradition, a story-teller; one who sits around a kitchen table or a campfire and tells a yarn, be it true or made up, for the sake of passing the time. This is one of the reasons I chose this story because it is a good yarn.

I wrote 'Sandcastles' in 1977 when I had a brief sojourn at WAIT—now called Curtin University of Technology. I wrote it in one afternoon in the library with the rain trickling down the windows and the dark pines swaying outside in the wind. It seems to me that winter is my best month for writing while rain is my best friend and soother of thoughts.

Also, my best stories—or favourites, if you like—are written in a torrent of energy, where the thoughts crowd in on me, urging to be released. Some of my stories are written over a period of several weeks at least but the very few I write in a matter of hours seem to hold the raw feelings that make that story great for me.

I like the style of 'Sandcastles', as told in the first person. Once again, it sounds just like someone sitting down and telling his story; just a story. There is no hidden message in any of my stories, although, of course, if one can be found then perhaps it will make the story richer. I never intentionally set out to preach or crusade, though.

Last of all, I chose this story because it holds a precious memory for me. Memories are strange things and you never know which one a colour or smell or sight will drag up. But my memory is of a day down at Albany, on the south-west coast of Western

Australia, when I was about seven or eight. Dad and my brother and I had intended to go to a secluded part of the beach for a picnic but I met my neighbour's kids and on the spur of the moment decided to stay with them. Mistake! They were nasty-minded, as children are, and I had a sad time. You see, I had thought I would be able to go to that beach when we went down the following year. But we never went down to Albany again and I hardly saw my father after that. There has been an empty spot in my stomach ever since, and I couldn't tell you why. Sometimes I think about the fun I must have missed out on. In all my life—from the age of six—I only saw my father in the holidays, and even then he was often too busy working on the farm. So that day on the beach would have been one of the few memories I'd have had of him and my brother and me all together. This is why it haunts me often.

So, I was sitting in the WAIT library where it struck me again and—with that thought as a lever—the story flowed from my mind as I thought of what might have been.

Archie Weller

SANDCASTLES

Hullo. My name is Tommy. I don't write too good, but I got all these things I want to say.

You know, when I walk down the street everybody stares at me. That's shame, like I was an escaped animal from the zoo, or a spaceman or something. I'm just a coloured boy. Maybe that is why they all stare at me, because they imagine I might steal their car, or knock them down and take their money.

I think of money a lot, when I don't have any. When I got it, I don't think of anything except having my piece of fun. When I got money then I'm someone, but when I'm broke I'm just Tommy Caylun, the boong, shuffling down the street, with an eye out for the monaych—coppers. With money in my pocket I can pretend I'm a main actor, you know? I walk around like Marlon Brando, big tough Tommy.

But their scornful stares, that look right through me, show me what I really am.

I hate white people—or maybe I hate myself because I'm almost white. And that is all I'll ever be—an almost man. Whenever I start becoming good and try to settle down, something always happens and I'm back where I come from. Like last time, when I had a Wadgula girlfriend, and a Monaro, and a steady job. I told myself: Tommy, this is it. You right now.

But my cousin, Clemmy—who was on the run—come around home, one night, with a carload of stolen beer.

We all got blue-drunk and gang-raped this girl Clem bought along. Well, not really rape because she was drunk too, and asking for it. But, when police busted through the door, it looked like rape. You can't tell police nothing, when it's part-aboriginals involved.

So I got three years in Fremantle, I was only seventeen. It hurt me; that's the truth.

Down the Central Station, five CIB blokes punched me and

Clemmy and the two Harrison boys up and down the room. But we give them our best because we only got our pride; when that's gone we may as well go out to some park to drink and die.

Any rate, I'm out now. I tell myself I will settle down now. But I am what I am. Or, rather, I am what the white people want me to be.

That white girlfriend of mine, she was pretty. She understood me, too. I met her at the Tech. school I was going to, where I was learning mechanics. One good thing about my Dad (and about the only good thing) was how he could fix up any old car. I learnt all I knew off him. I remember dusty days, in the hot sun, and rainy nights, with the electric light dancing with the wind. I would huddle into my hand-me-down clothes and watch every move his stubby, greasy fingers would make. I reckon he could of fixed an engine blindfold, he was that good. Every now and then he would glance down at me and explain, in his gravelly voice, what was where. Sometimes, he would raise a rare laugh and say I looked like a little joey 'roo. That was when he would forget the black skin my mother had given me and just remember I was his son and I could love him then.

He used to say him and me would go into partnership, when I got old enough and passed Tech. He was proud of me, you know.

Then Clemmy Jackson and Olman and Eli Harrison had to come along.

So, that was the finish of that; all Dad's dreams, I mean. It was the beginning for me. You might say I'd finally busted out of my white cocoon, hanging on a tree. But I wasn't a butterfly, you see. I was something bad, and black, and unsightly in my real world.

But I was telling you about my girl, I was going to marry.

One night, she and me took these pills. I learnt if you take pills with Coke, it makes you like you was drunk—well, happy really. Plastic joy, you might say. These Wadgulas have got funny tricks. Well, anyway, we was rolling around on the floor, laughing at nothing much, thinking about nothing much—at this party. Somehow, me and her got together. Kissing and cuddling, you know? Then we made love, and it was like nothing that had ever happened to me. She was so soft and gentle, and she gave everything. That's what got me, because most Wadgulas take everything off my kind. She quietened me down and showed me where I was going.

All that summer, me and her went everywhere together. I had this Monaro I bought off Uncle Butch for five hundred. Brother, she could move, all right! It made me feel like God or something, you know, to roar and rush up and down the streets. I hotted it up with floor shift, and foot-on-the-floor power, and mags, and bucket seats. I put a radio and cassette in it, and, with my knowledge, I kept the engine in good shape.

But you can't get away from nothing. One night, outside this pizza hut, these demons pulled us up. They tried to say I stole my Monaro, and shamed me in front of my girl. They had a good look at her, too, with a what-the-hell-are-you-doing-with-*him* sneer. They pulled me out, and trod on my toes, and scared the shits out of me. They made me look a fool, just to prove to themselves they was the men.

The people in the pizza hut stared, with hooded eyes, at another boong being picked up; the sluts in the one darkened car on the street (for it was past midnight) giggled at the two coppers—who promised, silently, to come back this way, later on, and pick them up for a quick free one someplace. The one Nyoongah there melted away into the shadows, not wanting to know about it. He knew that where there was monaych there was trouble: for him, or me, or any poor black bastard like us. You live and learn and live. The lights blinked down on me, bored-like. Even the jukebox couldn't give a damn, shouting out happily as I went through the third-degree, on the hot street.

I would like to punch the huge, fat policeman in the guts, and make him grunt. I would like to shout out, to all the world, that I am a man.

But I never did.

311

I put on my best aboriginal face, and closed my eyes and hung my head and called them sir—just as they wanted me to.

Afterwards, I could sense my girl, Jillianne, was just a little cold towards me. I think she was reminded that I was, after all, a quarter black. But I never cared. I was used to her kind of treatment. Any rate, it didn't last long. It did spoil our evening, though.

But when we went back to Tech., it was all right. It made me feel good making out I was a Wadgula. I met Jillianne's family, in their double-garage house at Subiaco. They thought I was number one, you know? Her old man got me a job in the Skipper Chrysler workshops.

But you can't keep being false forever. You can never escape from your people, either. They are always watching. Watching.

So my cousin come along and what happened, happened.

You can be what you like on the outside, but inside you are you.

In Fremantle, I met more of my cousins, and an uncle I never even knew I had. Nyoongahs, us south-west people, stick together in Freo, unless they are enemies. I never had no enemies, so I was right. I tell you, going into Freo is like having a bath. All the bullshit gets washed off you and you learn the truth. You come out clean, you might say.

That is why I do the given-up-don't-care shuffle around the streets and spend my dole money on getting drunk at Beaufort, or Guildford park, with my people. I live with my two cousins, and my woman, in a tent at Lockridge.

Not my Wadgula woman, Jillianne. A Nyoongah girl—Phyllis Kennedy—who I knew a little bit. *She* come to see me sweating it out in jail: Jillianne didn't. So what did you expect? She'd welcome me with open arms and a great big hullo-I'm-glad-you're-free-kiss? Buddy, she was off a month after I got put away, with a Wadgula lawyer. How she must of laughed at silly black Tommy, as she showed her aboriginal around to all the gawking squawking white crows.

Peck out your eyes. Peck out your life. Leave the bones to

bleach, lost and forgotten, in the corner of some paddock.

That's when I started hating the white people.

Phyllis is pregnant for Paddy Needles, who took off when he found out. But I love her. Sometimes, when she's rasping away in her harsh voice, I feel disgusted with her and wish she would speak softer, and better English. I wonder why I can live with her, with her torn, dirty clothes and untidy hair and her smell. But it's not our fault. We got no water here, only a tap—and a creek that runs dry in summer. When Phyllis come out of Niandi she was given all these new clothes by that Girls' Home. But you can't keep nothing clean in this place. Besides, all her sisters come and take her clothes off her. Then—she got this pretty way of throwing her arms about that makes her look like a ballerina. And her hair *is* beautiful and soft. Her eyes, too, look at me with such warmth and happiness and trusting. We are very happy together.

Sometimes, however, she doesn't understand me, because I never belt her around; and I share everything with her; and worry about her, like an old chook. Even when she gets me wild, all I do is go for a walk, somewhere peaceful, and think.

No one understands me.

They weren't me, brought up in my family.

Mum thought she was really good, marrying a white bloke, you know? She dressed in good clothes, and wore shoes when she went to town—and jewels. When we was given all our rights then she may as well have been a Wadgula. But before that, even, she could look a white person in the eye with pride.

Her first man, Freddy Jackson, was sitting back in Fremantle. (He was that uncle I never knew about.) What he done was get drunk on metho and paint cleaner (because coloured people wasn't allowed to drink legally, then) and run amuck in the Reserve, by the railway line. He got an axe and killed Mum's brother, who also had got drunk.

He got life for that, and had already done twenty years when I went there. He'd sort of grown onto the place, like a piece of fungus. He's not even a human any more. If they let him out tomorrow he wouldn't know where to go or what to do. They did let him out once, I remember; after he had done eight years, when I was about five years old. He come down to see Mum and his son Jojo, who was nine.

I won't never forget that night. Not that I knew what was going on. I didn't. It was just the violence, that was to be with me all my life, bursting in, that I remember.

It started off quiet. Dad, a couple of his mates, and Mum was getting drunk, playing poker around the kitchen table. Me and my true sister Geraldine, who was only two, and my half-brother, Jojo, was supposed to be asleep. But we always watched the Saturday Night Show.

We reckoned it was funny to watch Mum laugh, and stumble around the kitchen, and throw her body around in a dance for the white men. It was the only time Dad got happy.

They would listen to the radio, or Dad would drag out his guitar. Sometimes, one of Dad's mates would try to get a piece of Mum. We would giggle from our corner as the white fella fumbled Mum's heavy breasts, and threw floppy arms around her shoulders, and kissed her—and then dragged her, laughing, into the bedroom. Dad would laugh too: he didn't care. Only once, when Mum was pregnant, he got in one of his sudden violent rages, and tried to kill the unborn baby and Mum. But Jojo—who was fourteen then, but big and strong and sullen—stopped him.

But Mum only went with Dad's mates when she was blue-drunk and didn't know what she was doing. Next morning, when she was sober, she would straighten herself up and forget about it and pretend she was a white lady again. But Dad, over in his chair by the stove, looking like a cockroach, sort of, would cackle and grin, with his yellow teeth, and tease her about it. Then she would be ashamed and go away to cry.

Yeah, we *used* to laugh at the Saturday Night Show. But as we got older we became ashamed, then disgusted, then angry.

Nyoongahs lose their laughter young in life, you know.

But this night I am telling you about, we was laughing softly

314

as huge Morry Gascoyne, who was a ringer in the shearing shed, tried it on with Mum.

Then there was a soft knock on the door.

Skinny-Jim (who we called Dad's brother) opens it and there stood . . . Uncle Freddy. I could see the front door from where I lay. It was raining and the rain run down Uncle Freddy's ragged clothes and formed in a pool around his feet; so it looked as if he had risen up out of that dirty puddle. It run down over his face, so it glistened in the light from the kitchen and looked like tears.

Uncle Freddy mumbled something to Skinny-Jimmy, who snarled back:

'No, you can't. Piss off!!'

'Who's that?' Dad shouts.

'It's *'im*. Come back to see his Missus.'

Us kids was wide-eyed watching this new twist to the show. We hardly ever had any visitors here; especially not Nyoongahs, who Mum discouraged. Any rate, as far as I could see this bloke was a stranger. But Dad and Skinny-Jim and big Morry seemed to know who ''im' was.

We could see something was up because Dad looked uneasy, and big Morry was going to get up. But then Dad grinned and motioned the giant to stay where he was.

'Bring him in, Jim. We ain't ignorant.'

Mum, she didn't know what was going on because she'd been drinking Vio Port, and whisky, and straight gin, all night, and she may as well have been dead.

Uncle Freddy come shuffling up the hall, with his prison gait; hands nervously shoved in his pockets. His hooded eyes flicked glances around the room without seeming to move.

He was only about thirty then but, in my mind, he looked ten years older.

He looked up and seen Mum and Mum seen him. Mum tried to struggle to her feet, but only fell off the chair. Her dress went right up her legs so her old petticoat showed.

No one laughed. Not even us.

'So,' was all Uncle Freddy said. His eyes were bleared, like a fused light-globe! Then he shrugged and turned to go.

That would have been an end of it, except for Morry Gascoyne (who thought of us all as boongs, and not worth a spit unless they was girls).

'So—what!' he bellows, and hauls poor dizzy Mum up by the arm. She leaned against the giant, and gagged, and hung her head.

'What you think of your woman now, the drunk little gin? Too good for a crazy boong like you. What did he do, sweetheart? Kill his best mate just to show how friendly he was? But we don't care, do we boys? This lovely piece of Black Velvet has kept us warm many nights.'

Uncle Freddy's hands sprung out of his pockets: big, knobbly, killing hands. He threw his head back and his eyes cleared. He gave a yell as he come in, swinging and kicking.

Morry let go of Mum, who fell back on the floor.

Then there was all buggeries let loose. Morry went down to one of Freddy's rights. Dad smashed a bottle over the black-haired head, before ending up, groaning, in the corner—his kidneys almost busted on him.

Skinny-Jim made a grab for a bottle then, but Freddy picked up a butcher's knife and put it right through him. Then the dark angry man worked over Morry Gascoyne so he wouldn't shear a sheep for a long time.

Mum had crawled over to us kids and hugged us to her.

Uncle Freddy busted every bottle in the house, and smashed the painting of the sorrowful white lady dressed in funny clothes, before he calmed down. Then he looked over at Mum, before dismissing her. He limped over to frightened Jojo, smiling with only his mouth. From out of his pocket he bought a medallion on a chain.

'I'm ya daddy, son. I bet ya forgotten me, unna? Well, any rate, I made this thing for ya to keep to remember me by. I won't never see ya again—Jojo.'

He was right. The monaych picked up Uncle Freddy, over at the camp, the next day, after Mum had rung them up. He came quietly, resigned and given up.

Skinny-Jim died.

They never let Uncle Freddy Jackson out again.

When I was in there all his teeth was falling out, and he talked to himself, and pissed himself sometimes. He was the joke of the jail, walking up to every new face—black or white—and promising to get them out on bail. Some people believed him, too.

When Dad recovered from his flogging, he laid into Mum and Jojo—just because Jojo was Freddy's son. Jojo ran away and lived by the Reserve, with his Auntie, for the next four years. He grew up rough and tough and dangerous, like his Dad. He always had a soft spot for me and Geraldine, though. When Jojo was thirteen, he went to work as a rousie on a shearing team. He come back home almost as tall as Dad and as strong as a bull. It was all right after that, because Dad was afraid of big Jojo, so he left Mum and us kids alone. Before, he used to flog us for any little thing. That is why I won't never flog my kids or woman, out at camp.

Yesterday, me and Phyllis went down to the beach. We kept out of the way of all the Wadgulas trying to turn black. We found a reef and waded around, looking for shells, Phyllis thought it would make the tent look pretty if we got some good shells. I went out deep and found some beauties; like trumpets, they were, and all orange and green and yellow, you know.

Some surfie blokes went by and whistled at Phyllis. Any Nyoongah girl is easy meat, they reckon. Even one who is six months pregnant. Other Wadgulas stare at us with their pale eyes, like they always do. But we don't care.

We sit in the shade of some rocks and talk quietly about what is happening outside in the world and inside Phyllis's stomach. That is our world.

Phyllis sleeps and I watch some little kids build a sandcastle.

The last time I built a sandcastle was when I become fourteen. I had just started Tech. and it was my birthday. Mum still believed I could be all right, you know. Turn out good.

317

She took us on a picnic down to the beach, to a place only she knew about. She used to come here, with her brother and sisters, when she was little and maybe she wanted to grab hold of her lost youth, or something.

That was fun. Jojo's Uncle Ronny, who was only a year older than Jojo himself (but that's how it works in Nyoongah families) drove us out there in his newly bought car.

There was just them two, Mum, me, Geraldine and the three young ones: all Nyoongahs together. We run around and played chasey and hidey. We swam and lay around, and ate a big feed, out of the picnic basket Mum had made. Ronny caught a huge fish and we seen some dolphins way off shore. No one come to annoy us with their stares and muttered remarks. That was the best part.

Only one thing spoilt it when Mum bought out a flagon of wine. Jojo just stared at her and took himself off for a long walk.

But he came back to help us build the sandcastle. All us kids—even Ronny, who was twenty and a man, really. And Mum, too, sat at our side, running the white sand through her fingers, and giggling. It was a beauty of a sandcastle; with towers and walls and a moat; all covered in stones and shells and seaweed. Geraldine was Queen and I was King, whilst Ronny and Jojo was the enemies. The little ones ran everywhere, being nothing.

The King of sandcastles, that's me—all the way through.

When the sea come in and the sun went down, our castle was washed away, and we all went home.

I cried, and the others laughed. But, you see, for one whole day I had owned something beautiful, for the first time in my life.

Why do kids build sandcastles when they know the sea will come right in and wash them away?

Why do we dream, you might say?

All I ever do is dream.

I'm always going to do something, or be someone, or go somewhere—but I never move.

That's Tommy Caylun for you, all over.

318

INSIDE THE OYSTER

Morris Lurie

AUTHOR'S NOTE

'Inside the Oyster' leapt from my Olivetti Lettera 22 half a lifetime ago in a room in a brothel in Tangier—actually, more of a knocking shop, rooms by the hour, Spanish owner, clean sheets guaranteed—and I sent it to my agent in London and he sold it straight away to a magazine called *King* for twenty-five guineas (minus of course his ten per cent) and I caught the morning ferry to Spain and walked across the border into Gibraltar and bought whisky and cigarettes and a sports coat and books and magazines and ate a Chinese meal and was back in my room in the brothel that night. Those were the days! The writer's life for me!

I can't tell you the misery.

Because, for a start, it was so quick. I can't even remember it. One minute there was nothing and the next it was already old hat. I mean, in the sense of history, finished, what's next? My diary of those days says ten stories in five months, plus outlines, beginnings, false starts, try again, notes, hopes, ideas, plans, schemes, business correspondence, letters to pals, and the only way I can tell you I fitted in all that and still had time to brood, mope, stare, sit for endless hours at the Café Central in the Socco Petit with yet another *café con leche* and yet another Camel, and walk, and sleep, and read, and talk, and escape to Gibraltar on a practically weekly basis, and the movies, and more, much more, the fear I fitted in, the despair, is that when I wrote, when I finally wrote—boy, it was fast.

Because, for another thing, who the hell anyway was I, living in Tangier? Scared to pieces, I call tell you. You think it's a natural thing, a shy Jewish fellow from Melbourne Australia alone in the midst of every known drug and perversion, a veiled woman on every corner, boys grabbing your sleeve, Mr Naked Lunch himself measuring you with his empty eye? Or the larger conceit: that a boy with a typewriter could swim in this river called life?

So you see why 'Inside the Oyster' has to be such a favourite.

No, I don't mean just souvenir.

Nor keepsake neither, mere memento, though it is all that, to be sure.

Plus the technical wizardry, the whole tale told in a flash, in and out in fifteen hundred rushy words, character, place, mood, story, the entire box and dice, where I should also perhaps mention the Pop Art opening paragraph years before Warhol and Lichtenstein and all the rest of them were even invented, or I had anyway heard of them.

Well, I was into comics as a child, a hot reader of *Batman* where my peers were labouring with Proust.

Influence of J. P. Donleavy?

Absolutely!

But I was reading Chekhov, too.

And Nabokov, Borges, Salinger, Saroyan, Bernard Malamud, John Cheever.

The Marx Brothers.

The usual endless list.

But enough, to the marrow of the matter—the story's singular claim to my heart, why is that?

Because half a lifetime and a hundred stories later I discover, encoded in my frail frightened beginnings, in this seemingly slight tale of hopelessness and despair (albeit comically told), the largest reassurance.

The kid was going to be okay.

Morris Lurie

INSIDE THE OYSTER

The last time I saw Eddie Blish he was hanging by his fingertips (in a manner of speaking) from a fast-crumbling ledge over a black sea and the waves were smashing up on the rocks a thousand feet below. Wind howled. Rain poured. The sky was green with electricity. Gongs were sounding (so to speak) and time was running out—I saw his left hand slip and hang uselessly in dizzy space—and I could hear the evil doctor cackling madly and rubbing his hands in satanic glee, and just before everything exploded I got the hell out of there and exactly what happened after that I don't know, it's all blank, but it was a real cliff-hanger, believe me. He couldn't possibly have lived.

Old Eddie Blish. He used to sit next to me in Economics. With his eyes open but glazed and his bottom lip hanging down like a flap and I would have to kick him awake under the desk whenever Fitzpatrick pointed straight at him and said, 'You! What's the Balance of Payments?' And the amazing thing was, no matter how debauched the night before had been, no matter how much he had drunk and how many girls he had rolled on his sagging attic bed and then read them poetry in the early hours of the morning—'Keats is a good one,' he used to tell me—as soon as my shoe touched his shin, Eddie would be wide awake and the answers would pour out of his lips. He knew his Balance of Payments. He knew his Terms of Trade. There wasn't a thing you could catch him on about Sterling or the International Banking Scene. 'Very good,' Fitzpatrick would say. 'And you!'—pointing at me. 'Tell me all about Gold!'

But this last time I saw him. I bumped into him in the street and he said, 'Come along and meet the wife. You've never met her, have you? Ann.'

And I said, 'By all means, let's go.'

And Eddie Blish said, 'Hop into this, it's mine,' and we hopped into a brand-new two-tone blue Ford and started up the hill to

321

where Eddie lived, and there were so many things I wanted to ask him, because I hadn't seen him for a year, but for some reason neither of us said a word. I could see he was concentrating on his driving. His hands were white on the wheel. His foot was down hard on the accelerator. His mouth was a line. His eyes were fixed straight ahead. So we flew up the hill in this new two-tone blue Ford to where Eddie lived, but almost at the top of the hill the Ford ran out of petrol and Eddie Blish said, 'Come on, it's not far. We'll walk.'

When we got out of the car I saw that he had left the keys dangling in the lock and the windows wound down and then he ran around to the front of the car and kissed it on the bonnet and said, 'Goodbye, sweet Ford. This car now reverts to the ownership of the Something-or-other Finance Corporation,' and we walked the rest of the way. A mile. With that sweet Ford haphazardly angle-parked by the side of the road. And still we didn't say a word to each other.

When we got to Eddie's house it was no house at all but one tall-ceilinged room in a bleak old building and it was so cold inside you could see the fog coming out of your mouth.

'This is the wife,' he said, introducing me with a bow, and I thought she was going to have her baby right then and there. Sad eyes. Watery. 'I love you,' Eddie said, and she said, 'Eddie, I'm freezing, it's no good for the baby for me to be cold,' and he said, 'Wait just one split-second, my precious, and I'll steal a load of firewood from the Jew next door,' and so saying he departed, and was back before either Ann or I had spoken, the right leg of his trousers savaged by a dog and his face blood red. But his hands were empty.

'Remind me to buy some mastiff poison in the morning,' he said, and before Ann could say a word he had pulled out all the drawers from an old black dresser that was standing by the wall and having emptied their contents onto the threadbare rug, put his foot through each drawer and manufactured, before our very eyes, a great deal of very combustible kindling, and for heavier stuff he dismantled an antique-looking chair—'Save the cushions!' Ann cried—and when the blaze was nicely taking care of itself in the grate, we all sat down and stretched out our legs and looked into the fire.

'I'm afraid,' Eddie said to me, 'that we can't offer you a cooling glass of beer or a savoury sip of sherry or even a cup of black coffee, because, old man, you see, we're broke. Not a penny. Nothing. Nada.'

'Eddie, what'll we do?' his wife said.

'Sssh!' he hissed at her. 'I'm thinking. Hey, you don't happen to have a couple of—?'

'I'm absolutely broke,' I said. 'Been out of work for two months. As a matter of fact—'

'Eddie, this is serious,' his wife said. 'I'm hungry.'

Eddie patted her on the arm and said, 'There, there, precious, Eddie knows, Eddie understands.'

This was all somehow embarrassing to watch, so I looked around the room, but there was nothing there but an unmade double bed and two suitcases and a hat hanging on a rack by the door. There was precious little left to burn, if it came to that.

'I've got this absolutely marvellous prospect all lined up, tomorrow morning,' Eddie was saying, 'but how am I going to get into town? The car conked out of gas,' he said to his wife. 'I abandoned it.'

'Oh, Eddie,' his wife said.

'They can't touch us, precious,' Eddie said. 'I gave them a wrong address.'

Suddenly Eddie leaned over and tapped me on the arm and said, 'Real estate. Watch out for real estate.' Then he leaned back in his chair and gazed into the fire and his face became a mask. And this was the Eddie who had run away from home when he was seventeen to live in a tiny attic with a shaky floor, through which, he told me, he had crashed down and fallen into the bed of a young, still-grieving widow, who had put aside her copy of *Ellery Queen's Mystery Magazine* and nursed him through the long night. Well, that's how he told it, and he most certainly was covered in bruises in Economics the next day, and had almost faltered when Fitzpatrick had swung a trick question his way. Almost, but not quite. Out came the words, and Fitzpatrick had said, when Eddie had finished, 'I wish the rest of you knew what Blish knows, I'd have no worries. You! Tell me about Lord Keynes!'

It's a hard pill to swallow, about the widow, I know, but I did, and still do, because Eddie was a ballsy guy with girls, and once when I dropped in on him, unannounced, to his attic, he had two nurses with him, two, with one of whom he was dancing tangoes—I can see now his gliding steps—to the music of old 78s on his wind-up gramophone, while the other ironed his school suit. It looked good, and either nurse would have been all right for me, but then Eddie glided my way and whispered in my ear, 'There's nothing here for you, boy,' and I went home.

So we sat and stared into the fire and then Eddie said to me, 'Got any cigarettes?' and I had to tell him no, because I had only one left, and in truth I was wondering how I was going to get home, it was a good three miles, and I could hear rain falling outside. And wind.

Well, that was the last time I saw Eddie Blish, and his wife, both sitting in front of the fire, as I tiptoed out, with that long walk through the rain ahead of me and Eddie's wife about to have a baby and both of them hungry and Eddie not even having his fare to get into town the next morning to look for a job and, as I've said, he used to sit next to me in Economics and I've got his photograph in my School Year Book and under it it says, 'The world is his oyster,' and three months later I heard from a friend that his baby was a boy, so something must have happened. But I don't know what.

BLACK GENOA

Beverley Farmer

AUTHOR'S NOTE

Marjorie Barnard was on the cover of a 1987 literary calendar. She was the August writer: grim-jawed in profile, thin white plaits looped on her head, her hands very large and knotted, fore-shortened as they were. A tabby cat lay sprawled on the table beside her by a vase of flowers.

I first read her famous story 'The Persimmon Tree' seven or eight years ago and was puzzled, when my joy in it died down enough for thought, to realize that the story in fact contained no persimmon tree. A row of persimmons was put out to ripen on a windowsill, autumn persimmons although it was spring in the story. The woman in the story had a childhood memory of a persimmon grove. Still, no persimmon tree: unless it was the shadowy solitary woman seen behind the curtain in the flat across the street, holding her bare arms up to the sun, the spring.

Now I have a signed first edition of *The Persimmon Tree and Other Stories*, thanks to a pen-friendship with T. In her first letter, in which she enclosed a silky black leaf of the Chinese pear tree she was writing it under, she mentioned that Marjorie Barnard lived near her parents' place. T was going to meet her and her friend and companion, Vera, and do an interview for her thesis. When I wrote back that Marjorie Barnard was a living national treasure and that I loved 'The Persimmon Tree', she told them so, and they gave her a copy to pass on to me. (T: 'When I asked Marjorie a question about "The Persimmon Tree" she waved her hand about and said wearily, "It's all in the past . . ."') She died last year, before 'her' month on the calendar came up.

Black Genoa is the name of a tree, a variety of fig. When I planted a small one in my garden last winter, I had already begun on the story which I have since named after it. My 'Black Genoa' has its roots in death: two deaths, close to each other in nothing but time. That of a friend's father; but also, and this only became clear to me later, that of Marjorie Barnard. The tree's name sounded like a woman's—like Joanna (which is not the friend's name). As draft succeeded draft, the bare fig tree and the life and death it bore within it—'She was pregnant with her own great death', wrote Rilke of Eurydice—came to stand for a woman in mourning, my friend, 'Joanna'; much as Marjorie Barnard's stranger across the street was a shadowy embodiment of a persimmon tree.

The woman in the foreground of my story is a friend at a distance, only an observer, for all her sorrow and her wish to help. She writes her poems and dreams and letters. She listens, she reads. Particularly she reads the letters exchanged by two distant friends of sixty-odd years ago, the Russian poets Pasternak and Tsvetaeva, and finds in them passages that resound in her. She writes them down. If not to share the burden of the other's pain, then at least to bear witness to it, she keeps a diary. She stays in her place by the sea. In the end, this being all she can do by way of affirmation, celebration, she plants her fig tree there.

Most of my stories have been based on people remote in time and place. Writing them was like trying to step in and out of a scene in a film. During the writing of 'Black Genoa', for once there seemed to be no jolt, no transition between life on the written page and lived life. The people and places were there in my immediate surroundings; in their fictional form they still fitted without a crease into day-to-day time. Into this story I slid as if into a long mirror. From beginning to end the writing kept pace with the living: slow pace. Slow writing. *Adagio sostenuto.* A winter story.

Beverley Farmer

BLACK GENOA

IN MEMORIAM: MARJORIE BARNARD

She had moved to the south coast in autumn to live in the house she had bought, an old weatherboard with long windows and old trees growing against them into the sun. One room in particular, the one behind the apple tree next door, glowed all day as if there were a lamp on inside as the sunlight moved over one wooden wall after another. The walls smelled of incense and quivered in the light wind; on every sunny day a banner with large characters on thin gold silk went wavering in the wind on one wall or another with every flicker in the branches at the window. The characters changed in size and shape and so, no doubt, in meaning. She put her bed in here, and hung a dark blue paper blind with white gulls stencilled on it over the window, though as often as not, and without fail when there was a moon, she would roll it up again once her bedlamp was out. Day by day more apple leaves fell until, with all but the last few stained leaves gone, the whole beach showed at this window when she woke, opaque and still on some mornings, glittering on others, or turbulent, white and dark blue.

She wrote a poem about the window and on impulse sent it in a note to an old friend, Joanna, who lived in the city but had grown up on this coast. *There's a spare bed if you'd like to come down and stay,* she added. *All these clear cold beaches— that's if you can get away, of course.* (Joanna had three children still at school.)

WINDOW

Branches at this pane
turn it into gold lead light
in the winter sun,
they spread a large butterfly
on each wooden wall in turn,

who comes in early,
settling where she's supposed to,
poising each black-veined
wing at the right slant, only
twitching in a wind, or when

birds happen to perch
on a vein—all are black birds,
turned wingpatches. Black,
all the new buds. She'll be blocked
in, blocked out, when the leaves grow.

On full-moon nights, two slabs of white marble stretched under her two bare front windows; and the bedroom window was white marble, watered with shadows. So quiet was the wash of the sea that she heard the engines of boats in the Rip. Sometimes in the middle of the night a loud rattling made her sit up and switch the bedlamp on. It was one of the mirrors quivering on the wooden wall, and as she watched the other mirror began and the double sound shuddered in the hollow space between that wall and the wall of the next room, then in the spaces of the rooms themselves until the whole house was throbbing aloud for as long as it took for the ship to edge through the passage.

She slept lightly in the house and had more dreams than usual. In one, her friend Joanna wrote back that she had cancer. Soon afterwards they met by chance and stood talking, so weighed down with intense sorrow that Joanna had to lie down in the grass. She was impossible to lift; trying only made the bones come away out of her like a baked fish's, leaving the flesh, a soft mess of pink and pearly white. Seeds, she thought, but they had a black speck and began to move. *Maggots*, she spoke aloud. Joanna said nothing more. Dumbfounded, she woke and was herself lying stretched out, but in the gold box that was her room on a bright morning.

In one of the half-read borrowed books that she was always

leaving lying round she read an extract of a letter from Marina Tsvetaeva to Boris Pasternak, written in November 1922, an autumn letter, and copied it into her notebook:

My favourite form of communication is in the beyond: in dreams. To dream of someone. The second choice is correspondence. Letters are a form of communicating in the beyond, less perfect than dreams, but subject to the same laws.

Joanna rang in answer to her letter to say she would love to come down to the coast, but her father's cancer, which he had fought for months, had invaded his whole body. They had stopped the treatment and sent him home but now he was back in; now even he had to admit it was the end. She had promised to be with him while he died.

Every day she sat on the beach sketching ink edges around the pallor of it—a still scoop of water as thin as cold air, as if the bay were an empty shell, an earshell, pearl-pale and dotted inside with a line of rocks. When she was cold she walked on the sand. A wet spaniel's head she found one day at high tide in the hairline of the marram grass turned out to be a drowned penguin, its dense wings folded under and hanging out like earlobes. Between them were hunched feathers and there, poking out of them on a fine chain of bones, waggled a small skull, black-beaked, formed of fretty translucent folds like blood-stained paper. Carefully she snapped the chain and carried the skull home wrapped in a sheet from her sketchbook to dry in the sun. Every day there was sun, though a wad of fog materialized over the dunes and the sea in the afternoons and often was still there until late next morning. Her house was not far from the lighthouse on the point; the horn's relentless hooting haunted her sleep. Waking, she read in the lamplight or wrote on scraps of paper.

He slips on a muddy embankment. Beside him something emits a foul sweetish stink: a corpse swelling against its buttoned jacket. It has the head of a pig, blue-tinged, dark red on

329

the cheeks and snout. Dark red means that it is decomposing, he reasons, proud that he is still capable of reason. Everyone is starving. This is a terrain of war, covered with the dead and the dying. What did he last eat? The jacket of his uniform has a blue and dark red hand stuck in it. He climbs the embankment to a railway platform. He is busking, juggling balls, reciting a patter. He is waiting, as is his audience, to jump in front of a train when one finally comes. Meanwhile he juggles. A train hoots, hoots on a double note. It is out of sight, very far away still. The audience exclaims. A ball falls onto the gravel. Squatting to grope for it he sees in horror a thick brown pipe of flesh come out of him and prod the gravel. It disgorges a shiny brown mass. He sticks his finger in it to confirm what it is. He groans. His death has begun. He will miss the train.

After school on a dark afternoon. I am walking home from the railway station along the middle of the street between gutters full of puddles shining grey, rain-spattered, with silvery fish flickering to their surfaces. No cars come and none of the neighbours in front gardens has anything to say to me. The streetlamps blink on. I go to my room, collecting on the way clothes that my father has taken off and left on the floor. I hold his warm shirt and singlet to my face to breathe in the smell of him. My bed looks too small with him in it. There is sunlight in the flowers of the broom bush at the window; the rain has made them large and glossy as buttercups. His pyjamas are in a tangle on the floor. Scolding him, I pick them up. He turns his sleepy grey head towards my voice, his eyes still closed, waiting for a kiss. He has a grey fuzz all over his body except his knees and elbows, wherever the nap has worn off.

Joanna rang early one morning to say that her father had died quietly a few hours ago, as day broke. 'When I woke he must have just gone,' she said. 'That could have been what woke me, I suppose.' She had sat nine days and nights holding his hand. She thought she might come to the coast for a day or two, now it was over. The funeral was in four days.

Misty rain would cover the cemetery. Joanna would wear black. Old soldiers would hang around chatting, and old railwaymen, waiting for the priest to turn up; eventually a flustered substitute would arrive to mutter the words of the service while rain trickled from grey trees and a crowd of umbrellas. The box of darkness into which the coffin under its flowers would slip with a clunk was lined with creased, satiny clay.

Joanna came at nightfall and sat, unable to eat, drinking wine, crying, smoking with a tremulous hand that made her strands of smoke ripple; folding, unfolding her hands between cigarettes. When the lighthouse uttered a blast she yelled. Startled awake, a dog howled in the distance. Again it blasted; again the dog howled. They opened the window a crack and fog came wisping in. No question of sleep now. They pulled on boots to walk to the lighthouse, which was invisible but for the twisting lantern until they were on the last steps; then like a rocket on the launching-pad it showed thick white. The shed that held the foghorn pumped out flurries of mist as bellow on bellow slammed through the cement platform, through their bodies. Just under the lantern, red tide lamps burned. The tide was out of sight. From over the bay an echo came in thunderclaps.

They walked under blurred white lamps along the leggy pier, its piles gnawed black at the ankles, above black rocks and the sandy sea floor, a thong here and there of black kelp winding in a net of ripples. The lighthouse flared, boomed, flared, boomed. Under the last lamp they were met by a huge groan. The lighthouse spoke, and the echo. The whole wide shell of the bay, seafloor and lip of cliff, reverberated. They leaned on a wet rail as with a groan, a roar, a groan, a cluster of lights came into sight, slid past the end of the pier and disappeared. Chord on slow chord sounded over the water. Their two shadows stretched along the

331

seabed as far as the whirlpool of light where the ship had been.

The metal staircase up the cliff face from the beach spilled rain with a jingling at each step. The moon was a high bright smudge. A secretive soft dripping of water from the black trees seemed to fall silent whenever they halted; frogs were creaking. They came back in after midnight with their lips salty and their hair dank and strung with bright drops, having taken the rhythmic booms so far into themselves that they were no longer hearing them, they were no more bother now than breath, than heartbeat and eyeblink. They were soaked with fog, booming. Once or more than once in the night they woke to the deep music of a ship passing the lighthouse. Loud crows in the pines woke them when it was well into the white mid-morning, and still the horn was sounding.

They flung up their sleepy white arms and stretched and yawned and drank strong tea in the kitchen. 'Waking up in this house is like waking up on board ship,' Joanna said.

The lighthouse horn hooted all night on two notes (she writes in her notebook), *while I dreamed of a wrecked ship sunk into a pit so deep no light could wake it. Now in the sun the fog is lifting. The pines creak, heavy with crows.*

I opened the book by my bed and found this in a letter from Boris Pasternak to Marina Tsvetaeva in July 1926, a summer letter: 'The groan is the loudest note in the universe. I am inclined to believe that outer space is filled with this *sound rather than with the music of the spheres . . .'*

At lunchtime Joanna leaned forward into a hood of sunlight, offering a damp paper bag in her hands, which though large and strong always looked helpless; and they still had their slight tremor. The bag was full of large bruise-purple figs, with a red crack in each one, a glow of seeds.

'The last of them and look, I've squashed them. I put them in the fridge and forgot all about them,' Joanna said.

'They're only a bit squashed.' She kissed Joanna's cheek in thanks and washed them in a bowl under the tap, watching seeds move on the surface. 'I associate you with figs, you know, ripe figs, for some reason,' it occurred to her to say.

'Fat and seedy. That's me.'

'Opulent. Purple. Abundant, syrupy and gritty, bursting—'

'They called me the Purple Lady in at the hospital, did I tell you? I was a fixture. Everyone knew me. Here she is, they'd say. Hullo, Purple Lady.'

'You wore all purple clothes?'

'I wore this *one dress*. I've had it on day and night for the last two weeks. Do I stink? No? I didn't have the time to change. No, it wasn't even that—in my tiredness I just couldn't think what else to put on. Last night I could hardly walk. How did I get through it?'

'You'd put your mind to it.'

'The family are all against me. Anyone'd think all of us weren't Ray's kids too, only you were—that's what they're saying.'

'It's the strain.'

'You might as well go home, they said. It's not as if he can see or hear you, he doesn't even know you're there. But I promised Ray I'd be with him.'

'Yes. And you were.'

'He never came out of the coma.'

'Whether he knew or not, you had to stay. But I think he knew.'

'I'd lie in the armchair holding one hand then the other. I'd fall asleep and wake up holding a hand, listening to him breathe. Sometimes I dressed his wound. It was black and it stank. They stopped giving him water, did I tell you? For ten days we were wrenching his jaws apart and dabbing inside with swabs. He had a leather strap for a tongue.'

'He wouldn't have been in pain.' She tore a fig open and licked and bit flesh from its dark lining, pushing the bowl forward. Joanna grinned and shook her head, her eyes blurring again. 'Like a ripe fig, am I? I feel as dead as Ray inside.'

They went down the stairs and sat on the strip of sand in the sun while the tide washed in and the shadow of the cliff flowed down to meet it. Rocks raised their brown backs, scaled or furry, and dived under; weeds strayed in and out of channels. Joanna puffed at a cigarette. 'I keep thinking I have to get back,' she said. 'To the hospital.'

'I know.'

'I was worried every minute I wasn't in the ward. I would have to be asleep when he finally went, wouldn't I?'

'Don't you always have a feeling who's with you when you're asleep, though? In a coma, mightn't it be the same?'

'I keep feeling that the death happened to someone else, Ray's still in there waiting? There was always someone dying. I got to know them all, the visitors too, everyone talked in there. All of us smoking our heads off nonstop, funny, isn't it?' She sighed smoke. 'I'm stopping when this is over.'

'Is the funeral still on Wednesday?'

'Wednesday. Yes, Wednesday at ten. Oh God. You do still want to come, then?'

'Of course.'

'Thanks. You never even got to meet him. I used to wish—oh.'

'No.' She poured more tea. 'I had a weird dream the other night. I keep having these dreams—horror dreams, some of them, and wish dreams. I try to note them down, if I wake up in time. There was this old man in a railway uniform—'

'That'd be Ray. I have frightful dreams all the time. I'm scared to go to sleep.'

When she had seen Joanna off she put the skull of the penguin, which smelled like salted cod now, on a sheet of paper beside a shell she had found and taken at first for another small empty-socketed skull, so many birds there were now washed up on the sand. A hole in the dome of it opened the shadowy ribbed chambers and the white column inside. Carefully with a fine pen she drew the skull and the shell and washed over them, blurring lines to make a watery shadow. I am an empty shell, she thought, not bothering with a signature; while my friend is brimful of feelings which spill out of her, words and tears, hour after hour.

Later, in the flickering room, beside a glass of daisies that had curled up like dead yellow spiders, she scrawled on the back of the sketch.

Dear Joanna,

I wish I could take on some of your pain. You would have taken your father's on, if pain could be shared. There you are overflowing with suffering, while I sit on the beach, empty, an empty shell.

My own father died fourteen years ago. We hadn't been close since I was small. We were shy and uncomfortable alone together.

I remember as a very small child waiting in the bathroom one winter afternoon so dark that we had lights on, waiting for him to come home from work and punish me for some misdeed that had angered my mother. I heard the front door and their cheerful voices suddenly lowered. When he stepped wearily into the bathroom I was cowering under the basin out of the greasy lamplight. He unhooked the razor strop from behind the door. I have no memory of the thrashing (of which we were never to speak), nor of the pain. I cried, I suppose. What I remember is disbelief: each of us staring at the other afterwards in a consternation of disbelief. He was never to thrash me again, and that might have been in his face as well.

My father had a heart attack one winter afternoon twenty-five years later. He died suddenly, alone in the house.

The page was full. She wrote her initial, and sent it to her friend, whose white hands, folded, quivering, filled her mind. The day of the funeral she drove into the rain and back. Yellow day lilies opened and closed in the garden, a curled blue iris here and there, and daisies. In a low fork of the bare prunus tree she found a twig cup with nothing inside but dead leaves and broken shells, snail shells. Brown leaves lay all over the grass. Wandering into a garden shop one day—by then it was July, midwinter—she saw among plum and apple and apricot saplings a grafted stick with loose roots and no branches, as slender and dry as cane or dark bamboo. The label fluttered, a printed butterfly: a picture of figs, and a name a woman might have, she thought, in a book about the deep South: *Black Genoa*. She bought it and planted it where it would be a sunscreen at the kitchen window, digging a hole with four glistening brown walls, packing the roots in hard. As night fell the fog fell also; the lighthouse hooted. In the fuzz round the porch light, wet and cold, the skin of Black Genoa shone. Green hands would reach out of it one day, loose on spread arms; and a thousand pouches, purpling, oozing, burst apart.

Karlinsky, Simon, *Marina Tsvetaeva: The Woman, her World and her Poetry*, Cambridge University Press, Cambridge, 1985, p.161.

Pasternak, Boris; Tsvetaeva, Marina; Rilke, Rainer Maria, *Letters, Summer 1926*. Edited by Yevgeny Pasternak, Yelena Pasternak and Konstantin M. Azadovsky, translated by Margaret Wettlin and Walter Arndt, Jonathan Cape, London, 1986, p.157.

TO BE CONGRUOUS WITH THE SEA

Finola Moorhead

AUTHOR'S NOTE

When you write you wish to dig through time, so there is no dating. One should not be embarrassed by one's own work and a lot of serious craft goes into prevention of that in the future.

'To Be Congruous with the Sea' was in my estimation my first published story, though, of course, there were things published and produced before this. I had had poems in university magazines, Melbourne and Hobart; plays read at Monash and one work-shopped at the first Australian National Playwrights Conference in Canberra, which was produced in Brisbane later in 1973. In my four years as a teacher, I had adapted stories and written and directed performance-pieces for the students. Also, I'd won a couple of prizes—the State of Victoria Unpublished Writers prize in 1973 and joint first prize in the *Herald-Sun* Summer Short Story competition. There were little bits in little magazines. Those successes were out of town tournaments so to speak, and now dated.

My mother could allow herself few luxuries during the fifties, and one that was most prominent lying on the coffee table in the sitting room was *Meanjin Quarterly*. She was proud of her allegiance to this journal of arts and letters since its inception. I probably learnt a lot about Australian writing fairly young from reading bits and pieces, her prejudice towards its nobly local line and the critical work of the great A. A. Phillips. To please her was, I think, always a difficult thing. Being published in *Meanjin* was becoming a writer in my interpretation of her eyes. Not that she ever approved of such a risky existence.

Clem Christesen had a serious sense of history and his role in it. He was an interventionist editor and claimed to have helped many an emerging writer. I cannot speak for others or the heroic days of *Meanjin Quarterly*, but he was rigorous in making me craft this story. I must have written twenty or thirty drafts, tasting every word, phrase, sentence, positioning paragraphs and balancing mood and effect. I don't want to glorify the role of an argumentative editor who cares as much as you do for the right word but I appreciated this hard schooling, and always know in any of my work whether the final draft has been changed in the slightest way. Clem tested my commitment to every word in this story. One thing bothers me now and bothered me then. Somehow he managed to make me change her surname, from Bergen to Addams-Smith. It is still an irritation. For the rest, the priceless lesson in rewriting, he has my undying regard and gratitude.

It was not difficult choosing 'To Be Congruous with the Sea' for this anthology as I can honestly say it is not dated. I might have written it yesterday. I didn't. I was twenty-five or six then and now I am as old as the woman in the story.

Finola Moorhead

TO BE CONGRUOUS WITH THE SEA

On the cold pastel scene of sea and sand, silvergulls and driftwood, one human may have seemed incongruous. But she was not.

Gina Addams-Smith was tall. Forty. Grey hair, waving to her shoulders, framed an oval face, cool and smooth as if carved like glass in the ocean's tumble. The one thing sensuous about her was the way she ate. Ripe pears, wounded by a deep, wide bite, would spurt juices to her cheekbones and thickly down her chin. Grapes, held above her back-thrown head, were played with by teasing lips. Cherries tossed and caught. Pips spat. Chops, barbecued, held by their bones, were torn by strong, shell-white teeth.

Gina ate, always, alone.

As driftwood is, outcast and at home, she stood on the beach. The soldierly lines of Pacific gulls, oyster-catchers, terns and the pair of mollymawks were undisturbed. Each evening she shared their vigil at sunset. The birds and she faced the east, the sea. This way the change of light was not spectacular but subtle yet sudden. Some days she turned to make her way back up to the shack and it seemed as if she were turning into another dimension of time, the western sky unexpectedly bright, the shack a misshapen dark rectangle, back-lit, having no substance. It was the only dwelling on the north-west Tasmanian inlet for five miles. From the road which ran along the centre of the narrow peninsula this building seemed uncomfortable caught in the sandhills and salt-toughened tea-tree. In fact, its old concrete floor had broken in parts; sand and spear-grass were inside. In one place the masonite wall had surrendered to the tea-tree; on this curl of gnarled trunk hung her yellow oilskin, her shapeless overcoat, her red and navy striped blazer. A few stairs led from the concrete to the next level, which jutted out over the beach. This was her studio. From waist-high to the ceiling the walls were windows. Originally bought from wreckers, they comprised small squares of glass in wooden frames, larger panes which opened, sections of louvres and one panel of stained-glass. In careless order, hung, propped, stacked, were large canvases—most of them already bright with hard-edged primitive shapes of children, fruit, or birds. Gina painted with a thick brush in primary and secondary oil-colours.

Visitors used to come and go from the Addams-Smith household without having seen Gina, nor she them. Her mother had given her crayons, clay, paper, cardboard and the exclusive use of a shed. The little girl created her world. She learnt the meaning of four walls and outdoors. She roped all her experiences into the tiny compass of her understanding. Her work, when it had served its natal purpose, went up to the house and was greeted with generous encouragement. An old friend sold it on the sidelines of his business as a quaint diversion. Gina grew up in the living privacy of her shed. At school she sat quietly. Later she worked in an office—retiring, when her duties were finished, to deep within her mother's garden to model and paint. She could buy the groceries, execute her job, but she could not laugh with the other girls or engage in casual social interchange.

Mrs Addams-Smith died when her daughter was twenty-five. The house was sold. The loss brought to Gina the cold, grey realization that she could not communicate. She could paint her need, but few would know. Acquaintances to whom she had given nothing of herself could not understand what she was asking of them. She resorted to tears, to shouts, to incoherencies. To frowning observation. She began to distrust people—their laughter, their joviality. Their lack of concern turned them into monsters, a conspiracy of monsters. She lost her ability even to buy groceries. She began locking herself in her room at the boarding house, barring the door, refusing to go to work; refusing, eventually, meals. The room was so small her paints, her paper, her paraphernalia could not breathe. The paints first, squeezed over the walls. The paper, torn to tiny shreds, slap, stuck, strewn . . . talc, toothpaste, lipstick. Laugh-laughter. Colour confusion.

Blankets? Sheets? Pull, scream, scratch, bleed. The landlord burst into the room, breaking down her brittle hysteria to tears.

For five years they gave her tranquillizers and IQ tests. And, for occupational therapy, newsprint and water-colours. The nurses held her in distant respect because of her reputed intelligence and the fact that she communicated only through anger and tears. One Sister tried to love her, but already Gina's face had set into its cool, sea-sculpted lines; and the eyes, a deep green glass, threatened drowning. Under the influence of the drugs, she painted pastel gothic interiors.

The sea was still, a silver-blue. A cormorant dived, hardly shaking the water. Two herons stood on a jutting sandbar. Some of the birds around her shuffled at the ebbing tide. Now and then an argument about the sandy head of a fish would revive; the young mollymawk would win again, stand astride his prize and look out to sea. Gina followed his gaze to the surfacing cormorant, fish in beak. The smaller birds fluttered.

Noise shattered the cool intimacy. A car skidded around the point. Gina turned. A boy jumped out, bounced about on the sand, threw a stone at the water and shouted. A girl slid through the driver's door, awkwardly, trying not to split her short black skirt. He made her laugh, she slapped him and they tumbled fightingly toward the speargrass.

Gina stepped back to the sand-polished log, and sat. The car had upset her trance. She thought of the two men she loved. For Gina there was only love, or disregard.

Tony, his smart clothes crumpled—always crumpled from the five-hour drive. Uncrumpling them with elegant down-strokes. Striding from his station-wagon, smiling. Her agent. Always smiling. Always knowing. Gentle unnecessary words. A brush of the cheek with his lips. Play-acting his words with care: the effort to come every month, all the way from Hobart, dropping commitments, angry friends. So many friends, so many loves. Male names, endearments, unlikely female names. Esmerelda. Prim-Rose. Violet-heart. Following laugh, hand flowing to the south, letting the names with their flower-faces and absurd colours tumble away down the Derwent, dismissed for the weekend. Casting her money about in a dance. Often the banknotes lying about the studio until needed. Performing Tony. Performance dissolving into his clean-shaven concentration. The paintings absorbed through his fingers, the pores of his face, erupting back at her, refurbished, electric, nourished. Enclosing him in her world and he never captured, never fully eccentric, always realistic. Her bank-book, receipts, presents, a new radiator put in her path, so she trips. Notices. Shrugs and relies on him. The second lip-cheek brush—she inside stiff sculpture, a slight melt—he all outside, fluid, flexible, singing. Then a silent, empty studio—colour compressed into tubes on a tray—vermilion, cobalt, sienna, ochre—white canvases, white beach and moon. Lingering drifts of shaving-lotion snapped off in the bite of an apple.

Gina felt the bleached wood with the tips of her tanned hand. And thought of the other.

'You tell Poppa Peppi the matter, heh?' Fat, brown, hairy arms thrown into tragic gestures of sympathy. And tears laughing in her eyes. Her taut body compressing, in a single shiver, a psyche fragile and raw from the institution. Brim-green eyes drinking in the fruit-bright store. Frost-pale and wine-purple grapes in cane baskets hung from the ceiling, jonathans in crisp clean rows, valencias and navels vying for truest orange, spreading hands of bananas giving, grapefruit and sweetcorn by the door inviting entrance into a cave of treasure, pineapples encrusting the back wall, tomatoes red and cucumbers green and and . . . Gina laughs: POTATOS UNIONS PUMKIN. 'You lika my shop, heh?' With that a comic hug, enthusiastic chatter and a march this way and that. Words orchestrating the cascade of fruit and colour. And the warmth filling starved places.

Gina felt a quiet smile. Ten years and Mr Peppiniccini is now quite old, but the warmth new-season fresh, and her paintings: *Italian Girl Skipping* in the lolly-pink and aqua kitchen; *Bananas and Blue Grapes on Red* and *Pumpkin House* in the shop. Colour! Gina looked at the ice-iridescent sea. The birds began flying off. Shadows ceased.

She strolled through the heavy sand to the track. The car parked on the beach was forgotten. Her world and her dream were one. She, as the birds nesting in the scrub, belonged. A part of the order. A detail in the picture.

Giggles, grunts, mumbles. Gina stopped to listen, jolted. There, in a bush cubby-house, the boy and the girl. The boy standing, dropped his jeans and briefs. The girl, lying sideways, propped her head on an arm and looked up at him. The young male stretched out of his shirt, preening his nakedness. He gestured. The girl shook her head and shivered. He knelt and bunched the skirt around her waist. She touched him with her hand. Gina froze. They knelt, coming together. Gina gasped, felt hot and damp. She wanted to run, she wanted to stare. The couple sank onto the grass.

Gina stepped back, and a twig cracked. A sharp glance, but the pair were writhing undisturbed. Another step back, the familiar bush became frightening. Another step back. Darkness rushed in like liquid and silence dropped about her, a net. Another step. A yell from the boy. Gina jumped, the fright screaming to her nerve-ends, aching at her skin. She turned and tiptoed, terrified of a hand which might close about her throat. Twenty yards further on, determined to turn back striding and singing, to be discovered and to discover, she began to hum. Her mind exploded with bursts of confusion and excitement, molten whirl. But her body, calm as dry wood, hummed. She came to the open stretch of beach, alien in the last light; logs became murdered victims, the silence a brooding, a held breath. In the west a vibrant orange glow bound by a complementary blue was garish. The shack, laced to the ground by tea-tree, sinking into sand mounds, was an ungainly box. A huge piece of litter. Gina turned away from it, in disgust.

The phosphorescent fish twitched inside the water. The tide, at ebb, lapped. White moon called driftwood to driftwood. Human voices reached across the sand: a laugh, a shout; the car left the beach with a sweep of its headlights and a rumble of exhaust.

In the moonlit darkness Gina's taut body shuddered. Slowly she folded into the curled form of a woman crying—a human lost at the edge of the rising tide.

CHRISTOS MAVROMATIS IS A WELDER

George Papaellinas

AUTHOR'S NOTE

This is it. 'Christos Mavromatis is a Welder' is my favourite of the published stories. Of course, each of my published stories is a favourite of sorts. This has nothing to do with sentiment. Being a writer who tends towards the lengthy, there exist sufficiently few stories to allow for indiscriminate affection. I do reserve something more for this particular one.

Remember, I am a tyro. I'm learning as I go.

This is the story in *Ikons* in which I first came close to understanding my own creative purpose. In this collection, I was able to articulate it, in a way that I could clearly understand, in practice rather than in my mind in some sort of theoretical grunt. It's the story that is most obviously unbiographical, and, at the same time, the one in which I first knew that I came close to the personal and empathetic. At least as far as I'm concerned. I understood that I didn't like Christos or anyone in particular in this story, except maybe Garbis, and I couldn't in future simply like any of the Mavromatises ever again, but I did understand them, and so I loved them. I understood that I could do this in fiction. In fact I should. I was able to escape myself. I had tried to like them so much until then. And so I had made them straining creatures. I went back and relaxed them in previous stories in *Ikons* as a result, but I couldn't achieve the texture of them that I caught in this one. I really understood them here; they most clearly became my creation and distinct from me. And, I hope, dependent on me in no way. The Mavromatises became politically real because they finally became difficult, really difficult.

This is the story in which I realized, for the first time, that

I wasn't writing about being Greek in Australia. This isn't written from a tourist's point of view, after all. No, every one of everyone's experiences was purely Australian in this story. I was writing about being Australian. Not ethnic. Not multicultural. These are a politician's, a careerist's, a PR person's arid definitions. They aren't true political definitions at all because they mean nothing dimensional. Australian is not an antonym for Greek.

It's the story in which I think I captured the culture of class well enough, which I think will always texture my work.

It's the story in which I tried to describe work—labour—and the emotional involvement in it. The politic of it. And achieved a measure of satisfaction in doing so.

It's the story that persuaded me finally that the short story form, the very intention of the short story as a dramatic form, the formula of it, the reality it proposes, did not really suit me one bit. I realized it was the first story I had written that wasn't a failed short story at all. It just wasn't a short story in the purist sense. From this point on I became aware that I really wanted to write long fiction, more elaborate, more sweeping, complicated narratives that try to escape the simple causality of the short story.

This is why you get only the first part of 'Christos Mavromatis is a Welder'. Length considerations. It's why the first part was written separately to the rest. As a short story. And why it perhaps doesn't satisfy—because it never satisfied me. It only ever tantalized me and made me want to explore it all just a little bit more. Which became a lot.

I like this story because it isn't even one.

George Papaellinas

CHRISTOS MAVROMATIS IS A WELDER

Christos Mavromatis is a welder.

I'll tell you because he mightn't.

Try him.

Whaddayado, mate? Simple question. Ask him. You want to know, don't you?

And if *you* can get it out of him then you're doing better than the old bloke did. His overalls don't tell you much, dirt's dirt and dirty overalls could mean any one of a million jobs, couldn't they? So . . . whaddayado, mate? Sit down next to him. Take it easy, you only want half the seat. That's how the old bloke on the bus home got started the other day.

'Are you doin' well for yourself?' Voice like a South's supporter.

There's Chris sitting on the bus home, hard up against the window, pretending Cleveland Street's something new to him. A face on him that'd frighten kids at a bus stop. Chris as sour as the hops on the old bloke's breath. Nothing is what the old bloke got from Christos.

But you'd be polite, wouldn't you? Suit creased. Smile like a dentist.

Good luck.

My guess is Chris would keep to his window, scaring kiddies. You'd be left rattling your *Herald* and baking in the couple of whiskies that got you asking in the first place. Forget Christos. No speaka da English. Turn to page five, past what Fraser isn't doing and what Hawke's going to, to the bit on who's having to leave what country. Try and guess where Chris is from.

Shift over. You'd make room for him, wouldn't you?

But this old bloke just undid the top button of his King Gees. He arranged himself. He squeezed Christos against the window.

'Whadda *you* do, mate?'

Dopey wog, he thinks.

'What . . . you . . . do? Mate?' Voice like a magistrate. Old bloke with a circle of hair sitting up on his head as stiff as a grey hedge, wet blue eyes.

No wife, thinks Chris, who else would be drunk before he's even home, before he's even eaten?

Or knowing Chris . . . how can you tell with an Australian?

Christos does not have much choice.

'Job mate . . . like you, mate.'

The bus is filling by now, almost full, people standing and they're all trying to keep their eyes from wandering away from the windows, but if this old bloke doesn't keep his voice down, if he has to ask again and he *has* been drinking, then all those eyes . . .

Chris's mouth starts to work so much it should be on overtime rates. Somewhere between a stranger's smile and something a little bit too eager. Chris's English isn't too bad and he doesn't want to seem unfriendly.

'Work.'

Old fool, he thinks, these old ones especially. They are quick with their abuse and this one's been drinking . . .

Better whaddayado then whereayafrom.

'Job . . .' and Chris nods his head again, tries another smile, this one as hard as the old bloke's stare.

Again.

'Job, mate . . . like you.'

Again?

The old bloke's eyes swing away only they're slow eyes, impatient with a bad joke.

'Yeah, know that . . . but whaddaya*do*, mate?' and the old bloke takes a breath that swells his belly. For a good laugh? I mean, it's not a bad joke . . . well, he's had a few and you like a laugh after a few, don't you? I mean, it's a pretty simple question and Chris . . .

'Sorry, mate, sorry . . . I . . . sorry.'

Chris is going to trust to silence. Time for a bit of shush. Time to shut up, he shrugs his shoulders, points to his mouth.

He's a dumbie. No speaka da English.

Chris reckons it's easier.

Look. The old bloke's going to cop this, no speaka da English, he assumed as much anyway, before he started with his questions.

That's right. No speaka da English.

The old bloke's going to sit back in his seat now. It groans. Not a sound out of Chris.

The old bloke's going to maintain a silence too but a jolly sort of silence his, a private one, like a giggle, unless, of course, he happens to catch the eye of, say, another old bloke standing in the aisle when he might just choose to translate it into a joke, matey sort of joke, you know the type, the sort that'll cause a little bit of rocking in the seat or on the feet, the sort that you get to hear again, louder and funnier the longer Chris nods and smiles and shrugs and says nothing. Old blokes swaying and bumping into people, making a fuss over Chris. Can you see it? Chris grinning, no speaka da English, and the old blokes laughing like old mates . . .

Chris interrupts.

He can see it.

'Builder, mate . . .' and Chris who can't *really* see a joke sits up, tense, the way a tightrope walker looks, smiling like he's going to cry and never still. Well, Chris has been swaying ever since the old bloke sat down as easy as a loose punch. Chris sits up now, balancing, and sure on his feet now that he's started. Have you ever seen a pub fight starting?

Who does the old bloke think he is?

'I'm builder, mate . . . workin' out Werrington . . . houses . . . lotsa houses, lotsa work, mate . . .' And he sits back too.

'Yeah?' and the old bloke's blinking, he smooths his soft face with a wipe of a hand, he's been woken up, he was just getting settled, 'yeah?'

Chris's talking is an elbow in his ribs.

'Yeah . . . good, mate,' and he throws another look over Chris. Beer is waking him up as quickly as it almost put him to sleep.

Who's this wog?

349

'Whaddayado? . . . Brickie's labourer?'

He hasn't been listening.

Look at him, thinks our Chris.

Old fool. Five o'clock and already drunk. Who is he? What does *he* do? Is he a property owner, is he, out collecting his rents in clothes that have never seen soap? No wife even? Whose boss does he think he is? Is he a judge? Is he?

Chris might as well be as drunk as the old bloke now. He's forgotten where he is, he's forgotten he's on the bus. He doesn't even know what country he's in.

'Boss mate . . . I'm boss!' It's a game of darts, one after the other and Chris wants to take the chook and the half dozen bottles too.

'Twenty men, mate . . . boss for twenty men!'

Have you ever seen a drunk who's been punched in the head? The way they stand there saying nothing and shaking their faces? That's what Chris wants. He wants a silent old bloke. He combs his wavy hair with fingers.

'Boss, eh?' and the old bloke believes him, you can see that. All he wanted was Christos's silence and now Chris has got the old bloke looking like he believes him.

Chris can see this.

The old bloke rubs his nose. He swings his arm in a long arc.

Stares at his watch. Lost for words, eh?

'Long way from Werrington,' he pauses, 'still early,' and he smiles at Chris, he congratulates him.

'Make your own hours, do ya?'

'Yes, yes . . .' and Chris sees himself in his own story, 'yes, mate . . . boss.'

'Where's ya Rolls, then?'

And Chris looks like he's going to stand up and shake a hand now (twenty men!).

And the old bloke's chuckling, 'Rolls in the garage?' and Chris chuckles, doing well in his story, he's smiling and grinning, the old bloke's grinning and smiling. Old mates!

Chris is just about on his feet, taking bows. But it's the others on the bus. Chris checks them. That one, a secretary, she's staring at her feet, and that other one whose eyes keep dropping on Christos, he looks away, he's back to counting cars in lines outside the window. An accountant. In case they're listening, Chris keeps his voice low. This story is for this old bloke who thinks he's better than Christos, but isn't.

Who does he think he is?

'Done well in this country, 'ave ya mate?' and the old bloke's not keeping his voice down. A voice like he's calling the winner at a pub raffle, he's checking for an audience in the aisle too.

'Yes, mate,' nods Christos who fidgets.

'Yeah, I bet you done well ... yeah ...' and the old bloke shifts large-bellied in his seat, too large a belly to squeeze by easily. The old bloke can pick Chris.

He scans a tweed skirt, looks up for a face to nod with and questions Chris who's doing well out Werrington way.

'Done well enough for yaself?' and Chris watches the old bloke watching the accountant, watches him poke him in the leg, friendly.

'They do well outta this country, don't they ... these blokes do *bloody* well,' and the secretary is staring at Christos, he catches her doing it and the old bloke's cackling and she looks away, back out the window, everyone does, but they *are* listening, of course they are, and as soon as Christos looks away, she'll be looking at him again, or the accountant will or they'll be looking at each other and they'll be smiling, like you do at strangers when somebody's kid is being smacked.

'Well you'll be goin' back 'ome, won't ya? ... Won't ya?' and Christos sits silenced in the old bloke's trap, caught by the old bloke's leg, swinging and playing as the old bloke faces Christos.

And the old bloke crosses his arms, showing interest.

'Whereareyafrom?'

'My stop ... please ... my stop ...' and Chris is pushing past the old bloke's legs, slow as the arms of a turnstile, 'my stop, here, please . . .' and he almost drops his bag, it's slippery, vinyl, one of those Qantas ones, he catches it, pushes the accountant out of the way, a receptionist almost goes over, he pulls himself along the handrail.

"Scuse me . . . 'scuse me . . .'

'Well, go back there, you smart bastard!'

"Scuse me . . . 'scuse me!'

Ever seen a crab? Always in a panic. Avoiding things sideways.

So, there you go. He's off the bus. He has to walk the rest of the way home. And the old bloke isn't even looking out the window. You are.

But Christos wouldn't know that. He isn't looking up at it.

Christos just off the bus.

Christos holding his bag.

Christos. Back the other way, mate.

Go home, Christos.

A WORLD THIS SIZE

John Bryson

AUTHOR'S NOTE

In an exhibition of paintings (modern European, I seem to remember, a far vault in the state gallery, barely enough wall space to set the exhibits elegantly apart), I fell in with a group listening to a guide. He had us stand in the centre of the room while he spoke about the next picture on our itinerary, and he insisted on this procedure, I guess, so that a pause might still the jostling image of the last painting and hold from us the next canvas, the event to come, until we were ready for it. The same care guided the way he spoke. He told us nothing about the subject, or the organization, or the technique. It seemed to pain him when such questions were asked (a slight man, tapped his fingers to speed up his thinking), so he avoided them, as if we were far better to hold no expectations at all, right now. Instead, he suggested some questions we might keep in mind. How may a painting of one part of life suggest life beyond? If the eye were to follow some compelling line, maybe to a point outside the frame, how might it be brought back again to the assured hub? And so on. Then we walked to the waiting exhibit, our imaginations happy and free.

The next canvas was of a late-night dance hall (the boards glinty and mischievous, paper flowers on pedestals), like any you've seen in your hometown, or in Sydney, Marseilles, Seattle. Everyone in this scene was waiting for the musicians to begin another bracket. Of the crowd, I best remember a knot of skylarking sailors, a swanky couple practising a two-step during the break, and a tipsy commercial traveller crossing the floor to accost a coy whore. All these folk, or their kin, were known to me, so I was surprised they didn't seem to be as acquainted

353

with each other. And by the doorway, in tuxedo and mirror pumps, the promoter drew us inside, his smile a billboard of welcome, his eyes never leaving us, no matter where we stood (not a difficult trick for painters, I know), so the pleasing effect of this was that the beholder was now part of the event, arriving in time for the music.

I left the gallery, walking uptown, thinking about 'A World This Size' and the people in it, because I was content with the solitude that has something to do with crowds, it was evening, and I was heading for the restaurant in the story—a place familiar to you, wherever you live.

John Bryson

A WORLD THIS SIZE

There is a restaurant like this in every fast city. The street number has long been forgotten, but it has stood here for so long that buildings nearby are described by their proximity to it. The façade is narrow, and shadowed by office blocks and department stores. You would have difficulty remembering its colour. By the entrance is a brass bell-pull, shined so mercilessly that the griffin embossed on it has become vague. (In your city, this may be a vain, but now shortsighted, lion.) Inside, varnished bentwood hooks beckon along the length of the corridor. Only those at the far end are filled, so the passage ahead will seem to lead you back into a time when hats and well-fashioned topcoats were still popular.

The proprietor has a dark complexion, although he was born far north of the Mediterranean. The one I am thinking of was born in Cremona. It might be a year since you last dined here, but he seems only temporarily to have forgotten your name. The tiny woman in black, sitting at a table just inside the door, is his mother. Everyone calls her the Signora.

In the evenings, a table near the centre of the dining room will, commonly, seat a small party hosted by someone who looks familiar if you are a keen reader of financial journals. Another is more quietly occupied by the producer of some television programme, and his second wife. This should exhaust the list of celebrities. A table for two in a corner is taken by followers of a restaurant guidebook (who quickly feel they have made an expensive mistake) and another by finals students in law and architecture whose successes have given them expectations. The guide followers now rest their menu cards on the table, comforted that the evening is not beyond their means, and the students look around remorselessly for the drinks waiter.

The place is popular with those who work late. The fellow in the hound's-tooth jacket is responsible for the human interest pages in our morning newspapers. Two youngsters at his table have pencils in their shirt pockets, and take care not to hinder his anecdotes. Holding a novel open on the table, a neglectfully thin young woman (a research assistant, quite likely, from the Central Library) gives the waiter her order. She orders in Italian; her voice is American. She reddens when she speaks. A clothing manufacturer from the warehouse lanes downtown, and his hearty wife, have an older woman with them who fussily checks items on her menu. She isn't afraid to interrupt their conversation.

A little baroque music struts overhead.

A man sits by himself. He is waiting on a martini. His fingers drum the cloth. Soon he falls to searching faces at other tables for something to hold his interest.

His name is Freddy Unthank. Freddy would be hurt if we were to confuse his somnolent gaze with boredom. He has an eye for foible, and when he comes here (most Thursdays) he chooses his seat for the best view of the room. His curiosity about people around him has made Freddy a lot of money.

It is, for example, Freddy's judgment alone that has established those thirsty students as inchoate lawyers and architects (although he cannot see their faculty neckties clearly from here); that the TV producer's wife is too careful of her husband's attention to be his first spouse; that the hound's-tooth jacket spends much of its time hanging within tremor of the newspresses. The rag-trade merchant's wife has an appetizing tan which Freddy has put down to tennis on Wednesdays and Sundays, and he thinks the older woman with them is an aunt. Freddy has already named her Lottie.

Freddy is a salesman. His room in the apartment he shares with his mother is hung with mementos of sales competitions he has won everywhere. Freddy is proud of the ragged tapa-cloth he bought his mother on their holiday around the Pacific (at the expense of a satisfied air-freight company) and of a framed citation (for 52 new car deals in one month) hanging over his bookshelf. But his mother's strong hand would then draw you aside to stand for a moment before the golden dinner plate (one million frozen fish fingers) on her mantelpiece.

All this success is the result of his interest, he would tell you, in the human pageant. Every salesman can recall his first sale, and Freddy's memory of his own is vivid. He served as a sales cadet in automobiles under an Irishman known, because of his splendid baldness, as Hubcap Reilly. Reilly's fat address book was filled with the birthdays, with the names of wives and children, and with the hobbies of anyone to whom he had ever sold anything. It was so well worn that he held it together with rubber bands. Freddy bought himself an address book and rubber bands and waited for instruction. But Reilly was cunning and lazy. On the car lot, he left Freddy to those he knew, from many hard years in the trade, were the worst wasters of time.

Freddy wrote all their names happily into his book: the lunchtime browsers, the tyre-kickers and the breezy tinkerers. Reilly could stand it no longer. He drew Freddy away from his customer (a stooped clerk, soon to be pensioned off, so he had told Freddy, from his duties of forty years). 'Look,' Reilly said, 'the jacket. The shoes.' But where Hubcap Reilly saw a thready jacket and piebald shoes, Freddy was watching something else altogether. He saw clever and inky old fingers which, never still, found walnut fasciae and leather cushions delicious to the touch, fingers which had begun already to pry (from ledgers and provisions for loss) the nuggets which his employers wouldn't miss for years after his drab retirement party.

Twenty-eight days later he bought from Freddy a heady white roadster with scarlet trim, and paid not with a reckless cheque but with careful and anonymous banknotes.

Since then Freddy has sold office furniture, toys, waterfront subdivisions, fast-food franchises, management games, aircraft space, futures in sisal and flax, unit trusts, and insurance. On the way, his address book fattened, then burst into a flutter of yellow cards in a crested box. At the time we catch Freddy sitting in this restaurant, his hair has thinned, increasingly he needs his spectacles and he has a rumble of minor ailments, but he will write $100 000 more in insurance sales this year than his nearest rival.

Francesca, the waitress whom Freddy likes to have look after

357

him, has brought without the need for his order a platter of red tripe and his Insalata Freddo. This is a joke of long standing. Francesca is a northerner (none of Freddy's conjecture, this— she has told him proudly herself) descended from the Ghibelline della Scala, the powerful family of thirteenth-century Verona. When she walks off, her black hair swings from side to side like the peremptorily drawn curtain of a departing carriage.

Freddy admires Francesca's deep voice and strong hips but he knows her interest in him is merely kindly. He sees her point of view entirely. Some of his friends seem to Freddy to suffer childish and debilitating hungers, irrelevant to the real nutrients of adult life. His own sexual need is modest. He has been happy enough to have it uncovered briefly, from time to time, by girls who were sellers of services like that. The latest was a heavily freckled woman who worked evenings at a massage parlour. Freddy imagined her day job on some thundering production line. He had offered (during a cosy flush of gratitude) to take her to dinner. 'I've got things to look after at home,' she said. So Freddy then attributed to her, without her knowledge, an unheeding two-year-old daughter whose own freckles wouldn't become apparent for another twelve months, a bitterly silent mother-in-law who lived in a room at the back of the house, and a stringy husband with stagnant singlet and stained breath, tired from driving his truck interstate three nights in every five. The spectre of that abused and resentful family has kept Freddy away from the parlour since.

Evidently their waiter has forgotten the students' order. They can't seem to catch his eye. These things are only a matter of luck but Freddy has noticed that the clothing manufacturer hasn't the same trouble. That waiter (a curt Calabrian, won't last long) has his pencil poised aggressively. They all wait for Aunt Lottie to order first.

'What is it, Fresh Fish of the Day?' Aunt Lottie demands.

'Sole. Poached, Signora, lemons.'

'Fresh, it says. Fish market is Tuesday and Friday. Now is Thursday.'

358

'Give me the New York sirloin,' says the clothier. 'Rare.'

'Now is Thursday,' Aunt Lottie says.

'No,' says the clothier, 'make mine the eye fillet.'

'I'm still thinking,' his wife says.

That the clothier and his wife have neither guided Aunt Lottie through the menu nor dared to interfere with her definition of wholesomeness is all the clue Freddy needs. Aunt Lottie is the holder of the clothier's purse. It is her money that keeps materials on his shelves (floral rolls of Singapore synthetics, light cottons from Calcutta), her money that funds the stock (flounced dressing gowns, brunch coats in well-behaved queues) in his storeroom. On the last day of the month, with pince-nez and stumpy red pencil, she corrects his debtors-ledger and circles the entries beyond sixty days so they stand out like angry sores. These small business enterprises are familiar territory for Freddy. In his time he has sold them estate-wagons, coffee machines, insurances for seamstresses' perforated fingers. But this has not been his jurisdiction now for many years. That he has marked Aunt Lottie so surely as the hidden proprietor gives Freddy a delicious feeling of adroitness, like a gambler who (above his teetering city of counters) finds he is perilously addicted not to risk but to infallibility.

While he savours this there is, in the doorway, a movement of black organza. A tall woman, blonde, showy. Freddy finds it difficult to guess her age. However old she is, the man behind her is a generation older. An evening coat hangs from his shoulders like the folds of a cloak. This seems to Freddy an outdated and contemptuous elegance. It is evidently not yet the correct moment for him to enter the room, but this woman is unhesitating and makes toward the head waiter. She interrupts his welcome with an astonishingly youthful smile and the gestures of her quick hands are charming and intemperate. She has achieved the agreement she wanted and turns to the man in the doorway. She is used to preparing his way.

Freddy has them firmly placed by now: she the envied young wife plucked early, for this match, from a career in the theatre;

her husband the liege of some buzzing financial realm who, with the ascetic and perverse pride of his kind, owns nothing at all himself but stocks and shares (though all in faithful corporations and stealthy trusts with addresses off-shore which provide him with chauffeured limousines, splendidly crewed yachts, and vacations wherever the sun shines).

The house in which they live is surrounded by a wall of bluestone taken from servants' quarters demolished in the sixties; a well-drained quartz driveway is crisp underfoot; no mastiff scowls behind the shrubs despite a warning on the gate; and Freddy would expect a sunny display of annuals to border the path, and peripatetic whiffs of jasmine. Since the husband leaves early in the morning for his office, the only car by the house for most of the day is a dainty French two-door. Sternly clipped lavender sentries stand by the doorbell. A household secretary, whose obligation is to open the door, does it bluntly and her route then to her employer carries past cabinets of chilly porcelains and carefully warring ivory horsemen.

The room in which the mistress of the house spends most of her day was once the ballroom, with enough shellacked floorspace for a hundred waltzing couples. But there is something here a visitor would find strange. These chandeliers are now limp and dusty. All but the far end of the room is empty. Instead of the rare silver, vases and portraits indicated by the behaviour of the rest of the house, there hangs above the fireplace (a middle-aged addition, that, since the fire is gas) a familiar and cheery print of an alpine farmstead on a Tyrolean winter's day. .

On the timber mantelpiece below (a frozen brown fallow it makes here, since it hangs just under the painted snow-line) transparent bonbonnière geese, horses and swans in spiky poses wait for release at the coming of some northern spring. Arranged to face this vista are a couch and armchair (whose pattern of nosegays has run to seed where it sees the light), a nest of skinny tables and a standard lamp with a floral bonnet, all assembled like the draughty properties of a dressing room backstage.

The woman whose domain this is sits on an arm of the couch.

Instead of the invoices and receipts of household accounting, there lie on the table only the interrupted pieces of a jigsaw puzzle (the recent beginnings of a Breughel street scene, most of the crowd yet to arrive). Her hair is not now showy and buoyant. It is hard to imagine her richly dressed. She sits on the bolster side-saddle and, whatever her thoughts, they do not have the rhythms of gaiety.

This downhearted furniture and the brittle menagerie above the fireplace are all the property she has. Her husband's disdain for the traditions of ownership still alarms and mystifies her. The contents of their larder appear on some company's inventory, somewhere; the house, the mahogany settings, the objects of art, are not purchased because they are lovely things but because assessors she has never met believe they will accumulate in value. This seems to her an unbalanced and graceless way to live. Gracefulness was part of her nature. Before her marriage she was a performer. Her family took comfort in their possessions. They were circus people (from Innsbruck, from Salzburg) who built up a touring show here and were proud of all they owned. The name painted in silver stardust all over the trucks was their name. Admission prices, above the ticket box, were figures she wrote, herself, at the beginning of every summer until she was sixteen. When she ran away to join the theatre she took with her three costumes and dreams of fame and fortune. At the time she was later plucked from over the footlights to become the new bride of an ornate but miserly man, what dreams had she then? Now her chief concern is getting through each long and featureless day, until it is time again to appear in restaurants such as this, wearing furs and jewels still cold from the vaults they live in, leading her husband between these tables, preparing the way for this old ringmaster, who fiercely commands others to procure for him the west-facing slopes of the Andes or mining rights to the Bering Sea (and his eiderdown, his flannel pyjamas, his crimson nightcap). And Freddy wonders at the remarkable capacity she has for holding a smile at full pitch whatever the circumstances (like a glittery performer whose upflung arm directs us to watch her partner make his tricky steps along the high-wire, while she holds steady her own enchanting pose).

When Freddy calls for his check the students try to intercept Francesca first. Evidently they have been charged for some irritating item that must be challenged. The television producer and his wife have gone. The pressman fills his pipe (with wisdom, it seems, as much as with tobacco) while the novices beside him note carefully whatever it is he is saying, but none of it will be as worthy in the morning as it sounds tonight and these boys will snigger about it in the corridors. Lost still in the pages of her novel, Freddy's shy researcher seems somehow all the younger for those dampened explosions of acne pitting her cheeks. Freddy hadn't thought them significant before, these wounds of misery, blatant and irremediable for this vulnerable girl whose soft name (Jennifer?) is spoken aloud from a darkening patio by her lonely and bewildered father as he reads her meandering airletters. Freddy would bet money that this patio looks westward over Long Beach or Monterey Bay.

Freddy leaves Francesca a tip, but less than he would if he hadn't caught Aunt Lottie watching. She would think him a fool.

At the door, the Signora, the proprietor's mother, hails him. '*Signore. Un momento.*'

This is a surprise. Although she directs the staff, in urgent and flinty tones, it is not often she speaks to a customer. She puts to the table her goblet of mineral water with tiny but firm fingers, and it occurs to Freddy that a universal emblem of motherhood is this curious authority in the hands.

'You are quickly back to us. I am glad. You have lost, pardon Signore, *mi spiace*, your little pallor. The journey has done you good. The *cartolina*, the postcard, you can see it, is still on the wall.' But the wall is blank and her gesture fades. 'The *cameriere* must have taken it down, but you can see where it was.'

Indeed Freddy can see a pinhole in the lacquer. But the Signora had got him wrong. He has not been away. He has not, so far as a man can judge in the doubtful light of morning mirrors, had a pallid face. He has never mailed postcards home to a restaurant in his life. How has he become, for so discerning and reserved a woman, the man whose weak colour she notes with sadness, the traveller who mails her (from a dim and icy post-house in the border Alpes, or with a cycling letter-carrier on a road to Bassano in the solemn satchel hung from his frugal shoulder) a greeting so welcome that she pins it to her wall?

'The scene on the card, Signora?' he asks. 'It escapes me. Which did I choose for you?'

'The Uffizi. Beautiful.'

'Yes,' he says. 'I was at the kiosk by the doors. There was a young couple. They had been in to the exhibition and were still excited by the Botticelli. They laughed and held hands. The boy wore a matelot singlet but they spoke in English. The girl, I remember, had long red hair very like the Venus they admired so much. That would have amused you.'

'So. The wandering children. Or students, of the fine art, it is possible.'

'Yes, possible.' In a world this size, it seems to Freddy, the number of possibilities is not a problem.

ONLY A LITTLE OF SO MUCH

Fay Zwicky

I have chosen this story because it represents one more step in the process of what I've come to think of as the dismantling of the educated self. I don't mean the self that has undergone formal educational procedures of school and university (though these must play some part in shaping one's directions), but rather that timid, shrinking organism that, for survival's sake, has set itself to conform to cultural restraints of a mean order. The self that sought social approval through pedantic correctness of speech and behaviour at the expense of spontaneity, the self that denied its own variety and animation, its true origins and inclinations.

As a poet with an obedient ear, I have always been drawn to the dramatic monologue. Browning's vitality, his glancing psychological ironies, together with Donne's acerbic hyperbole embodied that balance between restraint and extravagance my temperament craved. As the autobiographically based protagonist of one of my early stories described herself, 'Forever rampant or prostrate, grace seemed well beyond my spiky grasp.' ('The Last Rites of the Nizam'.)

Some of my early poems were dramatic monologues, impersonations of characters as unlike my 'educated' self as I could manage. Poems written in later years were set in the American South, enabling me to use a simple rural vernacular to which my life, as a female academic in urban Australia, did not seem to entitle me.

But the casting-off of the 'mind-forged manacles' of self-consciousness is a long, slow process, and it's not finished yet. It involves a transfer of attention from one's own concerns to those of other people. You can't become responsive in mind and heart to other voices until the anxiety generated by the controlling ego has been dissipated. If you're fortunate enough to survive the lesson, time and experience will break down whatever it was you thought you knew.

Aunt Eva, the narrator of this story, is not a calculating woman. She is the undisciplined, half-educated youngest child of a respectable middle-European family, who speaks English with reckless disregard for definite articles and who mangles the colloquial idiom to comic effect. She has been, to some extent, the victim of her own spontaneous heart, but she's not sorry for herself. She has lived foolishly, with touch of naïve cunning, but her follies have been undertaken with headlong enthusiasm, a *joie de vivre* I can sponsor wholeheartedly on paper but which I find so hard to capture in life.

Nearing her death in a nursing home, courageously buttoning her dress like mad Lear, she's passing on to her niece those fragments of an impetuous small-time hedonism, her forays into life and levity. She is a cumulative portrait of ghosts from my own past—post-1939 European refugees with heavy foreign accents, musicians, painters, cooks who wrought culinary miracles in our drab Australian kitchens, and, of course, the *dramatis personae* of a family who is transplantable to any cultural context. All those brave, rash, expansive, lovable women who added so much colour and emotional nurture to my own life.

I see this story as a kind of reparation for my earlier willed resistance to irrationality and muddle. Living now as much with the dead as I do with the living, I can afford to let the Aunt Evas of this world have their say. She speaks for me when she concludes with, 'So what's to celebrate? Something, maybe, missing the first time around?' She's proclaiming, at one remove, the wasteful impoverishment of a mind fettered in absolutes, celebrating the knowledge of my own mortality, dismantling the trappings of that educated self. So I'm grateful to her for taking over, bringing to life again those rich presences that my younger self denied.

Fay Zwicky

ONLY A LITTLE OF SO MUCH

Help me up with the last button, says Aunt Eva, my mother's youngest sister. According to the scales even Krupp the Murderer puts his personal signature on I weigh exactly thirteen and a half stones, she says. It never poisoned the spirit to see a bit of flesh. Too much, they're telling me but who listens? The same all my life—for this I should be bereaved? Why eat, says nurse, the Brünnhilde, with respect mind you. Why sleep is my answer to Miss Rheingold. Legs and arms were never wicked to us stage people. Or bosoms, bursting from the good life wherever it was. What's wickedness I'll tell you is something else. Don't let that button become your emotional problem—a safety pin does in this place! Here! Please God you wonderful younger generation won't drop the cheese when the fox says 'Sing!' Plums all day if you want!

Your mother was the skinny one. Pickled in dill and vinegar like her cucumbers, stuffed into glass jars like stiff hussars. Living decently while the earth trembled, may she rest in peace! A ruin at thirty following you and that messiah, your brother, round with a Wettex. Your father couldn't come in the back door with his shoes on, and a colonel in the war! No wonder he looked other places, excuse me for saying so but you're old enough . . . you needn't search your soul for answers either. 'What's a little dirt in a family?' I'd say, sorry as usual. 'You always were a fool,' she'd come back like a tiger. 'You ought to know about dirt. You bring enough of it into this house.' Harsh you're thinking? She didn't eat enough for kindness . . .

Your father liked his food, poor thing. A hedonistic streak going nowhere. I'd run up a chocolate soufflé for support and other reasons. I made one the day after the ad came in the *Chronicle*. 'A celebration! Hello cello!' I said, my breath coming and going. 'They don't need this rubbish,' she shouted, swinging open the oven door with a bang. The soufflé sank in the sudden cold like a dead creature. 'He's putting on enough weight as it is. And your fanny needs now a duet stool!' 'It can't be your doing then,' I said under my breath, sharp fingers pinching my hammering heart. Don't look so worried, kid! *I'm* still here. Save worry for the final judgment. You're pretty enough for Miss Australia even if you are *her* daughter! A heap of cucumbers and four dead souls, ninety per cent water! Do you wonder I couldn't marry? Sisters! I could only take a little of so much . . .

It wasn't my first endeavour in the Personals, by the way. *That* was an Armageddon! The perilous primrose path any time but, remember, I was no vision according to the authorities. Plump however. Some said womanly but no man around to make sense of it. Everyone acting as if they knew a thing or two. And I believed! I believed. 'Always stuffing your face!' 'How much on truffles this week?' 'Get your fat bottom off my seat!' And so forth. A Goldilocks with bears and no porridge. A full life of nothing and me crackling inside my thin skin like a Christmas duck!

The first—that hiker and waltzer!—turned out a tuner and I'm not talking fish. A race dying for you lot with your televisions and nuke boxes rocking and rolling. No Beethoven but who is so lucky? Deaf he wasn't but blind, yes. That such a man could call himself special, humorous, substance and character and ready to match an attractive female—I wrote Rubenesque with the returnable photo—for refreshing interludes of levity. Levity! I used to think it was a Jewish word. Him, me and the guide dog and your mother's Wettex chasing us into every corner—a collaboration!

And who was he to say the family piano was finished? Finished! It sounded always good to me. You won't find filigree flowers and candle holders like that any more. Straight from the Steinway factory in Leipzig with your grandmother, I told him. Maybe the F sharp in the middle stuck a bit now and then. I could still get off lots of runs in the Minute Waltz—just under a minute in my prime—and plenty oompah and what-have-you on the left in the Tannhäuser arrangement. I practised like a fiend when your mother was out, pretending I never touched it. She always had to slave over her fiddle! Hours of scrape and scratch and for what? New hammers, he said, prodding away. That'll cost extra, he said. Who asked about cost? I started weeping like the fool that I was, thirteen and a half stones of autumn dream streaming like Niagara!

And what was Mr Substance and Character doing in the middle of the flood? Building an ark for my bones? Why, poking away at the F sharp stuck forever like it is today in spite of my runs. Who notices, kid? Your mother showed him the door. And to me, 'Don't bring any more of that trash into the house again!' with other profanities I won't soil your ears with. Screaming 'You need a psychologist!' and worse, waving her soapy rubber gloves over my plait like Mickey Mouse and him still on the path to the gate with his dog. Sorry as usual, I didn't bring anyone for a time, having trouble getting breath back . . .

All right, Miss Nosey. I promised no lies. The best last. Water drop by drop will also split stone. I was on the way to splitting when the colonel comes back from the war with his boots and medals and I start on the soufflés, making no demands on anyone. *Anyone*, mark you, patience my middle name almost. What was is what will be is by now my philosophy so no picture needed this time. Flesh may be flesh—how could I doubt?—but spirit no gherkin regiment either, even if I did believe everything for what it wasn't. I'm not religious, God forbid, but if I was, then God would be a musician. Or maybe an actor—Shakespeare only, with a little Schnitzler for luck! This time, please, a real *Musikant*! Beethoven he doesn't have to be. Never forget your musical talent comes from me, not your scratching mother! My prayer, kid, was heard and noted. Even a soufflé murdered couldn't wreck the day!

Every word comes back. Handsome professional cellist. And French! Twenty years under Toscanini. Warm and dynamic calibre to share hopefully dancing. Sense of laughter. Legally unencumbered. Photo appreciated but not essential—can you imagine?

Another late bloomer exactly my age and ready to romp, the French culture a bonus. *Ça va sans dire*, Flaubert! That surprises you, doesn't it? I took to languages like a duck to troubling waters. Not educated like your generation but honoured, yes, honoured to match this person in intellect and frolicsome invigorations. I hid the *Chronicle* from your mother and communicated immediately. A woman of passions and ideas, I wrote, and ready always for gracious dining and something personal.

I am in levitation hours after first meeting—a Jewish word I told you it must be!—no questions in my mind. Size, shape, IQ high or low, my fate was written in his fancy! Kismet come true, my heart in throat and sleeve together! See for yourself the picture—a life-member of the Pleasure Principle Club, isn't it? Wonderful dancer and diner, a prince of eloquence—the entire holus-bolus! A pity all those genius Jews took precious time trying to make us better than we are—Misery Marx, Sad-Sack Sigmund and the atom bomb person whose name I am forgetting forever. A woman has to measure things according to pleasant or unpleasant. How it feels is her final standards. Still, I am asking him to play me the sad Swan of Saint-Saëns and occasional Kol Nidrei to curb enthusiasm for more frivolity!

Even your mother, smelling excitement in my life, is impressed. Enough to forget to tell the colonel to take his boots off. The matter is not for laughing, kid! 'France my spiritual home,' she murmurs in her spotless kitchen, wandering round his chair. 'Ah, Paris,' she sighs, Wettex stranded on the sink. 'My dream place! Where men chase real women with life's experience and leave minors alone.' 'Who is minor in this house?' I say. 'Humph!' snorts the colonel waiting for his dinner in the corner. No soufflés these days, alive or dead, poor man!

Before I can nip her bud, he is telling her what a lot of this and that she has, a woman with life's contacts written all over her face—her *face*, mind you!—fine children, loving husband and military to boot, the works. 'Why so personal?' I ask. 'She's only my sister, the eldest, and can't play the fiddle for peanuts.' Thinking, of course, of my under-the-minute waltz. 'My youngest sister here,' she says, 'is only a baby in arms. She can't help it.' A baby? Thirteen and a half stones and fifty years? I want to shout but do not for fear of releasing my cat from the sleeping bag. My paramour is thinking thirty-eight but since the word marriage has recently arisen I let the sleeping dog lie . . .

What next you are wanting to know? So much so quick, my mind rocky with remembering. But never so dumb I couldn't tell who warned him off my grasses . . .

The day before we were booked for Paris, I get a postcard with the Eiffel Tower in colour which says for all to see, 'I have missed for so long France. Now I must miss you for the remainder of my days. Thanks for all the good times, never so good with my legal encumbrance but duties call me home, *adieu.*' I go to my room and shut the door, very quiet. Outside, I hear your mother, *my* sister, saying to the colonel, 'All for the best. He did the right thing.' 'Always right if you say so,' says your father, no smile in his voice. 'In this case, yes. It was for the best. She doesn't know her own good and never will!' *My* sister again.

I come out, swinging the door with a bang behind me. Ten feet tall and stronger than any tiger. '*You* asked him to stay away?' I say in a quiet voice unlike my own, coming slowly down the stairs. 'Yes,' she says, backing away. 'And he agreed with that?' I say, still coming down, still quiet. 'Yes,' she says again. 'And he just *agreed*? He didn't even *want* to see me again?' 'He said he would write to you.' 'What am I, then? A dead-letter office? And what,' I scream, no tears, 'are *you*?' Then I leap at her skinny throat, a creature dying of pain. I know she was your mother, excuse me, but also my sister! And they say women stick together!

Turn on the light, kid. It's getting quickly dark these winter nights. Over the basin is the switch! There goes the colonel again in his silver lining! No, he didn't break, dear. Put him carefully back with the others and we'll celebrate. The tablets go down easier with a drop. They won't find out, don't look so worried! You remind me of your mother when you look that way. Miss Rheingold will be along soon with that tuft of dog-grass she calls dinner. No, I won't calm down! Calm isn't my nature. Why calm when I'm nearly dust? Tomorrow's almost behind me and yesterday's here already! So what's to celebrate? Something, maybe, missing the first time around?

THAT ANTIC JEZEBEL
David Malouf

AUTHOR'S NOTE

I prefer not to write an introduction. My own feeling is that the story now has its own life to lead, among readers, and should be left to get on with it, with no further word of mine to speed it on its way. Any comment I could make now would be superfluous—if it isn't, it ought to have been in the story itself.

What writers have to say about their work is sometimes illuminating but is more often I think misleading. We do not always know more than a good reader will see for himself or herself—what we know are sometimes the wrong things, things that would get in the way; and our personal involvement with the events or characters will already have been transmuted into the quite different medium of fiction—or ought to have been— so there can be no significant residue, that is worth talking about, of *that*.

The story belongs now to the reader. The writer's part is finished and he had better retire and let it become part of the *reader's* life, in that passionate, private and instant relationship (if it happens at all) that needs no further mediation and to which the writer, if he has done the job properly, can add no single word.

David Malouf

THAT ANTIC JEZEBEL

Climbing to her seat in the organ gallery, up three flights of stairs, was such an arduous business, and she was so slow nowadays, that Clay had to begin early, even before the warning bells were sounded. She hated the thought of arriving breathless, of being locked out, or of looking, on the way up, like an old girl in need of aid. 'He's cooked his goose—let him lie in it'; that was one of her sayings. Messy of course, but life is, you got used to it.

Clay McHugh had learned her survival tactics in Europe between the wars. She had studied there how to present an appearance that was never less than elegant and might be mistaken by snobs, and by the undiscerning and unworldly, for affluence. You lived in the best part of town, had one outfit of perfect cut that went to the cleaners each week, one piece of jewellery, and you never let anyone past the door.

Her present apartment was at Elizabeth Bay and she had spent all she had on it. Within its walls, among the last of her loot, she practised a frugality that would have surprised her neighbours and made social workers, and other Nosey Parkers, cry famine. Clay despised such terms. She ate a great deal of boiled rice, was careful with the lights, and on the pretext of keeping trim, she walked rather than took the bus. Her one outfit was black; her one piece of jewellery a chain of intimidating weight that chimed rather than tinkled but was too plain to suggest ostentation. Hung with mint-gold coins, seals and medallions, it provoked questions and the answers told a story—in fact several stories, but never all. There was, each time, a little something-left-over.

This chain was her *curriculum vitae*. She shook it when she needed to remind herself that, whatever hole she was now in, she had once been in a different one and this was her choice. The chain spoke of attachments: of men young and old, back there in Europe, who had wanted at one time or another to present her with their blue eyes, their lives, their titles, or with little flats in Paris or London or country houses near Antwerp or Rome—all of which, for good reason, she had declined. The men had slipped away, leaving only a family seal or rare coin or medal. The weight on her wrist was bearable and she thought of it as a tribute to her intention to keep free.

That was one way of putting it. Put another way, you might say that the men had escaped and that these coins were the price they'd been willing to pay. Clay looked at it different ways on different occasions, but mostly she thought of herself as having come out of all this—of *life*—as well as could be expected: that is, badly. But her freedom was important to her. All those dull dogs and bushy-tailed buffers, if they were still kicking, would be as old now as herself. She would, if she had accepted their offers, be no more than an expensive nursemaid to an old man's incontinence—though she was not without affection and she wouldn't have complained, even of that, after a lifetime of some other devotion, if it had been her fate; or if the right man—Karel for instance—had asked it of her. Things had turned out otherwise, that's all. She was lying with the goose.

Besides, she told herself in her scarier moments, I'll soon be in that state myself, except that I won't be. I won't hang around to get up at three in the morning like poor Grandma and make scones for people who've been dead for thirty years. I'll finish it first. I'll take the bun and the pills . . .

(This grandmother had lived with them. As a grown girl of fifteen she had been sent out, burning with shame before the neighbours, but also before the old woman herself, to bring her in when she went aimlessly wandering. On several occasions that now seemed like one, they had stood shouting beside a fence in the overpowering smell of honeysuckle. The old woman whined, screeched, wheedled, tried to shake off the grip on her wrist; dogs barked, children stared, other old women shook their heads behind blinds—she could still feel the pain, the humiliation of it. But the centre of the occasion had shifted now from the unwilling and angry girl to the wilful old woman, who with her hair awry and her gown open stood barefoot under the streetlamp saying over and over, 'Why are you doing this to me?' The old woman was herself.)

She shook her wrist and the chain clanked against the gallery rail, as leaning forward she allowed her eye, which was sharp, to sweep the crowded amphitheatre.

Eleanor had just come in, high up in the stalls. Tall, in an emerald cloak, she was waiting for the people in her row to get up and let her through.

How like her! There was stacks of room up there, not like these gallery boxes—stacks of it! But Eleanor continued to stand, and when at last the whole row had risen to its feet, the silly woman, holding her cloak about her, moved through, gracefully inclining her head and smiling and thanking people. Settled at last, with the cloak thrown back for later, when the air-conditioning would turn the place into an icebox, she looked about; then cast her gaze upward to the gallery and waved.

Clay immediately relented. Oh God, she told herself, I'm such a *bitch*. It was touching really, Eleanor's little wave—a real leap in the dark. Too vain to wear glasses, and half-blind by habit (as who wouldn't be after forty years with the dreaded doctor) she could barely see her face in the glass.

Clay produced in response one of her brisk salutes, a real one made by bringing two fingers of her right hand up to the temple and flicking them sharply away. It was her trademark; from the days when she had modelled little suits of a military cut for Molyneux in Paris and was considered a sport. It too was a leap in the dark since Eleanor couldn't see it. But she made the gesture just the same—as an acknowledgement to herself of the old, the unkillable Clay McHugh, since there was, God knows, so little left of her.

(She had taken to avoiding herself in mirrors and in ghostly shop-windows; her eyes were too sharp, she hadn't, like Eleanor, developed the habit of not-seeing-clearly-any-more. But at some point back there she had let her attention wander, lost her grip on things, and the spirit of disintegration had got in. Well, she was fighting it—tooth and claw—she was holding on; she got tired, that's all. Your attention wandered. You got tired.)

She came quickly to the alert now. Eleanor was making a play in the air with her fingers that meant they should meet later and share a taxi home. They would—they always did—and Eleanor, who was generous and tactfully tactless, would see to it that they did not share the fare.

They were neighbours. Eleanor, Mrs Adrian Murphy, lived in a unit-block three doors from her own, and once a week, on Fridays, they went down in the Daimler (Eleanor drove only in daylight now) and had coffee together: down among the heavy-eyed Viennese, all reading air-mail papers that were two weeks old, and those deeper exiles who had been born right here, in Burwood or Gulgong or Innisfail, north Queensland, but were dying of hunger for a few crumbs of Sacher Torte and of estrangement from a life they had never known. What a place! What a country!

Years ago, in Brisbane, where they had been at the same convent school, she and Eleanor Ure had hated one another. 'That stuck up goody two-shoes' was the phrase she found herself repeating in her twelve-year-old's voice; though she couldn't recall how Eleanor, who had been mousey, could have deserved it—not then. It fitted her better twenty years later when the dreaded doctor appeared.

But that period too had passed; and now, with nearly sixty years between them and the girls they once were, she could accept Eleanor Murphy for what she was: a spoiled and frightened woman, too insistent on her own dignity, but generous, loyal, and very nearly these days a friend.

That first winter after they found themselves neighbours, Eleanor had slipped and broken her leg. Clay had gone across each afternoon to sit with her: not in the spirit of a little nursing-sister—she had none of that—but in a spirit of brisk cheerfulness, of keeping one's stoic end up, that revived the bossy schoolgirl in her. Eleanor was happy to be organized. They spent the afternoons playing cards (rummy) while the westering light touched with Queensland colours the baskets of maidenhair and the tree-orchids and staghorns of Eleanor's rainforest loggia, and Mrs Thring, who came in to clean, and who served when Eleanor entertained, made them scones and tea.

Things had levelled between them. She was no longer 'that Clay McHugh', unmarried and trailing clouds of dangerous appeal. And Eleanor, with the dreaded doctor gone, was no more the gilded and girlish dependent of a Household Word. They were alone, alive (widowed or not, what did it matter?) and had no one close but one another.

(Eleanor in fact had a son whom she doted on, worried over and never mentioned; a forty-four-year-old hippy and no-hoper called Aidan, for God's sake! who wore beads, wrote unpublishable poetry, had two broken marriages behind him, and lived in a rainforest—a real one—on sunflower-seeds, bananas and old rope. Eleanor's bedroom was full of photographs of him when he was an angelic six-year-old. Clay knew all this, but was meant not to. There were days when all Eleanor had to say in the long silences between them was, 'Aidan, Aidan, Aidan, Aidan.' It was hard then not to cry out, 'For God's sake, Eleanor, I thought we were friends, why can't we talk about him?' 'About who?' Eleanor would have said. 'Who can you possibly mean?')

The Year of Eleanor's Leg had been followed by The Year of the Rapist. For five months their Point was at siege. The rapist specialized in high unit-blocks and only assaulted older women (they had shared, she and Eleanor, a phone code that made Eleanor at least feel safe) and had turned out to be a twenty-two-year-old-cat-burglar, so round-chinned and mild-looking that nobody believed it was really him.

Clay did. Standing at the glass door to her balcony, with her old dragon-robe about her, she had come face to face with him. He was spreadeagled against the wall, his cheek flat to the bricks. There was only feet between them; he in the cold air, high up above the fig tree and its voracious flying-foxes, she safe behind glass. Below, the whole Bay was lit. The police were on to him. Their searchlights crossed and re-crossed the fern-hung balconies.

Let me in, his eyes had pleaded. He was blond, with a two-day growth that made a shadow above his lips. She shook her head.

He had smiled then and nodded; as if she were some silly old girl who could be fooled by a soft look and didn't know he was a tiger, a beast of prey, and these tower blocks were his jungle. Nervously his tongue appeared, just the tip, and slicked his lips. He was perplexed, he was thinking with it.

If she hesitated a moment then it wasn't because she was fooled but because she saw his animal mind at work. They were a pair. She too had been 'out there'.

She didn't let him in. Another night she might have, it wasn't final; but not that one. She stood and watched the searchlight play across the balcony; go on, back-track, then stop, isolating him like an acrobat, an angel, in its glare. He had his eyes closed. He was pressing his body hard against the wall, pretending, like a child, to be invisible.

Being more vulnerable than ever at that moment she had turned quickly away . . .

So there was Eleanor, safely settled in the stalls. And there, in their box, were the Scarmans, Robert and Jeanette, who always appeared for the first half but seldom for the second. Cool ash-blonds, very still and fastidious, they tried again and again but real players never came up to what they were used to on Robert's equipment. Robert had been Karel's favourite student (that was how she knew them), but he was fonder now of Jeanette.

She caught their eye, and Jeanette made little window-cleaning motions that meant See-you-later-in-the-usual-place. (That was the Crush Bar on the harbour side.)

All this was ritual. She watched Jeanette wave to the Abrams, and the Abrams a moment later caught her own eye, and Clay gave them her salute. Then Doctor Havek, whom she had known in Paris before the war, then in Cairo, and who was now her doctor at Edgecliff, shuffled to his seat in the third row—down in Middle Europe among the garlic and ashes; but before he was seated, he too waved to the Abrams and then leaned over and shook hands with the Scorczenys, whom she had also known in Paris but had nothing to do with here.

She began to tap her foot. Karel hadn't arrived. They had spoken on Thursday—no, Friday, and he had said yes, he definitely was well enough, he would be here.

It was just before eight. Downstairs the last bleeps would be sounding, like a nasty moment in a beleaguered submarine. But the seat between the blonde woman and the couple who hummed, Karel insisted, through all of Mozart and Beethoven and most of Schubert (though they were pretty well stumped by Bartók) was empty, the only one in its row.

'Would you like to see the programme?' the young man on her right was enquiring. He was a sweet rather effeminate boy who had struck up a conversation at the start of the season and chattered on now whether she answered or not. She thanked him, turned the pages politely and handed it back.

'Martinů,' the boy said with excitement. He had apple cheeks and a great deal of fluffy bronze hair.

Martinů too she had known for a time. She did not say so. She was too puzzled.

Down in the hall a character in a double-breasted suit had paused at the end of Karel's row, and, after turning his head this way and that to examine the ticket, was pushing in towards the empty seat. It was a mistake—he had the wrong row; she leaned forward across the tense air to inform him.

Short, fair, balding, he pushed his way along the row, pausing frequently to excuse himself, and seemed unaware of his error. When he reached the seat at last he stood flicking it with a handkerchief, then settled. But uncomfortably, sitting too far forward, and went to work now, with the same handkerchief, on his brow. He mopped, consulted his watch, mopped again—all the time in the wrong seat; then sat with the handkerchief crumpled up in his right hand like an unhappy child, and sitting too far forward, as if his legs would not reach the ground.

It was this vision of him as an unlikely middle-aged child that gave her the clue. She saw a plump nine-year-old with sloping shoulders in front of a row of newly planted poplars. The poplars were meant to civilize a wilderness, and the child, who wore khaki shorts and sand-shoes, was bearing a spade. It was a snapshot. He squinted into the sun. Well, those poplars now must be sixty, seventy feet high, sending their roots to block someone's drains. And the child would be—Nicholas. Nicholas!

Her heart thumped and she half rose to her feet. But the hall was ringing with applause now and the chamber group was trooping on, the lights were fading. Too late! There was a scraping and plucking as they tuned up, and she joined them with a hiss of desperation at her own slowness. It was loud enough for the boy who was her neighbour to swing his head in alarm. She made violent motions—no, it's nothing, nothing—and subsided into noiseless gloom.

That Nicholas. He had sided against his father, turned clean against him all those years ago, and now here he was occupying his father's seat. 'Traitor,' she wanted to shout down at him, 'you broke his heart!'

But on an abrupt and sickening change of key, old injustice and indignation gave way to alarm. Why wasn't Karel here, that was the real point. What had he said—on Friday was it?—no, Saturday. What had they talked about? What did they *ever* talk about, these days, these days! The music kept switching pace. She couldn't fit his voice to it. The violins were doing impossible things, leaping about off key, scraping below the bridge; no voice could be fitted to that! Oh my God, she thought, my God. The music was approaching a violent end. It ended. And the boy beside her held his hands clasped a moment, with his head thrown back and all his hair electrically tingling, before he joined the applause. 'Wasn't that terrific?' he breathed. Then, when she clenched her jaw at him: 'Are you all right?'

No, she was *not* all right! Where was Karel? Why hadn't he rung if he wasn't coming?

She got to her feet again, determined this time to rush down and call; but her head was filled with the sound of a phone ringing in an empty room, and she sat down again, plump, just like that, and covered her eyes. There was a hush. She steeled herself. Terrible Tchaikovsky bloomed all over the hall.

She managed to push her way through the harbourside bar without encountering Robert and Jeanette, or Eleanor, or the Abrams, and after an eternity of searching (where *was* the man? He couldn't spend the entire interval in the loo) she found him pacing up and down under the sloping panes that gave on to the dark; nervously consulting his watch and looking so like the child of thirty years ago that she immediately felt thirty years younger herself.

'Nicholas!' she accused.

He looked startled. His hands jumped and opened. There was no need to introduce herself.

'Where is he?' she demanded.

The man frowned and lowered his gaze.

The worst, she thought, it's always the worst. Damn him!

He was looking desperately about for a place they could slip away to that wouldn't be loud with people, all standing too close and with glasses in their hands, shouting.

For God's sake, she thought, why doesn't he get it over with? I know already, it's only words. The stoop of his shoulders and his look of pained, concentrated concern was too irritating; she would have preferred him to be cruel. (It struck her then that all the bad news she had ever heard had come to her in public places: in railway-stations, hotel foyers, bars, or over public address systems in crowded squares. It was a mark of the century.) Go on, damn you, she thought now, say it, shout it why don't you?

At last, in desperation, he did. He tipped his balding head towards her, and with one hand cupped to his mouth, bellowed softly: 'My father died this morning. I tried to ring you. He collapsed while he was out shopping. I'm very sorry.'

The vision of spilled parcels hit her harder than she expected; and Nicholas, made bold by the fear that she too might be about to fall down in a public place, took her, not quite firmly, by the elbow, and kept up a dismal muttering.

They had become a centre of concern. The crowd about them had drawn back. People were staring, she must have cried out. Nicholas, deeply embarrassed, was making little gestures towards them. He was explaining why he was clutching her, that it was not this that had provoked her cry. Meanwhile, to her, he was offering more complex explanations. 'You see,' he stammered, 'I found the ticket—and I—well I just didn't want the seat to be empty.'

His soft eyes appealed to her for understanding of his pious but perhaps foolish sentiment.

She did understand, and suddenly felt sorry for him—for his awkward emotion and the need to explain it, but also for his grief. But it hurt, that. They must have been closer than she had guessed, Karel and this grown-up Nicholas; who would be, of course—why had she never let herself think it?—the father of the grandchildren: of Elsa and Ross. She had known about the grandchildren—she even knew their birthdays, but had thought of them as having come to him without intermediaries. And now here he was, one of the *intermediaries*, thin, distressed, too formal, with the sweat breaking out on his bald crown—the bearer of a weight of filial piety that she did understand and which did after all do him credit, but which she felt like a knife in her bowels.

'Listen,' she said harshly, 'do you think you could find me a drink? Something good and strong. I'll be fine till you get back.'

She swayed a little but recovered. How odd it was after all the turmoil they had created—the promises, threats, curses, the real and imaginary violence—to have reached in a public place in Sydney this moment of utter aloneness: Elizabeth gone, that devout vindictive woman, now Karel also gone, and nothing left but this numbness before the brute fact. Karel! Tipped out on the pavements of a town he had never meant to live in, let alone die in, and the hot sky pulsing overhead as the angel zoomed, found his easy mark—there under the ribs—and pushed. She too felt it, the knife; and the closeness of his breath.

She looked up sharply at a gentler touch. Nicholas, with a double cognac and nothing for himself.

She smiled, thanked him, and playing the tough old girl, threw her head back and tossed it off. Then stood with the balloon resting lightly on her palm.

She looked at it—it was so fine. Tough but delicate. If she closed her fist and pressed hard enough it would splinter.

He must have felt the thought pass through her; she was surprised. He took the glass in his own pudgy fist, but had nowhere to put it.

'I'll see you home,' he was saying in that heavy, middle-European way, all breathless gallantry, that she had found absurd even in his father and which thirty years in Australia, the rough example of contemporaries, and the half mocking acquiescence of women like herself, had done nothing to change.

'No,' she said. 'The seat. You must stay.'

He looked down again and was embarrassed. 'The seat doesn't matter.'

'Oh but it does!' she said firmly. 'You've been kind enough already—Nicholas. I'll get a taxi.'

He did not insist. 'Then I'll find you one.'

Still holding the glass in one hand, and with the fingers of the other just pinching her elbow, he led her down the shallow steps. When they came to the foyer he made a wide arc towards one of the bars, and reaching in between packed shoulders, fumbled and set the thing down, grinning a little for the awkwardness of it.

At last they were in the open air. Out here she had no need of support. The night was fresh, and the sky, beyond harbour-rails and fig-trees, an electric blue. He stood with his hands clasped behind him, rocking gently on his heels.

'It seems a shame,' he began, 'that we've never—that we had to wait so long. I'm sorry.'

She shook her head. No good going into all that. Too late, too late.

But he was determined she saw, in his discreet, passionate,

pedantic way, to deal with it, an image of her that must have been, like her own picture of him as a slope-shouldered child in shorts, a stereotype: the flashy homebreaker and Jezebel who had stolen his father and left him to be the little man of the house, the resentful mother's boy. Or perhaps what he was dealing with was his father's nakedness. Well, either way, either way, he was too late.

'If you don't mind,' he was saying, 'I'll call up tomorrow and see how you are. It's no trouble.'

She shook her head and made deprecating motions with her lips. What was it—kindness?—was he *kind*? More of his filial piety?

Fortunately the taxi had arrived. The driver gave her a look—some old girl who'd had too much to drink, and while Nicholas was giving him the address, she heard, as often before, the sound of a note being passed.

'Thank you,' she murmured, eager for nothing now except to be moving on in the dark.

'You all right, ol' lady?' the driver asked over his shoulder. There was mockery in his voice.

'Get stuffed,' she told the fellow. That fixed him.

Eleanor's late-night telephone voice was full of concern. 'No, no, I'm okay, no trouble—I was tired, that's all. How was the Schoenberg?' Then, because she was tired of making mysteries, and because sooner or later it would have to be said, she let a voice that was not quite her own announce flatly: 'Karel died this morning—a heart attack. In the street . . .' Poor Eleanor! 'No, no, I'm okay—I promise. Yes, I'll call you in the morning.'

She replaced the receiver and stood for a moment looking down at the Bay. She must have been doing that for the last hour. There were no searchlights tonight; and no angel was clamped like an aerial frogman to the wall out there, with his animal eyes upon her and his angelic, unshaven cheek pressed close to the bricks. Only below, in the dark of the Moreton Bay figs—those exiles of her own northern shore—the flying-foxes, gorging on fruit.

She turned the lights out and went into her bedroom. Brightness and squalor of a small star's dressing room—den of a sorceress whose spells were expert and false according to the times, and whose powers had been worked up always out of improvident energies. Well, that spring was dry. All that was left were the half-empty bottles of the witch's fakery: cut-glass in what the boys these days called Deco, plastic jars full of liquors, creams, milks, balms, emulsions—unmagic potions. Unzipping the good black dress, she hung it like an empty skin in the closet—one of the rules—then sat and rolled off her stockings, leaving them anyhow on the floor; underclothes the same—she had always been messy. 'You're impossible,' people told her, 'you're such a perfectionist.' 'No,' she had sometimes answered, bitter at being misunderstood, 'I'm a slob.' The nuns had known. 'Clay McHugh,' she heard an old nun, Sister Ignatia, complain, 'if your mind in any way resembles your closet you're in for a hard time. We shall say nothing of your soul.' They had none of them said anything of her soul.

So she was naked.

She groaned aloud now, since there was no one to hear, and drew back the sheet. She lay her body out: the slack flesh of her arms and thighs, her wrinkled belly, her skull and her feet and her hands that were covered with blotches, patches of darkness that would spread.

I am lying with the goose, she told herself, that's how they'll find me. Only nobody dies of grief—grief doesn't kill us. We're too damned selfish and strong—and what we love in the end is the goose.

She unsnapped the chain. It was too heavy to sleep with. It dragged you down into your dreams. With a solid clunk it hit the night-table, all her stories, her insoluble mysteries: a dead sound, *clunk*, just like that—the last sound before silence.

BIOGRAPHICAL NOTES

Jessica Anderson was born in Queensland and now lives in Sydney. She wrote radio scripts for many years, and in 1963 her first novel was published. In 1987 she won the *Age* Book of the Year award for her first collection of stories, *Stories From the Warm Zone and Sydney Stories*. Her latest novel is *Taking Shelter*, published in 1989.

Barbara Hanrahan, acclaimed equally as a printmaker and writer of fiction, was born in Adelaide in 1939. She returned there after several years in London. The first of her nine novels was published in 1973, and her short story collection, *Dream People*, was published in 1987.

Michael Wilding was born in England in 1942 and now lives in Sydney, where he is a writer and academic. *The Man of Slow Feeling* is a selection of his widely anthologized short stories, and his most recent book, *Under Saturn*, consists of four novellas.

Glenda Adams was born in Sydney in 1940 and now lives in New York. In 1988 she was awarded a three-year Senior Fellowship by the Literature Board of the Australia Council. Her books include the 1988 Miles Franklin Award novel, *Dancing on Coral*, and the story collections *The Hottest Night of the Century* and *Games of the Strong*.

Peter Carey was born in rural Victoria in 1943 and now lives in Sydney. He has received international recognition for his short stories (collected as *Exotic Pleasures*) and the novels *Bliss*, *Illywhacker* and *Oscar and Lucinda* (winner of the 1988 Booker Prize).

James McQueen was born in Tasmania in 1934. He has written on conservation issues, and his novels include *Hook's Mountain* and *The Floor of Heaven*. His short stories, collected in *Uphill Runner* and the forthcoming *Death of a Lady's Man*, have won many awards.

Helen Garner was born in Geelong in 1942 and now lives in Melbourne, where she is a full-time writer of fiction and scripts. She has won major awards for her novels *Monkey Grip* and *The Children's Bach*, and for her short story collection, *Postcards from Surfers*.

Joan London was born in Perth in 1948 and lives in Fremantle. She has been awarded a writing fellowship from the Literature Board of the Australia Council, and won the *Age* Book of the Year award in 1986 for her first book, the short story collection, *Sister Ships*.

Garry Disher was born in rural South Australia in 1949 and now lives in Melbourne, where he is a full-time writer. He was awarded a creative writing fellowship to Stanford University in 1978, and won the national short story award in 1986. His books include *The Stencil Man* (a novel) and *The Difference to Me* (short stories).

Murray Bail was born in Adelaide in 1941 and, after several years overseas, during which he began writing stories, he now lives in Sydney. His book of stories, *Contemporary Portraits*, has been republished, and he won major awards for his novels *Homesickness* and *Holden's Performance*.

Gerald Murnane was born in Melbourne in 1939, where he has lived for most of his life. He is the acclaimed author of *The Plains*, *Landscape with Landscape*, *Inland* and other works of fiction, and is highly regarded as a teacher of fiction writing. A collection of his short stories will be published by Heinemann in 1990.

Jean Bedford was born in England in 1946 and grew up in rural Victoria. She has worked as a journalist, reviewer and teacher, and is the author of the novels *Colouring In* (with Rosemary Creswell), *Sister Kate* and *Love Child*, and of a short story collection, *Country Girl Again.*

Barry Hill was born in Melbourne in 1943 and now lives in the Victorian coastal town of Queenscliff. He is a full-time writer of fiction, reviews, radio scripts and media commentary. His books include two novels and the short story collections *A Rim of Blue* and *Headlocks.*

Thea Astley was born in Brisbane in 1925 and for many years taught in schools and at Macquarie University, Sydney. She is the author of nine novels, three of which won the Miles Franklin Award, and two short story collections, *Hunting the Wild Pineapple* and *It's Raining in Mango*, winner of the inaugural Steele Rudd Award for short stories in 1988.

Gerard Windsor was born in Sydney in 1944, where he now works as a writer and reviewer. He is the author of a novel, *That Fierce Virgin*, and two highly praised short story collections, *The Harlots Enter First* and *Memoirs of the Assassination Attempt.*

Frank Moorhouse, regarded as one of Australia's most important practitioners of short fiction, was born on the south coast of New South Wales in 1938 and now lives in Sydney. He is a writer of fiction, scripts and articles, and his books include *The Americans, Baby; Room Service;* and the 1988 *Age* Book of the Year, *Forty Seventeen.*

Kate Grenville, author of the acclaimed novels *Lilian's Story, Dreamhouse* and *Joan Makes History*, was born in Sydney in 1950. She lived for many years overseas, studied creative writing in the United States, and now lives in Sydney. Her short stories are collected in *Bearded Ladies.*

389

Elizabeth Jolley, regarded as one of Australia's foremost writers of fiction, was born in England in 1923 and moved to Western Australia in 1959. She is the author of several award-winning novels, and of three short story collections, *Five Acre Virgin, The Travelling Entertainer* and *Woman in a Lampshade.*

Peter Goldsworthy was born in rural South Australia in 1951 and now lives in Adelaide, where he is a GP. He has won awards for both poetry and short stories, and is the author of three story collections, *Archipelagoes, Zooing* and *Bleak Rooms.* His first novel, *Maestro,* will be published in 1989.

Robert Drewe was born in Melbourne in 1943 and now lives in Sydney. A journalist for many years, he is now a full-time writer of fiction. He is the author of three highly regarded novels and the best-selling short story collection, *Bodysurfers.*

Carmel Bird was born in Tasmania in 1940 and now lives in Melbourne. Her books include two story collections, *The Woodpecker Toy Fact* and *Births, Deaths and Marriages,* a novel, and the acclaimed writers' handbook, *Dear Writer.*

Tim Winton was born in Perth in 1960. A graduate of the notable WAIT (now Curtin University of Technology) creative writing course, he is the author of such prize-winning novels and short story collections as *Shallows, That Eye The Sky, Scission* and *Minimum of Two.* His first book for children was published in 1989.

Archie Weller was born in rural Western Australia and is now based in Perth. His novel, *The Day of the Dog,* was highly placed in the Vogel Awards, and his short story collection, *Going Home,* is regarded as a classic in black Australian writing.

Morris Lurie, well-known for his children's books and humorous stories and articles, is the author of an award-winning autobiography, *Whole Life*, several novels, and collections of short stories, including *The Night We Ate the Sparrow*. He was born in Melbourne in 1938, and returned there to live after several years overseas.

Beverley Farmer was born in Melbourne in 1941, spent several years in Greece, and now lives at Point Lonsdale, on the Victorian coast. She is a full-time writer of fiction, poetry, articles and reviews, and author of the acclaimed story collections, *Milk* and *Home Time*. Her most recent book, *A Body of Water*, will be published in 1990.

Finola Moorhead was born in Melbourne in 1947 and now lives in Sydney. Her stories and prose pieces have been widely anthologized, and her fictional innovations, particularly in the novel *Remember the Tarantella*, have been highly praised.

George Papaellinas, author of the short story collection *Ikons*, was born in Sydney in 1954. He was awarded a writer's fellowship from the Literature Board of the Australia Council in 1987, has taught creative writing at the Tranby Aboriginal College in Glebe, Sydney, and organized the successful Sydney writers' festival, Carnivale, in 1988.

John Bryson was born in Melbourne in 1935, trained as a barrister, and later became a full-time writer. His books include *Whoring Around* (stories), a collection of journalism, and the acclaimed and influential study of the Chamberlain case, *Evil Angels*.

Fay Zwicky was born in Melbourne in 1933 and now lives in Perth, where she works as an academic and a writer of poetry, essays and fiction. Her books include collections of poetry and the short story collection, *Hostages*.

David Malouf was born in Brisbane in 1934 and he now divides his time between Sydney, Brisbane and a village in Tuscany. He has earned international recognition for his novels and won many awards in Australia for his poetry and fiction, including the inaugural Vance Palmer award for his first story collection, *Antipodes*.

OTHER TITLES AVAILABLE IN IMPRINT

FERAL PALIT
Robin Wallace-Crabbe

Alan Palit, mad and incarcerated, is trying to make sense of the events in his life that made him a hermit, that translated his innate isolation into forcible exclusion from the world. Memories that are morbidly witty, sometimes sentimental and often funny as Palit looks for intimations of his own relevance to the universe. His universe—a small country town in the Gippsland district of Victoria.

'It is the undercurrent of continual self-analysis and questioning that is so unusual in a modern Australian novel . . . I suspect it will be a sleeper, gradually and deservedly gaining a reputation among those who chance on it as a finely written and significant novel.'

Jean Bedford, The National Times

'Gradually it became talked about. David Campbell urged me to read it, Patrick White sent me a copy. It is a very good book, a notable addition to Australian literature.'

Geoffrey Dutton, The Bulletin

THE INITIATE
Justin D'Ath

Stephen Quintus is young, white and middle-class, unsure of his future and dissatisfied with his present. Rafael Roebuck is black, a college student, lonely in Melbourne's white society, and yearning to be back among his people at the Aboriginal Corpus Christi Mission near Alice Springs.

Stephen's life changes when he takes up an invitation to manage the Mission club and learns that if he is to be accepted into the community he must he must pass a fundamental test: he must become a Man. Rafael, too, must make the transition, but his test is far more complex: he must be initiataed, and this initiation has a double edge.

The Initiate is a deeply satisfying, intricate and powerful portrayal of two very different lives and sets of beliefs and what happens when they converge.

UP ALL NIGHT
Heather Falkner

Silvana grew up in wartime Italy, but now lives alone in Kings Cross, where she runs a late night cafe. This offers her more peace than marriage with the dubious Victor, whose associates were probably gangsters. Then Griff comes back into her life, an old lover with new troubles. Out of their night together emerge new problems and new solutions . . .

'A writer who is cool, wise, amused, reporting with compassionate accuracy on the way many of us live right now.'

Kate Llewellyn

'Taut tales of loving and losing, raging and boozing, set in contemporary Sydney. Heather Falkner tells it like it is, with wry humour and a sharp eye for the foibles of inner city life.'

Elizabeth Webby

CAVIAR FOR BREAKFAST
Betty Roland

In 1933 Betty Roland went to Moscow with her lover Guido Baracchi, a member of the Australian Communist Party. Roland broke all the rules and stayed for fifteen months, sharing a room with fellow Australian writer Katharine Susannah Prichard.

Her diary details the excitement of her introduction to Russian theatre and her life in Moscow. She has a few privileges which almost compensate for the bedbugs and the fierce Russian winter. As Roland smuggles literature through Nazi Germany or stands in endless queues at thirty degrees below zero, she experiences the false dawn of Stalin's new revolution. When she leaves in 1934, Stalin closes the country to the West.

Caviar for Breakfast follows Roland's first volume of auto-biography, *An Improbable Life*, in a setting that is both exotic and macabre.

BOYS BY THE SEA
Barry Donnelly

No one speaks. Being strong and silent is a mark of manhood. I feel like yelling, calling them fools, but my chest is heaving so much from running, and that crazy engine is coming already. I take my place next to Ferdie ... These russian roulette kind of games are Ferdie's specialty, and it is written over his face that he is the reigning champion of the train-on-the-bridge game.

First girl, first job, first motorbike, first jump in the train-on-the-bridge game ... *Boys by the Sea* is a novel of teenage initiations. Set on the New South Wales Central Coast during the Korean war, five friends play their own part in this turning point in Australia's history. For these teenagers, all stumbling into manhood, it's a time of innocence and frustration, when a single glance from a girl can cause paralysis. It's a time of excruciating boredom and delicious yearning, with deep-set fears about staying then leaving this seaside town. On the beach, on the road, in the billiard halls, Barry Donnelly has evoked a remarkable portrait of Australian adolescence.